OBSESSION

OBSESSION

Anthony F Coster

Matador
9 Priory Business Park,
Wistow Road, Kibworth Beauchamp,
Leicestershire. LE8 0RX
Tel: 0116 279 2299
Email: books@troubador.co.uk
Web: www.troubador.co.uk/matador
Twitter: @matadorbooks

ISBN 9781789013764

British Library Cataloguing in Publication Data.
A catalogue record for this book is available from the British Library.

Printed and bound in Great Britain by 4edge Limited
Typeset in 11pt Minion Pro by Troubador Publishing Ltd, Leicester, UK

Matador is an imprint of Troubador Publishing Ltd

By the Same Author

Security in Commerce and Industry
(Butterworths)

Profile

For twelve years the author was a member of the Royal Military Police and became an investigator with the Special Investigation Branch (SIB) of the British Army where he investigated most types of serious crimes including murder. He worked in the UK, Northern Ireland, France, Asia, and Germany. On leaving the SIB, he was appointed Head of Security for a major international bank where he managed fraud and criminal offences within the United Kingdom and many overseas countries including India, Thailand, South Africa and Hong Kong. He later became a consultant and investigator, dealing with high profile commercial crime. He has written several articles relating to criminal matters, and is the author of Security in Commerce and Industry (Controlling Losses for Profit) published by Butterworths in the UK and the USA.

Elements of this book are based on actual events experienced personally by the author. He now lives in retirement in South Wales enjoying golf, chess, piano, reading, writing and charity work.

PROLOGUE

When a responsible person decides to commit a crime, as opposed to a hardened criminal, the psychological effects of the wrongdoing cause a staggering change in behaviour. The fact that this change will take place is not usually considered by the potential criminal but it often has far-reaching implications. A person intending to commit their first crime who has a comfortable life, financial soundness and no real problems will not necessarily realise the total and staggering change in their personality which often leads to arrest. Nearly all people who commit their first serious crime show personality changes of some sort. Many criminal investigations are carried out successfully with little evidence but the experienced investigator will assess the behaviour of those persons interviewed. He or she will use intuition, watch for responses, and identify stress factors. This is often enough to lead to a confession.

When potential criminals "press the button", so to speak, there is no going back, the crime is done, nothing can be changed and suddenly they are not the same person. They will be in a different world, alone with their worries and will experience sleepless nights. Their emotional state will show at home and it will be noticed by others. They will be stricken by fear and nervousness and their downfall often follows.

Henry Walters, QC did not consider the personality changes when he was faced with a major problem, a problem that involved wrestling with a decision as to whether or not to carry out the most heinous of crimes. Only he could decide, there was nobody to assist – it was a discussion with himself but a discussion and a decision of life-changing proportions.

One

Irene looked at her daughter smiling broadly with excitement. 'I think I've found him, I'm really excited about this one.'

Jayne, her daughter, was a beautiful young lady who turned heads wherever she went. Her aim was to marry a man who could offer her the luxurious lifestyle she desperately desired and her mother was totally committed to help her.

'Who is he Mummy?'

Jayne had an expectant look on her face but she had heard it all before. She was nearly 25 years old and over the past few years had been close to marrying the ideal sugar daddy, but her plans had never worked out.

'He's a QC, one of the most successful, and he's taken silk.'

'Sorry, I don't understand, what does that mean?' Jayne was confused.

'It means he's Queen's Counsel, one of the highest paid barristers in the country. He's 47, divorced and loaded. He lives alone in a beautiful house and doesn't go out much socially.'

'He's getting on a bit, isn't he?'

'The wealthiest usually are, but he's not bad looking for his age.'

Jayne smiled. 'I'm not that bothered about looks as long as he's not revolting, how can I meet him?'

'Well, my latest boyfriend Robin is a solicitor and he has asked me to accompany him to a Masonic Ladies' Night at the Greenhill Hotel. He's also invited Henry the barrister as his guest. His name is Henry Walters and he's in the same Masonic Lodge. I asked if you could come with me and he was fine about it, so it's all fixed for next Saturday.'

'He isn't expecting me to be his partner for the evening is he?'

Irene smiled. 'I'm afraid not that would make things too easy so I'm afraid you will have to look dead sexy and flirt like mad. If we think he looks interested then we can use our usual ploy, and cross our fingers hoping he takes the bait.'

On the Saturday, Robin, Irene and Jayne arrived at the hotel and found a table in the bar. Jayne looked stunning in her tight-fitting dress, high-heeled smart shoes and blonde freshly shampooed gleaming hair. Even Robin was struggling to take his eyes off her, much to the annoyance of Irene. Henry Walters arrived, shook hands with Robin and joined them. He was a smart, tall and refined looking man.

'Henry, may I introduce Irene,' said Robin.

She leaned forward in her seat and Henry bent down and lightly kissed her cheek.

'Very pleased to meet you,' he smiled pleasantly.

Irene smiled, 'likewise,' she said, turning to Jayne.

'Mr Walters, I'd like you to meet my daughter Jayne, I do hope you don't mind her joining us tonight?'

'Not at all, and please call me Henry.'

He put out his hand and Jayne gently took it with a mild shake. He smiled and looked into her eyes for a moment longer than necessary and she held his gaze smiling in a slightly sensuous manner.

Henry hadn't been looking forward to that night, but things were looking up as he was delighted to be in the company of such a beautiful young lady.

'I'm delighted to meet you, my dear.' He spoke in a very cultured voice but as soon as he had said it, he regretted his patronising and rather old-fashioned response.

'Would you like a drink, Henry?' Robin enquired.

'I think they are calling us in,' he replied. 'I'll have some wine with the meal.'

They made their way to their table in the dining area and Jayne deliberately walked ahead to give Henry a view of her stunning figure from the rear.

Irene was pleased to spot him glancing down at Jayne's eye-catching body as she exaggerated her walk. Once at the table she manoeuvred herself into a seat opposite him.

During the meal Jayne turned on the flirting, she laughed at his jokes, gave him sexy looks and asked him questions about his work. Irene noticed that he hardly took his eyes off Jayne, in fact she thought he looked a little embarrassed as he was having trouble avoiding the odd glance at her and Jayne knew it.

After dinner they were entertained by a singer and pianist but when the performances were coming to an end, Irene suddenly stood up. The plan was going to be put into action.

Irene spoke quietly whilst feigning head pains.

'Gentlemen, please excuse us but I have a dreadful headache so we will have to leave early.'

Robin got to his feet. 'I've had a bit to drink but I think I'm OK to drive you home,' he said, looking concerned.

'We won't hear of it, there are always taxis outside. We're not going to spoil your evening, you haven't even finished your drinks. Thank you for a lovely evening Robin, I'll ring you tomorrow.'

Irene and Jayne both pecked him on the cheek and Jayne then walked around the table to Henry. She leaned down close to his face with her luscious blonde hair falling forward and gazed into his eyes with an alluring look, speaking slowly in her practised sultry voice.

'It's been an absolute pleasure to meet you Henry. I could listen to your fascinating stories all night. I do hope we meet again.'

'It's been a delight to meet you too,' he whispered. 'Perhaps we will meet again, my dear, but I cannot imagine where.'

He thought she smelt divine.

Henry hadn't bothered with the opposite sex since his acrimonious divorce several years earlier as he never moved in the right circles to meet anyone. However, he thought Jayne was one of the most enchanting and beautiful young ladies he had ever met, but unfortunately one too young to be interested in him.

The ladies left the table and as they passed the reception desk, Jayne gave the receptionist an envelope.

'Would you be so kind as to hand this envelope to Mr. Walters on table 8? I forgot to do so earlier.'

'Of course, I'll take it now.'

This was a ploy that they had used before and it was part of the plan. Irene and Jayne then took a taxi home.

When the ladies had left, Henry casually brought up the subject of Jayne.

'Pretty little thing, Irene's daughter, didn't you think, Robin?'

Henry was smitten and made the remark in the hope

of drawing a response. He wanted to know more about her but knew immediately that he had tried in a clumsy manner, with obvious motives.

'Yes, very pretty, half the fellows in Nottingham have been chasing her for a couple of years but as far as I know she doesn't put herself about much. Very fussy I hear. She is what you would call a sophisticated young lady.'

'I gathered that,' said Henry. 'Nice girl though.'

Henry made an attempt to change the subject. 'Pleasant evening wasn't it?'

'You liked her, didn't you?' Robin smiled mischievously, ignoring the question.

Henry didn't answer but he knew that his attraction had been obvious and it annoyed him immensely. However, he was unlikely to see her again, and as a man of his age wouldn't interest her, he decided to put all thoughts of Jayne out of his mind.

He was about to say something to Robin when the receptionist appeared.

'Mr Walters?'

'That's me,' said Henry.

'This envelope was left for you sir.'

Henry had no idea what it could contain but he opened it and covertly glanced at a note inside containing just one sentence – a sentence that would change his life forever.

I would like to talk to you, can you please ring me on 0602 496040.
Jayne Saunders

He closed the envelope and put it in his inside jacket pocket, trying to appear nonchalant.

Robin couldn't suppress his curiosity. 'What on earth was that, Henry?'

'It's nothing, I'll deal with it later.'

Henry's voice had a serious tone to it so Robin did not pursue the matter.

When Henry got home, he examined the note again. He stared at it trying to drag more information from it. He couldn't think of any reason why Jayne would want a further meeting other than to discuss a legal problem or something like that. Deep down he was hoping that she liked him, but he thought that was preposterous. He hadn't bothered with women since his divorce mainly because he didn't really come into contact with single ladies.

He rang her the following evening.

'Hello, Jayne speaking.'

'It's Henry Walters. I've telephoned in response to your note.'

He tried to think of something more exciting to add but failed, accepting that he could have made a better job of his opening remark.

'I'm pleased you rang. May I see you sometime to talk?' Jayne enquired.

'What about?' he responded sharply and wanted to kick himself.

'If it's difficult, I'll leave it if you like,' she replied.

'No, no, let's meet,' he said, slightly panicky. 'Just say when and where.'

'There's a small tea shop in the square, Harriet's it's called, could you meet me there about three o'clock on Sunday afternoon?'

He knew he would have agreed to any suggestion she made.

'That's fine, I'll be there.'

His curiosity overcame him. 'What's this all about? Is it regarding a legal matter?'

'Do you want it to be?' She replied tantalisingly.

Henry now guessed the meeting was nothing to do with work and he was feeling quite excited. He knew he couldn't resist meeting her to see how things would develop, to him she was the most lovely looking young lady he had ever met.

'No, I don't mind if it's nothing to do with the trial, I just assumed it was.'

Jayne then surprised him.

'I'm not being silly, but I got the feeling that we both wanted to see each other again, and as my mother mentioned that you were single, I wanted to find out if you felt the same way. Am I right?'

'Yes,' said Henry, 'I'm both flattered and delighted, I'll be there at three o'clock on Sunday.'

*

On Sunday, Henry thought about what to wear and finally decided to dress casually, but dressing casually did not come easy to Henry. He eventually plumped for grey slacks and a plain collared blue shirt without a tie. To Henry, an open neck shirt was extremely underdressed but he did wear his favourite blue blazer and felt he looked trendy.

He arrived at Harriet's early and chose a table in the corner which gave some privacy. He ordered a small pot of tea and waited nervously – he was more nervous than he sometimes felt in court.

He spotted Jayne approaching the teashop looking just as lovely as he remembered and he couldn't believe she was coming to meet him. She was dressed casually with trainers and sports top which made her look even younger than when they'd met at the dinner. She came over to Henry who rose politely. To his amazement and delight she offered her cheek towards him inviting a welcome kiss – Henry leaned over and pecked her on the cheek, he thought she smelt divine.

He tried hard to think of something exciting to say as they sat down but failed miserably.

'It's so nice to see you again Jayne, have you come far?'

'No, I live fairly local. How about you, do you live alone?'

'Yes, I live alone. I was married and we lived in a house called Tudor Manor just out of town but my former wife left me some time ago and I live there on my own now – we're divorced.'

Jayne knew he was divorced and she also knew where he lived. She had been to see Tudor Manor with her mother and they both loved the look of it. She obviously kept her snooping to herself.

Henry started to relax and began to open up a bit.

'Shall we have some tea and cakes?'

'That would be lovely.'

Henry ordered some from the waitress and looked into Jayne's eyes. He tried to speak in a sensuous voice but it didn't work, it simply wasn't his forte.

'I was very flattered to get your note. May I ask why you made contact?'

Jayne smiled, she seemed so confident to Henry for one so young.

'I find you a very interesting man and the work you do fascinates me. Of course, I'm not being rude but young men don't interest me – I prefer mature real men like you really.'

He tried to suppress his delight at hearing such a response. He had never received such a compliment and he loved it. He wanted so much to see her again and thought a compliment might be a good move. 'I must say, Jayne, that you look just as lovely in your sports kit as you did at the dinner. Have you been training?'

'Yes, I was in the gym earlier and then I went swimming. Do you swim Henry?'

'Yes, quite a lot really.'

'Which pool do you go to?'

Jayne sounded interested but wasn't really until she got the reply.

'I swim at home – I have a large indoor pool.'

Jayne could not suppress her pleasure at hearing this remark. *His own swimming pool*, she thought, *what a bonus.*

Henry spotted her delight and thought he would try to move things on.

'Would you like to come round for a swim sometime?'

Jayne jumped at the offer. 'I'd love to,' she said without hesitation.

'How about coming over next weekend, say about three o'clock on Sunday?'

'Wonderful, I'll be there.'

Jayne was delighted with her progress.

Henry eventually walked with her to her car after having spent one of the most enjoyable afternoons he had spent for years. After their swimming date at Tudor Manor, he took her to dinner, arranged theatre visits and their relationship slowly became more serious as the weeks passed. Henry became totally obsessed with her and he didn't want to be without her.

Weekends were spent together and within six months of their first meeting they were married. They enjoyed a honeymoon in the up and coming resort of Marbella in Spain staying at a large villa owned by Diego Garcia, a Spanish friend of Henry's.

When Jayne moved into Tudor Manor, Elsie Moyle, his housekeeper for many years, did not like the new arrangement at all as Jayne made her presence felt. She was lazy, selfish and loved the good life but Henry was prepared to put up with anything to please her. Mrs Moyle had to work harder due to Jayne's laziness, washing up was left and there was more washing and ironing to do. She felt that she was being treated as a true servant rather than enjoying the pleasant working atmosphere that had existed before Jayne had arrived.

Henry was oblivious to all of her frustrations. Their marriage was wonderful for Henry as he loved being with Jayne and he couldn't spoil her enough. There was nothing in his life more important than her and he hated it when they were apart. He was determined to increase his wealth so that he could retire early in order to spend more time with her.

Jayne more or less had everything she had ever wanted, she loved having access to plenty of money, going shopping and enjoying holidays with her good friend Moira or her mother. She was also into fitness and when she asked for an annexe to be built onto Tudor Manor for a solarium and sauna, Henry arranged it immediately.

A few years after their marriage, her mother went to live with a friend in Australia and although it upset Jayne, she understood her reason was due to loneliness now that Jayne had married.

Two

Nearly four years of blissful marriage had passed for Henry and he had enjoyed taking Jayne for a special meal on every wedding anniversary. As he sat in the kitchen having his breakfast with her, he was aware that the next day, the 16th February 1982, was their fourth anniversary and he would unavoidably be in court in London. He was extremely upset.

'You are looking particularly nice this morning, my dear,' he said.

Every morning he liked to say something complimentary to Jayne. It was his way of assessing her mood which he judged from her response.

'Thank you, darling.'

She smiled as she replied and he knew that she was in a good mood. Jayne was totally unpredictable, some days moody and others full of life. He never knew what she would be like from one day to the next. She tormented him really, knowing how much he wanted to keep her and she took advantage of everything, his feelings, money and his inability to say no to her every wish. Yet he didn't mind so long as he pleased her. He still felt the same as the day they married and come what may he would never let anything ruin their relationship.

One thing Jayne always did was to prepare his breakfast of boiled eggs and toast when he was home – four minutes precisely with the toast slightly burnt. He liked his tea in a teapot, he couldn't stand tea bags. He was an old-fashioned perfectionist and he knew many people found him boring, but try as he might, he was unable to change his ways at this stage of his life.

'Where did you say your new trial is being held?' Jayne asked the question without even looking up from her newspaper.

'London, my dear. I should be there for about six weeks.'

He was always pleased when she seemed to take an interest in his work. In reality she wasn't interested in the slightest.

'I'll miss you, especially as I'll be in London on our wedding anniversary. I'm really upset about that,' he added.

'I'll miss you too, I feel the same.' She still never looked up.

'I had better get ready.'

Henry made his way upstairs. He never concerned himself about Jayne's disinterested attitude; he simply chose to ignore it. It was just her way and he accepted it.

He liked to do his own packing and he laid out shirts, underwear, socks and other necessities. Being Queen's Counsel he had a court wig, a silk gown and other court regalia which he kept in a purpose-made bag together with a brief case for the appropriate documents for the trial.

He was now ready to leave so he picked up his bags and made his way downstairs.

As he reached the foot of the stairs, his housekeeper, Elsie Moyle, arrived. She was a fit and hardworking woman who looked after most of the household chores. She came in every weekday at about 9 a.m. Henry was always astounded by her fitness as she was now 67 years old and Henry thought the world of her but Jayne did not like her at all and was sometimes quite rude.

Mrs Moyle had looked after Henry and his first wife Anne for many years and Jayne resented her more intimate knowledge of Henry's likes and dislikes.

'Good morning to you, Elsie,' he said, glancing at his watch, it was 9 a.m. and he should have known that as she was never late.

'Good morning sir, I thought you'd have left by now.'

'I'm leaving right away as I want to be in my hotel by lunchtime. I have some papers to go through this afternoon.'

'When does the actual trial begin?' She asked with genuine interest.

'They start by sorting out the formalities and swearing in the jury which will take all of tomorrow and possibly some of the next day. The actual trial itself will probably start later on Wednesday.'

He put down his cases and went into the living room where Jayne was sprawled out full length on the sofa with Candy, her cute looking white poodle. Henry put up with this totally spoilt little dog, which he disliked immensely but he kept that thought to himself.

Jayne was reading with her long shapely legs showing off her superb tan courtesy of the solarium he had installed for her. Although she looked radiant, Henry knew she had probably done nothing to enhance her looks whatsoever.

To him, she always looked absolutely gorgeous but he hated it when men flirted with her in his presence. Sometimes he thought she played up to them by deliberately walking seductively and wearing sensuous dresses that tantalisingly showed the outline of her body. Men often took little notice of him as they thought he was either her father or a business acquaintance and his defence was to hold her hand or make a physical gesture to show the predator that she was his.

Henry stood in the doorway. 'I'm leaving.'

'Come here.' She spoke seductively.

He walked over to her obediently and she laid back on the sofa opening her arms as if she were offering her body to him. He leaned over her and kissed her gently on the lips. She smelt divine as always.

Suddenly she broke away. 'Off you go then or you'll be late.'

'Jayne, my dear, you do remember that it's our wedding anniversary tomorrow, don't you?'

'Of course I do but I didn't want to upset you by mentioning it.'

In reality, Jayne had completely forgotten already, she had more important things on her mind of a private nature.

'I've been upset since you told me you would be away this week but what can I do?' She was good at acting.

'I'll make it up to you darling.' Henry was trying to make her feel better.

'I know you will, you'll be home Friday, won't you?'

'Yes, as early as I can.'

As he walked through the hall Mrs Moyle glanced at him disapprovingly. She hated his readiness to crawl to Jayne's every whim, she remembered him with his first wife, strong and masterful. Henry knew Jayne wanted to dispense with Mrs Moyle's services and he knew it would improve the atmosphere but Elsie knew his needs and he would miss her terribly.

As he drove his Jaguar out of his gravel drive through the light snow, he glanced back at the house. It was mock Tudor and Anne had named it Tudor Manor. With the light covering of snow it looked to him as if it should be on a Christmas card. He loved the place and it would take a lot for him to move.

Once in London, he booked into his hotel and began to read the papers relating to the current defence he was to handle. The solicitor dealing with the case was Bryan Mathews and Henry met him later at the hotel. Whilst they sat having coffee in the bar, Bryan remarked that he thought Henry looked a little sad.

'You look a little down in the dumps Henry. Is everything OK?'

'I'm all right, it's just that it's my wedding anniversary tomorrow and I always spend it with my wife. We've been married four years.'

'Perhaps you shouldn't have taken this case after all then – I suppose I did persuade you a little.'

'It's not that, I had to take it – after all it's very lucrative for both of us.'

Henry was defending a man named Geoff Rawlings who had been charged with GBH (Grievous Bodily Harm).

'You can say that again,' said Bryan. 'Rawlings is very wealthy and he told me he would pay whatever it takes to get you.'

'It won't be so bad,' Henry smiled, looking unconvincing.

'I've made arrangements for flowers to be delivered for Jayne around noon and I've also left a beautiful necklace and anniversary card with my housekeeper to hand to my wife tomorrow morning.'

'That should make up for it old chap,' said Bryan, smiling.

As far as Henry was concerned it didn't, he wanted to be with her on this special day.

When his meeting with Bryan finished he went to his room and rang Jayne around 6 p.m.

'How are you my dear?'

'Not too bad but I do have a bit of a headache.' She put her voice on to sound a little poorly.

'I'm sorry to hear that dear. I won't keep you talking long, I just wanted to know that you are OK.'

'Thank you Henry – I'll be all right. Was the journey OK?'

'It was fine but I can't help being upset about missing our anniversary – I usually take you for a nice meal.'

'I know. Let's make up for it on Friday.'

'Yes, let's,' said Henry, 'I'll ring you tomorrow. Goodbye dear.'

'Goodbye, darling.'

That's that out of the way, she thought.

Henry then had dinner, checked a few more points about the case and retired to bed early.

The following morning he was due in court at 10 a.m. for the opening day and he rang Jayne before leaving, having given Mrs Moyle time to give her his gift and card.

'Happy anniversary darling,' he said as she answered.

'Thank you very much for the lovely present Henry. I only wish you were here to spend some time with me on our special day.'

'That's exactly how I feel,' said Henry, 'what are you going to do today?'

There was a slight pause.

'I'm going to Moira's this afternoon and Dawn and Harry have invited me to dinner tonight but I don't really feel like going.'

'I'll ring you about six o'clock and I'll make things up to you at the weekend.'

Henry hoped he had cheered her up.

'OK, must go, love you,' she said as she rang off.

Hearing Jayne's voice brought home even more how much he wanted to be with her that day of all days. He hastily made his way to the court's changing room feeling a little uncomfortable as he was unusually late.

Whilst sitting in the court he had a brainwave. As this first day would be taken up with swearing in the jury and other formalities, they would undoubtedly be finished by 4.30 in the afternoon. If so, he could get changed quickly at the hotel, ring Jayne and be on his way by six o'clock arriving home before 9 p.m. They could then have most of the evening together. It would be a lovely surprise for Jayne. The following morning he could leave home about 6.30 a.m. in order to be back at the hotel in time to prepare for the 10 a.m. start.

The day went as predicted and nothing occurred which would interfere with Henry's plans. The court closed at 4.20 p.m. and after several formalities, he returned to his hotel, showered and rang Jayne, it was about 5.45 p.m.

'How are you my dear?'

'I'm OK Henry but I've still got a headache although it's not as bad as it was earlier.'

Henry chatted a little more before asking her the main question.

'Are you going out tonight dear?'

'No, I'm staying in to watch a film.'

Henry was delighted to hear that and once the call was ended, he left immediately for Tudor Manor to spring his surprise. He was sure it would cheer her up.

*

On the day of Henry and Jayne's anniversary, Elsie Moyle handed Henry's card and present to Jayne in the morning and noticed that there was little sign of any gratitude. The flowers were delivered later which Elsie arranged in a vase with water but she noticed that Jayne was not particularly bothered about those either.

"Ungrateful cow," she thought.

Jayne read for a while on the sofa and then took Candy for a short walk, after which Jayne drove to Moira's for a coffee and a light lunch. She was back home by three o'clock. Mrs Moyle finished her work around 4 o'clock and went home shortly after.

Jayne now had the house to herself.

Around six o'clock on her wedding anniversary, Jayne was stretched out alluringly on her oversized bed totally naked. The bedclothes were pulled back and her bronzed body appeared firm and well formed in the faint romantic lighting she had organised. Lying next to her on the bed was John Stevens, a 29 year old fitness mad insurance representative who had arrived shortly after Elsie Moyle had left. After nearly an hour of sex, they had both dozed off. She stroked his muscular arm.

'Are you awake?'

Her question was answered with a moan as John reluctantly stirred but made no response. Jayne shook his arm a little more aggressively, she wasn't used to being ignored.

'John, you'll have to wake up because he'll be ringing shortly,' she ordered, with some concern.

'You don't need me to speak to your husband.' John gave the curt reply without moving.

'I know that, but I don't want you doing anything silly when he rings. I'd rather you went into another room as he's bound to ring in a moment. It's our wedding anniversary so he'll ring on time.'

Jayne had met John Stevens at the local fitness club where he used to work part time and she saw him purely to satisfy her sexual desires, nothing more. However, she had met someone even more exciting so shortly she intended to finish with John completely.

John Stevens had received a call from Jayne around lunchtime that day, asking if he fancied coming over later that afternoon. Whenever he got the chance to see Jayne he jumped at it and that day was no exception. He always obeyed Jayne's instructions by driving to the house and parking in the next street away from the Tudor Manor.

John was a handsome blond man and his regular training at the local fitness club had enabled him to develop a well-toned body. Being over 6 feet tall and good looking, Jayne welcomed his physical attention. As far as he was concerned he was enjoying weekly sex with a beautiful woman of substance and he got a kick out of it, but knew better than to boast about the arrangement.

He had a puzzled look on his face. 'So as it's your wedding anniversary, do you want me to leave?'

She looked at him with a wry smile.

'Certainly not, I want you to stay tonight but I must get Henry's call out of the way as I can't feel comfortable until I have.'

As she spoke, the telephone rang, it was about a quarter to six.

'That's him, be absolutely quiet. In fact, clear off.'

She flicked her free hand in a shooing motion and John wrapped a towel around his waist and moved to the door.

She let the telephone ring for a moment and answered the extension beside the bed. As she did so she turned her back on John.

'Hello,' she said quietly, predictably it was Henry.

'How are you, my dear?'

His opening line was always the same, *boring,* she thought.

'I'm OK, Henry. I've still got a headache but it's not as bad as it was earlier.'

She lied blatantly to shorten the call.

'I'm sorry, my dear, I do hope it improves – I won't talk for long, so you liked my present?'

'Oh yes, as I mentioned this morning it's absolutely beautiful and I loved the flowers too, thank you again.'

She could see John out of the corner of her eye pulling faces and blowing kisses. She found him childish sometimes, quite immature – she knew she could do better.

'Are you going out tonight dear?' Henry asked.

'No, as I mentioned earlier, I'm staying in to watch a film.'

Jayne attempted to please him and end the call.

'Happy anniversary again, and thanks again for the necklace.'

'I'm so glad you liked them, my dear. I do try to make your day better when I'm not able to be there. Special occasions are not the same when we are apart. I just wish I was there with you tonight, don't you?'

'Absolutely, I miss you so much, but I do understand – I love you. See you Friday.'

She lied blatantly and didn't sound very convincing but she had got to the stage where she automatically said what he wanted to hear.

'I love you too,' said Henry and rang off. He had no intention of spoiling the surprise he had in store for her so as soon as he had replaced the receiver, he began his journey home.

Jayne felt relieved that John's larking about went unnoticed. She replaced the receiver and stared into space for a moment pondering as to whether she was doing the right thing. She did have the occasional feeling of guilt, but it was her life and the feeling never lasted for long. John's voice jolted her from her deep thoughts.

'Everything OK, you little fibber. When's he coming home next?'

'Not until Friday.' Jayne looked annoyed.

'John, I'm fed up with you messing around when I'm on the phone, I really am – you're like a big kid, pack it up.'

John looked amused. 'It's only a bit of fun. You don't like him much anyway so what's the big deal?'

'It's a big deal because it's my life and I don't want it ruined so don't do it again.'

John snapped to attention and saluted with a broad grin on his face. 'Sorry madam – I shall obey.'

Although Jayne had decided to finish with him she couldn't help smiling. 'OK, let's have some more champagne.'

John filled up two full flute glasses whilst Jayne went to the kitchen.

She returned with a plate full of prawns, crisps and sandwiches.

She smiled as she put the plate on the bed.

'Tuck in, I thought these might get our strength back. I love prawns with champagne, don't you?'

'Fantastic. I love seeing you and it's great how you

provide snacks as well – it saves me having to get a meal when I see you.'

'That's typical of you John. I think the sex and meals is all you want me for.'

'I think you're the same about the sex bit, truth be told.' He didn't know how right he was.

Jayne was getting weary of his attitude but the atmosphere changed as he reached out for her again and she gently slid against him. She responded immediately to his desires by passionately kissing him and encouraging his sexual advances. Within seconds they were violently making love again. This was the only thing Jayne liked about John – his powerful sex drive which never seemed to diminish. When it was over, they fell back on the bed exhausted and both fell asleep.

Jayne awoke suddenly to the sound of the doorbell. Drowsily she glanced at the clock and saw it was after 8.30 p.m. She shook John but he merely grunted and remained asleep.

She got out of bed and put on a dressing gown whilst furiously thinking of how to handle this problem. She knew she had to answer the door as she was supposed to be at home and the bedroom light was on. She looked in the mirror, straightened her hair and raced downstairs. The bell rang again, this time more urgently.

"All right for Christ's sake, I'm coming," she whispered to herself.

She reached the door and peeped through the side window, it was her friend Moira. She was about to open the door when she spotted John's jacket hanging over the chair in the hall. She grabbed it and threw it onto the living room sofa before rushing back to the door.

'Are you all right Jayne? Is everything OK?' Jayne paused momentarily before calmly opening the door.

Moira was standing there with a card and parcel in her hand. 'Are you all right?' she enquired.

'Yes, I'm sorry, you caught me in the bath.'

'I'm sorry' Moira said, 'when you came around earlier I forgot to give you these.'

She held out an envelope and small package wrapped in presentation paper.

'Happy Anniversary.'

'Thank you very much,' said Jayne, feeling edgy as to what Moira would do now.

As she took the present, she could see that Moira expected to be invited in so Jayne had to think fast, if she comes in John might wake up and shout down the stairs. Also, his jacket was in the living room. Nevertheless, it would be suspicious to leave her on the step in the cold. Jayne held her head and feigned another headache and decided to take a risk.

'I've got a dreadful headache Moira, it came on after I left you today but you can come in if you like. I'll just have to let the bath water go. Do you want to? I could see you tomorrow for a chat if not?'

'Oh no, I won't stop. I won't spoil your bath, I only wanted to drop your gift off. Yes, meet tomorrow if you're feeling better. I hope you get rid of that headache by then.'

Moira left as Jayne waved. *"What a relief,"* she whispered. She closed the door, relaxed and went into the kitchen taking another bottle of good quality champagne from the fridge. She then joined John in the bedroom who was sitting up in bed. He had been waiting patiently knowing there was a visitor.

'Who was that?'

'No problem,' said Jayne casually. It was just a friend with a present which she forgot to give me earlier. Look, I've brought some more champagne up.'

She smiled, trying to recapture the atmosphere they were enjoying earlier. John laughed and began to relax.

'Give me the bottle!'

He took it and went into the bathroom. There was a crack as the cork popped and he appeared at the bathroom door with the bottle oozing foam and a wide grin on his face.

'More champagne?' he said, pouring two glasses. He then straightened up dramatically and made an announcement.

'Let's have a toast – to us!' They held their glasses up high and chorused.

'To us!'

As Jayne said it, she knew she would be ending their relationship for good.

She had met a more desirable lover and she had been seeing him behind both Henry's and John's back. He was Jonathan Bond, a wealthy 38 year old business man who owned the luxurious Roman Rooms, a local night-club. There was nothing childish about him. To Jayne he was a real man, mature and masterful and she liked him a lot. She was sure that he was fond of her too, so the relationship had a promising future. Jonathan was taking her out to dinner the following evening.

Jayne and John sat in bed sipping their champagne. There was silence for a few moments before John spoke sounding more serious.

'When will I see you next, later this week, Thursday perhaps? I'd like to see more of you, we have such a good time when we meet don't you think?'

'I'm not sure when,' she replied, guardedly.

Jayne was stalling him. She was seeing Jonathan the next evening and was hoping to develop a more serious relationship with him.

'Leave it for a few days; I've got things on my mind.'

John detected her feelings for him were cooling.

As Jayne lay on the bed sipping her champagne, she was secretly considering how she could end this relationship without any bad feelings. She knew that the happy go lucky relationship she had with John was getting more serious on his part. Consequently, she was not prepared to sacrifice her affair with Jonathan, or her marriage, for what she considered to be little more than a bit of fun. Jonathan knew she was married but she was sure he was under the impression that he was her only lover and Jayne had told him that her marriage to Henry was purely platonic – another lie.

Three

Henry saw the house looming up as he caught it in his headlights. It was just before 9 p.m. and he had made good time. To be home when working at court was an unheard of treat. He could hardly believe that he was back home having only left the previous morning. He almost felt guilty, like a schoolboy playing truant. He intended to leave early the following morning to ensure he was in court in good time but in the meantime he looked forward to spending the night of his anniversary with his beloved Jayne.

On his journey from London, he had stopped on the way with the intention of buying chocolates but spotted a late night garage where he bought another bouquet of mixed flowers instead. He was quite excited about his rather out of character plan. They had both accepted that they would be apart on this special day, he being in London and she at their home in Nottingham, but here he was, complete with flowers, ready to spring his surprise.

He parked on the road so that Jayne wouldn't hear the engine and picked up the flowers and a small overnight bag, closing the car door quietly. It was a clear night and the house was in darkness other than lights shining in the hall and their bedroom. The snow on the roof stood out in the moonlight – it looked picturesque. The gravel crunched under his feet causing him to tread lightly.

He was excited and quite proud of his adventurous plan which was totally out of character – he thought it might be a good idea to be more like this in the future as Jayne often accused him of being staid and old-fashioned.

As he was about to put the key in the front door he stopped. He began to think about what he should say and how he should announce his surprise? He didn't want to frighten Jayne so he pondered for a moment and after a few seconds decided to creep up the stairs and shout 'happy anniversary!' A burglar would hardly do that. He knew she was awake as he saw that the bedroom light was on.

Carefully he opened the door and entered quietly, depositing his bag in the hall. Clutching the flowers he moved to the foot of the stairs. The hall was gloomy in the half light provided by a small lamp. When he was halfway up the staircase, he was about to shout but stopped abruptly. A male voice came from the bedroom. He froze, listening intently. There it was again. Surely it was the radio, he thought. Let it be the radio, he prayed. His heart was beating rapidly, something was clearly wrong as he could hear Jayne's voice. There was a conversation going on and it was no radio, there was a man in the bedroom.

Henry was glued to the spot and felt sick. His well intended surprise was shattered. Could this be a mistake? He frantically searched his mind for a logical explanation but to no avail. Should he enter the bedroom? Henry's experience had taught him to be calm in these types of situations and analyse the position before doing anything hastily.

He decided to investigate further so he carefully placed the flowers on the stairs and tiptoed along the dark landing. He felt like his heart was in his mouth as he moved along the landing and as he approached the bedroom door the voices became clearer. His heart was pounding so much he felt sure they would hear it inside. He listened outside and heard a man's voice say 'more champagne?' He then heard the man asking when he could see Jayne next. Henry felt completely destroyed.

Standing on the landing he cut a pathetic figure, he had experienced something that he had never contemplated and he could hardly believe it. As he stood there, listening to the romantic talk behind his own bedroom door, he felt a tear running down his cheek but he was angry and his anger was intense. So much so that if he had a weapon he could have burst into the room and killed the man without any compunction whatsoever. Even whilst standing there he thought of a case of murder he prosecuted successfully years earlier with more or less the same circumstances, and yet he caused the culprit to spend his life in prison. Little did he understand until now the motivation that caused the defendant to take a life.

He resisted doing anything and quietly went downstairs into the lounge where he flopped into an armchair to think. There he sat, tears trickling down his cheeks whilst he thought about what course of action to take. One thing was certain, whatever action he decided upon, the man in his bedroom would suffer.

"*What action to take?*" He thought to himself.

Divorce was unthinkable, he was obsessed with Jayne. If he could not have her, nobody else would. He considered how he would feel if it were an isolated incident, perhaps a one off sexual encounter. If that were the case he thought that if he challenged Jayne perhaps she would end the relationship. His mind was in turmoil but as he sat in the gloom his eyes became adjusted to the darkness and they eventually rested on a man's jacket lying across the sofa. Henry arose from his seat and examined the jacket. It looked modern, something a younger man would wear, even trendy. He found a wallet in the inside pocket which he removed and went under the hall light.

There were a number of credit cards and some business cards inside. Henry examined a business card and saw the name on the card was John Stevens, an insurance representative with a business named "*Lench Insurance Services.*" The address was local in Matton Street in Nottingham. The credit cards were in the same man's name. Henry put one of the business cards in his own wallet and replaced everything.

Despite a daunting second journey, he decided to drive back to London that evening and get some sleep before court in the morning. As it was about 9.30 p.m. he reckoned that the traffic would be light so he should be at the hotel soon after midnight. He would try to think things through and come up with a plan on the way.

He replaced the jacket, picked up the flowers and quietly opened the front door. He collected his bag from the hall and took one last look around before walking back to his car. He felt lonely, sick and cheated. He was determined not to do anything rash until he had considered the position rationally. He tossed the flowers on the back seat and glanced once more at the house before climbing in.

Henry thought he might become tired driving back so soon, he even thought he might have to stop at a hotel to get a few hours sleep but he had so much to think about, the time just flew by. Over and over again he re-lived the moment outside the bedroom door. Time and again he tried to come up with a sensible method of dealing with the situation. He needed to keep Jayne at all costs and his ideas were all focussing on that important point. The question he couldn't answer was whether he should come right out and tell Jayne what had happened and then see her reaction. However, he was worried that if he did that, it might inflame the situation and she might leave him.

Another alternative would be to warn off Stevens, threaten him if he didn't leave her alone. Then the terrible thought crossed his mind that she might be in love with him. That really frightened Henry as the danger of losing her was far greater in those circumstances. If it were merely a fling for sex then provided she didn't get involved and the relationship did not develop, he might be able to live with it. He was a wealthy man and despite being only 51, he was seriously thinking of retiring within a couple of years so that he could spend more time with Jayne. Once he had retired, he felt he could spend so much quality time with her, she wouldn't need anyone else.

He went straight to bed when he arrived back at his hotel but he couldn't sleep and he certainly was not looking forward to the following day in court. He felt well and truly tricked, deceived, and he had no idea what to do. He had always believed that there would be no other men as long as he spoilt Jayne and gave her everything she wanted.

He glanced at the clock at his bedside and was horrified to see it was 3.30 a.m. and he hadn't slept a wink. He still hadn't worked out what to do, but he had formulated the start of a plan. He had to establish the strength of Jayne's feelings for this man. Was she in love with him? Were they planning anything or was it just a fling? He thought these were the sorts of questions that needed to be answered before he could decide what action to take.

He had spent most of the night thinking it all through time and time again. By morning, as was often the case in worrying situations, he was sound asleep at last but he was woken by his alarm. He reckoned he had been asleep for about twenty minutes and he had decided to say nothing to Jayne until he had discovered more about her relationship. He proposed to telephone her as usual that evening as if nothing had happened. The problem was how to find out more about John Steven's but as Henry was stuck in London, it would not be easy.

When he got to court, he joined Bryan Mathews the defendant's solicitor.

'Good morning Henry, you look a little run down this morning if you don't mind me saying so, is everything all right?'

Henry knew he looked tired and so he tried to appear more cheerful and alert than he felt.

'I've had a rough night, I'm afraid. I don't really know why, something I've eaten I think. I'll be all right Bryan.'

'The good thing is,' said Bryan, 'we are only likely to be finishing off yesterdays formalities and there may be time for the prosecution's opening speech– not much for us to do fortunately.'

'Yes,' Henry replied, 'that's good news.'

With John Stevens in mind, Henry thought Bryan would probably have the details of private detectives used for gathering evidence, most solicitors have them. When the court adjourned for lunch he approached him again.

'Bryan, have you got any details of investigation firms in your office? I've got a little enquiry that needs doing.'

'I've got a little book of them – you can borrow it if you wish. Mind you, it doesn't just cover Nottinghamshire.'

'That doesn't matter.' Henry thought a firm located away from Nottingham might be preferable.

'Come over and borrow it now if you wish, my office is just down the road.'

'Thanks, Bryan, I will.'

Henry took the book back to his hotel after the day in court had finished. He went through the pages and his eyes fell on a firm in Luton named Oakfield Investigations Ltd with a Director named K. Williams. They advertised private detective work throughout the UK. Henry intended to use a false name. He liked the idea of using a firm not so close to home so he jotted the number down with the intention of ringing them the following day.

That evening, Henry had to make his first call to Jayne since his awful discovery. As he dialled the number he took a deep breath and tried to shut out his true feelings – he was determined to sound normal.

'Hello,' she sounded a little breathless, as if she had been jogging or something.

'Darling, it's me,' he said, trying to keep his voice light and breezy.

'Oh Henry!' she said. 'I've just had a swim, it's so nice to hear your voice. How has your day been?'

'Busy,' he said, 'the case is slightly overwhelming but I keep on going as always.'

He struggled to feign cheerfulness but he knew he had to sound happy, as though nothing unusual had happened.

'How has your day been, my dear?' he asked.

'Oh, things have been as quiet as ever.' She was lying and he knew it.

'I rarely see anyone while I'm rattling around here on my own.'

'Well, I'm looking forward to seeing you on Friday.'

'Me too Henry, I must go now. I'm still a bit wet.'

Henry usually said he loved her when he ended his call but it was sticking in his throat this time. He took a deep breath.

'Bye Jayne, I love you.' He forced the words out.

'I love you too,' she said.

After the call, he went to the restaurant where he had a quick light meal and by 9 o'clock he was in bed. Once again, he struggled to get to sleep.

*

John Stevens left Tudor Manor early on Wednesday morning as Jayne always insisted on that to ensure nobody spotted him. He had enjoyed being with Jayne as always but he had the distinct impression that she was deliberately cooling down the relationship and he wasn't actually sure what to do in the circumstances. He didn't want to lose his weekly rendezvous and so he decided to ring her later in an attempt to demonstrate his feelings for her. He knew he couldn't ever see her on a permanent basis but he was most reluctant to lose what he had.

After he had left, Jayne made herself some coffee and decided to sit down quietly and do some serious thinking. She was seeing Jonathan later that day and was sure that the relationship with him was becoming quite serious. Sometimes they saw each other two nights a week when Henry was away. She made a decision – John would have to be eliminated from her life and she decided to tell him the bad news as soon as possible.

That evening she had arranged to drive to an intimate restaurant about eight miles from Tudor Manor to meet Jonathan there at eight o'clock. After a meal and a few drinks, they intended to go to Jonathan's club for a nightcap before going on to Tudor Manor. Jayne had never been to his club before and had no idea what it was like but she imagined it was not classy enough for her liking.

Jayne had a lazy day, she read, took Candy for a walk and had a nap after a light lunch. Mrs Moyle cleaned the house and left around four o'clock in the afternoon. Jonathan rang about half past four.

'Hi babe.'

Jayne liked to hear his voice as he was always lively and never miserable.

'How are you doing?'

'I'm fine,' she replied. 'OK for tonight?'

Jonathan replied sounding sad. 'Afraid not, bit of a problem at the club. I have to go to Reading to do a deal and it's important. I've got to go tonight and stay over, I'm so sorry.'

Jayne's heart sank. 'Oh no, must you?'

'I can't get out of it honey, but I'm back tomorrow, can we make it then instead? We'll have a great night.'

Jayne was very disappointed but she always tried not to show it, she thought that was a sign of weakness.

'OK,' she confirmed, 'shall I meet you at the restaurant around 8 o'clock tomorrow evening instead?'

'That's fine, can't wait,' he replied. 'Take care and don't be late.'

He then rang off before she could reply.

She put down the receiver thoughtfully. It was a blow to have the date postponed but she decided to have an early night instead and looked forward to Thursday.

The telephone rang again almost immediately, it was John Stevens.

'How are you?' he asked.

'I'm all right, a little tired.'

She mentioned that she was tired as a precaution against being asked to meet him and she was right to do so.

'Are you doing anything tonight?' he enquired with false casualness.

Jayne was keen to commence running down the relationship.

'Sorry, John, but I'm really tired, perhaps we could make it another time?'

'Sure,' he said, 'I understand.'

"If only he did," Jayne thought.

Now that her evening had been ruined she relaxed in the house. She began to think that it might be quite pleasant after all, have a swim, enjoy an easy meal and watch a film. She began to like the idea thinking that there was no need to go out every night.

She spent some time swimming and was drying off when Henry rang, it was six o'clock.

'Hello.' She was breathing heavy whilst still trying to dry herself clutching the telephone.

'How are you?' Said Henry.

'I've just had a swim, it's so nice to hear your voice. How has your day been?'

Jayne always tried to sound interested but she thought he sounded different, more abrupt, as if something was troubling him. This was particularly apparent when they ended the conversation. She thought Henry didn't sound so sincere when he said he loved her but she dismissed it, thinking he was down in the dumps as he had missed their wedding anniversary.

Four

The next morning, Thursday, Henry was back in court listening to the prosecution barrister delivering his opening speech. The barrister was Ralph Hopkins who Henry knew well. It was a very impressive delivery and the case for convicting Rawlings of GBH seemed convincing. Henry noted that the jury looked equally impressed. He was still struggling to concentrate fully as he couldn't shake off his stressful feelings. Not only was Jayne's infidelity playing on his mind constantly, but the trial itself was now bothering him as well. He knew he wasn't in the right frame of mind and he would have never accepted this case if he had known of Jayne's infidelity at the time.

He spent lunchtime with the defendant's solicitor, Bryan Matthews, where they discussed certain issues before the afternoon proceedings opened. Like many solicitors,

Bryan had great respect for Henry being a QC of renown. They met in a comfortable private room and had coffee and sandwiches delivered.

Henry lit a cigarette and leaned back looking studious.

'Bryan, the prosecution barrister gave a good opening speech but we didn't learn anything new. I'd just like to go through our case again so I'm sure I've got everything right in my mind.'

'Do you know this prosecution barrister, Hopkins?' asked Bryan.

'Yes, he's pretty sharp I'm afraid.'

Henry took some papers from his briefcase.

'The accused is Geoff Rawlings, we know he's a wealthy man facing the serious charge of GBH and…'

Bryan interrupted him with a grimace. 'You have to remember, he is a wheeler-dealer and he's been in trouble before, you did know that didn't you?'

'Yes, I did know that but I now know he's been in prison. I know he's not a nice man but you told me that he especially wants me to defend him and that he would pay whatever it cost.'

'Yes, he did say that.'

Henry looked embarrassed. 'I've got a confession to make, Bryan.'

Bryan was a little bewildered, to him Henry did not seem to be his usual self.

'What is it?'

'I think you were right when you said that perhaps I shouldn't have taken this case.'

'Why on earth not – I was only joking when I said that?' Bryan looked shocked.

Henry took a heavy drag on his cigarette and looked embarrassed. Bryan had never seen him like this.

'Well, between you and me, I've got issues going on and together with Rawlings being a little rough and ready I'm not happy. Also this fellow can be awkward.'

'What sort of issues have you got?'

'I can't say old chap, stuff at home, but it's affecting me a little. I'll be OK, don't worry. It's just that you may have to assist me more than usual.'

Bryan was surprised but pleased Henry was prepared to confide in him.

'I'll do whatever is required,' he said.

'OK,' said Henry, 'let's recap. Go through it with me again.'

'Well nothing much has changed, we know Rawlings found out that the woman he lives with, Irene Howell, had been playing around with a man named Tomkins from London who came up North on business once a week.'

Bryan pulled out some notes from his bag which he went through.

'Rawlings knocked Irene about and got Tompkins' contact details. He then warned him over the telephone to leave her alone.'

'Yes, I got that.'

'Shortly after, Tomkins was beaten up in London and the result was two broken legs and injuries to his head, one leg is ruined for life. The attacker wore a balaclava but Tomkins is adamant it was Rawlings.'

'Well, the evidence for our defence is pretty good, don't you think?' Henry had been through it and was confident.

'It certainly looks good. Rawlings can prove he was playing cards at home with two friends. They say they were playing cards with him on the evening of the attack.'

Henry thought for a moment.

'Our key witness is Irene Howell and she confirms she was at home with Rawlings and he is just as adamant that he is innocent.'

'Don't forget Robert Free,' said Bryan, 'he was in the card game in Rawlings' house and he's a good witness too. It's a pity we couldn't get the third card player but he has gone abroad and we've got no chance getting him in court.'

'I don't think it matters, these two witnesses will win the case for us I'm sure.'

Henry then went silent as he took a couple of sips of coffee.

'Well, everything sounds OK to me.'

After another pause, Henry said, 'You will remember I asked you to have a word with Rawlings because he comes over very rough and ready. You know, tell him no bad language in court and get him to wear a suit. You said you would try to get him to look polished as normally he looks a bit like a thug. Did you do that?'

'Yes,' said Bryan, 'I spoke with him the other day and he gave me the impression that he would comply.'

'Good, let's go.'

The meeting ended and they entered the courtroom.

*

When Henry took his place in court, he noted with disappointment that Rawlings had taken no notice whatsoever of Henry's advice concerning his dress or his demeanour.

He turned to Bryan with an anguished look on his face.

'Rawlings is wearing jeans with a bomber jacket over a grubby sweatshirt – what happened to the request to smarten up? Did you tell him?'

'I told him, I honestly did and he said he'd think about it so I thought he would comply. He did say he couldn't see the point as the trial wasn't about his dress but I wrongly assumed he would do what we asked anyway.'

Bryan looked embarrassed and Henry was furious.

'This is a real set back, Bryan. The prosecution are delighted as I've just caught Hopkins glancing at me with a smug look on his face. They have to prove he's a violent man and straight from the start he looks like one – this is a disaster. Remember, Hopkins is no mug so we've got a problem.'

'What can we do?'

'Nothing, but I don't think we can let Rawlings take the stand dressed like that.'

Their whispering was interrupted by the judge.

'Mr Walters is everything all right?' he sounded irritated.

'I'm sorry, Your Honour.'

The witnesses for the prosecution began their evidence, with Hopkins introducing the injured Tomkins first. He was using a wheelchair and was rather dramatically wheeled into court with Hopkins trying to exaggerate his pain and injuries whilst taking him through his evidence.

Henry was delighted when the judge made his announcement after the conclusion of Tomkins' evidence.

'This court is now adjourned until two o'clock.'

Henry couldn't get out of the court quickly enough and as he left, Bryan Mathews tried to speak to him but Henry merely brushed past him.

'Sorry, Bryan, must dash.'

He hurried into the changing room and removed his court regalia before rushing to his nearby hotel in order to make the call to Williams of the investigation agency. A female voice answered reciting the number.

'May I speak with Mr Williams please?'

'One moment, I'll see if he's free,' was the reply.

After a few seconds a rather gruff male voice spoke. 'Yes, can I help you?'

'Is that Mr Williams?'

'Yes, Keith Williams speaking.'

'Well,' started Henry somewhat nervously, 'I want a job done. Can you help?'

'What sort of job?'

'Detective work, in Nottingham, I'll pay well. It's finding out some details about somebody.'

'Yeah, we do that sort of work, can you give me some brief details?'

'Of course. Have you a pen handy?' asked Henry.

Somehow he knew he was making a mess of this call. It wasn't really his line of country, put him in court and he was usually brilliant but with something like this he was like a fish out of water.

Williams was quite abrupt. 'I just want a basic idea of the job, if you give me a few details over the 'phone we can meet later. What's your name for a start?'

'Jenkins.'

Henry said the first name that came into his head.

'Address and telephone number?'

'Is all this necessary at this stage?'

As he said it, Henry knew this wouldn't work so before Williams replied he put the receiver down and cut off the call. *What a mess*, he thought. He needed to sit down and think his strategy through properly. He sat quietly in the hotel bar with some tea and sandwiches, and decided it would be better to carry out the investigation himself.

*

Henry returned to the court for the afternoon session. The doctor who saw Tomkins immediately after the attack gave evidence and Henry struggled to concentrate, his mind kept drifting back to the Stevens problem, trying to work out how he could find out about him. Suddenly he had a brainwave; he realised that he needed some sort of bug, a gadget that would record conversations in his bedroom. He knew he should not be thinking about such things whilst in court but try as he could, he was unable to stop.

Devices for eavesdropping were on the market, he had seen them in the Exchange and Mart, a popular weekly sales magazine. He knew a colleague who used one such device for evidence in an earlier trial.

He was still deep in thought when the judge suddenly spoke sounding irritated.

'Mr Walters, are you all right?'

The clear and powerful voice of the judge resounded across the courtroom and it jolted Henry from his thoughts.

He looked at the judge with a look of extreme confusion and embarrassment.

'I'm sorry, Your Honour. I'm not feeling at all well which accounts for my demeanour. I cannot apologise enough.'

'I'm sorry to hear that. Would you like an adjournment for today?'

'I would be extremely grateful, Your Honour.'

'Very well, this court is adjourned until ten o'clock tomorrow morning.'

It was adjourned nearly an hour before the normal time. *Wonderful*, thought Henry.

He decided to take advantage of his good fortune and visit the nearby newsagents to purchase an Exchange and Mart. He had a coffee in the court café intending to change in his room before going to the newsagents. As he sat with his coffee going over things once more he was deep in thought when his thinking was interrupted by the voice of a friend, Donald Bates, who was passing. A barrister of some repute, Donald had studied with Henry many years earlier and they had often found themselves staying together and sharing the odd beer or meal.

'Hello, Henry, nice to see you,' said Donald, pulling up a chair.

As he started to get comfortable, Henry responded.

'Sorry, old boy, but I've got to go somewhere urgently.'

With that, he rose abruptly and left Donald sitting there rather taken aback.

Henry made his way straight to the newsagents in the next street. Nothing could distract him from his quest to resolve the problem regarding Jayne and her lover – Jayne was everything to him and he knew that he was totally and utterly obsessed with her no matter what she had done. He was in the shop within minutes and on his way back to his hotel room with the Exchange and Mart.

Donald had been chasing him and caught up with him. He looked anxious. 'Henry, is everything all right?'

Henry knew he had been rude.

'I'm sorry to have been so abrupt Donald but I have a little personal issue that I must deal with quickly, are you staying overnight?'

'Yes, I am.'

'Shall we dine together?' Henry wanted to put things right.

'I'd like that. Shall we say 8 o'clock in the hotel restaurant?' said Donald.

Henry agreed and made his way to his room. He made himself comfortable and began to scour the Exchange and Mart for the equipment he felt he needed. He was not disappointed with what he saw as there were numerous advertisements for surveillance equipment. He spotted a company in Enfield called Professional Security Services which advertised all types of surveillance devices and investigation work. There was a telephone number but rather than get caught out as he did on the first attempt, Henry had prepared false details in readiness. He needn't have bothered as this firm was far more amenable.

He rang the number.

'Is that Professional Security Services?'

A friendly voice answered. 'Yes, Peter Andrews speaking. How can I help?'

'I'm after some listening equipment. Do you sell that sort of thing?'

'Yes, we have all the latest surveillance equipment. What are you after?'

'Well, I want to secretly record some conversations in a bedroom. Is that possible?'

'Of course, no problem. Why don't you come in and see what we've got? We're open every weekday until 6 o'clock in the evening.'

Henry liked the way this was going.

'Would it be all right if I came on Friday afternoon before six o'clock, although I may be slightly late?'

'I'll stay open until you get here.'

'Splendid, thank you very much. See you Friday.'

Henry was pleased as he would pass Enfield on his way home and six o'clock shouldn't be a problem.

Five

Thursday was a busy day for Jayne. She intended to make a special effort for Jonathan and that afternoon she had an appointment with her hairdresser. She hadn't seen him for a while and was looking forward to the night immensely. She decided to ring him before her hair appointment to make sure there were no problems. As she would be leaving about 7.45 p.m. for the restaurant, she wanted to get Henry's usual call out of the way before getting ready. She felt pretty good that afternoon and was pleased with her hair. She was going to wear a relatively new outfit that Jonathan hadn't seen before.

She rang Jonathan that afternoon.

'Hello, sexy,' she spoke in a sultry voice when he answered.

'Hi, babe. I'm really looking forward to seeing you – we'll have a blast tonight.'

Jayne was truly excited but she always tried to appear relaxed and composed. 'I'm really looking forward to seeing you as well, I'm feeling really hot tonight and I'm taking my feelings out on you.'

'Be my guest, can't wait.' Jonathan chuckled down the phone.

'See you at eight, honey.' She rang off.

Henry rang just after six o'clock. Jayne felt that he sounded a little different than usual, as if something was troubling him. She tried to cheer him up.

'You sound a little down darling, the trials obviously getting to you. Don't be sad – you'll be home soon. What time do you think you'll finish tomorrow?' she asked him.

'We'll finish in court a bit later than usual I think, around five in the afternoon but I should be home before 9 o'clock. I'm looking forward to seeing you,' he added.

Henry had built in some time to collect the listening device from Enfield on his way home.

He knew somehow that he didn't have the same sincerity when he spoke to Jayne but kept telling himself that he must try to sound as though nothing had changed. However, it had, and how he knew it.

Jayne had noticed the change in Henry, she also thought he was a little frosty and she put it down to tiredness. Knowing he would be home the next day depressed her no end as she hated weekends but she had to act the loving wife as that was the price she had to pay for the luxurious life style she enjoyed the rest of the week.

She started to get ready at half past six as she intended to make a supreme effort. From her well-stocked wardrobe she took the relatively new shimmering blue dress which was tight and low cut. She knew this subtly displayed her generous breasts. She laid out the dress on the bed and then examined her large choice of shoes, wondering which colour would be best. She loved getting ready to go somewhere special and with Jonathan, it was always special. She liked to sexually tease him so having selected her blue high heeled shoes, she laid out her underwear complete with silk stockings and suspenders. To complete everything she added her new gold handbag that she had bought the previous week.

She always left the selection of jewellery until she was ready to leave and so having placed everything on the bed, she went for a shower in the en suite bathroom.

At seven o'clock she was refreshed and began putting on her make up before starting to dress. When she had finished she stood in front of the full length mirror in a somewhat admiring manner.

'Not bad,' she whispered to herself.

From her jewellery case, she took her gold watch, an expensive bracelet and the new necklace that Henry had bought her for their anniversary. Large dangling earrings set it all off nicely and she was decidedly pleased. Her eyes did rest on Henry's anniversary present, the necklace.

'*Christ*,' she whispered, '*it must have cost a grand at least.*' She wondered if she should wear it. Was it right to do so?

Sod it, she thought, *why not*? She picked up her bag, flicked off the light and left.

She had visited the restaurant previously with Jonathan and it was very upmarket. She liked it a lot and had got to know the manager as he always made a point of speaking to Jonathan. It seemed to Jayne that Jonathan had many connections throughout the area, presumably due to the popularity of his club. She never went anywhere like this with John Stevens – in fact she never went anywhere at all with John, only her bedroom. That tended to make her feel cheap and was an added reason for finishing with him.

On the odd occasion Henry took her anywhere, she made sure they kept away from Jonathan's favourite establishments. This restaurant, called *The Beech Tree*, suited her and Jonathan very well as it usually never closed until the last clients had left so they could eat a leisurely meal with good quality wine, rounding things off with a coffee and a brandy or two. Drinking restrictions concerning drink driving were much more relaxed in the eighties.

She got to the restaurant at ten minutes past eight but she couldn't see his car. 'Damn,' she said to herself.

Jayne hated arriving first for a date. She thought it made her look too keen to see him when in fact she was very keen indeed. There was also the unpleasant moments being in the restaurant alone looking like a pick up. She therefore drove down the road and parked on the kerbside. She waited impatiently for a full ten minutes before driving back to the restaurant and she was pleased to see that his car was parked just outside.

She parked up, looked in the mirror of the car and made one or two unnecessary adjustments to her hair before leaving the vehicle. Confidently she strode over to the main door and through into the bar. Jonathan was there, ordering a gin and tonic. He didn't see her approach and so she was able to sidle up and tease him by purring in his ear whispering, 'Hello, sexy'. She deliberately and shamelessly stepped back so that he could see a full length view of her efforts.

Jonathan turned, smiling broadly. 'God, you look wonderful.'

She could detect the genuineness in his voice. He ordered her a vodka and tonic and as their table was ready, Jayne sat down and waited for him to bring the drinks. She felt good and knew she was going to enjoy the night. Jonathan joined her and they were immersed in deep conversation when the waiter arrived with the menus which they studied and selected their meals.

The manager then came to their table.

'Good evening, Mr Bond, it's lovely to see you again. Are you well?'

He was grinning from ear to ear and appeared to be overly ingratiating.

'Yes, Mark, I'm fine. You remember Jayne, don't you?'

'Yes indeed. Lovely to see you again and may I say how lovely you look tonight.'

Jayne thought his smile was kind of creepy but she loved the compliment. 'Thank you so much, Mark.' She felt slightly embarrassed.

Jonathan looked at her with obvious affection. 'He's absolutely right of course, you do look gorgeous tonight, even ravishing.'

'Perhaps you might do some ravishing later?' Jayne was beaming with pleasure at his compliment.

'Yes please,' he replied.

She knew she wanted to see much more of him. She found him a most fascinating man.

As Jayne was enjoying the meal and wine, she suddenly looked into Jonathan's eyes with a mischievous-looking smile.

'Do we have to go back to your club tonight?' she asked in a hopeful voice.

'Not if you don't want to. Keith, my manager, is there and if I ring him he can deal with any issues tonight. Don't you want to go for a nightcap there then?'

Jayne put her hand on his arm gently. 'I know where I want to go,' she had a playful smile on her face as she spoke.

'Shall we go to your place, is that what you mean?' he said.

'Why not, let's have a great night together. We can open a bottle of champagne and not have to worry about driving once we are home.'

'I'm always at your place, don't you want to come to mine for a change?' he suggested.

Jayne wouldn't want that.

'Jonathan, I can't really do that because I get worried if I'm not at home to sort a few things out before the cleaner arrives or, heaven forbid, if Henry should ring due to some sort of problem.'

'I understand, I don't know why you stay with him. I sometimes wish we could be together without sneaking around – I do think quite a lot of you, I'm sure you know that.'

'I'm feeling the same about you, it's bothering me too,' she said.

'Well, let's have some dessert and a nightcap here,' said Jonathan. 'We can then go straight to your place.'

She stared into his eyes as he spoke and she knew that to anyone watching they looked like a couple in love. Jonathan suddenly looked at her seriously.

'There's nobody else, is there?' he enquired urgently.

'Of course not,' Jayne lied. 'Apart from Henry, there's nobody in my life, and as I've told you, that's purely platonic.'

She felt guilty as she said it, but thought that as she had decided to give up John permanently, it was half reasonable. In her heart though, she knew she was lying. This conversation had quite an impact on Jayne as she was terrified of losing Jonathan and knew she had to get rid of John quickly and permanently. She was even thinking about how to handle that when Jonathan suddenly asked a very pertinent question.

'So where do you think our relationship is going do you think?' he asked.

'My,' murmured Jayne, 'we are serious tonight.'

'Do you mind talking seriously about our future?' As he asked a voice cut across their conversation rather abruptly.

'Excuse me, Mr Bond, are you ready to order desserts?'

They both turned to see the waiter standing poised with his order pad and pen at the ready. They gave their orders before a relieved Jayne was forced to respond to his rather awkward question which he appeared to have forgotten.

The evening had been wonderful for Jayne. They had talked incessantly as usual, enjoying the good food and wine. It was easy to feel romantic in the atmosphere created by this particular restaurant – the whole surroundings made the place somewhere special. The intimate nature of the place, with its subdued lighting and tables fitted into private alcoves, generated an ambience of relaxation. Now that they had both enjoyed a couple of large brandies their feelings for each other began to come to the surface.

Jayne thought that she had avoided the poignant question Jonathan had posed earlier and she was pleased about that as she wanted more time to think about her answer. However, clearly he hadn't forgotten as he suddenly looked earnestly into her eyes.

'I asked you earlier where you thought our relationship was going. It's important for me to know. How do you *really* feel about me?'

Jayne looked closely at his sincere expression. She knew there was no escape from answering but she took her time and blatantly made him wait while her mind raced, searching for an answer whilst holding his gaze. There was something much more than a sexual attraction here, she knew that, but was she in love? Was that the answer he was looking for? She wasn't going to commit herself by saying that she was in love, until she was totally sure. She put her hand gently onto his.

'I think so much of you, darling, more than I have ever thought about anyone.'

He looked disappointed. 'But you don't love me, do you?'

'Do you love me?' she said, anxious for a nice reply.

'Yes, totally and utterly.'

Jayne was shocked and taken aback by his frankness but she believed him, and deep down she was pleased. Before she had time to reply, he excused himself from the table.

'Sorry, Jayne, I've just noticed the time. I must ring the club to make sure all is well.'

Good, Jayne thought.

She correctly figured that he had deliberately left at that critical moment and she welcomed that to collect her thoughts. She lit a cigarette and leaned back to think about this development.

She thought about her feelings for Jonathan in the light of his surprising admission. If she spurned him, she might lose him altogether. It was inevitable to her that she would fall in love with him, indeed she felt that she might be in love with him already – how does one assess the difference between love and deep feelings for someone? It all seemed close enough to her, especially as she would be finishing with John.

Whilst she was thinking, the manager came to the table.

'Good evening again, is everything all right, madam?' he enquired.

'Absolutely,' Jayne replied. 'I love your restaurant, it's the best I've been in around here.'

'You've never been to Mr Bond's restaurant then?'

'I didn't know he had one, I've not known him long you see.'

'He has a lovely restaurant in his club, beautiful it is.'

'Really?' Jayne was surprised as she was under the impression that it was simply a nightclub and nothing special.

'I've known Mr Bond for years and he's one of the most generous and helpful men I've ever met. He paid several thousand pounds for my wife to have a life-saving operation and he never asked for a penny back.'

'I don't know that much about him but I do like him very much, he must be very well off to be able to do that.'

Jayne was hoping for some information on his financial situation.

'He is very wealthy and he helps no end of people and charities, extremely generous he is. Mind you, you wouldn't want to cross him, that's a different story.

Anyway, I'm so pleased you are enjoying the evening and I hope to see you again soon.'

The manager left.

Jonathan returned from the telephone and Jayne wondered for a moment if he had rung anyone at all, perhaps he was just giving her time to think. Jonathan sat down and looked at her searchingly. It was clear that he was after an answer to his earlier question which seemed to confirm that the call was contrived. Jayne took the initiative, placing her hand on his once again, she stared deep into his eyes.

'Darling,' she said, 'I don't want anything to happen to our relationship. I want us to keep seeing each other and to be together as much as we can. I don't want either of us to see anyone else, I want us to make that commitment. If that's love, then I'm in love with you, but I do get confused and I don't think I really know the meaning of the word.'

'That will do for me for the moment.' Jonathan looked very pleased.

They were holding hands across the table, looking at each other knowingly when Jayne made a profound comment.

'One thing is certain, if anything happens regarding Henry, there is only one person I would want to be with and that's you.'

Jonathan was delighted with this disclosure.

'Why can't you leave him then, we could then be together properly?'

'I can't at this time, please don't put any pressure on me at the moment.'

'OK, I'm happy for now,' he said, smiling.

Jayne was being selfish. She wanted to make sure everything was going to work out OK before she took any decisions which might spoil her life. Henry was very wealthy and at the moment she was having her cake and eating it. She wasn't ready to give it all up until she could see how it would be if she was with Jonathan permanently.

Jonathan signalled to the waiter who came over with the bill.

'Shall we go?' Jonathan said to Jayne.

'Everything all right, sir?' enquired the waiter.

'We've had a wonderful evening, thank you,' Jonathan said, more to himself than the waiter.

He paid with his usual generous tip and they drove straight to Tudor Manor. Jonathan followed Jayne's car and parked a short distance from the house. She parked on the drive, let herself in and collected a bottle of champagne from the fridge. She then went into the living room and put on the dim light of the standard lamp. As she was collecting a couple of champagne glasses, from the cabinet there was a gentle tap on the front door. She put the flutes on the table and let Jonathan in.

He immediately kissed her in the hall. It was a kiss of affection but it soon developed into something more as she felt his body pressing strongly against hers. They were soon kissing passionately and she felt him fumbling with the zipper on the back of her dress. As they were still in the hall, it all seemed a little unromantic and she momentarily thought she should stop him, but it was a half-hearted thought which she quickly dismissed from her mind. She felt her dress go loose at the shoulders and the dress fell to the floor. She now knew she couldn't resist him and so she stepped out of the dress and took his hand leading him up the stairs to the bedroom.

The champagne glasses were still on the table and they stayed there all night.

*

Jayne awoke early on the Friday morning when the alarm rang. She was always edgy on Fridays as she had to get psychologically prepared for Henry's homecoming that evening. He usually arrived between seven and eight o'clock but that night he'd told her that he would be late. He always expected dinner when he arrived which was usually prepared by Mrs Moyle and left ready to be heated up by Jayne later. She hated Fridays.

It was around six o'clock in the morning when the alarm woke her and she saw that Jonathan was still stretched out beside her half awake. She pushed him and he came round.

'Hello, babe,' he murmured affectionately. 'How you feeling?'

'Great, I'll show you.' Jayne kissed him passionately and within seconds they were making love again. She simply couldn't get enough of him and as they fell back on the bed in each other's arms, he started breathing heavily.

'Don't go to sleep,' Jayne ordered, 'it's nearly seven o'clock and you must leave soon.'

'God, I hate this creeping about,' he said, irritated. 'I'd love to be with you and not have to worry – do you think that will actually happen one day?'

'I really hope so too,' she said truthfully. 'In the meantime get dressed.'

She pushed him from the bed jokingly and he fell onto the floor laughing. She looked at him seriously for a moment thinking how much fun they have together and it made her think that perhaps she really did love him. He wanted her to say it and so she decided now was the time. She leaned over and cradled his head in her hands, staring into his eyes.

'Jonathan, I love you, now clear off!' she said, jokingly.

He looked at her with disbelief. 'You don't know how happy that makes me feel to hear you say that. I'll go now, it was a wonderful night. When will we see each other next?'

Jayne pondered. 'Henry will be back tonight for the weekend, he's on a big trial in London but any night next week is fine, maybe even two nights?'

'Wonderful. What about Tuesday?' ventured Jonathan.

'Fine by me,' she said, 'but for Christ's sake get ready, I need to tidy up before Moyle arrives – she'll be here within the hour.'

Jonathan showered, dressed and left discreetly just after eight o'clock. He left through the rear door and it was still a little dark.

'I'll ring you Monday to fix things up,' was his parting remark.

She watched him creep to the side of the house and as he was about to go through the hedge to walk discreetly to his car, Jayne cautioned him.

'You can't stay this late again, we must make it earlier in future because Moyle could come early for some reason. We must remember that next time.'

'OK,' he replied turning round momentarily, 'but I just wish that one day we won't have to put up with all this sneaking about, I really do.'

With that, he disappeared through the hedge.

Jayne put on a dressing gown and made some coffee. She then cuddled Candy for a moment and picked up the papers which were lying on the mat. She sat down at the kitchen table and had been reading for some time when she heard a key being turned in the front door.

'It's only me,' Mrs Moyle's voice was distinctive and loud.

Jayne rose from the table and went into the hall.

'How are you?' Jayne enquired, more out of politeness than interest.

'Fine. My word, you look a little rough. Have you been to a party or something?'

Mrs Moyle thought she had been up to something, she often thought that.

'I went to a friend's house and had a few drinks. I came home later than I intended.'

It was the best excuse Jayne could muster up.

'So what,' she whispered under her breath, 'it's only the bloody maid, what's it got to do with her anyway?'

She knew she probably looked rough so whilst Mrs Moyle was hanging up her coat in the cupboard, she went into the living room and examined herself in the mirror.

'My God,' she whispered, 'I do look rough.'

Then, horror of horrors, she spotted in the mirror the reflection of the two champagne flutes which were still on the table from the night before. Desperately she spun round, picked up the flutes and put them hastily in the drinks cupboard. She just managed to shut the cupboard door as Mrs Moyle walked briskly into the room carrying cleaning materials and a duster. Jayne glanced around the room to make sure that there weren't any other signs of her evening's activities.

Satisfied, she announced, 'I'll leave it to you then.'

She then strode out of the room and went to her bedroom. She knew she had plenty to do that day in readiness for Henry's homecoming and she was not looking forward to that one jot.

Six

Henry found it extremely difficult to concentrate in court during Friday as he kept thinking about his visit later that afternoon to the security firm. He was determined to get a suitable device to record what was going on when he was away. The day in court was mainly spent continuing with the evidence of the injured Tomkins, followed by the start of the doctor's evidence who was the first to examine his injuries. Henry saw nothing contentious in the evidence and so he declined to cross examine. He was convinced that the evidence of Irene Howells and the Robert Free would sway the jury enough to deliver a Not Guilty verdict.

The judge adjourned the trial at four o'clock precisely and Henry collected his bag, checked out of the hotel, and left for Nottingham via Enfield to purchase the listening device. He had located the street he wanted on his map and he made good time as he had managed to leave just before the traffic got too heavy. Unlike his last clumsy attempt, he had prepared false details of himself and had collected some cash from the bank at lunchtime. He wanted to pay without using a cheque as he didn't want to disclose his identity.

He arrived at the premises and parked in a communal car park. The building housed several firms and they were listed in the doorway. The writing was small so he put on his glasses and stooped, looking closely at the names. Suddenly a door opened and he felt somewhat foolish in his ungainly position. A tall man in his thirties stood in the doorway.

'Can I help you?' he enquired.

Henry looked up. 'I'm looking for Professional Security Services,' he explained, almost apologetically.

'That's me. What can I do for you?'

'I rang the other day and was told you could sell me the equipment that I'm looking for, if so I'd like to buy something.'

'Come in,' invited the man.

It was a small office with well-used furniture comprising a large ugly desk and a number of chairs and cabinets. It was badly in need of decorating. The man walked behind the desk and sat down. He was relatively smart and seemed pleasant enough, almost out of place in the scruffy surroundings. However, none of that mattered to Henry – he just wanted a suitable device.

'Won't you sit down?' the man said, motioning to a seat.

Henry sat down in a rather worn but comfortable chair. He felt uneasy as he knew this sort of thing was out of his comfort zone.

'I'm Peter Andrews, the owner of this business. Professional Security Services carries out all types of investigations and we also sell most types of security equipment. We have a storeroom through that door there with a large stock.'

He motioned to a door in one corner.

Henry got straight to the point. 'I understand you sell items for recording conversations and as I have a problem, I'd like to buy something that's appropriate to deal with it.'

'We have plenty of those devices. Why don't you tell me the problem you have and I'll recommend the best way forward?'

He took a pad from a drawer and poised over it with his pen. 'Let's start with some details, what's your name?'

'Does it matter?' enquired Henry.

Although he had already prepared his false details, he thought he would try to get away without having to disclose anything if possible.

Andrews put down his pen. 'Look, if you want this all to be discreet and you don't want to tell me who you are, then I couldn't give a toss. As long as you pay me with cash that's all I care about. Why don't you tell me the problem and we'll see how we get on from there.'

Henry sat back feeling a little more relaxed.

'Well,' Henry started somewhat hesitantly, 'it's all to do with a friend of mine. He didn't want to come himself as he's very nervous about the whole situation so he asked me to deal with it, is that OK?'

'Sure, it doesn't matter to me.'

'Well, my friend thinks his wife is having an affair and she takes the man back to their house when my friend is away working. He thought a good idea would be to put a bug in the bedroom to try to find out what their relationship is like, you know, whether he's in love with her, that sort of thing.'

Henry knew he was no good at this at all. Once again he thought how strange it was that he could control a packed court room with a jury, and confidently speak with authority to the extent that the courtroom would hang on his every word. Yet here he was, stumbling along with this fairly simple explanation.

Andrews stared knowingly into Henry's eyes for a few seconds. He gave the impression that he didn't believe the story about it being a friend.

'This friend,' he said slowly, 'surely he doesn't need to know anything else if he knows she's having an affair?'

'Yes he does,' replied Henry, 'because he needs to know whether or not they are serious, whether or not it's going to affect his marriage. In other words he wants to know whether they are likely to plan a future – maybe even run off together. If it's just a fling he thinks he might be able to get through that. See what I mean?'

Henry realised he was beginning to speak excitedly, trying too hard to get his point across.

'I see,' Andrews responded, 'why don't you just hire us to tail them and see what goes on in the relationship. We'll get your friend the answers he's looking for?'

'No, no, that won't do at all,' Henry said positively, 'he's adamant he wants to control it himself. Anyway, he doesn't think they go anywhere much so why can't you just sell me the required device to put in the bedroom of his house, or even one to tap the telephone line? Maybe I could get both for him?'

'That's all very well but these devices are not all that easy to set up and control. The other thing is you're not supposed to use them in the UK without a licence from the Home Office and it won't be possible for your friend to get one. It's an offence to sell transmitting devices of this nature knowing that they are to be used in the UK.'

Henry looked worried. 'Does that mean I can't buy anything?'

'No, all you've got to do is sign this form to confirm that they are going to be used abroad and I'll be happy to sell you what you want – for your friend, of course.'

Henry felt he added the last remark slightly sarcastically. He wasn't familiar with this law but felt he had to comply so he signed the form in a name that was indecipherable.

'Well, I do remember him saying that it would be used in Spain,' said Henry as he signed.

Andrews looked at him approvingly. 'Nobody will know you used the items in the UK so let me show you what I've got.'

As he spoke, he rose from his seat and motioned Henry to follow him through the door in the corner.

When they entered Henry couldn't believe the change from the office he had left. It was a well-decorated large room displaying different kinds of security equipment comprising cameras, recorders, locks and many other items. He was very impressed as the items were laid out more akin to a museum, with explanations relating to each product.

As they stood in the room, Andrews had a query. 'What room did your friend say he wanted to bug?'

'The bedroom, really, I think.'

'Does your friend–?' Andrews stopped suddenly. 'Look, can we stop messing about, I couldn't care less who the stuff is for so if it's for you will you please say so. It will be easier to get things done, OK? I don't need to know anything about you or even who you are, get it?'

Henry came clean straight away. 'Fair enough,' he said, somewhat relieved.

'This man is seeing my wife when I'm away during the week. They use our bedroom and obviously sometimes talk in there. I want to know what they are saying for the reasons I explained earlier. It's as simple as that.'

'Good, it's easier now, come with me.'

Andrews led him to the display table. 'These devices are the latest you can get, some have only just come on the market from the States.'

Andrews seemed very proud of his products. 'Look,' he said, whilst picking up one of the items.

'If you put this little transmitter secretly inside a telephone it will record both sides of any telephone conversations that take place.'

He then picked up a pen.

'This looks like a normal pen but it has a hidden transmitter inside it which sends anything said in the room to a remote recorder, so beware if someone leaves a pen on your desk when they leave the room. There are all sorts of gadgets to choose from but this one here is best for your job.'

He picked up an item which appeared to be a three-pin plug.

'This looks like a normal three-pin plug and it can be used as such. However, it has a concealed transmitter in it which will enable you to record conversations up to about 100 yards away. As it is powered from the mains, it will transmit indefinitely to a remote receiver. No batteries are therefore required.'

He then picked up a radio which had a cassette recorder in it.

'This is a normal looking receiver and radio, but it has been adapted to receive signals from most transmitters, including the three-pin plug I just showed you. It will record onto a tape at half speed which increases the recording time available.'

Henry liked what he was hearing and was beginning to think Andrews would be able to provide exactly what he was after.

'This is fascinating,' he said, as he continued to concentrate. Andrews carried on explaining.

'If you put the plug in an electric socket in the bedroom, and you hide this receiver somewhere nearby, say a garage, it will pick up any conversations that take place in the room where the plug is. To save tape time, it won't record unless someone is speaking or there is a loud sound. You won't even need to be around, when you get home you can simply take the tape out and listen to it at your convenience.'

He took from a shelf two boxes containing the items.

'Do you have an electric socket in the bedroom to put this three-pin plug in?'

'Yes,' said Henry, 'there are a few spare sockets.'

'Good, the signal will transmit through walls so the radio receiver can be quite a distance away. Use a socket that's unlikely to be noticed or used in the bedroom if you can.'

'Can I have a demonstration?' asked Henry.

'Of course.'

Andrews removed both items from their boxes and set them up. He plugged the three-pin plug into an electric socket and switched on a radio. He then took Henry outside of the building and switched on the receiver. He tuned it in and within seconds they could hear the radio perfectly. He put a cassette tape in it and recorded the voice talking on the radio. Andrews then turned the radio off in the room and the tape stopped.

'It's perfect,' said Henry, obviously impressed. 'What worries me is that someone who has a radio nearby could inadvertently tune in and listen, say a neighbour?'

'No, not possible, this receiver works on a megahertz frequency outside of normal radio frequencies. It sometimes picks up police messages and that's why you should have a licence.'

'It's marvellous, just what I need. How much is it?'

'The receiver is expensive due to the voice activation so its forty-five pounds for the transmitter and the plug is thirty pounds.'

'I'll take them both if that's OK,' said Henry.

'OK,' said Andrews, packing them in their boxes. 'Do you want a receipt?'

'No thanks.'

Henry took a wad of notes from his pocket and counted out seventy-five pounds. He picked up the goods feeling very pleased with his purchases.

'Thank you very much, you've been most helpful.'

'That's OK,' said Andrews. 'I hope it all works out, let me know if you need any help with any enquiries.'

'I might take you up on that,' said Henry.

Henry was in his car and on his way to Nottingham before six o'clock. On his way, he stopped at a telephone box and rang Jayne.

'How are you, my dear?'

'I'm fine, looking forward to seeing you,' she lied brazenly, 'where are you?'

'I've had a small problem, I'm running a little late so I won't be home until about half past eight. I'm looking forward to being with you.'

'Drive carefully,' she said. 'See you soon.'

*

As Henry pulled into his drive, he was somewhat apprehensive about seeing Jayne for the first time since his dreadful discovery. He was determined to act as if nothing had happened and he was not intending to say or do anything about Jayne's relationship with Stevens until he had established the strength of it.

'I'm home!' he shouted as he opened the front door.

'I'm in the living room!' Jayne shouted in reply.

He left his bags in the hall and walked into the living room and he felt apprehensive as he walked in. She was lying on the sofa reading a book, with Candy on her lap and he thought the dog seemed to look at him with disdain. It jumped off the sofa as Jayne put her book down and smiled.

'Hello, darling,' she said tantalisingly.

She rose from the sofa to greet him, kissing him lightly on the cheek. As she did so Henry pulled her towards him with his arms firmly around her. He spoke instinctively without thinking, simply saying what was on his mind.

'Jayne, you'll never leave me will you because I always want to be with you.'

He then found himself rambling, telling her how much he loved her and he realised that he was being uncharacteristic and might be arousing her suspicions that he had something to hide.

She pulled away from him.

'Whatever is the matter, Henry? Why are you talking like this? I'm not going to leave you. Why should I? I love you much too much to do that.'

Henry calmed himself down.

'I know, dear,' he said, trying to be more casual, 'but as I've been away all week, plus missing our anniversary, I'm worried that our marriage might be becoming insecure and I wouldn't like that to happen.'

Jayne looked at him in an understanding way.

'Come and have a drink with me.'

She took his hand and led him to the drinks cabinet where she poured two large whiskeys. She popped in a couple of ice cubes in each from the ice bucket.

'Sit down here with me,' she ordered.

They sat on the sofa and Henry began to relax.

'I've cooked your favourite meal,' Jayne announced suddenly, 'I cooked it myself, not Elsie.'

He looked at Jayne admiringly and asked himself how she could be having an affair when she was so nice to him. He didn't want her to know he knew about her affair because he was worried that it might cause her to leave him. Even so, sometimes he thought about telling her but no, it wasn't worth the risk. When he could get Stevens out of his mind, things seemed normal and he even thought that he could handle their arrangement if it were purely physical and provided it stopped when he retired. However, the thought of losing her was more than he could bear and that was his major worry.

They sat down together to enjoy Jayne's cooking and Henry knew it would be a chicken stew as it was about the only meal she ever cooked. He never found it appetising but he would never dream of saying anything detrimental. However, the wine Jayne had chosen was his favourite; a fruity smooth red Spanish Rioja. Jayne knew Henry's mind was elsewhere as she half filled their glasses so she attempted to lighten the mood.

'Henry, drinking this Spanish wine reminds me of the time we spent in that Spaniard's lovely villa.'

She gave him a warm smile as she said it.

'When we stayed with Diego, you mean? We had some lovely times there.'

Henry remembered their early holidays together with fondness.

'He's still a good friend of yours though, isn't he?' asked Jayne.

'Yes, but he was a client first and a friend later,' said Henry.

'He has a lovely villa, I loved it there but didn't he steal lots of money or something?' Jayne reminded him.

'Allegedly,' Henry said, smiling. 'I think we were at our happiest there,' he added, trying to remind her of the spark he believed they once shared and, perhaps, could share again.

They both had a brandy with coffee and Henry enjoyed a cigar. Despite everything, he loved nothing better than being with Jayne when he was able to put the problems out of his mind. He was tired due to the driving and was pleased to get to bed but once there he put his arms around Jayne and kissed her fiercely. She thought about pushing him away but knew it might seem suspicious to do so. As Henry's lovemaking never took long, she let him get on with it as she thought that with luck, this might be the only session during the weekend. She was more upset about cheating on Jonathan than anything else and that made her think that she must be in love with him. She did a bit of acting and within less than ten minutes it was all over and Henry was sound asleep. She wished she was with Jonathan.

Saturday was usually a quiet day as far as the Walters were concerned. Elsie Moyle didn't come in so they usually ate out in the evening. Jayne often went shopping whilst Henry enjoyed a lazy swim and then he would read the newspapers. Sometimes he took Jayne's beloved poodle Candy for a walk, much to her reluctance. However, this weekend would be far from quiet for the both of them. Henry was anxious to set up his transmitter and receiver ready for the possibility of John Stevens visiting Jayne during the week. Ideally he would like to test it.

After breakfast, Jayne announced she was going to the shops that morning. As soon as she had left, he took the opportunity to go to his car to take the three-pin plug up to the bedroom. In the corner behind a cabinet there was an electric socket which wasn't used. He put the plug with the transmitter in it and switched on the socket. He then stepped back to examine his handiwork – it was fine and unlikely to be noticed.

His idea was to place the receiver in the corner of the garage behind the workbench as Jayne rarely went in there and the chances of her finding it were remote. He found a suitable spot and plugged it into a nearby power point. The receiver came to life and Henry twiddled the dial as Andrews had shown him, but apart from some shipping forecast and other channels, he couldn't get anything from the transmitter. He then realised he needed some noise in the bedroom.

He went back to the house and switched the radio on in the bedroom. Someone was discussing train spotting so he left it on that channel and returned to the garage. He moved the dial again slowly and suddenly, to his delight, he heard the train discussion as clear as a bell. It was going to work, he thought. He put an empty cassette tape in, made sure it was on half speed and switched the receiver off. It was now ready to go with several hours' recording space. He would turn the receiver on as he left Monday morning.

There was something else he needed to do whilst Jayne was out. He looked at John Stevens's business card and rang Lench Insurance Services. A female answered.

'I'm trying to contact John Stevens. Is he there?'

Henry was hoping he wasn't as it was the weekend.

'I'm afraid he doesn't come in on Saturdays, you'll get him on Monday. Can I help you?'

'Not really, I need to see him urgently, I've got a parcel for him,' said Henry.

'Do you want to bring it in here?'

'No, it's urgent. If you would kindly give me his home address, I'll drop it round to him this afternoon,' said Henry hopefully.

'No problem. Have you a pen?'

'Fire away,' said Henry.

'4 Ely Street, Beeston.'

Brilliant, thought Henry.

'Would you like his telephone number?'

'Thanks very much, that may be handy,' he said, jotting down the number.

'Who shall I say called?'

Henry rang off. He felt pleased with himself and so he changed and went to the pool for a dip, he felt he'd earned it.

Later that morning, whilst Henry was in the pool, Jayne arrived back with some groceries and other items. She could see Henry through the large pool windows. She decided to join him to give the impression that she cared as she wasn't ready to spoil her good life just yet until things became clearer regarding her relationship with Jonathan. As soon as she put the shopping down in the kitchen, the telephone rang. It was John Stevens.

'What the hell are you doing ringing me at home on a weekend?'

She almost snarled, keeping her voice low.

'You know my husband's at home. For Christ's sake, say what you want to say and get off the phone.'

'Are you going to see me again or is it all over? I got the impression the other day that you're dumping me. I need to know. It's not fair stringing me along if it's all over.'

Jayne decided to take the bull by the horns.

'I'm sorry, John, its pointless beating about the bush, I want to end it.'

'Just like that,' he responded aggressively, 'you end it over the telephone; you really are a hard cruel bitch, that's all I can say.'

Jayne was upset to hear John talking like that but was determined to end it. She went to the door and checked Henry was still in the pool.

'Listen, John, I know it's not the best way to do it but that's how I feel. We've had some good times together so let's just leave it at that.'

John kept on. 'I don't want to finish, let's have a meeting with dinner one night and talk things over, you owe me that.'

'No,' said Jayne, 'I don't owe you anything, it's finished and I don't want you contacting me again. Get it?'

'Well, sod you!' said John.

There was a click as he rung off and she would never see him again. In a way she was pleased with the call even though it was on a weekend.

'I've done it,' she whispered, 'John is out of my life.'

Jayne abandoned her intention to swim and instead prepared a light lunch for them both which they enjoyed with a glass of wine. She had decided to be nice to Henry as she didn't want to rock the boat until she knew what she was going to do long term. After all, she thought, he did give her a good life and if she could keep him sweet, she could pretty much do what she liked including seeing Jonathan when Henry was away. She would turn over a new leaf, she told herself.

They had a lazy afternoon and went to Henry's favourite restaurant in the evening. Unbeknown to each other, they were both pleased with the individual achievements they had made that morning.

Seven

Henry was up and dressed very early on Monday morning as he had to leave at 6.30 a.m.

Jayne was carrying out the only chore she ever had to do, preparing Henry's usual breakfast.

'I'm just taking some things to the car, dear,' Henry announced.

He went to the bedroom and collected his bags and some files. Before leaving the bedroom, he switched on the radio, turning the sound down relatively low, and strangely enough Rachmaninoff's Prelude in C sharp minor, his favourite piece, was playing. He glanced at the three-pin plug housing the transmitter making sure the switch was on.

He went to his car and put his bag and files on the back seat before going to the workbench in the garage where he switched the receiver on. He immediately heard the faint strains of the prelude which confirmed it had stayed on the frequency that Henry had set on Saturday. He then pressed the record button and the tape started to record so he tucked the receiver behind the bench out of sight and left the garage.

Once indoors, he went upstairs and turned off the radio. That caused the tape to stop as no noise was coming from the bedroom. It was now ready and he heaved a sigh of relief thinking he had done a good job.

He went into the kitchen for breakfast, knowing that he could listen at the weekend should anything be said in the bedroom. He knew that Jayne rarely used the radio so space on the cassette tape wouldn't be wasted by radio broadcasts. He continued to try to act as normal as possible despite being aware of Jayne's infidelity and he made small talk over breakfast.

'Are you doing anything special this week, my dear?' he asked.

'I'm going shopping tomorrow with Moira and my other friend Deidre, I don't think you know her. She has actually asked me to go for a meal at a restaurant tomorrow evening.'

'Are you going?' Henry enquired.

'She's supposed to ring me today and if she does, I think I'll go. How about you, are you still on the same case all this week?'

'Yes, I'll be on this for a while longer.'

'I guess you won't be back until Friday, will you?'

Jayne wanted to confirm Henry's absence for the week.

'Yes, I'll be back on Friday,' he replied. 'It's quite a complicated case so I won't get home until about eight o'clock. Of course, I'll ring you as usual around six during the week. I'm actually getting fed up with leaving you like this and I'm hoping to be in a position to retire early, maybe in a couple of years, life would be totally different if I were here with you all the time.'

You're telling me, Jayne thought worryingly.

Henry then frightened Jayne by making an announcement.

'You should come down to London whilst I'm there and we could have some evenings out in town. You could do some shopping as well while I'm in court, you'd like that wouldn't you?'

That was the last thing Jayne wanted. 'No, I don't think so. It's not the same when you're working.'

'Fair enough,' he said, sounding disappointed.

Henry had finished his breakfast and it was nearly 6.30 a.m.

'Well,' he announced, 'I'm going now. I'll ring you as usual.'

'See you Friday,' Jayne said as he left the room.

As soon as Henry had gone, she sat down on the sofa with Candy and lit a cigarette. It annoyed Jayne that he expected her to get up at an uncivilised hour just to make his breakfast and see him off. It seemed selfish to her and quite often she went back to bed with Candy until Mrs Moyle arrived.

Jayne had a reasonably uneventful day. Mrs Moyle busied about cleaning and ironing and left about four o'clock. Jayne had a swim in the afternoon and then waited for Jonathan's call; he usually rang after Mrs Moyle had left. Jayne stripped down to her bra and panties and lay on the bed dozing but was soon woken up by the telephone.

'Hi, babe,' Jonathan's voice was distinct.

'Hello, darling,' she replied drowsily.

'What are you up to? It sounds like you're having a sleep, are you getting fit for me?'

She came around quickly. 'I'm fine, great to hear from you. OK for tomorrow?'

'Yeah, I'm really looking forward to seeing you. Shall we go for a nice meal at our favourite restaurant and then go back to your place? If you like I'll pick you up around the corner and that will save you driving.'

Jayne liked that idea. 'Lovely,' she said, 'I'll meet you on the corner of Salisbury road if that's OK, shall we say eight o'clock? It's far enough away from the house, but don't be late because I'll feel like a tart standing there waiting and if someone sees me it could be embarrassing.'

'I'll be there before eight, I promise,' he replied positively. 'Are you able to meet me again later in the week?' he asked.

'Of course. Henry's away until Friday evening so any night's OK.'

Now that John was out of her life she felt she could make a heavier commitment to Jonathan.

'Good,' said Jonathan. 'I'll try to fix something.'

'That would be lovely, I'll see you at eight tomorrow, bye.' She rang off.

Jayne glanced at the bedside clock. It was just after five o'clock so she got up and poured herself a whiskey whilst waiting for Henry's call. He rang just after six with nothing special to say. She patronised him and reminded him she was going to dinner with her friend Deidre the next evening. She then settled down to watch a movie on the television.

The next day, Tuesday, Jayne was excited to be meeting Jonathan. She made another special effort to look good with a different dress but just as stunning. By eight o'clock she was ready and by five past she was at the corner of Salisbury Road. His car was parked at the roadside and he flashed the lights as he saw her approaching. She glanced around and as nobody was about, she got in the car and pecked Jonathan on the cheek by way of greeting.

'Babe, do you mind if we change the plan for tonight? It's very important that I am at my club.'

'Not at all,' she replied.

'The thing is, babe, there are a couple of important new patrons coming in and I'm anxious that they are looked after. I don't need to do anything but if the staff know that I'm in, they stay on their toes more and work better. We can eat there as the club's restaurant is nice. I don't think you've eaten there before.'

Jonathan knew Jayne loved the restaurant they planned to visit and he didn't want to upset her.

'I'm so sorry, Jayne, for changing things.'

'Don't worry, I've never been to your club and I certainly didn't know you had a restaurant in it until the other night when the restaurant manager told me – I'm looking forward to seeing it.'

'It's tucked away, you'll like it,' he added.

Jayne had always had the impression that the Roman Rooms were sleazy and down market, not her style at all. However, after speaking with the restaurant manager the other night, it appeared she was wrong. Since being with Jonathan she had noticed that people seemed to respect him and it was hard to believe that he would have anything other than the best. She also made a few casual enquiries of friends who told her that it wasn't possible to get in the Roman Rooms unless accompanied by a member.

She was now looking forward to walking into an exclusive members' nightclub on the owner's arm. Showing off her looks was right up her street. This would give her the opportunity of using her sexy walk and do a bit of posing which made her feel glamorous. She thought she might feel like a gangster's moll, someone to respect, and she he liked the idea a lot.

Jonathan drove them straight to the Roman Rooms and as they approached, Jayne saw a smartly dressed uniformed doorman who recognised Jonathan's top-of-the-range Mercedes which he drove straight up to the door and parked right outside. He got out of the car and the doorman opened the door for Jayne. She got out of the vehicle feeling like royalty and Jonathan tossed the car keys to the doorman.

'Park it up, Ralph,' was all he said.

'Certainly, sir,' the doorman replied, with obvious respect.

Jayne loved to walk in through the ornate doors with statues of Roman Emperors either side. The doors were opened for them by one of the club's security team, who gave a little bow to Jayne.

'Good evening, Mr Bond.' Jonathan nodded.

'We'll go straight into the restaurant to eat shall we, or would you like a drink at the bar?' he asked.

'I'm starving,' said Jayne, 'can we eat now?'

'Of course.'

He nodded to a smartly dressed man who came over and shook his hand. Jonathan introduced Jayne to him.

'I'd like you to meet Jayne, a very good friend of mine. Jayne, this is my manager, Keith.'

'Very pleased to meet you, Jayne, follow me.'

Keith led them through the club and Jayne couldn't help feeling that he had probably escorted many other girlfriends into the place over the years. However, she dismissed that thinking to herself, *So what, I'm here now, and unlike the others, I intend to stay.*

Jayne was astonished at the lavish surroundings. The Roman Rooms were outstandingly decorated in Roman style with statuettes and pictures adorning the walls. It also had beautiful curtains and exuded an intimate and relaxing theme. There were busts of Roman Emperors strategically placed throughout and other artefacts from Roman times and she was truly impressed.

Jonathan took her hand. 'Let me show you the casino.'

He led her through ornate double doors into a casino with roulette, craps and card games. It was beautifully furnished again with a Roman theme and even the croupiers and waitresses were dressed in Roman-style uniforms.

'What do you think of it?'

Jayne smiled with pleasure. 'Your club is absolutely beautiful, I never realised it was like this.'

Jonathan was delighted with Jayne's compliments. 'Come on, let's eat.'

As they walked through the club towards the restaurant located at the rear, a trio was playing with a crooner singing on a stage. Couples were dancing to a slow romantic song on a small dance area.

'Are you the owner of all this, Jonathan?'

'Absolutely,' he replied proudly, 'I'm the sole owner which means I can pretty much do as I wish to the place.'

Jayne's mind was taking in what this could mean for her future. She was now keener than ever to develop her relationship with Jonathan.

'What time does it have to close?'

'I have a licence that allows me to keep this nightclub open late, in fact it usually shuts when the last customer has left.'

As they walked on their way to the restaurant arm in arm, several clients acknowledged Jonathan with verbal greetings or gestures. He was clearly respected by the customers and staff, so much so that as soon as the band spotted him, it changed from what it was playing to a very striking powerful piece of music which Jayne thought was the *James Bond* theme. The music was clearly acknowledging Jonathan's presence and this intrigued her as she listened whilst walking through the dance area. She turned to him looking impressed.

'Why do they play that music when you come in, Jonathan?'

'They always play that every time I come in, I don't like it myself, it makes me feel uncomfortable, but if it makes them happy I just let them get on with it and play it if they wish. I think it's a bit cheesy myself. Of course, the other reason they play is to let everyone know, including the staff, that I'm in the club and I do like that. You know where the tune comes from, don't you?'

'It's the James Bond music, isn't it?' said Jayne.

'Yes, after the first film, *Dr No,* they made a couple more called *From Russia with Love* and *Goldfinger.* I've a feeling this character will be big for many years to come and that piece of music is the *James Bond Theme* from the films.'

'Of course it is, but why do they play it?'

'You know my surname is Bond, don't you?'

'Of course,' said Jayne. 'How stupid of me. That's why they relate it to you.'

'There's also a rumour going around that as I did quite a bit of acting years ago, I auditioned for the James Bond part, load of rubbish that was of course.'

Jayne looked at him intently and thought, *Nothing would surprise me about this man.*

She was absolutely fascinated by the whole set up and she told herself how stupid she had been not to come to the club before when he had previously invited her. She was beginning to realise that there was much more to Jonathan than she realised and she wanted more of it. She loved all the attention she got when she was with him, and she also liked the admiring looks from several male clients who eyed her up and down as she passed.

Jayne was so obsessed with looking glamorous that she copied the famous Marilyn Monroe *bum wiggle*. Like Marilyn, she had one high-heeled shoe made with the heel slightly shorter than the other which caused a sexy wiggle when she walked. Jayne had brazenly copied Marilyn's idea and milked it, as this trick looked spectacularly sexy, especially from behind.

They went through an elaborate archway into a beautifully decorated restaurant in a large separate room. Jayne was very impressed with the exclusive feel of the dining area with its low romantic lighting and pleasant music piped through from the band in the main room at a low sound level. The tables had crystal glasses and crisp white tablecloths together with tasteful candles. The waiter produced some menus immediately.

'Good evening, Mr Bond, and good evening to you, madam.'

He spoke in a somewhat subservient manner. Jonathan ordered a couple of glasses of champagne.

They ordered their meals which were accompanied by a bottle of burgundy. Jayne thought every evening spent with Jonathan was absolute heaven, but she tried to remain fairly matter of fact without appearing unappreciative. She had detected that he seemed to prefer people who were not constantly fawning over him and so she tried not to do so. One thing was definite; this was the way she wanted to live and if possible, with this man.

They enjoyed the meal, followed by coffee, and Jayne lit a cigarette and took a big draw on it.

'I think I'll join you,' said Jonathan who raised his hand beckoning a waiter. As the waiter had hardly taken his eyes off Jonathan, he arrived in a flash.

'A cigar, please,' he said.

The waiter disappeared and returned with an expensive looking box of Cuban cigars offering Jonathan the choice whilst holding the lid open. He selected one and gave it to the waiter who clipped it and lit it for him with a large match whilst the cigar was in Jonathan's mouth.

'Jonathan, I didn't know you smoked.'

'There's a lot you don't know about me, Jayne,' he replied, smiling.

Jayne thought to herself, *Is there no end to the surprises that this man springs?*

'Incidentally, I notice that you still call me Jonathan?'

'That's your name, isn't it?' said Jayne, curiously.

'Yes, but my close friends call me Jon. I don't really like others shortening my name though but I do think it's about time you joined my close friends now though, don't you?'

'Yes, Jon, I do,' she proudly replied. *A sort of breakthrough*, she thought to herself.

'I'm surprised at the size of your club,' Jayne said casually. 'It really is impressive.'

'I'll show you around sometime, and then you can see where I live. I've asked you enough times to spend the night at my place but you always say you can't. You can have a look around though.'

'Are you saying you live on the premises? I thought you had a house somewhere?' Jayne was surprised.

'Just shows how little you know me, I have a great apartment built on the roof, stay tonight, why not?' he offered.

Reluctantly Jayne declined. 'I'd love to, but I can't. As I've explained before, I have to be at home just in case something happens and Henry rings. Also I've made no arrangements for my poodle, Candy.'

'Bloody Henry, I'm fed up with hearing about him. I just wish we could be in a proper relationship. Do you think we could at least think about being together one day?'

Jayne didn't answer but she knew she would have to give some thought as to how she might be able to spend more time with him or she would lose him. He was clearly losing patience regarding Henry's influence on their relationship.

After coffee, they left the restaurant and Jayne noticed nothing was said about the bill. As they walked to the car Jonathan had a suggestion.

'I can't do tomorrow or Thursday but can we meet next week. Is that any good for you?'

'That would be great,' said Jayne. 'Henry's away during the week for a while. What about Tuesday?'

'OK, I'll pick you up again, that's a much better way of meeting. Leave things to me, I'll sort something nice out for us.'

Jonathan drove them back to Tudor House and dropped Jayne off nearby. He then parked around the corner and walked back to the house. Jayne poured a couple of whiskeys which they took to the bedroom but before they could enjoy the drinks, they were back in each other's arms vigorously making love and Jayne loved it. She thought Jonathan was full of passion and afterwards they fell back on the bed and talked a little whilst drinking whiskey. However, much to Jayne's disappointment, Jonathan returned to the earlier subject.

'I'm sorry, Jayne, but I really can't help thinking about our future, if we have one.'

'What do you mean if we have one? Listen, Jon, of course we have a future. Just give me some time to think things through. I'm sure we can work something out.'

'I do hope so,' he said. 'I really would like us to plan some way of being together properly. That's what I want more than anything.'

'We'll work on it, but in the meantime let's enjoy being together now.'

She reached out for Jonathan who responded with a passionate kiss and they fell asleep in each other's arms.

The tape in the garage was filling up.

Eight

For Henry, the week in court really dragged. He could think of nothing but his wife's infidelity. It really hurt him to think of her with Stevens but his main concern was the possibility of losing her. He still felt that if it were a fling with John Stevens, and nothing more than that, he could win her back when he was retired, as he would be spending more time with her. He hoped that there would be nothing on the tape when he returned home to suggest that it was a serious relationship.

The trial continued throughout the week with the prosecution witnesses. The victim, a medical specialist, the police, and character witnesses all gave evidence with Hopkins trying to show that Rawlings had ferociously attacked and wounded Tompkins. There was also the witness who saw the attack from his window. He had picked out Rawlings at an identification parade. Henry cross-examined every witness and some were re-examined by Hopkins. Henry concentrated as best he could, trying to suppress the dreadful strain that he was under, but his performance did not impress Rawlings who listened and watched the accusations played out from the dock.

A few months earlier, Henry would have relished a trial of this sort but not now. The tape was on his mind constantly and it was affecting him badly and he knew it wasn't fair on the defendant. Was the tape recording properly? Had Jayne found it? Was it used up yet? Over and over, Henry wrestled with the factors connected with Jayne and her lover.

Friday finally came. He had telephoned Jayne several times during the week and was sure that he hadn't raised her suspicions. Now he wanted to get on his way home and he was able to do so shortly after four o'clock.

By five, he was on the M1 motorway aiming to be at Tudor Manor by eight o'clock and he made good time pulling into his drive as planned. Despite his craving to get the tape from the garage, he resisted the temptation and stuck to his usual routine.

He rarely put his car in the garage and although doing so would give him an excuse to remove the tape, he resisted. However, he did need to turn the receiver off. He therefore parked in his usual spot, quickly went into the garage and turned it off, took out his cases from the car and walked to the house. He let himself in, placed the bags on the floor and shouted for Jayne. She glided down the stairs looking as lovely as ever and to his surprise began kissing him passionately on the lips for what seemed like an eternity. Henry couldn't believe it.

'Hello, darling,' she purred. 'I've missed you.'

'I've missed you too,' he replied instinctively.

She kissed him again and as she did so he wondered why she was being so affectionate. Could it be that her affair was over and he now had nothing to worry about?

Jayne looked into his eyes whilst her arms were draped around his neck. 'I've prepared a special meal for us tonight,' she said.

'Thank you, dear. I'd love that,' Henry said, feeling special.

'Go and freshen up while I get it ready,' she added.

She slipped her arms from around his neck and went into the kitchen. Henry stared after her for a moment trying to work out why he was receiving such superb treatment.

Why worry, he thought, *just enjoy it.*

He took his cases upstairs to the bedroom but couldn't resist checking the plug housing the transmitter. It looked fine and he was sure it hadn't been disturbed.

He undressed, unpacked his bags and hung his clothes in the wardrobe and turned on the shower.

After showering, he dried off and put on a pair of slacks and a light shirt. Years earlier, he would have dressed more smartly as dinner was always a jacket and tie occasion, certainly with his first wife Anne, but that was a habit

Jayne had managed to break. It was one he was pleased to have changed as he now enjoyed the comfort.

He was very keen to get to the tape but decided to do nothing until the next day, Saturday. He just wanted to enjoy the evening. As he came down the stairs he thought again about Jayne's affection that night. Maybe she had finished with Stevens, or was she after something? These thoughts caused him to stop halfway down the stairs to contemplate the possibilities.

Yes, he thought, *that could be it. She was going to ask him for something expensive that she wanted.*

He stood on the stairs for a moment trying to think it through before settling down for the meal. His thoughts were interrupted by Jayne's voice.

'Are you all right, Henry?'

Jayne had appeared at the foot of the stairs.

He felt rather foolish standing on the stairs apparently doing nothing.

'Yes, I'm OK. It's just that I've thought of something I should have done in London but it doesn't matter. I'll make a note of it and do it on Monday.'

He guessed she wouldn't be interested in any details so he was now prepared to be a blatant liar, another new habit he had picked up since being with Jayne.

She served an excellent meal instead of her usual chicken stew. However, he was suspicious and was sure it had been prepared by Mrs Moyle with Jayne heating up the main course. He didn't care and gave her the benefit of the doubt. Delicious avocados with prawns followed by lamb cutlets and assorted vegetables. She had opened a very nice bottle of claret to accompany the meal. To follow, there was raspberry cheesecake, coffee and brandy. Henry thoroughly enjoyed the meal especially as Jayne maintained her affectionate attitude. She lit a cigarette and Henry joined her with a fine cigar.

It occurred to him whilst she was speaking that when he had heard the tape, he might be able to test the authenticity of her account of her week's activities but at that moment he simply wanted to enjoy her company and forget the background issues. When she was like this he knew of nobody who he would rather be with. He remained totally obsessed with her which once again confirmed his determination to make everything right for his future retirement. He felt very mellow with the wine and brandy and he smoked his cigar staring at her and taking in her looks without hearing anything she was saying. He was thinking how bright and sparkly her face was with her shining hair still tumbling attractively over her shoulders as it had years earlier when he'd first met her. To him she was simply radiant. As he was deep in his own world, he suddenly realised she was asking him something.

'Don't you think so, darling?'

He hadn't been listening and he hadn't a clue as to what she said, he decided to chance it.

'Yes, I do,' he replied, hoping that was the right response as he didn't want to upset her when she was in such a good mood. It obviously was the correct reply as she smiled.

'Would you like another brandy?' she asked.

'Why not,' he replied.

After a further brandy, they retired to bed and Henry put his arms around her attempting to make love, but the long drive and the brandies had got to him and he began gently snoring.

Jayne was delighted when she saw he was in a deep sleep and she managed to gently release his arms without waking him – she was pleased to have learnt that the secret of dodging lovemaking was wine and brandy.

Saturday was fairly uneventful. Jayne went to the shops and rang one or two friends, whilst Henry went to his club lunchtime. After lunch, he read the papers and had a doze for an hour in the afternoon. Although he was keen to get the tape from the garage, he didn't want to hear it until Monday as it might upset him and spoil his weekend.

In the evening, they went to Henry's favourite restaurant.

Jayne tolerated the place as it wasn't her cup of tea at all. Very stodgy with a poor tired out atmosphere but she always put up with it if they went there for a meal. She still found it hard to forget how fantastic it was in The Roman Rooms and how fabulous the evenings were with Jonathan. When they retired to bed she was disappointed to find that Henry expected sex and she submitted with some fine acting.

On Sunday, Henry went to bed early as he was due in court the next morning. He prepared his necessities for Monday, polished his shoes and other chores. He had agreed to attend a Masonic meeting during the week which was a social evening that he was looking forward to very much. The members of Henry's local Freemasons Lodge were well standing members of the community and he was a senior officer. Although he couldn't attend regularly, he did enjoy the male camaraderie at the meetings. On Wednesday he had been invited as a visitor to a Lodge in London whose members were mainly in the legal profession. He would therefore be taking his Masonic regalia contained in an oversized purpose made briefcase.

Jayne didn't like Sundays because Mrs Moyle never came in on the weekends and therefore she had to make the bed, cook meals and carry out some household chores. She hated that but tried to suppress her feelings from Henry.

He was anxious to get the tape from the garage as he intended to listen to it whilst driving to London in the morning. It was relatively easy to get as he invariably went into the garage for something on the weekends. After lunch, which was the usual mediocre chicken stew, they washed up together and Jayne announced she was going to read the papers for a while. She stretched out on the lounge sofa with Candy, and Henry took the opportunity to make his move.

'There are a couple of things I need to do in the garage, dear. Nothing much; I'll only be 20 minutes or so.'

Jayne glanced up at him. 'OK, see you in a bit.'

Henry went out to the garage feeling quite nervous. He approached the work bench and saw that the receiver was in exactly the same position as he had left it on Monday morning. He switched it off and eagerly examined the spool on the tape. Quite a lot had been used up and that concerned him slightly as it suggested Jayne had been up to something. He would be disappointed if that were true because as she had been so nice to him over the weekend, he had hoped that she had finished with her lover.

Henry put the receiver back with a fresh tape inside to record the forthcoming week's activities, should there be any. He checked that everything was back as before and went to his car. He put the tape in the glove compartment and returned to the house and as he walked in, Jayne shouted from the living room.

'That didn't take you long.'

'I know, I only wanted to oil the mower ready for the spring. It didn't take as long as I thought.'

He went into the lounge and picked up the Sunday Times.

'I think I'll have a read,' he said.

He sat down in his favourite armchair but after five minutes was asleep.

How boring, Jayne thought to herself.

＊

Henry got off to his usual early start on Monday morning after having gone quickly into the garage to turn on the receiver. Once he was on the road, he couldn't wait to hear the tape. He pressed play but to his annoyance he couldn't hear a word. He even began to curse Andrews as he thought he might have sold him faulty equipment. It suddenly dawned on him that the tape needed to be wound back so he fiddled around to rewind it and nearly hit a bollard in the road. Henry then realised that driving whilst fiddling with the tape was a bad idea so he pulled over into a parking spot at the side of the road.

He successfully rewound the tape and pressed play. Initially he heard different noises and the sound of the telephone ringing three times. Unfortunately when Tudor Manor was called, all of the three telephones rang in the house until one was picked up, usually the one in the kitchen. The tape picked up some other louder sounds in range as well as speech. He did eventually hear Jayne pick the telephone up in the bedroom but she only discussed some garments at the dry cleaners. He was beginning to get a little frustrated when the telephone rang again and Jayne spoke.

'Hello, darling,' he heard her say.

She then replied to something else with, "I'm fine, great to hear from you. OK for tomorrow?"

Jayne spoke again. 'Lovely, I'll meet you on the corner of Salisbury Road if that's OK, shall we say eight o'clock? It's far enough from the house, but don't be late because

I'll feel like a tart standing there waiting and if someone sees me it could be embarrassing.'

Henry stopped the tape. He knew she had been unfaithful with this man but it shocked him to hear more proof of her infidelity.

He couldn't help mumbling to himself. 'How could she treat me so wonderfully over the weekend and then kick me in the teeth like this?'

He was glad he had stopped the car as he needed to concentrate in order to take this in. He pressed the play button again but was annoyed that he couldn't hear both sides of the conversation; obviously the receiver could only pick up sounds in the bedroom itself.

Jayne then responded to something else the man had said.

'Of course, Henry is away until Friday evening so any night's OK.'

She went on to reply to something else.

'That would be lovely. I'll see you at eight tomorrow, bye, Jon.'

She finished the telephone call with that remark.

Henry worked out that they were meeting Tuesday. *Christ,* he thought to himself, *that's tomorrow.*

It was dawning on him already how serious the relationship was becoming and it truly worried him.

There was now some crackling and the tape stopped. Henry sat back in his car seat to digest what he had heard. He was totally dismayed and it took him a full five minutes to regain his composure. He then pressed the play button again and this time he was subjected to worse news as it was clear to him that Jayne had returned home with her lover. Furthermore, the noises told him that they were making love with considerable effort in his own bed.

He was shocked. He knew she was having an affair but it sounded far too serious for his liking. He was determined to put an end to it but had to think out his strategy. It seemed to Henry that he had three options:

- Tell Jayne he knew of her affair and ask her to stop seeing him.
  This he quickly dismissed as he felt this might inflame things and she might leave him.
- Get someone to threaten her lover with physical harm.
  He didn't like that as it meant getting someone else involved and it was a crime.
- Offer him some money to leave her alone.
  This seemed the best option to consider.

Henry thought for a few moments and decided to consider the latter course. Being a wealthy man, he decided to offer him a substantial sum to leave her alone but he wanted to be sure that the agreement would be honoured. He needed to come up with some way of making sure her lover didn't simply pocket the money and then continue seeing her.

He didn't have any idea how to prevent that happening so he decided to give it more thought later. Suddenly he caught sight of the clock in the car and panicked. He had been sitting there far too long and was almost certainly going to be late in court. He started the engine and risked speeding the rest of the way.

Despite his best efforts, he was still over thirty minutes late. Henry didn't go to his hotel, he drove straight to court and pulled into a barristers' parking area. He literally raced into the changing room with his bag and files, dressed and went into the courtroom. He had kept the proceedings waiting for a considerable time and he apologised profusely. His apology was greeted by silence and frosty glares.

Henry tried hard to concentrate as the prosecution witnesses continued to give their evidence, but his cross examinations were weak and he continued to struggle.

When the recess for lunch was announced, the judge motioned for him to join him in his office within the court chambers. Henry was an eminent barrister and knew the judge personally but he was concerned that his reputation might become damaged. He knew he could possibly be reported to the Bar Standards Board for being late and this would really be a worry.

Judge Julian Hayes looked stern.

'Henry, what is going on, it is most out of character for you to hold up the proceedings by being late?'

Henry felt like a schoolboy being admonished.

'I'm so sorry, Julian, but I was held up in traffic, there was an accident which held me up considerably.'

'How so? That's the reason we pay expenses to those living away to stay the previous night. Did you not do so?'

'No, I wasn't able to for personal reasons. I drove down this morning.'

The judge looked at him sternly.

'Not good enough, Henry. I've also noticed that you seem to be pre-occupied with other matters whilst in court, not like you, is there something going on?'

Henry did not wish to disclose his worries with anyone.

'I have had a few issues but I'm confident they are sorted out. I will be fine now, I give you my word.'

'Fair enough, we'll say no more about it but make sure you apologise to your client's solicitor, Mr Matthews, as it's not fair on either of them.'

Henry gave a sigh of relief and went into the court tea room where he spoke with Bryan Mathews.

'Bryan, I need to apologise to you, it was unforgivable for me to be late today and I am so sorry.'

Bryan looked surprised, an apology from someone of Henry's standing rarely occurred.

'You've obviously got something on your mind and I suspect it is to do with the issues you mentioned the other day, whatever they are, they must be serious.'

'I can't tell what the problems are but I am on the verge of solving them. Going forward I'll be a different person. Please kindly bear with me.'

Henry spoke confidently but he knew he was no nearer to a solution.

'Apology accepted, I'm glad things are working out for you.' Bryan spoke in an understanding way and smiled, but he felt he had little choice.

Henry forced himself to pay more attention and he was more professional that afternoon, but the worries he had concerning Jayne's lover kept nagging him and he felt under enormous stress which was affecting him terribly.

*

Henry was certain that John Stevens was Jayne's lover, it was obvious to him, so he had therefore decided to offer him a lump sum in cash. Henry was anxious to meet him as quickly as possible to try to get a deal finalised.

When the court adjourned about 4 p.m., he went straight to his nearby hotel and booked in. He ate a quick sandwich and prepared himself for the conversation with Stevens. He was not comfortable with this call but it had to be done. He was feeling surprisingly nervous, and for the first time, he noticed a slight shake in his left hand as he picked up the telephone. He rang Stevens at the insurance company where he worked desperately hoping he would be in his office and as luck would have it the lady on the telephone managed to get him.

'He's just leaving for an appointment, I'll see if I can catch him' she said.

A few moments later, Stevens spoke. 'Hello there, can I help you?'

'Is this John Stevens?'

'That's me,' came the reply.

'I don't think you know me Mr Stevens? My name is Henry Walters.'

'Never heard of you, how can I help? Are you looking for some insurance?'

Henry took a deep breath and forced himself to speak in a positive and commanding voice.

'No, nothing like that, listen. I'll get straight to the point. I know that you are having an affair with my wife Jayne. I want the affair to stop immediately so I'd like to meet you personally to talk about it.'

'I don't know what you're talking about, I'm not having an affair with anyone. The best thing you can do is bugger off.' Stevens had his hand over the phone and was whispering.

Henry suddenly had a rush of bravado and somewhat out of character he began to speak quite aggressively.

'Now you listen to me. I know you're having an affair with her, don't ask me how, but I do. Her name is Jayne Walters and I want it to stop and I'm prepared to offer you a way out.'

'All right,' Stevens whispered, 'fair enough, I admit it but–'

Henry interrupted him with an aggressive tone but he would suffer for that interruption because Stevens was about to tell him the affair was over.

'Listen to me,' said Henry, 'I'm prepared to offer you a one off payment to get out of her life.'

Stevens stopped in his tracks.

Christ, he thought to himself, *I nearly buggered that up*. He was now very interested in what Henry had to say.

'What sort of one off payment are we talking about?' he whispered excitedly down the phone.

'We can't talk about this over the telephone, can I come to your house and discuss this properly?'

'Yes, when?'

'Can I come this Friday around seven thirty in the evening?' Henry suggested.

'Yes, that's fine,' said Stevens. *Money for nothing*, he thought.

'OK, see you then.'

'Don't you want my address?'

'Yes, of course. I have a pen, fire away.'

Henry didn't want him to know he had the address already, so he paused pretending to write it down.

'See you Friday,' he said and rang off.

Henry suddenly had a thought. He remembered Andrews offering to carry out enquiries for him if needed so he wondered if personal information about Stevens could be obtained, especially details of his finances. If he could get that before he met him on Friday it would be extremely useful. It was a tall order but worth asking so he rang him to see if it were possible. Peter Andrews answered the telephone personally.

'I wonder if you remember me, I bought some items from you recently, a three pin plug and a receiver? I wanted to record some conversations in a bedroom.'

There was a silence for a few moments before Andrews replied.

'Yes, I do remember, nothing wrong is there?'

'Not at all,' said Henry, 'however, I do remember you saying that if I wanted any enquiries carried out you could oblige.'

'No problem, what do you want done?' he asked.

Henry explained. 'I need to know as much as possible about an individual in the Nottingham area, his background, financial situation, you know, things like that.'

'We can give you the complete run down on the guy, just give me his details.'

'The problem is I really want this information by Thursday evening, is that at all possible?' asked Henry.

'It's possible, but there's quite a lot of work, we would have to drop everything. Also there's the distance aspect as well. Can't you get someone up there to do it? If we do it from Enfield it will cost much more, especially due to the time frame.'

'I'd rather get someone like you further away from Nottingham to do the job, I don't mind the extra cost. He won't know anything about you making enquiries, will he?'

'It will be absolutely discreet; he won't know anything about it at all. Of course, there's a lot of work to be done in just a couple of days so you could be talking around £100.'

'That's fine,' said Henry, 'go ahead if you can do it by Thursday. I'll bring cash like I did last time. Would I be able to pick the report up around six o'clock on Thursday, or is that too late?'

'That's OK. We shut at six but we'll wait for you.'

Henry gave Andrews the details of John Stevens, where he worked and his home address. He intended to go to Enfield after the court closed on Thursday.

Andrews had exaggerated the difficulties to enhance his bill as the method used for these types of enquiries was, in fact, fairly simple. The investigators used by Andrews were spread across the UK. Most were self employed and they carried a business card with their photograph on it but a false name. The company shown on the card was *P. A. International Research* a bogus company dreamt up by Andrews. The investigator had a clipboard with a number of questions on it. Armed with these items, he would visit the premises of the person under investigation.

Andrews used David Morgan for the Nottingham area and he rang him straight away, gave him the details, and asked if he could do the enquiry by Wednesday for an extra fee. David put his mind at rest.

'As long as Stevens isn't away, I'll do the job tomorrow. On Wednesday I can ring and dictate my report to your secretary if that's OK. You could then get her to type it up ready for Thursday. Is that all right?'

'Fantastic,' said Andrews.

The following evening, Tuesday, David Morgan arrived at 24 Ely Street around seven thirty in the evening. He preferred this time as the target was usually at home. He knocked on the door and it was opened by a very fit looking young man in a gym slip.

'Good evening, sir. I wonder if you would be prepared to help me as my company have been engaged by your local council to identify areas that could be improved to help the residents. It's simply a short questionnaire that I need to complete. Would you kindly help?'

David Morgan handed Stevens his bogus card which Stevens examined and handed back to him. He seemed unimpressed.

'Not really,' said Stevens, 'I've just got back from the gym, bit knackered. Can you call another day?'

David was used to this knock back. 'I can't really call back, I've got quite a lot of surveys to do, it's a shame you can't help as the council gave us the names of those they thought would be the best to use, and you were one of them. They must value your views you see, you are John Stevens, aren't you?'

'Yes, that's me.'

'Look, it won't take long but you will be able to suggest improvements for certain areas like transport, shops, and sports facilities. You look like a sportsman yourself so you may be able to improve those facilities. Also your name will go into a draw for a £50 prize.'

David knew this tactic usually worked.

'OK,' Stevens said, 'perhaps I should help. You'd better come in; it's freezing out here.'

David noticed the house was a little scruffy, clothing placed over chairs, grubby carpets and dirty dishes in the sink, typical of a man living alone he thought. They sat at a kitchen table and David started asking his views on a list of subjects which were printed on the form including:

- Shopping facilities
- Sporting and recreational facilities
- Medical and quality of doctor's surgery
- Transport
- Family and marital status issues
- Type of residence, council, owner occupier, mortgage.

The list did cover other areas and was quite comprehensive. Being an experienced investigator David had spotted the gym vest and guessed that he was probably into sports and fitness. He therefore started the survey on that subject.

'Let's start with sporting and fitness facilities. Do you think they are of a good enough standard? Remember, any points you have will be considered by the council.'

With that, Stevens told David several shortcomings he had noted about the council's recreation centre which housed fitness equipment, and David took copious notes. As with many surveys of this sort, once Stevens got into it he became quite helpful and began to enjoy it. Investigators, with skill, were able to extract many pieces of useful information and David was no exception. When it was concluded they left on friendly terms with David confirming that the council would consider his concerns. He gave him a date for the non-existent £50 draw and left, shaking Stevens's hand whilst thanking him. As he left, he noted the number of a fairly old Ford car parked on the drive.

The next morning, Wednesday, he went to Stevens's place of work. He guessed that being mid-morning he was likely to be out on calls and he was correct, his car was not there. Morgan went to a call box and rang the firm's number. When he had been talking with Stevens, he had managed to discover that there were only four employees at the insurance company, a piece of information he now intended to use.

A lady answered the telephone.

'Good morning, my name is Mr Reynolds and I am a Tax Inspector from the Customs and Excise. I am hoping you can assist me with a wage query involving income tax relating to one of your employees?'

'I can't. I'll get Debra. Just a moment, please.'

After a few seconds another lady answered. 'Debra Collins speaking. I understand you are a Tax Inspector?'

'Yes, that's correct. It's a simple query really which will save us visiting your premises if you can help to clear it up. We have four employees shown at your premises which comprise the owner, yourself, another lady and a John Stevens. Is that correct?'

'Yes, that's right.'

'With regard to John Stevens, we have him down as having annual earnings for the last tax year of £15,260 but we believe that is incorrect. We simply need to clarify.'

David plucked the figure out of the air, it was just a guess close to the average annual wage.

'Just a moment, I'll check,' said Debra.

After a couple of minutes, she returned to the phone.

'John Stevens actually earned £16,480 which was made up of his basic salary and his commission.'

'That's fine, we've no need to trouble you again, thank you.' David rang off.

He then rang Hire Purchase Information and checked the Ford car on Stevens's drive to see if it were clear of finance and he discovered that Stevens had a hire purchase agreement which he paid monthly. Later that day, David used all of the information to compile a report which was very comprehensive. On Thursday morning, he dictated it to Andrews's secretary as arranged and she then tidied it up in time for Henry to collect it at six o'clock that evening.

*

On Tuesday, Henry was thinking about the amount he would offer Stevens. It would have to be cash of course as then there would be no trail. He was a wealthy man with cash deposits at his bank, building society accounts and shares but he wasn't yet sure of Steven's financial position. However, he wanted to make sure his offer was accepted so he decided upon a generous payment of four thousand pounds. He decided to ring his bank during the first recess.

His bank was in Nottingham and Henry was a respected and well known customer. When he rang, he made it clear that he needed this sum transferred from his deposit account to a branch in London from where he could withdraw it. The transfer was arranged and Henry collected the £4,000 plus the money for Andrews's enquiries. He put the cash in his Masonic case as there was no safe in his hotel room.

That evening he went to the arranged Masonic Lodge meeting with the money in his locked case. Most Masonic meetings consist of a ceremony in a Temple followed by a meal in the Masonic dining room. He actually enjoyed the meeting as it took his mind off his worries for a while.

When Henry went to bed in his hotel that night, he couldn't get off to sleep for a long time due to his worries. He had now thought of a flaw in his plans. What if Stevens was wealthier than he seemed and wasn't interested in four thousand pounds? There was also the possibility that as he loved Jayne so much no sum would persuade him to leave her alone. He dismissed that worry and thought that if Stevens would not do a deal, he would have to try to find another option.

Nine

Back at Tudor Manor on Tuesday, Jayne was meeting Jonathan again as arranged. He was picking her up and taking her to his apartment for the first time. She assumed they would be dining in the club's restaurant. Once again, she took care to make herself as glamorous as possible before going to the corner of Salisbury Road as before. She was deliberately ten minutes late to ensure he was there. However, she could not see his Mercedes car, but there was a glorious American Cadillac parked there which made her curious.

"Surely that isn't Jonathan, is it?" she thought.

As she began to walk towards it, she saw that Jonathan was sitting in the back.

'Good evening, babe!' he called. 'What do you think of this little beauty?'

'Christ,' exclaimed Jayne, suitably impressed, 'it's fantastic.'

'Hop in,' he said, opening the rear door. 'I thought we'd take this for a bit of fun tonight.'

Jayne saw that he had a chauffeur driving him as she climbed in the back.

Jonathan explained. 'I got this shipped in from America, Ralph's driving us tonight.'

Ralph turned around and looked at Jayne. 'Good evening to you,' he said, smiling.

Jayne recognised him as one of the doormen at the club. 'Nice to see you again, Ralph,' she said, feeling a little superior.

'Jon, where's your Mercedes? Have you changed it?'

'No, I've always got two or three cars, I like them' he explained, 'I feel like a loser if I only have one car – never be a loser, I say.'

Ralph drove to the club causing several people on the way to stare at the flamboyant car. Cadillacs were associated with brash wealthy Americans, they were certainly not often seen in Nottingham. Jayne loved the journey as it was a very comfortable drive with elegant leather seats, fancy chrome wheels and all sorts of unusual extras. Jayne was seeing pound signs for a car this luxurious, especially with the added cost of shipping it over from the States.

'Jayne, I've arranged for us to have a nice meal at my place.' Jonathan sounded pleased to be able to show her his home.

'However, when I run you back I can't stay over tonight because I have to be at the club early in the morning as I'm having some new carpets fitted and there are some preparations that I want handled correctly. I must be there to supervise.'

'Oh dear,' said Jayne, disappointed. 'I dare not stay overnight at your place, you know why, I've also got Candy to think of,' Jayne explained.

'Don't worry, I'll get you home by about eleven thirty tonight.'

Jayne leaned over and whispered in his ear. 'That would be fine but no jollies tonight then?'

She thought Ralph couldn't hear but she saw in the driver's mirror a knowing smile appear on his face.

'I don't know about that, we'll have a nice meal and still have time for some fun. It's only about twenty minutes to your place,' said Jonathan quietly.

Ralph drove into the club's grounds and Jayne was surprised to be driven to the back of the premises where he parked, got out and opened the rear door for her. Jonathan had left the vehicle and was unlocking a discreet-looking door in the wall of the building which he opened and signalled for Jayne to join him. Ralph wished them a pleasant evening and drove off. Inside the door was a small hallway and Jonathan pressed a lift button and the door slid open.

'What's happening?' Jayne asked, slightly nervous.

'No worries babe,' he replied, 'this is the private lift to my apartment on the roof, it's a penthouse suite really. I don't go through the club to get there as I'd have to put up with that bloody Bond theme every time if I did.'

'I thought we were eating?' said Jayne with concern.

'We are, we're dining in my apartment.'

Jayne was a little sceptical of that idea; she couldn't imagine how that would work with Jonathan cooking and all that goes with that chore. She was used to being waited on.

The lift door opened into another small hallway where Jonathan hung their coats. He then opened a door which revealed an absolutely splendid living room. It was so stunning she gasped with surprise and impulsively let out a loud 'wow!' When she had composed herself she thought her reaction had been a little childish.

The room was lavishly furnished with expensive sofas and armchairs. Lovely paintings adorned the walls. The carpets were clearly expensive and tasteful, and there were large picture windows offering lovely views of the countryside which was at the rear of the building. She could see a large balcony with a dining table, barbecue and garden loungers. To her surprise there was a baby grand piano in the corner which prompted her to ask who played it. With that Jonathan sat at the piano and quite casually played a beautiful rendition of *I Only Have Eyes For You*.

Typical, Jayne thought to herself, *is there anything this man can't do?*

'You play beautifully, Jon. How on earth did you get some of this stuff up here, particularly the piano for example?'

'It came up on a crane onto the balcony and through the patio doors.'

Jonathan smiled. 'Come through to my dining room, follow me.'

He led Jayne through another door into a dining room which had a large elaborate table with twelve matching carver chairs. Two lovely candelabras were romantically alight, one each end of the table and soft wall lamps enhanced the delightful ambience.

A member of the club's staff was carefully placing crystal glasses on the table and making other preparations. Jayne was totally taken aback by the beautiful room.

'Jayne, would you like a drink, vodka and tonic perhaps?'

'Yes please, anything will do.'

She was still trying to get over the extravagance of the wonderful suite.

Jonathan signalled to the waiter.

'Will you oblige please? I'll have a scotch and soda. Jayne, this is Pierre, one of my trusted staff from downstairs.'

'Good evening, madam. Charmed to meet you,' he said.

He bowed slightly as he took her hand kissing it lightly. Pierre then gave them their drinks.

'Bring your drink and come with me. I'll show you around,' said Jonathan.

He led her through two of the apartment's three lavish bedrooms both with en suite stunning bathrooms boasting gold taps, walk in showers and fluffy yellow towels. He showed her his offices and a small gymnasium.

'This is my piece de resistance, my bedroom,' as he opened the door to another room.

'Fantastic,' exclaimed Jayne, 'what a wonderful room and a super king size bed. I love it.'

'You can try it out later, if you fancy it,' suggested Jonathan mischievously.

Jayne smiled knowingly. 'I don't mind if I do,' she said with a cheeky looking smile.

'Come and look at this.'

He invited her through the large patio doors onto the roof top garden.

'It's a bit chilly and I don't use it this time of the year, the pool I mean, it's covered at the moment but I would still like you to see it.'

To Jayne's surprise, there was a large swimming pool which was surrounded by several sunbeds which were spread around it. A small garden area with winter shrubs was at one end and Jonathan pointed out a Jacuzzi and a small building housing a sauna and steam room. She was absolutely amazed by how much she had underestimated his wealth. Even as she stood there she knew she had to keep this man, she could see he was even wealthier than Henry and had the looks as well.

'Jon,' she said, 'I think this penthouse is stupendous and I am delighted to be here with you.'

'Glad you like it, come and meet Carlos.'

Jon led her back into the apartment and into a well equipped large kitchen where a continental looking chef was busily cooking.

'Jayne, this is Carlos. He's from Barcelona and cooks the meanest paella on earth. He's not working in the club restaurant tonight as he's preparing paella for us. Carlos, this is Jayne.'

'Pleased to meet you, senorita,' he said in a Spanish accent. 'If you go to the dining room, I'm ready to serve, but I have prawns and avocado to start.'

They made themselves comfortable in the dining room where Pierre had opened a quality bottle of Spanish Rioja red wine. With the wine they enjoyed a superb meal of prawns, paella rounded off with crème brûlée.

When they had finished, Pierre poured them their chosen liquors and brought them coffee. Whilst the two staff members washed everything up and tidied the kitchen, Jonathan enjoyed a fine cigar and Jayne had a cigarette.

A few minutes later, the waiters asked Jonathan if anything else was required. He thanked them and asked them to return to the club. Jayne saw them open a door in the dining room and disappear through it.

She asked, 'Where does that go?'

He explained, 'That's a lift that goes straight down to the club, very handy.'

Jayne thought it was a fantastic place to live.

The time was now nine thirty and Jayne was thinking maybe bedroom action was looming from what he had said in the car. However, she felt she needed a little while for the fabulous meal to digest. She needn't have worried because Jonathan was about to drop a bombshell.

He suddenly spoke in a serious tone. 'Listen, Jayne, I want to talk to you about something very important.'

Jonathan looked into Jayne's eyes with a disturbing stare.

'It's about this Henry situation which has been troubling me for some time, you know it's bothering me, don't you?'

'I do realise it bothers you, yes.' Jayne felt uncomfortable, she wasn't sure what was coming.

'The thing is we haven't got a proper relationship, we're always creeping about, ducking and diving, so much so that we don't really know how it would be if we had a normal relationship. I'm not used to it and I don't think I can go on much longer looking over my shoulder like this.'

Jayne began to feel extremely concerned. 'What are you getting at? You're not thinking of ending things are you?' She was now feeling decidedly uneasy.

She certainly didn't want to lose him, particularly after the extravagance and high living she had experienced that night. She wanted to have some of that for herself, permanently if that were possible.

Jonathan was still clearly unhappy.

'You must know I don't want to end it and that I think the world of you. It's just that I can't see any end to your marriage on the horizon. You talk of Henry's age but he's not that old, he could live for many years yet and if he retires, as you say he will soon, we will see each other even less.'

'But, Jon, it won't be forever, it's just a matter of waiting a while to see if we could be as happy together all of the time, isn't it?'

Jayne was almost imploring him.

'No,' he said sharply, 'I'm not sure about this waiting business. Wouldn't you like to live a normal life with me? Live a life not worrying about being caught by him? Let me ask you something straight. If you knew we would be just as happy as we are now being together every day, would you leave him? Is it that you are uncertain of how things would be if you left him?'

Jayne went into deep thought for a moment and Jonathan said nothing.

Eventually she spoke. 'I suppose that's probably right if I'm honest.'

'Do you know what I think?' Jonathan mused, 'I think you're frightened of giving up the life you have in case the alternative doesn't work out. You've got a pretty good set up really, Henry giving you whatever you want and me on the side providing the things missing in your marriage, am I right?'

'Yes, if I'm honest with myself you're probably dead right,' she conceded.

'Right, well, here's my suggestion, come abroad with me in the sun for two whole weeks. Let's find out how we would get on when we're together every minute of every day with no Henry lurking in the background. If we're the same after those two weeks, then I'm sure you would leave him and we could be together for the rest of our lives.'

Jayne looked at him as if he had gone mad. 'Are you serious, I'd have to leave him permanently to go away for two weeks without him? How long in the future are you expecting this little jaunt to happen?'

'In two or three weeks' time,' he said, still looking totally positive.

Jayne was shocked. She was worried as she had the impression that if she didn't agree he would finish with her.

'I'd love to do it, but surely you know it's impossible?'

'Listen to my idea.'

Jonathan relaxed a little.

'It's not as daft as you may think, consider this idea. You told me that your mother is living in Australia, am I right?'

Jayne nodded, she was becoming engrossed with his line of thinking.

He went on.

'Does Henry have anything to do with her, you know, phone calls or letters?'

'No,' she replied, 'he met her years ago but she went to live with a friend in Perth, Sandra I think, and he's never heard or spoken to her since. What are you getting at?'

'Well, supposing you told Henry that you had received a phone call from Sandra who told you that your mother was seriously ill in hospital with cancer and that she was asking for you. The hospital also told her that your mother may not make it, so she felt you should know in case you wished to see her before she died.'

'Bloody hell, Jon, that's not very nice, is it?'

Jonathan ignored her and continued.

'You would have to tell Henry that you'd be gone for two weeks but instead of going to Oz, you come with me to the sun on a great holiday. You'll have to put it on when you tell Henry, you know, be all upset and that but he's bound to agree with you going, what do you think?'

Jayne was quite thrilled with the idea of spending two whole weeks with Jonathan, especially as it could save the relationship, but she wasn't convinced it would work.

'Well, I have to admit that it could work. Mind you, the lies are a bit shitty to tell Henry, aren't they?'

'That's a bit rich coming from you, don't you think?' Jonathan said, 'Shagging me once or twice a week behind his back isn't shitty at all then, is it?'

He had a point so Jayne smiled. She really wanted to go but she needed time to think.

'Maybe I could think it through. How long have I got?'

'It's Tuesday today, I'll have to know this week as I'll have loads of arrangements to make, is that OK?' he asked.

'Yes, I'll ring you but as it's only March I can't see how we'll get much sun, where would we go?'

'Las Vegas, the weather is lovely at the end of March. I'm looking to go on a Monday March the 22nd.'

'Las Vegas!' Jayne exclaimed with a loud laugh, 'you're kidding me.'

'I'm not, I have some business to do there but that won't interfere with our trip, trust me.'

'How come you have business to do out there?'

'Listen, Jayne, I will explain but only if I know you're coming with me. I'm not going through my business details if you're not coming because this is a precursor to us being together, possibly for good.'

Jayne didn't know what a precursor was but thought it sounded good so she made a note in her mind to look it up in the dictionary when she got home.

'OK,' she said, 'I understand, I'll ring you later in the week and tell you when I've thought it through. I really want to come with you to such a fantastic place.'

Jonathan suddenly looked flustered.

'Jayne, we've only got about an hour before you have to go and I was thinking of showing you the delights of my super king bed.'

'That's fine by me,' said Jayne, smiling broadly.

'Good,' he said, 'let's take a brandy to the bedroom.'

By eleven thirty, they had given Jonathan's bed a real pounding and he was driving her home. He dropped her near Tudor Manor and returned to the club.

'Don't take too long with your decision – Monday the 22nd we take off' were his last words.

Jayne realised today was Tuesday the 2nd March so Jonathan was planning to go in less than three weeks' time.

*

By Thursday, the 4th March, Hopkins had presented all of his evidence and he was confident of achieving a conviction especially as he had noticed that Henry hadn't performed to his usual standard and that his cross examinations had been weak.

However, Henry knew that Irene Howell and Robert Free would be taking the witness box for the defence the following week and he was confident that their evidence would win him the case. He was however slightly worried about Rawlings as he had not been looking at all pleased as he watched the proceedings from the dock.

After the court recessed on Thursday, Henry drove straight to Enfield to collect the report from Professional Security Services. On arrival he saw Andrews who advised him that the enquiry had been a success. He gave Henry the report and he glanced through it and saw that it was extremely comprehensive.

Henry was very impressed. 'I am very grateful for this splendid report. I simply don't know how you can obtain all of this information in such a short time. How do you do it?'

Andrews was beaming with pride. 'As I said before, I can't tell you that but suffice to say that it's better you don't know how it's done.'

'Is it accurate?' Henry queried. 'Can I rely on all of the content as being correct? I don't mean to question it, but it's so important to me.'

Andrews looked annoyed. 'Of course it's accurate – everything in this report will be one hundred percent correct.'

'That's good to know. Here's the payment.'

Henry gave Andrews the cash, thanked him again and left.

Henry returned to his hotel and read the report in comfort over dinner in the hotel's restaurant. The report gave a clear and comprehensive account of Stevens's lifestyle. He saw that his fitness programme, diet, family situation, daily activities and much more were all covered. He was delighted to have so much detail but for the moment he was only looking for information which would help him seal the deal with Stevens tomorrow. He spotted it quickly.

He could dismiss his worry that Stevens might be wealthy enough to turn down his £4,000 as he could see in the report that Stevens was paying hire purchase instalments for his car, mortgage payments on the house, and he only earned just over £16,000 annually. Henry would read the remainder of the report more closely after he had seen Stevens. 'Fantastic report, money well spent,' he said to himself. He now felt more comfortable about meeting Stevens the next day.

*

The next day, Friday, Henry began his defence case with his opening speech and his first witness but once again his performance was lack lustre and this was noticed by Bryan

Mathews and Rawlings. Henry knew he had Stevens to face on his way home that evening and he couldn't get that meeting out of his mind.

During the break for lunch, he did some planning ready for it and when the court adjourned he was able to get on the road by 4.30 p.m. Beeston was not far from his home and he calculated that he would be there before 7.30 p.m. as arranged.

He had the cash in envelopes in his Masonic bag and he found Ely Street on his map without a problem. He drew up outside number 24 and turned the engine off.

He sat for a few moments taking a look at the property. He was surprised to see that it was a rather scruffy semi-detached house in need of painting, with a neglected garden. A Ford motor car was parked on the drive. The front gate was hanging off and the grass was overgrown so he simply could not believe that Jayne would exchange Tudor Manor for this standard of living. He took his case with the cash inside and walked to the front door and knocked. The door was opened by a young man who Henry guessed was around thirty. He was undoubtedly handsome and his body suggested that he was into fitness and possibly weight training. He struck Henry as being very proud of his looks as he was wearing a tight-fitting gym vest which was not normal in the winter.

'John Stevens?' said Henry.

'That's me. I guess you're Henry?'

'Correct,' Henry replied. 'I'm here to follow up on my proposal regarding my wife.'

Stevens held his hand out and Henry ignored the offer to shake it.

'You must be joking if you think I'm shaking hands with you. This isn't a social call you know.' Henry spoke rather curtly.

'Please yourself,' said Stevens, 'you'd better come in.'

Henry followed him into his kitchen and they sat facing each other over a small table. He noticed that the hall and kitchen were in need of decorating and Henry was now even more confident that his proposition would be attractive to Stevens as he clearly was not a wealthy man.

'Do you want a cup of something: tea, coffee?'

'No thanks,' Henry said with distain, 'I just want to get this out of the way. The reality is that you've taken advantage of the fact that I'm working away a lot and I have to do that in order to keep Jayne happy, she doesn't come cheap you know.'

'Whatever,' said John.

'Right,' started Henry, 'let's put our cards on the table. I know you're having an affair with my wife. Don't ask me how I know but I can assure that she didn't tell me, furthermore she has no idea I am here today. I am going to insist that as part of this deal you must never tell her the reason you are going to stop seeing her, got that?'

John paused before he replied.

'Yes, that's OK with me, but how much are you going to offer me to pack her in? I must tell you that I'm not at all happy to give her up as we had some plans of our own and they are all going out of the window now.'

Stevens lied in an effort to get a higher offer. In his mind he was thinking of perhaps five hundred pounds and he was just about to mention that amount when Henry interjected.

'I'm sorry, but if you think you can squeeze a fortune out of me you are wrong, I'm offering you four thousand pounds and no more, that's it. Take it or leave it.'

Stevens was shocked and he tried to stay calm. He was literally dumbstruck and speechless for a moment.

Four thousand pounds, he thought to himself, *I can't believe it. It would change my life.*

He tried to suppress his delight and gather his senses.

'I'll take it,' he said, trying to sound casual.

'It won't be quite as simple as that,' warned Henry.

'What do you mean, it will be cash won't it?'

'Yes,' said Henry, 'but you don't think I'm simply going to give you four thousand pounds and walk away in the hope that you do what I asked, do you?'

'Well, what else can you do?'

Henry leaned forward and looked at him with a stern and serious look.

'Listen carefully, these are the stipulations, firstly you must tell her you are never going to see her ever again. After that call you mustn't talk to her on the telephone, write or visit her again. In fact you must totally break off all connections with her. Furthermore, you must do it this coming Monday as I'm away.'

'Blimey,' said John, feigning concern, 'I guess I'll have to comply. Mind you, I don't see how you will know if I've done it unless you talk to her.'

'As I told you, she mustn't know about our arrangement but believe me, I'll know if you've reneged on the deal and things will get very uncomfortable for you.'

John looked at Henry somewhat aggressively.

'Are you threatening me with violence, old man? Not a good idea, believe me.'

Looking at the muscles on Stevens, Henry knew violence was not an option. 'No, I don't need to do that. I have another type of insurance in case you try to trick me.'

Henry opened his case and took out a document he had prepared.

'Read this,' he said.

John took the paper and read it and he was disturbed by what he read:-

To Mr Henry Montague Walters of Tudor Manor in the county of Nottinghamshire.

This letter is to remind you that I am still having an affair with your wife

Jayne Walters. She and I have been discussing how we can be together permanently. You have asked me to break off my relationship with your wife but I'm not prepared to do so unless you pay me 4,000 pounds in cash.

Failure to pay this money in cash will result in your wife leaving you permanently.

Your choice?

Signed............   Date............

John examined the wording. 'What's it all about? I don't get it.'

Henry took pleasure in explaining. 'Blackmail, that's what it's all about. I need you to write this out in your own handwriting then sign and date it. I will then retain this note and should you keep my money and my wife, I will go to the police and tell them that you delivered this threat to me. Clearly, this would be considered a serious offence, blackmail, or demanding with menaces. That carries up to fourteen years' imprisonment and that's what you will be risking. As I'm paying you cash, you can't prove I paid you the money.'

John Stevens was taken aback. *Perhaps this old boy is not so daft after all*, he thought to himself.

'What if I don't want to write this out. I'm not happy about it?'

'The deal's off if you don't.'

Henry knew it was a risky thing to say but he followed the remark with an explanation.

'The thing is what does it matter whether you write out the threat or not? Provided you stick to the deal it will never be used, that would only happen if you welsh on the arrangement which I assume you don't intend to do.'

John went silent and looked thoughtful. 'I suppose you're right,' he eventually said.

There's no way I'm giving up four grand, he thought, *especially as I don't actually have to do anything at all except write out the note.*

'OK, I'll do it.'

Henry produced a blank piece of paper and slid it across the table with a pen.

'Why do I have to write all this out, can't I just sign the one I'm copying?'

'No,' said Henry, 'if you write it all out, the police can prove that it's all your handwriting should you deny sending it to me, it won't come to that though, will it?'

'Of course not, I just thought you'd trust me that's all.'

Henry smiled. 'Come on old chap, me trust you? Think about what you've been up to.'

'Yeah, I guess you're right but I'm not signing anything until I've seen the money, it could be a trap.'

'Fair enough.'

Henry opened his case and took out the envelopes which were stuffed with notes. He put them on the table giving John a glance of the notes inside.

'Write it out and sign it and you can take the money.'

John wrote it out, dated it and signed.

Henry pushed the envelopes over to John and rose from his seat looking Stevens in the eye.

'That's us done, I guess, but remember, you must do it on Monday, preferably after four o'clock as the housekeeper will have gone home by then. Of course, you probably know all about that.' Henry was being sarcastic. 'Anyway, on Monday, Jayne's at home and I'm away, but remember, you must never contact her again after that in any way whatsoever.'

'OK,' John said, 'I won't.'

They walked to the door and John held his hand out again. This time Henry took it and they had a handshake.

'Don't think this handshake is anything else other than to seal the deal, nothing more than that. Good day to you. I never want to see you again.'

Henry then drove home, feeling pleased with himself.

Ten

Due to his secret visit to Stevens's house, Henry had told Jayne that he would be home later than usual on Friday. Not being sure of his arrival time, she had prepared a cold meal of salmon, salad and accompaniments with chilled white wine followed by a cheesecake with cream. She had made a special effort to please him because during their evening meal, she intended to talk about her alleged trip to Australia.

When Henry arrived, he went straight into the garage, switched off the receiver and let himself into the house.

As he put down his bags, Jayne heard him and went into the hall.

'Hello, darling,' she purred. 'How was your journey?'

She was overly pleasant whilst wearing a rather sensuous dress and acting rather flirtatiously.

'Not too bad,' said Henry rather glumly. 'I had to attend a meeting and it took longer than expected.'

Jayne helped him off with his coat and kissed him on the lips.

'How is the trial going?' She pretended to be interested.

'Not all that well really.'

Henry was too tired to respond to Jayne's amorous behaviour and this surprised and upset Jayne as she had planned to spoil him before springing her important piece of news.

'I'm sorry, dear, but I'm very tired and I just need to go to bed early.'

Jayne made one more attempt.

'I'd really love to go with you, my darling,' she said, smiling seductively.

'Sorry, Jayne, I'm simply not in the mood.' She gave up.

'You'll have something to eat though, won't you?'

'Yes, that would be nice but then I must sleep.' He looked exhausted.

Jayne served their meal and although he was tired, Henry enjoyed it as he had hardly eaten all day.

'Henry, something has come up that I need to discuss with you' she said, gingerly.

Henry smiled politely and looked disinterested.

'If it's all right with you, dear, I'd rather leave it until the morning as I am ever so tired, do you mind?'

'Sure, that's fine,' she replied.

The holiday with Jonathan was too important to discuss unless she could have Henry's full attention so she decided to leave it until morning.

He kissed her goodnight and went upstairs relieved to get into bed.

On Saturday, Henry was refreshed and feeling good. In fact, it was the best he had felt for some time as things seemed to be improving in his life. John Stevens should be ringing Jayne on Monday to break off their affair and with luck the trial would end either that week or the next. When this trial was concluded he intended to spend more time with Jayne in an effort to prevent the need for her to engage in any more affairs. In addition, he had now decided to only accept work that was near to his home.

After breakfast, Jayne had a bath and Henry took the opportunity to check the tape in the garage. He was very pleased to note that there was very little on it, just a couple of insignificant telephone conversations and a little snoring from Jayne. He was pleasantly surprised because there was no reason why Stevens couldn't have seen Jayne during the week as his and Henry's deal wasn't done until Friday afternoon. He then turned off the receiver for the weekend.

Jayne prepared a light lunch and as Henry seemed more relaxed she decided to introduce the possibility of her false trip to Australia. She thought this would certainly bring to an end Henry's good mood.

'Do you remember I mentioned last evening that I wanted to talk to you about something important?' She felt a little nervous as she had never tried anything like this before.

'Oh yes, what is it, my dear?'

'I'm terribly upset.' Jayne assumed a distressed look. 'I didn't want to bother you last night but I've had a call from my mother's friend Sandra in Australia.'

Henry looked surprised. 'Really, that's unusual.'

'Yes, apparently my mother is seriously ill – she may not make it and she's asking me to visit her. What do you think?'

Jayne was trying to assess his reaction before getting into details.

'Oh dear, that's terrible. What's happened? An accident?'

'No,' said Jayne, 'cancer, I'm afraid.'

She feigned extreme sorrow, dabbing her eyes with a tissue as if she was tearful. She actually felt very uncomfortable with the conversation but was determined to act her way through it.

'Do you feel you should go?' he asked.

'Well,' she explained slowly, 'I don't relish the journey and it won't be a holiday, but I would like to see my mother again if she's going to pass away. You do understand that don't you, darling?'

'Of course, you must go, how long would you be away?'

Jayne hesitated for a moment, she was actually thinking that the conversation was going well, but she couldn't help feeling a twinge of guilt at her deception.

'I'll be gone for about two weeks, I suppose. The journey will be about two days each way, so that would give me ten days there. I think I would need that amount of time. Sandra told me that I could stay in their house so I'd only have to pay for the air fare.'

'I'll pay that,' offered Henry. 'When would you go?'

'Thank you for that Henry, you are so understanding. If she's that ill I can't leave it for long, I'll probably have to go within the next two weeks so I'm thinking of going on the 22nd of March, which is a Monday and coming back two weeks later.'

Henry went to his diary and examined it. 'The trial will be over by then and I'll be working locally, so that's all right.'

He then dropped a bombshell.

'Would you like me to come with you, the trial will be over so there's no reason why I couldn't join you?'

Jayne had to get rid of that suggestion.

'No, it's not fair on you Henry, you didn't really know my mother and there's nothing to be gained.'

Henry looked disappointed so Jayne continued, almost displaying desperation.

'I'm perfectly capable of making the journey, I really am. I would fly from Heathrow so I'll go down on the train and get a taxi from St Pancras to Heathrow.'

'Fair enough, at least let me drive you to the station here.'

'OK,' said Jayne, 'let me organise possible flights this week and then we'll talk again. I'm so shocked by this.

I do have enough in my bank account to get the return ticket so I'll sort out a date and buy it this week.'

'I understand, I'll reimburse you,' he said, with genuine sympathy.

Henry had always paid Jayne a monthly allowance which was credited to her own separate bank account. Although it had a modest balance, there was enough to buy the ticket. Jayne was a tough lady but even she felt a twinge of guilt about her deception.

On the Saturday evening, they went to another one of Henry's favourite restaurants. The mood was fairly sombre due to Jayne keeping up the pretence of being upset about her mother's fake illness. Due to the upsetting news, Henry did not make any sexual advances and Jayne was pleased about that.

On Sunday morning, Jayne was reading the newspaper when Henry appeared at the door of the living room.

'Jayne,' he said, rather seriously, 'I need to talk with you about this trip to Australia you are planning.'

His tone worried her and she felt a little nervous.

'Come and sit next to me,' she said, pushing Candy off the sofa.

Henry sat down looking concerned.

'What's the problem, darling?' Jayne was apprehensive.

'Well, there are a few things that bother me about it all, like where are you buying your ticket from, what about Australian currency, what about Candy, how will I contact you if I need to speak with you? You know, things like that, there are many other issues we need to sort out as well.'

Jayne wasn't expecting this; she was relying on Jonathan to take care of everything and she didn't realise Henry would question her so thoroughly so she had to think fast.

'Yes, darling, I know there are a number of points to explain to you but I was thinking that if you give me a list of those bothering you, I'll sort them all out this week and have the answers when you get home on Friday. How would that be?'

'Yes, that's a good idea. I'll do a list this afternoon.'

Jayne heaved a sigh of relief but realised she had to speak with Jonathan urgently and get the answers.

On Monday morning, 8th March, Henry left earlier than usual as he was still conscious of the criticism he had experienced the previous week from the judge. Henry couldn't afford to be late again as he risked being reported to the Bar Standards Board which regulates the behaviour of barristers and that would be disastrous. Prior to getting in his car he quickly went into the garage and switched on the receiver as he thought he might have been lucky enough to record Stevens's call on Monday, ending the affair with Jayne. He wasn't very optimistic about hearing this conversation as she was likely to be downstairs when he rang. Nevertheless, it was worth a try.

He drove to his hotel, checked in and unpacked. He was in court early and feeling better about things now that Stevens was out of the way. That day was important for Henry as he would be putting Irene Howell in the witness box. He was sure her evidence, supported by Robert Free, would win him the case but his world was about to crash again as Bryan caught up with him in the corridor.

'I'm glad you're early as I need to talk with you. We have a problem.'

'What's the matter?'

Henry could see that Bryan looked concerned and it worried him.

'Rawlings is in the meeting room and he wants to see you. Can you come now?'

'Of course, what's it about?'

'He thinks you're not dealing with the case properly and he's pretty furious. He says, dare I say it, you are bloody useless.'

Henry was dumfounded.

'Do you think he's right, Bryan?'

Bryan looked at Henry sheepishly without answering.

'You do – don't you?' Henry looked furious and Bryan's face was flushed.

'Will you see him? If you don't, he may well embarrass you in court, he's very unpredictable and you know he is a very aggressive man.'

'All right.' Henry realised he had to do something. 'I'll see him.' He sounded extremely reluctant.

They went into the meeting room where Rawlings had been waiting and he immediately confronted Henry staring into his face in a most threatening manner. Henry was frightened but tried to appear unruffled.

'So you've come, have you. Well let me tell you something, matey, I'm not happy with you at all and I want to know how the fuck you think you're going to get me off this bloody charge when you're day dreaming most of the time and asking stupid questions?'

Henry was visibly shocked. He had never experienced anything like this and the colour was literally draining from his face. Bryan said nothing.

'Mr Rawlings, do not speak to me in this rude manner. I must remind you who I am, and I will not stand for that sort of language. I am carrying out–'

Rawlings interrupted and pushed his face into Henry's. He could smell his foul breath and could see his nostrils moving as he breathed with anger.

'I don't give a shit about what you're carrying out. I've paid you a lot of dosh upfront and what have I got for it? Bugger all. I'm going down unless you shape up and I don't get it. I was told you were the best.'

Henry tried to stay composed whilst trying to calm him down.

'Listen, things are going OK,' he said, but deep down he knew Rawlings was right.

'I think we'll win, just leave it to me.'

Bryan looked on in disbelief, he privately thought they had no chance of winning.

Rawlings had a look of confusion. 'How the bloody hell can you think that? You must have a secret I don't know about. Let me tell you something, if I go down you'll bloody well pay for it, that I promise you.'

Henry looked shocked, this was all new territory. 'Is that a threat, Mr Rawlings?'

'Of course it's a threat – now get cracking and get me off, I mean it otherwise you'll pay.'

With that, Rawlings strode out of the room slamming the door.

Henry was speechless. He simply stood as if in a trance trying to come to terms with the situation. He now felt that he was defending an animal, a man who was clearly capable of carrying out the bodily harm he was accused of, and there was no doubt that given the chance, Henry would walk away from this trial immediately.

Bryan tried to console him. 'I think we took on the wrong case here and I take the blame. I knew Rawlings was a violent man but I didn't think he had a temper like that, it was frightening.'

'It's not just your fault, Bryan, I agreed too. I don't like the threat he made though, I think he was talking about physically harming me. Unfortunately I can't do much about it, he would just deny it if I told the police. I think we just have to push on as I'm sure with the witnesses we have today we can win the case and then he'll be happy.'

'I hope so,' Bryan said, sounding doubtful.

The court opened with Henry continuing with the case for the defence and after some preliminaries, the first of the two important defence witnesses took the stand.

These witnesses were crucial to Henry if he was to achieve a 'Not Guilty' verdict. The first was Irene Howell who lived with Rawlings and cheated on him. She had categorically stated that at the time of the attack, Rawlings was nowhere near London as he was playing cards in their home in Nottingham. The key moment for Henry arrived as Irene took the stand but he was concerned to see that as she took the oath, she was nervous and her voice was trembling.

Bryan turned to Henry.

'I hope she's going to be OK. She looks petrified.'

'I think she will be all right.'

Henry stood up to take her through her evidence. He introduced her and led her along carefully so that she was able to explain her background and her relationship with Rawlings. He then built things up to reach the most important key fact.

'Miss Howell, on the evening of the attack on Mr Tomkins, I would like you to tell the jury where you were.'

'I was at home.' She still appeared nervous.

'That would be the home in Nottingham that you have shared with Geoffrey Rawlings for several years, would it?'

'Yes.'

'The attack on Mr Tomkins took place about nine o'clock that evening in London. Can you tell the jury where Geoffrey was at that time?'

'He was at home playing cards with his friends Robert Free and Kelvin Jones.'

'Did you speak with them whilst they were playing?'

'Yes, I took them snacks and drinks.'

Henry was pleased to see that she was a little more relaxed. 'Did Geoffrey Rawlings leave the house at any time during the evening?'

'No, he was at home all evening and we slept together that night.'

'Was there any way at all that he could have been in London?'

She looked a little bemused. 'I've told you, none whatsoever.'

'Do you think that he was capable of attacking and causing the terrible injuries to Mr Tomkins?'

'He would never do that, and in any case, it wouldn't have been possible because as I've told you several times, he was in the house all evening and night. It's a ridiculous accusation.'

Henry glanced at the judge with a satisfied look on his face.

'No more questions, Your Honour.'

Henry sat down feeling confident, he couldn't see anyway Hopkins could hope to get a conviction now as his next witness was Kelvin Jones who would be confirming Irene's evidence.

As Irene went to leave the stand the judge held his hand up.

'Miss Howell, where are you going?'

'I thought I had finished.' She looked confused. 'I've told all that I know.'

'You must return to the stand as Mr Hopkins wishes to cross examine you.'

She went back into the witness box looking a little nervous again.

'Remember, you are still under oath,' said the judge.

Hopkins rose to his feet with a smug smile on his face. His hands were clasped behind his back as he slowly walked up and down twice in front of his desk before he spoke. It seemed to unnerve Irene as she wasn't sure what was going on.

'Miss Howell, you've lived with Geoffrey for about six years, haven't you?'

'Yes.'

'How has the relationship been during that time?'

'I don't know what you mean.' She looked confused again.

'Well,' said Hopkins slowly, 'has it been a nice, friendly and a loving relationship?'

'Yes, I like to think so.'

'Really?' Hopkins said rather sarcastically. 'But he beat you up sometimes, didn't he?'

'Not really.' Irene was looking uncomfortable.

'What do you mean, not really? Tell the jury why you gave him your lover's telephone number and address.'

'Well, he was upset that I had been seeing him.'

'Your lover, Mr Tomkins, was the victim in this case, and shortly after you gave Geoffrey his details, he was badly beaten up. Do you know anything about that attack?'

'I know nothing whatsoever.'

'But you do know that once you had given Geoffrey the details of Mr Tomkins he rang him up and threatened him.'

'So I believe.'

'Why did you give Geoffrey your lover's details, not the sort of thing a woman would normally do, is it?'

Irene looked flustered, she hesitated and before she could reply, Hopkins became more aggressive.

'Geoffrey beat you around to get the details, didn't he. You've told people that, haven't you?'

'Well, it wasn't too bad; he just slapped me a little.'

'Slapped you a little, did he? I wouldn't call it that because enquiries about your injuries have shown that they required treatment, isn't that correct?'

Irene hesitated and looked nervous.

'Isn't that correct!' Hopkins raised his voice.

'Well, yes, but I soon recovered.'

She was clearly becoming a little distressed with Hopkins's aggressive questioning and Bryan looked at Henry expecting him to try to save her. He expected an objection regarding the aggressive style but nothing happened.

'I know you recovered but that's not the point – the point is that if he wants you to do something for him, he beats you up, doesn't he?'

'Not really,' she said.

'Of course he does. We have evidence that he's done it before – it's true, isn't it?'

She paused, clearly flustered.

'Isn't it!' Hopkins almost roared.

At last, Henry rose. 'Objection, Your Honour.'

'Overruled,' said the judge.

'Thank you, Your Honour,' said Hopkins smiling smugly.

He carried on with the questioning and Irene looked more nervous than ever.

'I asked you a question: he has done it before, hasn't he? Remember you're under oath.'

'What if he has? It's got nothing to do with this case, has it?'

'Miss Howell, what it means is that if he beats you up, you do what he says and that's what has happened here – he beat you up to say that he was at home when in fact he wasn't, was he?'

Irene was now looking very uneasy and clearly wasn't sure how to respond. Bryan kept looking at Henry expecting him to object again but nothing happened.

'You must remember you are on oath. It's dangerous to lie. Tell the jury what happened – he beat you didn't he?'

Irene paused for a moment but Hopkins went on.

'Didn't he?' Hopkins kept going. 'Why are you hesitating, you know the answer, tell me – he got you to lie about being at home by frightening you and hitting you, didn't he?'

Irene looked frightened and bewildered.

'Miss Howell, if you're worried about the accused

beating you up again for telling the truth, don't be, because he'll be in prison out of the way, you'll be free of him.'

Henry jumped up. 'Objection, Your Honour!'

'Objection sustained,' said the judge. 'Mr Hopkins, please do not make assumptions of that sort.'

It was too late. Hopkins had made his point and Irene appeared to realise she could be rid of Rawlings if she told the truth. She suddenly broke down and tears ran down her cheeks.

'Yes,' she said through the tears, 'he hit me and threatened me – that's why I lied. He was in London that night. He told me he was going to beat him up.'

There were gasps around the court and Henry's head fell to his chest.

Bryan turned to him. 'I don't believe it, we've no chance now.'

Rawlings was shouting something from the dock and was restrained and Hopkins looked across the court at Henry with a wry smile; he knew Henry had little chance of winning now.

The court was adjourned early and Henry went for a drink in the bar with Bryan to drown their sorrows.

The remainder of Henry's defence witnesses' evidence was of little value as Hopkins used Irene Howell's confession to his advantage and broke down Robert Free as well. Hopkins and Henry delivered their closing addresses and the judge summed up on Friday morning.

The jury were sent to deliberate and they only took an hour to reach a verdict.

The foreman of the jury stood up and the judge looked sternly at him.

'Do you find the defendant guilty or not guilty?'

The foreman replied immediately. 'We, the jury, find the defendant Geoffrey Rawlings, to be guilty of the charge of grievous bodily harm.'

The judge adjourned the court to deliberate on the sentence and when it was reconvened at 3 p.m., Rawlings was sentenced to 6 years in prison.

'Take him down,' said the judge.

As Rawlings was escorted from the courtroom, he stared straight at Henry giving the sign of a throat being slit.

Henry felt threatened by the sign and he turned to Bryan.

'Did you see that?'

'Yes,' Bryan replied, 'I wouldn't worry about it, he's been put away for six years.'

'It's a good job he has,' said Henry, with a sigh of relief.

After the trial, Henry was advised that he was required at court on the following Monday and Tuesday for administration purposes and a discussion regarding a possible appeal. When the court closed on Friday, he was able to commence his drive home at 4.30 p.m.

Eleven

Once Henry had left on the morning of Monday the 8th March, Jayne was anxious to ring Jonathan with the news that he had agreed she should visit her mother in Australia. Deceiving Henry had bothered her initially, but the guilt was fading fast and she was now looking forward to the holiday. Two weeks together in Las Vegas would test their relationship and if it were to be a romantic success, she would feel secure if she left Henry. Jayne couldn't ring Jonathan with Mrs Moyle in the house so she had to get to a call box.

'Elsie, I'm going to take Candy for a walk in the woods,' she announced as she put her on a lead.

'I'm going to do some ironing,' Elsie replied. 'Will you be long?'

'About an hour. See you later.'

Jayne walked to the nearest call box and tied Candy's lead to the door. She rang Jonathan at the club hoping he was there and she was lucky.

'Jon, it's me,' she said.

'Hi, babe. What's happening?'

'Well,' exclaimed Jayne excitedly, 'I've done it. I've told him. I can't believe I'm going to Las Vegas with you for two weeks but I think I've got away with it.'

'Fantastic, how did he take it?' asked Jonathan.

'OK, but I didn't like it at all, I really didn't. I felt a bit lousy even though I want to go. Still, it's done now but there are loads of queries he's firing at me and I'm struggling with the answers.'

'Don't worry,' Jonathan sounded unconcerned, 'we can have a meeting and come up with suitable answers. Are you free during the day on Wednesday?'

'Well, I suppose so. Henry's trial won't finish until next week and I can tell Moyle that I'm going to lunch with friends.'

'Great, how about if you drive to my place?' said Jonathan, 'I can't pick you up, your cleaner is crafty enough to watch where you go. However, if you can get here for noon I've got a couple of friends I want you to meet. We can have a quick drink and then all go to a special horse-racing meeting at Nottingham Racecourse. How's that sound?'

Jayne was a little worried.

'Great, but when can we clear up these queries Henry has? He's going to grill me again on Friday. I really need to confirm dates and all sorts of stuff – it worries me.'

'It'll be fine,' Jonathan said calmly. 'My friends will be gone by six o'clock and then we could spend an hour sorting out dates and answers, you can stay until seven or eight, can't you?'

'Yes, that's OK. What should I wear? Is it posh? I've never been to a race meeting before.'

'Just wear something nice. I want to show you off.'

'I'll be there at noon on Wednesday, darling.'

'I'm looking forward to seeing you,' said Jonathan as he rang off.

The races would be something new to Jayne and she thought they would be exciting but she had to think of an excuse to be out all day. She was determined to go as not only would she enjoy the races, but she would also get the answers she needed before Henry came home on Friday.

On Wednesday, the race day, Jayne needed to leave around 11.30 a.m. to meet Jonathan so she spoke with Mrs Moyle when she arrived.

'Elsie, I'm going to be out for most of the day and I won't be home until after you have gone.'

'Going somewhere nice?'

'Yes, I'm going to meet some friends and we're having lunch at one of their homes. I don't think I'll be back until after six.'

Elsie Moyle was as nosy as ever. 'That's some lunch, isn't it?'

'Yes, well we're going to see her holiday pictures and other stuff. It should be nice.'

'I see,' she said, sounding unconvinced.

Mrs Moyle often had her suspicions about Jayne's activities but she took the view that it wasn't anything to do with her.

Jayne gave Henry the same excuse to prevent him worrying when he rang her at his usual time. She left a message at his hotel. She intended to make an effort so she started getting ready around 10 a.m. with a bubble bath. She put on one of her many glamorous dresses, made herself up nicely, and selected some suitable jewellery.

She left on time and as she made her way to the door, Jayne detected that Mrs Moyle was surprised at her appearance. It seemed to her that she looked like she was attending a black tie function or something.

I don't give a shit what she thinks, Jayne thought to herself as she strode through the door.

'Look after Candy, please. I'll be back about seven this evening.'

Mrs Moyle had a look of distain and said nothing.

Jayne drove straight to the Roman Rooms and parked in the front car park. She made her way to the entrance and the doorman, who she hadn't seen before, greeted her.

'Miss Jayne?'

'That's correct,' she replied.

'You are expected,' he said, 'please follow me.'

Jayne followed the doorman through the club. There were a few people having aperitifs before lunch but it was not particularly busy. She was surprised to be led to a door at the rear of the large kitchen where the doorman pressed an intercom button.

'Yes, who is it?' someone said through the intercom.

'Miss Jayne is here to see Mr Bond,' said the doorman.

There was a pause followed by a click as the door was activated and opened. The doorman signalled for Jayne to enter the lift, whereupon the door closed and she was transported to Jonathan's suite. The door at the top opened and she was confronted by a smiling Pierre who she remembered from the recent dinner she enjoyed there.

'Welcome, nice to see you again,' said Pierre.

'Good to see you too,' Jayne replied, with some relief.

'Mr Bond is expecting you. Please come this way.'

She went into Jonathan's splendid living room where she saw a smartly dressed couple who were drinking elaborate-looking cocktails. She noticed that they were both smiling whilst undoubtedly sizing her up.

Jonathan introduced Jayne. 'I'd like you to meet the love of my life, Jayne.'

He then turned to her.

'Jayne, allow me to introduce Antonio Rossi, a very good friend of mine, and his wife Martina.'

They both rose and Martina kissed her on both cheeks as did Antonio, clearly a continental greeting.

'Very pleased to meet you,' said Antonio, 'we've heard so much about you.'

'Nice to meet you both,' Jayne replied a little bemused and wondering how they fitted into Jonathan's life. Jayne had felt quite flattered by Jonathan's introduction. *The love of his life*, she thought to herself, *I like that*.

The couple were very Italian looking, probably both around forty. Looking at the way they were dressed she was certainly glad that she had made an effort with her appearance. Pierre suddenly appeared and invited her to have a drink and Jayne made things simple.

'I'll take a vodka and tonic please, if you have one.'

'I think you'll find Mr Bond has pretty much every drink available in his bar,' Pierre said, smiling.

Jayne ignored that remark thinking it was a stupid thing to ask for on her part. She sat in an armchair with her vodka and made some small talk with the couple.

'Are you here on holiday?' she enquired, trying to be polite.

'No, we live in America. We emigrated there from Sicily about fifteen years ago,' Martina replied.

'How did you meet Jon?' she shortened his name to demonstrate how close they were.

'Jon and I do a bit of business together,' Antonio said smiling. 'He comes over quite a lot.'

Jayne thought they seemed a nice couple, she quite liked them.

When their drinks were finished, Jonathan told Pierre to organise a car whereupon they went into the lift and down to the car park. The driver turned out to be Ralph, who she knew from her previous visit.

'Hello, Miss Jayne,' he said, respectfully.

She felt influential by his acknowledgement and nodded to him saying, 'Nice to see you again, Ralph.'

He was driving the Mercedes and it took them about half an hour to get to Nottingham Racecourse. They pulled into a member's car park and Jayne could hardly believe the attention they received; it was if they were royalty. Stewards opened the car doors, and one smartly dressed steward escorted them to a private box in the stand. They simply left the car for Ralph to park. Jayne was beginning to realise that Jonathan was well respected and she wasn't really sure why. However she loved being with someone so powerful and this was truly the man she had dreamt of all her life.

When they arrived at the private box, there was a tray of assorted drinks and nibbles plus a runner who took care of all their bets. This was just what Jayne enjoyed and it once again confirmed that she would truly enjoy a future with Jonathan – he seemed to live the life she yearned for.

Both Jonathan and Antonio placed several heavy bets as they had wads of bank notes which Jayne saw them taking from their pockets. Both of them gave generous amounts to Martina and Jayne so that they could have a wager, but neither of them was lucky and they lost it all. It didn't seem to bother Antonio or Jonathan, they just carried on with heavy bets and Jayne didn't know whether they had lost or won. One thing she did notice was the rather reckless way they treated money, it didn't seem to matter whether they lost or won as long as they had a good time. They laughed all the time and seemed to have fun whilst consuming quite a lot of alcohol.

When they left their box, Jayne noticed that Jonathan was tipping stewards and waiters as they made their way to the car which Ralph had parked in readiness for their appearance. He drove them back to the club where they had another drink before Antonio and Martina left around six o'clock. Jayne heard Jonathan making arrangements for dinner at eight o'clock with Antonio and she was disappointed not to have been invited.

Jonathan noticed the look on her face. 'Sorry, babe, but I couldn't invite you tonight as it's a business meeting, you'd be bored anyway.'

'I understand, you've had a bit to drink for a business meeting haven't you?' Jayne ventured.

'It's nothing, we'll be fine. Don't concern yourself about my drinking habits.'

Jayne detected a slight warning from his tone. She attempted to try to find out more. 'Are you in business with Antonio then?'

'Yes,' said Jonathan, 'we own a club in Las Vegas as partners which offers shows, gambling and girl escorts. It's a nice club, we've had it for years so when we go over to Vegas you'll see them some of the time, you did like Antonio and Martina, didn't you?'

'Yes, they seemed nice.'

'So you've got another club, Jon. How exciting. Will we go there?'

'Of course, I'll take you there but one of the things I must do is check out one the hotels. It's called Caesar's Palace and it has fantastic Roman themes running through it. I want to see if I can get some ideas from it for the Roman Rooms. You'll love it; it's got everything.'

Jayne thought to herself, *This guy is amazing, clubs in Vegas now; it gets better all the time.*

Jonathan looked serious for a moment. 'I need you to get on with Antonio and Martina as they are my business partners.'

'Yes, I got on with them well, it was a great afternoon.'

She felt she dare not say anything else.

'They'll be plenty more great afternoons when we go to the States. Talking of which, even though we are a bit pissed I think we need to clear up those worries you mentioned regarding Henry, don't you? I've only got until about seven thirty before I have to get ready for the meeting with Antonio.'

Jayne was relieved. 'Yes please, the sooner I get the answers the sooner I can relax.'

Jayne produced some notes from her handbag. 'I've made a list.'

'Christ,' exclaimed Jonathan, 'it really is bothering you so let's sort it out now. Fire away.'

'Right,' said Jayne, 'the first problem is flight tickets. What if Henry asks to see my ticket? I wouldn't know what to do.'

Jonathan smiled mischievously and opened a briefcase which was on the table. He took out an envelope with travel agent's details printed on the outside and handed it to Jayne.

'Give him this to look at if he asks.'

Jayne opened it and saw a flight ticket inside. She read it and it was a ticket from London to Perth with the flight leaving at 1605 hours on Monday, 22nd March 1982.

'This is great,' she said. 'It looks just like a real ticket.'

Jonathan smiled again.

'That's because it is a real ticket.'

Jayne looked surprised, 'I don't understand.'

'Well, you are booked on that flight but we know you're not going. You just tell Henry that you ordered this flight early in the week from a travel agent in town and you collected it, I don't know, say tomorrow.'

Jayne looked confused.

'Don't be worried,' explained Jonathan. 'We'll just tell the check in desk when we're in Heathrow airport that you can't take the flight due to family problems and that's that.'

'What do I do with the ticket?'

'Just bin it,' he said.

Jayne looked shocked. 'This ticket must have cost a fortune.'

'So what' queried Jonathan. 'It doesn't matter. For you to feel comfortable, it needs it to be authentic so you can show it to Henry, don't you think?'

'I guess you're right. It just seems wasteful.'

'Don't worry about it. Our flight to Las Vegas, via New York, takes off at 1800 hours so we'll cancel this Australian flight and then we can have dinner in the airport and board our flight.'

Jonathan then took some bank notes from the briefcase.

'Here's some Australian currency for you. There's not much but if he asks you if you have any, at least you'll be able to show him some. It would look strange if you were going without any. Just change the notes back to sterling at the bank when you get home.'

Jayne was impressed how he could come up with the answers, and amazed at the money he simply threw around. She was feeling better about her worries already.

'You seem to have thought of everything, Jon. I feel so much better.'

'I try my best,' he said smiling broadly.

'There's something else bothering me,' Jayne looked concerned again. 'Henry said he would pay for the ticket. Shall I tell him I paid for it from my own account and when he reimburses me I can give you the money back?'

Jonathan looked at her sternly. 'Everything on this trip is on me. I don't want you paying for anything. Keep the money Henry gives you and use it as spending money whilst we are away. I'll give you a grand in dollars when we get to the States.'

'That's a lot of money, Jon,' she said.

'Don't worry about it. I'll have plenty of money in dollars when we get to Las Vegas from my club – never be a loser, that's what I always say.'

Jayne felt much better and moved onto another worry. 'He insists on driving me to Nottingham railway station, so how do I get to link up with you?'

'The St. Pancras train from Nottingham stops at Leicester so just get off there and I'll be at Leicester station to meet you. We can then drive the rest of the way to Heathrow, no problem.'

'You seem to have covered everything, however, just one other thing, what if he wants to speak to me on the telephone whilst I'm away? He could ring Australia.'

'Just tell him there's no phone in the house in Australia,' suggested Jonathan. 'Tell him your mum's friend said that overseas calls from Australia are very difficult for her to make, especially as she lives in a remote area. She has to go through an overseas operator and it's all a bit unreliable. Tell him if you have a major problem, which is unlikely, you'll send a telegram.'

'Thanks for that, Jon. You've covered everything as I knew you would.' Jayne was genuinely grateful.

'Is Henry coming home Friday evening?' Jonathan asked.

'Yes, I think this will be the last full week of the trial. Early next week it will be finished and he said he would probably be home either Wednesday or Thursday. That means if we want to see each other before we go to the States, we need to meet at the beginning of the week.'

'Right, well, let's arrange something. I'm not sure what I have on early next week but I'll definitely sort something out. I'll ring you after four o'clock tomorrow, after Mrs Moyle has gone, to fix something up.'

'Good,' Jayne felt much more relaxed about facing Henry's questions.

'By the way, it looks like things are going to get difficult for us to meet when we get back if he's not going to be working away so much.' Jonathan said, looking concerned.

'I guess you're right.'

'Like I said earlier,' he continued, 'we've got to talk about our future when we return from Vegas, don't you think? We definitely can't carry on like we are now.'

Jayne felt he seemed to be getting more and more serious about that lately. 'Absolutely,' she replied, 'let's have a great time together and make some decisions after the trip – I'm all for that.'

'I've got our flight tickets and I've booked the hotels in America,' said Jonathan, 'you won't be in the States long enough to need a visa but make sure your passport is OK.'

'It's fine,' she confirmed. 'I'll wait for your call tomorrow, bye.'

She pecked him on the cheek and drove back to Tudor Manor.

*

On Thursday, Jayne took Candy for a long walk in the morning and did some thinking. She loved the fact that Henry gave her everything in terms of the material things in life, but she wanted excitement and love as well. Jonathan was refreshing, exciting and she was sure that he would give her everything she wanted, and more. He had made it clear that he wanted a permanent relationship with her, and on this very walk, she made her decision. If the holiday in Las Vegas was a success, she would agree to leave Henry for Jonathan. She had always worried about burning her boats but now she was ready to risk it.

She returned to the house with Candy, had a light lunch and read the newspaper. Mrs Moyle had been busy with some outside chores including cleaning the swimming pool. Henry had asked her to deal with those jobs and when she had completed them, she prepared a meal for Jayne which she could heat up in the evening. She then left about four o'clock. Jayne went into the bedroom to change when the telephone rang. It was Jonathan ringing as arranged.

'Hi, babe. How's things?'

'Hello, Jon. I'm fine,' she replied. 'How did things go last night?'

'OK,' he said. 'We sorted out some business and it was a successful meeting. Listen, I'm OK for Tuesday if you are. He won't be home by then, will he?'

'No. Where shall we go?'

'How about the Beech Tree for a meal, what do you think? I'll pick you up if you like about eight on the usual corner?'

'That's fine,' she said.

Jonathan continued. 'I really enjoyed yesterday as always. I love us being together so Las Vegas will be a real treat. I think we will be spoilt by having such a long time together. I can't help thinking about us and I've a feeling we will want to make some decisions so I'm going to have to give some serious thought to our future when I get back.'

'Absolutely, when I get back I'll talk to you about getting together for good but I need more time, I just need to know that being together will work.'

'It will, I'm positive. I honestly think we will be living together soon, See you at eight o'clock on Tuesday. Bye, honey.'

'Bye, Jon. See you next Tuesday.'

The tape was recording in the garage.

Twelve

During his drive home on Friday, Henry was feeling less stressful now he had reached a deal with Stevens. He had been initially upset about Jayne's trip to Australia but having had time to think about it during the week, it didn't seem quite so bad now. After all, he would have a couple of weeks to himself during which time he could reflect on the situation, relax, and enjoy being at home. Also, if John Stevens had any ideas about upsetting the agreement he had made with him, he could deal with it as Jayne would be out of the country. He left the court disappointed with the verdict but pleased to be going home, particularly as he would only have to be in London two or three days the following week.

He arrived at Tudor Manor about seven thirty on Friday evening and was particularly looking forward to seeing Jayne now that Stevens was out of the picture. He had stopped on the way and bought some nice flowers for her. Before entering the house he went quickly into the garage and switched the receiver off as he didn't want to hear himself on the tape. Of course, there was no time to listen to any recordings at that time. He smiled broadly as he entered the house.

'I'm so pleased to see you, darling. I've had a rotten week and I lost the trial.'

He got that piece of news straight out of the way. Jayne took the flowers smiling and she kissed him gently on the cheek.

'How thoughtful of you. The flowers are lovely. I'm so sorry about the trial, I'll try to cheer you up. Elsie has cooked us a roast dinner and it's all plated up to put in the oven, it just needs heating up. Come and have a drink with me before we eat.'

Henry was surprised at the nice welcome. He hadn't been sure what to expect so this was an encouraging start to the weekend. He put his bags down, took off his shoes and flopped in an armchair in the living room.

'I'll sort things out later,' he said. 'I fancy a scotch.'

As the trial was over, Jayne was now worried about her date with Jonathan on Tuesday. She was anxious to know whether Henry would be needed the following week. 'So as you lost the trial, does that mean you won't have to go back next week?'

'I'm afraid I will; I've got matters to attend to regarding appeals and financial issues so I won't be home until Wednesday or Thursday,' he replied.

Jayne suppressed a sigh of relief as she put the flowers in a vase and poured two whiskies.

'Tell me about your week,' she said.

Henry felt that she was genuinely interested but then he always did.

They talked for a while and Henry felt much more comfortable now that most of the pressure was gone. Jayne heated up the dinner that Mrs Moyle had prepared, and they had a bottle of red wine as an accompaniment.

'No more news about your mother is there?' Henry asked.

'No, her friend did ring again during the week and asked me if I was able to come. I told her I'd fixed it for the Monday, the 22nd, and she was really pleased. I can't ring her because she hasn't got a home telephone, she goes to a friend but even that's difficult with poor lines and stuff. Anyway, I've sorted it now and I need to catch the ten o'clock train on the Monday morning to St. Pancras station.'

'I said I'd take you to the station and as the trial will be finished, it will be OK for me to do that for you. Are you sure you can get to the airport all right from St. Pancras?' queried Henry.

'That's not a problem, I'll get a taxi.'

'What about your flight ticket?'

'Oh, I contacted a travel agent in Nottingham and got it all fixed up. I picked up the ticket the other day.'

Jayne proudly produced the ticket that Jonathan had given her and showed it to him. Henry examined it.

'How much was it?'

Jayne was casual. 'It's on the ticket, I paid by cheque. It's an awful lot of money, Henry.'

'I'm going to reimburse you – I did promise. I'll give you a cheque.'

'Thanks. That's very kind of you.'

'That's OK,' he said.

Once again, Jayne felt she was being cruel by deceiving him, however, as usual the feeling did not last long.

After dinner they had coffee and brandy before Henry went to bed tired. He apologised to Jayne once again for being so tired but she was secretly delighted; no sex.

On Saturday morning, Jayne took Candy for a walk after breakfast and Henry took the opportunity to hear what was on the tape. He took it from the garage receiver and sat in his car from where he could see Jayne if she came back early. He felt quite anxious as he was hoping to hear her respond to the call from Stevens breaking off their relationship. He agreed to do that on Monday but if he did ring he thought she might have taken the handset into the bedroom in order to get out of Mrs Moyle's earshot. Initially once again there were several telephone calls which were obviously answered and dealt with from other telephones, but eventually he heard Jayne speaking.

'Hello, Jon, I'm fine. How did things go last night?'

Henry stopped the tape. 'It's him,' he said to himself, 'I'm lucky, I think he's going to finish with her as promised.'

'No, where shall we go?' Jayne said next.

Then she said, 'That's fine.'

He stopped the tape again.

That's fine? thought Henry. *What does that mean?* He was really frustrated at not being able to hear the other side of the conversation. He started the tape again.

'Absolutely, when I get back I'll talk to you about getting together for good but I need more time, I just need to know if being together will work.'

Henry stopped it again. He didn't like the sound of the conversation at all. He pressed the play button again and heard Jayne again.

'Goodbye, Jon. See you next Tuesday.'

Henry was totally shocked. He truly believed John Stevens would honour the arrangement as he was sure he was frightened of the blackmail threat that Henry had over him, yet it appeared that he was prepared to ignore that. Henry felt totally sick and furious that he had been cheated. He was in such an emotional state he felt he could do anything – he was mentally in a very dangerous state of mind. He was literally shaking. He knew he had to calm down, think his strategy through sensibly. It seemed to him that Jayne had told Stevens that she was going to Australia too.

'When I get back I need to know if being together will work,' he had heard her say.

He was worried by that remark because it implied that they were considering getting together on her return. He thought through the timings but there was no doubt –

this conversation was after his meeting with Stevens when the deal was agreed, he knew that because he had put a new tape in since he had seen him.

'*This has got to be stopped,*' Henry whispered to himself.

His options were limited as he couldn't really use the blackmail threat. He didn't want the situation to blow up as that might cause Jayne to leave him for Stevens because she would know Henry had been deceiving them both. As he wouldn't be back home until Wednesday or Thursday of next week, he decided to put the tape on again to see if there was any possibility that he had reached the wrong conclusion. He now knew that they were meeting on Tuesday and even considered for a moment returning from London to confront them. However, once again he was frightened of driving Jayne away. He checked that there was nothing more on the tape and rewound it. He then put it back in the receiver intending to switch it on before leaving on Monday morning.

He went indoors and flopped on the sofa in the lounge feeling terrible but he knew he must look natural when Jayne returned.

During the rest of Saturday and Sunday Henry was very poor company and Jayne was unable to understand why. She put it down to the fact that he was upset about her leaving him for a couple of weeks so she decided to say something about it.

'Are you all right, Henry? You seem very sad. Is something bothering you?'

'Sorry, dear. I'm feeling a bit down. I'll be all right when this trial is well and truly over. By the way, I'll be home on Wednesday or possibly Thursday but I'll ring you to confirm.'

Once again, he wanted to tell Jayne what he knew but he always managed to suppress the desire.

'OK, when will you be away after that?' Jayne asked.

'I think I told you, I'm cutting down on long distance work. I'll be mainly working locally and slowing down. I want to spend more time with you.'

Jayne didn't like the sound of that. 'Oh, I see,' she replied, 'that will be nice,' she added rather dismally.

Jayne left it at that.

*

On Monday morning, Henry went off early reminding Jayne that he would be home Wednesday or Thursday. He said he would ring to confirm which day. He was still feeling cheated by Stevens and was struggling to come to terms with it. Before getting into his car, Henry went quickly into the garage and switched on the receiver. He wanted to see if Jayne would bring Stevens back to the house on Tuesday and if she did, Henry knew nothing will have changed, other than being £4,000 worse off.

Jayne lazed about on Monday whilst Mrs Moyle cleared up all of the weekend mess and started doing some washing and ironing. After she had taken Candy for a walk, Jayne read the papers and went to lunch with Moira. In the afternoon, she had a swim before Mrs Moyle left about four o'clock. Jayne then sprawled out on the sofa with Candy reading her book, but her mind kept drifting back to the wonderful holiday with Jonathan which was coming up the following week. Suddenly the telephone rang and she answered it in the living room.

'Hello, Jayne speaking.'

'Hi, babe. Jon here. How's things?'

'OK, she said, 'you all right for tomorrow?'

'Yes and no,' he replied. 'I can take you home after the restaurant but I can't stay overnight as I've got to be at the club very early Wednesday.'

'What a shame, no shenanigans then?' said Jayne, giggling.

'I don't know about that, I don't have to leave you that early,' he said.

'Oh good,' she responded, 'so I'll see you at the usual spot at eight o'clock, OK?'

'I'll be there, we can also make sure we are all set for our trip. See you tomorrow.'

'Look forward to it,' she replied.

The next day, Tuesday, Henry rang about six o'clock and told Jayne he would definitely be home late afternoon on Wednesday.

Jayne was looking her usual glamorous self as she walked to the corner of Salisbury Road on Tuesday evening. Jonathan was in the driving seat of his Mercedes and had been waiting for a few minutes. She got in the car and kissed him on the cheek.

'Great to see you, honey,' she said, genuinely.

'Good to see you too, babe. How's Henry?' he asked.

'He's gone to London as arranged and he won't be back until tomorrow. He's agreed to take me to the station on Monday though.'

'I'll sort some timings out with you tonight.'

He drove to the Beech Tree and they spent a nice evening with fine food and wine.

After the meal, Jonathan had his usual Cuban cigar and Jayne smoked a cigarette whilst they both enjoyed a brandy and a coffee.

'Is everything under control for next Monday?' he asked.

'Yes, Henry has seen the ticket and he seems OK with it all, I don't think he suspects anything. I've also explained the telephone situation and he accepts that he won't be able to speak with me whilst I'm away. So really I'm all set to go.'

Jonathan looked pleased.

'OK, Henry thinks you are catching the 1605 hours flight to Australia from Heathrow so we must plan for that. Therefore you've got to give yourself at least 6 hours what with the train journey, the taxi from St. Pancras and the wait after check in. That means Henry must get you to the station for the 0950 hours train from Nottingham.'

'OK,' said Jayne, 'I'll tell him that. Do I get off at Leicester?'

'Yes, get off there and I'll be outside with the car and then off we go.'

Jonathan sounded unusually excited now.

Jayne was eager to get started on this fabulous holiday and she wanted him to know how excited she felt.

'I'm so looking forward to this, Jon. Can we speak before Monday?'

'I suggest that you leave the house and ring me from a call box over the weekend just to make sure all is still OK for Monday morning.'

'Will do,' she confirmed. 'Let's go to my place now, shall we?'

'Can't wait,' Jonathan said, as he paid the bill.

They then left for Tudor Manor.

When they arrived, there was no doubt about their intentions. Jayne shut the front door behind them and they went brazenly straight to the bedroom without saying a word. They literally threw off their clothes and embraced each other wildly whilst crashing onto the bed. Sexual excitement quickly took over and within seconds, Jonathan was fiercely making love to her. Jayne loved all the raunchiness of it and when it was over, she fell back on the bed.

'Christ, Jon, that was fantastic.'

Jonathan looked at her with a flushed face and a wide grin.

'You're telling me, it really was. I'm sorry if it was rather unromantic. I don't know what came over me.'

'Don't be sorry,' she replied. 'I loved it.'

'Listen,' said Jonathan, somewhat seriously, 'I must be at my place first thing in the morning. Do you mind if I clear off now?'

'Not at all, I'm going to sleep after that session.' Jayne smiled and held his hand affectionately. 'I do love you.'

Jonathan smiled. 'I love you too.'

He got dressed without even showering and pecked her on the cheek.

'I'll let myself out, OK?'

'Sure, I'll ring you as arranged,' Jayne replied.

As he left, Jayne rolled over and fell asleep with the light still on.

On Wednesday morning before Mrs Moyle arrived, Jayne tidied everything up and checked to ensure there was no sign of Jonathan having been there. When Henry was coming home, Jayne usually changed the sheets but as he would be home later on that Wednesday, she examined them and thought that they were good enough to leave on the bed.

He rang after lunch.

'Hello, my dear,' he said, sounding slightly miserable.

'Henry, darling, you sound tired. Are you OK?'

Jayne's response made him realise that he was affected more than he thought by Stevens's failure to end his relationship with Jayne. He therefore deliberately spoke more cheerfully.

'Yes, dear, I'm fine, just a bit tired but looking forward to seeing you.'

'Me too, would it be OK, darling, if we dine at a restaurant tonight as nothing's prepared here?'

'I'd enjoy that. We'll go wherever you wish,' he said cheerfully, 'I'll be with you between five and six.'

'Great, I look forward to seeing you.'

During Monday and Tuesday, Henry had meetings with Bryan and court officials and it was agreed that an appeal was pointless. Other matters were finalised, including outstanding fees. Before leaving on Wednesday, Bryan asked Henry to have a coffee with him in the court tearoom.

Henry wanted to get on the road but was curious.

'What's on your mind, Bryan?'

'I'm a bit worried about Rawlings, I can't see us getting the rest of the fees.'

'The bulk was paid up front,' said Henry, 'we'll just have to write off the rest. I'll make sure you're OK as I feel I let you down somewhat.'

Henry felt embarrassed by his performance.

'It's not just that, I've heard from an officer at the prison that Rawlings is absolutely furious about you and he says you are going to pay. He's been warned to stop these threats but he's still adamant that you're going to suffer, it just worries me.'

To Bryan, Henry appeared unperturbed, but deep down he was a little worried knowing Rawlings' terrible reputation. However, he knew he would be in prison for many years.

'I'm not too bothered, Bryan. By the time he gets out, he'll have forgotten all about his grievance, I'm sure.'

They shook hands and Henry left.

When he arrived home, he went straight into the garage and switched off the receiver. He then went indoors, put down his bags and gave Jayne a welcome kiss. He was determined to suppress his worries.

'It's lovely to be home, darling.' He spoke with a chirpy voice to reassure her all was well.

'You sound better but you must be tired after that long drive.'

'I'm not too bad, looking forward to a nice meal tonight. Have you decided where we are going?' He had left it to her.

'The Walnut Tree, is that OK?'

'It's fine, wherever you like."

Henry was intrigued to know what fake story she would give him regarding the previous Tuesday evening.

'Did you go out last night?' He asked the question casually.

'No,' she replied, 'I just watched a film and washed my hair.'

This made him wonder if there had been a change of plan. He hopefully wondered if she hadn't seen her lover after all.

They went to the Walnut Tree restaurant and after the meal they went home and straight to bed. Henry was asleep in no time.

On Thursday, Jayne put her suitcases on a bed in a spare bedroom and started her packing. Jonathan had told her not to worry too much about weight, so she was able to use two cases for herself. She selected a number of glamorous dresses, beach wear, erotic lingerie as well as all the usual necessities. She had a feeling that there would be plenty of bedroom action.

Mrs Moyle was curious and asked Henry what was going on and when he explained, she was delighted to be free of Jayne for two whole weeks and she couldn't resist making a rather cheeky response.

'It will be just like the old days,' she said, quietly chuckling.

By Saturday, Henry was quiet and pensive. He was no company for Jayne at all. It was so obvious that Jayne had to say something.

'Are you all right, Henry? You seem in a strange mood?'

'Sorry, I'm feeling a little miserable. I'll be OK later.'

Jayne put it down to the fact that she was going away for a couple of weeks.

In reality, the Stevens situation was really beginning to bother him. It was literally eating away at him and he knew he was going to have to take some positive action.

Jayne took Candy out for a walk on Sunday morning and rang Jonathan from a call box. She wanted to speak with him and confirm Henry was taking her to the station on Monday morning. Henry took the opportunity to remove the tape in order to listen to it in his car.

He put the cassette tape into the car player with some trepidation as he was nervous as to what he might hear. He made sure the car was facing the gates so that he could see Jayne if she returned. As he pushed the play button, he was decidedly edgy as he hadn't liked the sound of the telephone conversation he had heard the previous Tuesday. Nevertheless, he had this remote hope that he had got it wrong and that Stevens had honoured the deal after all.

The tape started with the telephone ringing twice but it was not answered in the bedroom. The rings were then followed by some groaning and shrieking, obviously generated by Jayne and her lover but nothing was said. Henry stopped the tape and felt sick.

After a moment spent composing himself, he listened with reluctance and sadness to the rest of the tape – he simply couldn't afford to miss any of the conversation that might take place. When the noise ended Henry heard Jayne say very softly, 'Christ, Jon, that was fantastic.'

Henry was totally shocked and filled with anger. He knew he had been well and truly deceived. He was in a rage and he wanted revenge. He truly thought Stevens would honour the agreement especially as his threat of reporting him to the police for blackmail seemed to worry him. In reality, Henry never intended to go to the police at all. He realised that not only was he now in danger of losing the love of his life, but he had lost £4,000 as well. It never crossed his mind that her lover was anyone other than John Stevens, why should it?

Henry sat for several minutes trying to take it all in.

He listened to the rest of their conversation but there was nothing of any real interest. However, he had got what he wanted, absolute proof that the money he had paid Stevens was brazenly pocketed with the intention of simply carrying on as before. Despite everything, there was no question of letting Jayne go to him. Henry was convinced that if he could spend quality time with her, even woo her as he had when they'd first met, take her to nice places and on luxury holidays then she would stay with him and have no need for other men. He had to win her back. He knew from Andrews's report that Stevens's modest income could never give Jayne the life she loved. She liked his body, his physical fitness, his good looks and his youth. In Henry's mind it was purely sexual, nothing else.

From that moment on, Henry vowed to totally destroy him.

He had to get Stevens out of her life and Henry was prepared to do anything to achieve it. Paying him off hadn't worked but violence was another option. After Stevens's deceit, Henry would have no qualms about violence. There were people he could pay to inflict physical injury which would cripple him. This wouldn't bother Henry whatsoever; he absolutely detested the man for what he had done. However, he couldn't risk anyone else being involved as he needed to incapacitate Stevens himself. He racked his brains to come up with a method and started to think about some of the many trials he had handled.

He recalled a poisoning case many years earlier. In that case, the accused mixed poison into the victim's food over a period of time which eventually rendered him helpless. Henry liked that idea. He would get his revenge and he would ensure Stevens would be ill for months, maybe he would never recover. The thought of that pleased Henry immensely. The poison used in the case was strychnine which he remembered as being odourless. He wondered if he could get hold of some and more importantly, if there was a way of getting it into Stevens's body. He decided to go to the reference library to do some research after he had taken Jayne to the station on Monday. As he hadn't taken on new work, he was free to do as he wished, particularly as Jayne was away for two weeks.

He was determined to act natural when Jayne returned from Australia, despite knowing what she was planning when she arrived back home.

He returned to the house and made himself a pot of tea which he sipped sitting in his favourite living room armchair. He was staring into space trying to come to terms with the dreadful dilemma he had when Jayne came back with Candy in a jovial and happy mood.

'Hello, Henry. You look very studious sitting there. What are you thinking about so deeply?' She had a wide grin on her face.

Henry couldn't help thinking that she appeared to be surprisingly cheerful for someone whose mother was dying – she would have a shock if she knew his true thoughts.

'I'm not thinking of anything much, just resting for a moment.'

'Shall we go out to dinner tonight?'

'I don't fancy it really,' he replied, 'I don't feel that well.'

'What's the matter?'

'I don't know really,' he answered glumly, 'I just feel a bit down in the dumps.'

Henry couldn't face sitting in a restaurant with her after his discoveries.

Suddenly he took her hand whilst gazing into her eyes.

'You do still love me, don't you?'

'Of course I do,' she replied. 'Whatever's come over you? Is it because I'm going to Australia?'

'That doesn't help, but setting that aside, I get the feeling that you may leave me,' Henry said mournfully.

Whatever she did, he would always forgive her. He couldn't help it, he was absolutely besotted with her and he truly believed life would not be worth living without her.

Jayne was becoming a little nervous about this conversation. She certainly didn't want to tell Henry that she was in the process of deciding whether to leave him for Jonathan, certainly not until she had spent two whole weeks with him to test the relationship.

In a way both of them were in a similar position as Henry didn't want to disclose to her that he had discovered her infidelity or her plans. He couldn't take the chance that she might leave him if it all came out into the open. He needed the chance to make her life so wonderful she would only want to be with him.

Jayne looked at him intently.

'Henry, I'm not going to leave you. I'm sorry I have to go away for a little while but I'll be back soon.'

She was buying time to make her decision really, she knew that. Henry then perked up a little.

'That makes me feel better, dear. Maybe we should go out for a meal tonight after all. I am tired though, so perhaps we can make it a short evening?'

'I'm fine with that,' said Jayne, thinking, *Good, no sex again.*

On Monday morning, the 22nd March, Henry drove Jayne to the station. He helped her with her luggage from the car and went onto the platform with her. When the 0950 train to St. Pancras, London, pulled in, he helped her onto it and felt tears welling up – Jayne noticed.

'Don't be sad, Henry. I'll soon be back.'

When she saw how sad and depressed he was she began to feel upset herself. She couldn't really understand why she felt so guilty and upset as this was what she wanted. She too was now close to tears so she thought to herself, *For Christ's sake pull yourself together. What's going on?*

She pulled the train window down and kissed Henry goodbye through it. Tears were still trickling down his cheek and she was touched by his feelings. The train pulled away and they waved to each other until Jayne was out of sight. She then relaxed and soon forgot about Henry's sadness – she was excited now about what was to come.

*

Henry stuck to his plan. He was now a free agent and he intended to use his freedom to good use. The first thing on his agenda was to deal with John Stevens and it was going to be much easier now that Jayne was away. He went straight from the station to the reference library in order to research the poison named strychnine. Henry looked it up and discovered that humans will suffer symptoms after ten to twenty minutes.

He sat in the library reading intensely about strychnine and what it could do if ingested and he liked what he read. The body's muscles begin to spasm, starting with the head and neck and then the spasms spread to every muscle in the body, with almost continuous convulsions, and they get worse at the slightest movement. As the convulsions progress they increase in intensity and frequency until the backbone arches continually. These convulsions lead to severe depression and if untreated, death will follow due to the paralysis of the pathways that control breathing, or by exhaustion from the convulsions. Death normally takes two to three hours and it's extremely painful.

Henry read these descriptions several times and he imagined, with joy, the suffering Stevens would endure if Henry was able to get the poison into his body. He didn't have the slightest concern about the pain he would inflict upon him, in fact he would delight in causing it. So much was his vengeful feelings towards this man. He would strive to keep a low dose so as to make him suffer, preferably for weeks or months which would destroy the body and the handsome looks that were attracting Jayne to him. This was the poison he wanted and he explored ways of obtaining it.

Further research revealed that farmers were permitted by law to use strychnine for the control of moles and rats on their farms. This was excellent news for him as a member of his Masonic Lodge, Roger Spears, was a dairy farmer who lived nearby. Henry had known him for many years and so he rang him as soon as he got home.

'Good morning, Roger, it's Henry Walters here.'

'Henry,' he exclaimed, sounding pleased, 'haven't spoken to you for ages. How are you?'

'Fine,' Henry said falsely, 'I wonder if you can help me?'

'What's up?'

'Well, I'm overrun with moles in my back garden and I wondered whether you might have an idea about how to get shot of them, you know, poison or something?'

Henry deliberately tried to avoid sounding knowledgeable as he wanted Roger to feel that he was helping him. He got the answer he hoped for.

'I use strychnine myself as I get loads of moles on the farmland, bloody nuisance they are.'

Henry said, 'I didn't think you could buy it?'

Roger explained. 'We can't, but farmers are allowed by law to use strychnine as moles are a major problem. You have to have a licence to get the stuff and I haven't got one. Most farmers use a professional mole killer like I do.'

'So you can't get me any then?' said Henry sounding disappointed.

'I do have a jar because the mole killer I use, Simon Bull, gave me one in case I had a problem when he wasn't around, he's not supposed to do that. It's in liquid form and I can let you have what's left in the jar, but you really must keep it strictly to yourself otherwise I'll get Simon into trouble. I think he actually deals with the mole problem on over twenty five farms over quite a wide area in our district. He also gets called to some golf clubs and racecourses.'

'If you could let me have some it would be very kind of you, Roger.' Henry felt relieved.

'I'll bring the jar over shall I and do it for you. I'll sort the little buggers out.'

Henry responded somewhat seriously with a blatant untruth.

'No need, I'm in your area tomorrow morning, could I call in and collect it say about ten o'clock?'

Roger hesitated. 'I'll be taking a risk but as it's you I'll help, it'll be good to see you and I'll put the kettle on.'

Henry was delighted. 'I'll be there around ten tomorrow.'

Roger added a warning.

'Listen, Henry, you mustn't mention this to anyone because its only for use on our farms due to the high numbers of moles affecting our livelihood, it's definitely the most effective way of killing them but people like you are supposed to use mole traps, get it?'

'I won't say a word,' said Henry, truthfully. 'I look forward to seeing you in the morning.'

Henry was feeling pleased. He felt revenge was truly in the air and he was certain that it would soon be time for Stevens to wish he had never crossed him.

Thirteen

The train was approaching Leicester station and Jayne had already forgotten Henry's sadness. Her thoughts were now totally focussed on her forthcoming adventure with Jonathan.

As the train chugged to a halt, she looked through the window anxiously for him but he wasn't anywhere to be seen and she had a terrible thought that something had gone wrong. She clumsily managed to get her cases from the train and stood by them on the platform still looking around for him. With a sigh of relief, she saw him stroll out of the cafeteria smoking a cigarette and looking as suave as usual. He strolled over and kissed her.

'Hello, babe, this is it,' he said. 'Together at last. Any problems?'

'No, everything went OK.' She felt totally relaxed now that she was with him.

'Ralph is outside with the car. Let's go,' he said.

They took her luggage out of the station and she saw Ralph sitting in the Mercedes right outside.

'Hello, Miss Jayne,' said Ralph. 'Nice to see you again.'

'You too,' she replied.

'Let's go, Ralph,' Jonathan ordered.

They arrived at Heathrow airport in good time with Ralph parking right outside the terminal. He helped them to unload their cases and told Jonathan that he intended to have some lunch nearby before driving back to Nottingham.

'That's fine, Ralph. Tell Keith to look after the place for me. I'll be ringing him from the States to make sure all is well.' Ralph then drove off.

Jonathan called a porter and they made their way into the terminal and then to the check-in desk for the flight to Australia which Jayne was booked on. She told the check-in officer that she had a family problem and that she wouldn't be able to fly and added that she would be claiming on her insurance. The officer was casual about that and cancelled her flight without any questions.

'That ticket is no good, Jayne. Obviously you'll just have to tear it up and put it in the rubbish bin,' said Jonathan.

Jayne was upset to do so but he didn't seem bothered about the loss of the fare so she complied.

'It seems an awful waste of money, Jon.'

'I know,' he said 'but its all part of the plan. Remember, it was only a single and you had to convince your old man. Just forget it, babe.'

He suddenly had a thought.

'I'm thinking, I know we're early but I think we may be able to check in for our flight to New York now, let's try.'

Jayne had never flown long haul before and as they made their way towards the New York check-in area, she spotted the queue for economy and made her way to the end of it. Jonathan took hold of her arm.

'We don't go there, babe. We're going first class. I never travel any other way.'

Once again, Jayne was taken aback by Jonathan's lavish lifestyle and she was enjoying being a part of it.

They reached the first class check-in which had a red carpet leading up to the desk, and the porter placed their luggage on the conveyer belt as they checked in. Once the bags were gone, they went to a luxurious lounge where Jonathan fetched two glasses of champagne. Jayne noticed that there was an array of fine foods, soft drinks and a large selection of alcoholic beverages.

'Let's relax,' said Jonathan, flopping into a comfy armchair. 'We've got plenty of time, we'll have something to eat and drink shortly, OK?'

'Sounds great,' said Jayne, thoroughly enjoying the luxury of everything around her. She thought it was a different world and she loved it.

They touched glasses and Jonathan looked at her grinning broadly.

'Here's to a fabulous holiday and I'm hoping our time together will be so wonderful that we will want to be together forever.'

'What a lovely thing to say, Jon. I totally agree.'

In reality, Jayne had pretty much made her mind up, this was the life and the man she wanted.

They sat talking and picking at the food whilst enjoying several alcoholic drinks. Being in the first class lounge, they were not called to board their flight until all of the other passengers had boarded. Jayne felt like royalty as she made her way onto the aircraft and into the first class cabin which was very impressive. The aisles were wide and the seats reclined to full length beds and they had plenty of legroom. Constant free drinks were offered and she and Jonathan were handed impressive menus with a choice of fine wines.

She thoroughly enjoyed the flight; it was one of the most exciting experiences of her life. Jonathan was wonderful company and the time just flew by as they talked, had a sing along with drinks in the cocktail bar and slept for a few hours. The flight time to New York was lengthier in those days with the time in New York five hours behind the UK, but despite that, Jayne felt great on landing, she thought it must be the excitement.

They landed at John F Kennedy International Airport in New York, renamed after the assassinated President.

'I've booked us into a nice hotel to get some well-needed sleep before we go onto Las Vegas,' Jonathan explained.

'Is Las Vegas a long drive then?' Jayne enquired.

'I think it might be better to fly there,' he replied chuckling. 'It's about two and a half thousand miles.'

Jayne said, 'just joking' in an effort to cover up the stupid remark, but it didn't work.

Jonathan casually remarked, 'I think I told you we would be meeting Antonio and Martina whilst we're in Vegas, didn't I?'

'I seem to remember you saying something about that,' she replied, but in truth she had forgotten.

'He's my partner in the nightclub and I thought I told you that too. Don't look so worried, they won't be with us all the time. We'll have bags of time to ourselves.'

Thank God for that, she thought.

They stayed overnight and after a few hours' sleep checked onto the flight to Las Vegas, again first class. Las Vegas time was another three hours behind New York and the flight was another several hours, all very tiring, but Jayne loved the whole experience. On landing they made their way to the arrivals hall and Jayne heard a man shout loudly.

'Mr Bond no less!'

She turned and was surprised to see Antonio Rossi and Jonathan throwing their arms around each other in a real 'man-hug' with Martina looking on. They then turned to Jayne and both hugged her with continental-style kisses whilst telling her how delighted they were to see her again.

'Come on,' said Antonio, 'let's go.'

He nodded to a porter who put their luggage onto a trolley and they all made their way outside. Antonio had a Cadillac and his own chauffeur waiting and as they got in the car Antonio took a fat-looking envelope from the glove compartment and handed it to Jonathan.

'You'll need this to be going on with,' he said smiling. 'It's the amount in dollars you asked me to get. Let me know if you want any more.'

'Thanks, I will.' Jonathan stuffed it in his jacket pocket.

They were then driven slowly through the Las Vegas streets and Jayne saw that they were littered with brightly lit clubs, bars, casinos, theatres and restaurants. Jonathan, assisted by Antonio, gave a running commentary on the buildings and surroundings for Jayne and she was fascinated by it all and totally spellbound. She tried hard to appear relaxed but her excitement was obvious.

The chauffer then drove slowly past the most impressive hotel Jayne had ever seen and she spotted the name Caesars Palace on a huge sign. She remembered Jonathan telling her how impressed he was with this hotel.

She turned to him.

'You're right, Jonathan, it's a fabulous looking hotel, and it must be a terrific place to stay.'

Jonathan was smiling broadly.

'You'll find out what it's like to stay there – we're in one of their suites.'

Jayne struggled not to make a fool of herself as she was like an excited schoolgirl.

'That's absolutely fantastic. I can't believe I'll be staying there. I really, really can't.'

She tried to stay calm but failed to control her elation. Antonio and Martina appeared to be slightly amused by her rather childish reactions, and for the first time, Jonathan seemed to find her a little embarrassing.

'It is a fantastic-looking hotel, I love it, is it new?' Jayne was curious.

'No,' replied Jonathan. 'Caesars Hotel is probably the most famous and prestigious casino hotel in the world and it was opened in 1966. It's all about depicting life during the time of the Roman Empire and that's why I love it because I get ideas for my club, The Roman Rooms.'

Jayne was impressed by the many columns, statues and other features reminiscent of the Roman period. The entrance was particularly outstanding as nearby there was a twenty-foot statue of Julius Caesar.

Martina was intrigued. 'What sort of ideas do you hope to pick up from this hotel, Jon?' she enquired.

'I've already pinched some of them like the toga-type waitress costumes, the logos used, the parchment-like stationary, and stuff like that. I haven't been for a while so I'm hoping to see something new.'

'Have they got a swimming pool, Jon?' asked Jayne, demonstrating once again her naivety.

Jonathan smiled. 'The hotel has several wonderful swimming pools, fountains, lavish suites again all depicting Roman themes. Its casinos attract the world's high rollers and engage the world's top stars. In fact, Frank Sinatra began performing here having signed a three-year contract about fifteen years ago shortly after it opened.'

Jonathan clearly loved the place.

When they were shown to their room, Jayne was once again overawed by the opulence and extravagance of everything in it. They had a separate lavishly furnished lounge, a beautiful bedroom with the largest bed she had ever seen, a large bathroom, a separate guest toilet, a full-length picture window with views of the pool, a drinks cabinet, and many other lovely features. The whole suite was in a Roman theme including small items like table lamps, taps and paintings. They also had a personal butler on call. Jonathan then pleased Jayne immensely by confirming that this would be their home for the whole holiday.

Jayne had the best holiday ever with Jonathan; they swam, sunbathed by the pool, and were driven around the Grand Canyon. They were also given a tour of the Liberace Museum. In the evenings they had wonderful meals in the best restaurants, sometimes joined by the Rossis and sometimes romantically alone. Jayne was able to pamper herself in the hotel spa, gamble with the generous amount of money Jonathan had given her, and enjoy a few evenings at Jonathan's own club which was also very stylish. The club had its own living accommodation, restaurant and lovely swimming pool. She loved that as she was able to show off her figure and make it known that she was the owner's girlfriend.

Another highlight was having front row seats at a major boxing event and she was also taken to see world-famous artists at some of the best show venues. The highlight of it all was the show at The Sands Casino as after the performance, being club owners, they were permitted to use the VIP bar where there were several celebrities drinking and socialising. Jayne was star struck when she spotted several well-known performers and film stars drinking there, and as Jonathan knew several of them, she was introduced to them. She was now totally on cloud nine and simply couldn't get over the evening. This confirmed her decision – she was going to leave Henry and the sooner the better.

To Jayne, everything about the holiday was marvellous except an incident that gave Jayne food for thought. One day, Antonio and Jonathan went to a business meeting and left Jayne and Martina by the pool as they wouldn't be back until later that afternoon. Jayne was looking strikingly gorgeous and getting plenty of admiring glances from several young men and as usual she enjoyed the attention. She and Martina took a couple of sun beds together, laid out their towels, ordered some soft drinks and prepared to read their books whilst catching the strong sun. A good-looking athletic well-built young man, who had been constantly eyeing up Jayne, suddenly decided to chance his luck by talking to her. He came over in a somewhat cocky manner and sat on the end of her sun bed, completely ignoring Martina.

'How's it going, gorgeous?' he asked, with a kind of lecherous look in his eye.

Jayne took an instant dislike to his rather rude approach.

'I'm fine, thank you,' she said looking irritated.

'Fancy a bit of lunch with me later?' His manner was very brash and cocky.

Jayne tried to give him the brush off. 'My boyfriend is at a business meeting today, he'll be back this afternoon. I'm trying to read so if you don't mind, I'd like to get on with my book.'

'At a business meeting, is he? You sound like a Brit to me. How's he in business here?'

Jayne was getting more irritated. 'Listen, just leave us alone will you, we just want a quiet day and you are becoming a nuisance.'

He didn't seem at all phased by the rejection and pulled up another sun bed and sprawled out on it next to Jayne's.

'Don't be such a misery, baby. Loosen up and I'll take you to lunch.'

Martina looked at the man fiercely. 'She's told you once so clear off.' She looked livid.

'What's it got to do with you? It's a free country so I think I'll stay for a bit, see if I can get you to change your mind.'

He grinned and seemed to be enjoying tormenting them.

Jayne noticed a large burly man in a suit strolling towards them. He had a continental look, Italian probably, and he didn't look very pleasant.

'Is everything OK, Miss Jayne?' he said.

Jayne didn't understand how he knew her name but she was so annoyed at being pestered by the young man, she didn't care.

'Not really,' she replied, 'this man is bothering us.'

The man looked up from his sun bed.

'What do you want? If you've got any sense you'll beat it, OK?'

The stranger stared down at the young man on the sun bed. He looked very much like a man used to violence and he certainly didn't look like the sort of person anybody would want to mess with.

'Let me tell you something, arsehole.'

He spoke calmly but his face looked very threatening and as he spoke, his jacket fell open and Jayne spotted a holstered revolver.

'If you don't get your arse off that bed and leave right now, you're going to regret ever meeting me, so leave while you can still walk – capeesh?'

The young man looked the Italian up and down as if considering taking him on, but thought better of it. He rose up from the sun bed and walked off in compliance saying nothing.

'Don't let me see you near these ladies again!' he shouted after him.

'Thank you,' said Jayne.

'Thanks, Gino,' said Martina.

'That's OK. Enjoy your day.' He then left.

Jayne turned to Martina. 'Do you know him then?'

'Well, yes. He's one of Jon's minders, they are always keeping their eyes on us when we're over here. They keep out of the way but if there's any bother it's good to know they are around. They don't mess about either if they have to get violent, that fellow knew that and was sensible.'

Jayne thought back to one evening in a restaurant in Nottingham. She never forgot the manager telling her something about Jon.

"He's helped no end of charities, he's extremely generous but mind you, you wouldn't want to cross him – that's a different story."

Thinking about it she quite liked the idea of having someone around should she run into trouble, but she couldn't help wondering if there might be more to Jon's businesses than met the eye.

The holiday was coming to a close and although they had discussed their future briefly, they didn't speak seriously until they were on the flight home. Sitting comfortably in their first class seats, Jayne opened up with a profound statement.

'Jon, I want you to know that the past two weeks have been the happiest days of my life, how about you?'

Jonathan paused before replying.

'Jayne, I love you and I now know I want us to be

together forever. I'd like you to divorce Henry and marry me. Will you do that?'

Jayne was over the moon. 'Absolutely, I'd like nothing better.'

'Does this definitely mean you'll ask for a divorce?' Jonathan was clearly anxious to get confirmation from Jayne.

'Yes' she replied in a determined voice, 'when shall I tell him?'

'You've got to do it as soon as we get back, why wait?'

'I'll do it tomorrow, Tuesday. I'll have to tell him there's someone else, shall I tell him it's you?' Jayne was uncertain.

'I wouldn't' said Jonathan, 'what's the point? Just get him to agree a divorce and once the process has started you can come and live with me at my club until we can get married.'

'Really?' this was just what Jayne wanted, 'I'd love that Jon' she cooed.

As much as she dreaded telling Henry that she wanted a divorce, she knew she had to do it. "Tomorrow morning I'm going to tell him" she told herself confidently.

On Monday the 5th April, the aircraft landed safely at Heathrow airport and Ralph was waiting with the car to drive them home. Jonathan had given him the flight numbers before they left. Jayne estimated she would be at her house during the afternoon and so she rang Tudor Manor from a call box. Mrs Moyle answered and Jayne asked her to tell Henry roughly what time she would arrive, she was abrupt and when Mrs Moyle asked how things went in Australia Jayne ignored the request.

'I'll tell you when I get home,' she said.

When they approached Nottingham, Jonathan made a suggestion.

'I don't think we can chance driving you near to Tudor Manor as you have a lot of luggage to carry. It's best to drop you at a taxi rank and you can make out you've come straight from the station, don't you think?'

'Yes,' agreed Jayne, 'that's best.'

She got out of the car at the taxi rank and kissed Jonathan.

'Thank you so much for such a wonderful time. I'll ring you tomorrow and let you know how it went with Henry.'

He looked at her sternly.

'Don't chicken out – it's our future you're dealing with. I'll look forward to your call.'

Jayne left in the taxi, feeling nervous and apprehensive about the ordeal she had to face.

Fourteen

On Tuesday the 23rd March, the day after taking Jayne to the station, Henry drove to Roger Spears' farm as arranged to collect the strychnine, allegedly to kill his moles. He knew this would be a lengthy meeting because sadly Roger had recently lost his wife in a car accident and he was therefore understandably lonely. He would take any opportunity to have a good chin wag with friends. Roger was a popular member of Henry's Masonic Lodge and he supported its activities fully, including the commendable charity work.

Henry usually only met Roger at lodge meetings when he was always immaculately dressed with a clean crisp white shirt thanks to the local laundry. He always wore a bow tie, white gloves, and polished shoes, all finished off with smart Masonic regalia. However, like many farmers, at other times he was just the opposite and today was no exception. A worn-out cloth cap, shoes covered in mud, trousers and a sweater full of holes together with the stench of cows. Henry understood it was all due to his farming work, but it was still a shock to see the contrast.

He was delighted to see Henry and invited him into his grubby kitchen which smelt like a farmyard. This wasn't surprising as he and his farmhands were constantly in and out all day for cups of tea and snacks whilst working with sheep and milking cows. They sat at his well worn kitchen table on uncomfortable chairs and Roger made them tea in a couple of stained mugs. As he was pleased to have company, Roger immediately started giving Henry a rundown of the recent events in his life, followed by quizzing Henry about his, but Henry simply wanted to get on with the real reason for his visit. However, he didn't want to appear rude by making a big thing about his sole aim, to acquire some mole poison. Eventually the conversation was exhausted and it was Roger who changed the subject.

'Over run with moles, you say. Are you sure you don't want me to come over? You have to be very careful with this stuff, you know?'

'No need,' said Henry. 'If you explain what I should do I'll be OK, I'm sure. What's the best way to make sure I kill them all?'

'The best way is to find the mole run, dig a hole above it down into the run, put gloves on, dip the worms in the strychnine using tweezers and drop them into the run,' explained Roger.

'Seems straight forward enough,' Henry remarked, casually.

'Don't take this lightly, Henry; this is really dangerous stuff, you have to be really careful – I mean it.'

Roger sounded concerned at Henry's rather relaxed attitude.

'I'll get the jar now.' He disappeared outside and returned with a jar which he placed on the table.

'This is strychnine and I'll give you this jar but again I must stress that you have to keep this to yourself as strychnine is only for farmers' use. I've used some of it but there's still plenty left in the jar, and there's no need to bring it back afterwards, you can dispose of it carefully.'

'What's the safest way to do that?' Henry asked.

'It's best to bury it. You must be very careful when you are using it, like when you're dipping worms in it. Don't open the jar unless you are going to use it and when you do, make sure you wear gloves and a mask because even inhaling it can be dangerous.'

'It really works well, Roger, does it?' asked Henry.

'It's fantastic, but we farmers are worried because it's likely that we will also be banned soon from using strychnine, and that would be terrible for us. It would actually put my licensed mole killer out of business.'

Henry thanked Roger as he took the rather old well-worn strychnine jar which he examined.

'It's been hanging around a while, looking at this jar. Is it still OK?'

'Of course,' Roger assured him. 'The reason it looks old is because Simon Bull, the licensed mole killer, mixes up liquid strychnine and puts it in his old empty jars, there's nothing wrong with it.'

Trying to appear casual, but genuinely interested for obvious reasons, Henry decided to ask a pertinent question.

'As a matter of interest, what would happen if a human did accidentally come into contact with it, you know, like swallowing some by accident for instance?'

'Well,' explained Roger, 'a little amount won't necessarily harm you, but if you take too large a dose you could be dead within an hour. We were told at a farmer's meeting that even if you're absorbing little amounts over a period of time, you will suffer a slow illness and if it's not treated, death will eventually follow. Apparently it's a dreadful death with excruciating pain.'

Thinking about Stevens, Henry liked the sound of that.

'I must be careful then,' he said.

'Absolutely,' confirmed Roger. 'It's a strange poison because there have been athletes and weightlifters who have taken strychnine deliberately to improve their performance under controlled conditions.'

'Really?' said Henry somewhat astonished. 'That's hard to believe.'

'Believe me, it's true,' said Roger. 'It's been used by athletes in the Olympic Games and years ago some competitors were banned for using it. It's peculiar, I know, but it's true.'

As Roger was explaining, Henry's mind was racing. This was excellent news because Stevens's illness could be put down to strychnine being used by him in an attempt to enhance his weight training.

Henry said his farewells and left with the jar which he hid in the garage when he got home. He then went indoors and had a chat with Elsie Moyle who made him a coffee which she brought to him in the living room where he sat thinking things through.

He wanted to get the Stevens problem out of the way before Jayne returned home but his main problem was how to get the strychnine regularly into his body for several days in a row. His aim was to put him in hospital for a long time at the very least but if he became very bad, or even died so be it, he had ruined Henry's life and stolen his money – he had no sympathy whatsoever. He spent a long time trying to come up with an idea and as he was reading the report from Peter Andrews for the umpteenth time, he had a brainwave.

In the report there was a section on Stevens's shopping arrangements in which it mentioned how he had a pint of milk delivered every morning. Doorstep deliveries of milk came in glass bottles with foil tops. The milkman went on his morning round in a milk float seven days a week very early, usually before six o'clock. His customers could also have eggs and other dairy products delivered if they ordered them. He would deliver the milk by placing the bottles on doorsteps whilst taking away the previous day's empties. This meant that Stevens's milk was on the doorstep early in the morning and all Henry had to do was to get the strychnine into the bottle.

Henry purchased two syringes from the chemist and two hypodermic needles. He was asked why he wanted the needles and he explained that he had some delicate paper items to glue and the needles, with the syringes, were ideal for that job. Being very thin, hypodermic needles were ideal for Henry's plan which was to inject the poisoned liquid into the milk on Stevens's doorstep.

After Mrs Moyle had left for the day, Henry went into the garage and put on rubber gloves. He then thoroughly cleaned the jar in case anybody's fingerprints were on it. He had read at the reference library that 30mg to 60mg could cause death and he decided he would use 45mg. He wrapped a cloth around his mouth and nose, put on a huge pair of Jayne's sunglasses, and very carefully opened the jar. He then practised drawing up ordinary water into one of the syringes, until he was confident enough to draw up some of the liquid strychnine. Once he had one of the syringes nearly full of the poison, he was ready. He intended to administer the first dose into Stevens's milk bottle the following morning, Wednesday. Henry put the full syringe into a plastic bag which he closed tightly with a knot.

He assumed that Stevens would consume the milk throughout the day so if Henry was able to inject the liquid into the milk for several days, Stevens would soon become incapacitated. He had read that strychnine did not smell but it had a slight bitter taste. However, he assumed that if Stevens had cereal, he would put sugar on it which would override the taste and if he had tea or coffee it wouldn't be noticed either. In case the authorities discovered poison in his body, Henry intended to plant the jar somewhere on Stevens's premises. The container would hopefully be found leading to the belief that he had accidentally poisoned himself whilst trying to improve his weight training.

'*Foolproof,*' Henry whispered to himself. As Jayne was away, the timing was ideal as he had few commitments, just a couple of meetings at his local chambers which required him to give advice to solicitors, nothing else.

Tuesday night, Henry struggled to sleep. He tossed and turned, constantly, thinking about his plans for the following day. He had never committed a crime before but considered this to be payback time, or revenge, not a crime in the true sense. He was sure his plan was foolproof; no roads would lead to him. He had no sympathy for Stevens whatsoever and considering how he had ruined Henry's life, Henry was totally committed to destroying him. Being involved in law he did know the important things to consider – to do the "what if's" and make sure the reasonable excuses were in place. The only "what if" he could think of was being asked why he was parked at the address so early in the morning. He tossed around in bed and came up with his reasonable excuse, he would take Candy, and he could then say he was taking her for a walk if challenged as there was a park nearby.

On Wednesday, he left Tudor Manor well before six in the morning having hardly slept a wink. He took the dog lead and woke up Candy, his reasonable excuse. She was most upset by this early disturbance and made her feelings known by growling and snarling at Henry as he took her to the car. They'd never liked each other which was why most of the feeding and dog walking was done by Jayne or Mrs Moyle.

He arrived in Ely Street about 6.15 a.m. and parked outside number 14 at the kerbside, he came as early as possible to be sure it was dark. He felt confident the milk would have been delivered by now. He put on rubber gloves in case there was any slight spillage and he had an empty syringe in one overcoat pocket and the one full of strychnine in the other pocket still in the closed bag.

He looked at Candy stretched out on the rear seat, she was fast asleep. He got out of his car and closed the door quietly so as not to wake the dog. It was slightly foggy and dark, except for a few weak street lights. Henry's heart was pounding and he felt tense and nervous which was making his hands tremble a little. The street seemed so quiet at that time, positively eerie, and he didn't expect to feel so edgy or uncomfortable – he was not as confident now he was confronted with the reality of the situation. Nevertheless, he was determined to go through with his plan. He walked carefully through the open gate of number 14 without making a sound in the soft shoes he had deliberately worn. He could positively hear his heart beating.

He reached the porch and glanced around. There were no lights on whatsoever and Stevens was obviously in bed as his car was on the drive. He looked down and sure enough, there was his daily pint of milk. "*This is it*" Henry whispered to himself, "*no turning back.*"

He took the empty syringe from his pocket and squeezed it between his finger and thumb. He then pushed the needle into the bottle carefully through the foil. When the needle was in, he released his grip and the syringe slowly drew up some milk into the empty syringe leaving over a quarter of an inch of emptiness at the top of the bottle. He had to pick the bottle up and angle it to get the right result.

As he withdrew the needle, he felt an uncontrollable tremor coming on and so he stopped, panicking in case he damaged the foil, however, he managed somehow to compose himself in time. He wasn't concerned about the very tiny hole in the foil as birds often pecked the milk tops.

He put the syringe with the removed milk in his pocket and tore open the plastic bag, taking out the other syringe full of the poison. He inserted it into the same small hole in the foil and just as he was about to squeeze the liquid strychnine into the bottle, he hesitated momentarily. Sweat was running from his brow, but squeeze it he did, filling the small empty space he had created full of poison.

He withdrew the syringe, placed it back in the plastic bag and then into his pocket. He knew there was no turning back now, the deed was done. He walked quietly back to his car, got in and drove back to Tudor Manor.

When he got home it was about 7.30 a.m. and he went straight into the garage. He carefully put the rubber gloves into a drawer and put the needles and syringes into a plastic bag which he placed on a high beam out of sight. He went back to the car and Candy was still asleep on the back seat. He woke her up, much to her displeasure, and they both went indoors. He was quite pleased with himself as he had felt remarkably calm during his journey home.

He made himself some tea and noticed his hands were starting to tremble again so he sat in a comfortable chair to think. Suddenly he had a terrible thought. "What if Stevens makes tea for a visitor? Christ, I might make an innocent person seriously ill."

Panicking, he took out the Andrew's's report again and discovered, to his delight, that he was a true loner, he lived by himself and rarely had any visitors. Henry felt better for seeing that but his calmness was short lived because once he had sat down, he seemed to be stricken with nervousness again and all sorts of thoughts flooded into his mind, he even started whispering to himself. '*What if I'm caught, what if I've forgotten something? Did anyone see me?*'

He was rambling and he didn't feel the same person, he could feel the sweat on his skin again, his heart started beating madly and his pulse was racing. He knew he was frightened but he never expected it to be so bad. He told himself the old saying "There is nothing to fear but fear itself" but in reality he didn't believe that anymore. Henry knew there was no turning back now, he had to carry on. 'Pull yourself together,' he said to himself. Mrs Moyle would be arriving shortly and he had to be back to normality. He had some cereal but his throat felt dry and the trembling was back. He had finished his cereal and was still not right whilst sitting at the kitchen table when Elsie Moyle came in.

'Hello, sir. Everything all right?' she asked.

'Yes, fine,' he answered instinctively.

'You're not looking too good if you don't mind me saying so. Did you sleep badly?'

'I think I must have. I don't know why.'

Coincidentally, Candy looked up at him as if she was frowning, and Henry rather stupidly thought it was a good job she couldn't talk.

Later that morning, Henry went to his local chambers as he had a booked session with a solicitor who required advice.

Henry soon realised that it was wrong of him to go, especially as his fees for such advice were substantial. What he had done that morning had taken over all of his thought processes and the meeting was something of an embarrassment. He was stressed, tired and nervous, and his handling of the meeting was unprofessional, so much so that the solicitor actually asked him if he was ill. Henry therefore apologised, postponed the meeting, and made no charge.

He was back for lunch which Mrs Moyle had prepared but he wasn't hungry so he went into the living room and had a sleep in the armchair. Mrs Moyle knew him so well and she soon detected that he had a problem of some sort.

Determined to push on with his plan, on Thursday and Friday he carried out the same procedure without incident. On Saturday morning however, when Henry went to inject the fourth portion of the liquid strychnine, he noticed that there was a police car parked a little further down Ely Street. It was nearly 6.30 a.m. and still dark, but the sight of the car unnerved him so he decided to stay in the vehicle as clearly something was going on. He dared not risk getting out of the car with the police about.

Suddenly a second police car arrived and two officers got out and went into one of the houses further down, probably number 22 he guessed. Henry waited for about ten minutes but as it would soon be light, he drove back to Tudor Manor.

As Mrs Moyle was having a day off, he took Candy for a short walk and then fed her. He then went back to bed. He was sure that missing one day's poison wouldn't make any difference to the outcome.

On Sunday morning, he took Candy again and set off to inject the fourth portion. All was quiet and he had no problems except he couldn't stop the stressful feeling he kept suffering. He was surprised to see a new bottle of milk on the step which suggested that the poisoned milk had been used and this led him to believe that something should be happening to Stevens by now. Henry was struggling to appear normal as he showed obvious signs of agitation and worry.

He wasn't eating much at all as his appetite seemed to have deserted him so he decided to try to eat a Sunday lunch at his local pub.

After walking Candy and feeding her, he went to the pub and had a drink at the bar whilst waiting for a table. He knew the barman from previous visits.

'Did you hear the news about the GBH?' enquired the barman, Jerry.

'No,' said Henry. 'A fight in here, was it?'

'No, there was a burglary in Ely Street yesterday morning and the burglars were disturbed. They attacked the occupant and he was seriously injured, life threatening I'm told. You're in the legal game, aren't you. Not worth tackling them, is it,' he said.

'Absolutely right,' Henry confirmed. 'Just let them take what they want and claim on your insurance.'

He now knew what the police presence had been all about on the Saturday morning and he therefore dismissed it. His table was ready and he did manage to eat some soup and part of a roast beef lunch.

On the Monday and Tuesday, he was surprised to see a fresh bottle of milk both days on the doorstep as usual so he was concerned that nothing seemed to be preventing Stevens from drinking his milk.

'Surely something should be happening by now?' Henry said to himself.

To his delight, on Wednesday morning there were two full bottles of milk on the step. This suggested that Stevens hadn't used Tuesday's and with luck, Henry thought, he might be ill at last. He couldn't leave yesterday's poisoned milk on the step so he picked up the bottle with the tiny needle hole in the top, and put it under his overcoat. He quietly went back to his car with it and drove home.

When he arrived, he put on gloves and carefully emptied the poisoned milk down the drain and put the empty bottle in the rubbish. Later that day, he intended to ring Stevens's place of work and try to discover whether he was ill.

Once again, his stress was getting to him and he simply couldn't stop the occasional shaking in both hands. Also the sweat would run off his forehead and he kept suffering from headaches. He really did feel ill but he was determined to see his plan through.

Around eleven o'clock that morning, he rang Lench Insurance Company and a woman answered.

Henry tried to stay calm and composed. 'May I speak with Mr Stevens please?'

'I'm sorry,' she replied. 'I'm afraid he isn't here today.'

'Is he out on calls?' Henry asked with his fingers crossed.

'I'm afraid not; he's quite ill. In fact he was taken into hospital yesterday. Are you one of his customers?'

'No,' Henry replied, 'I'm a friend. I'd like to visit him though, do you know the ward?'

'You can't visit I'm afraid, I can't say any more.'

Henry felt a strange rush of excitement come over him. *It really sounds bad*, he thought to himself. *Marvellous, it's worked.*

'Are you still there?'

Henry pulled himself together. 'Thank you for your help,' he said and hung up.

He was pleased – Stevens was suffering at last.

Henry went back home and entered the garage. Wearing gloves to ensure there would be no fingerprints, he took the jar of strychnine which was nearly empty. He also took a fairly large empty box on which he wrote Stevens's name and address before driving to 14 Ely Street. Knowing Stevens was in hospital, Henry knew he was safe to visit the house and put the strychnine jar in a suitable spot on the premises. He went round the side of the house carrying the box, hoping there was a garden shed or somewhere suitable to put the jar.

Sure enough, there was a shed with no lock on it and Henry went inside and put the strychnine jar on a shelf. If he was challenged about this visit his reasonable excuse would be that he was trying to deliver the parcel he was carrying. Satisfied, Henry went back to the car with the parcel and drove back to Tudor Manor.

On Friday, he realised he knew he had to overcome his feelings of stress and worry as the next Monday, Jayne would return home. He was excited about seeing her but conscious that he might appear strange, as he could not stop thinking about what he had done. He kept telling himself that he had nothing to worry about, everything was covered, and there was nothing to link Henry to Stevens's illness. He realised that Jayne would soon discover her lover's plight, but she wouldn't be able to link anything to Henry. Also he guessed she would soon get over it all, especially as he would be making her life much more enjoyable. He was aware that if and when Stevens recovered, he would struggle to resurrect their relationship as Henry would not be working away overnight in the future.

When he managed to put the Stevens situation out of his mind, Henry was really excited because he had all sorts of plans to please Jayne on her return. Once she was over her mother's illness, he intended to take her away for a luxury holiday in Marbella where they had had their honeymoon years earlier. He had already looked at hotels but wasn't sure whether to stay in one or ring his friend Diego and see if they could stay with him. Henry had also planned some days out together, including a weekend in London. Things would be totally different from now on.

Elsie Moyle had left him cooked dinners to heat up for today and Saturday, but on Sunday he planned to have another Sunday lunch at the pub. He had no idea of what time Jayne would arrive on Monday so he intended to stay in all day.

When he fed and took Candy for walks over the weekend he felt that something strange was going on. It was as if she was taking to him a little. He also began to like the little creature himself – he sort of looked on her as an ally as she had accompanied him on his unlawful activities. When he sat on the sofa during Saturday, he was shocked when Candy jumped onto his lap and started licking his hand. He then found himself stroking her and it was hard for him to believe what was happening after all those years of hate.

'God knows what Jayne would make of this,' he said to himself.

Henry went to the florists and bought a lovely bouquet of flowers and a "welcome home" card.

He was truly excited on Monday morning, so much so that he managed to put the Stevens situation out of his mind and he spent the afternoon constantly looking out of the window waiting for the arrival of her taxi.

Fifteen

On the Wednesday that Henry had carried out his first early morning injection into the milk, John Stevens had got up as usual at 8 a.m. He had his wash down, shaved, cleaned his teeth and dressed for work. He then filled his breakfast bowl with cornflakes and sprinkled a generous portion of sugar over the flakes. He then went to the porch, picked up his milk, tore off the foil and poured about half a pint of milk. He made himself a cup of tea which he drank whilst enjoying his cornflakes. The subtle bitter taste which concerned Henry went unnoticed due to the sugar and tea overriding it.

He drove to work feeling fine but later, he felt agitated for some reason. He also noticed that he had a slight twitching in his muscles. He thought nothing of it and went to the gym straight from the office for his usual weight training, but he seemed to struggle a little, he was not his usual self due to the constant feelings of agitation and nervousness. When he went to bed that evening he did not feel too good at all and slept badly with more muscle twitching. It is hard to imagine a more horrendous and gruesome death than that of strychnine poisoning, and had Stevens known of his forthcoming plight, he would have contacted a doctor immediately.

The next day, Thursday, he had his breakfast cereal with more milk, accompanied by a mug of tea but he noticed that the twitching in his muscles had got worse, now he was getting more regular spasms. Nevertheless, being the man he was, he drove to work but during the morning he could feel that more of his muscles were now affected. Also, he was experiencing a peculiar taste of metal in his mouth and he felt constantly restless but didn't want to sit down, it was a most peculiar experience. He was asked by Debra in the office if he wanted to go home as she had noticed something was wrong, but being the macho man he was, he declined.

He went to the gym again after work, but was unable to do anything meaningful as he was now feeling terribly ill and was in great pain so he gave up and went home. The pain was now so terrible that he just about managed to make a coffee and a sandwich, which he couldn't eat, before going to bed.

On the Friday, he did manage to have breakfast again but when he got in his car, he realised that he couldn't possibly drive as his calf muscles were stiff and they periodically jerked. He also noticed that when he moved his head, flashes of light darted across his eyes. Driving was impossible but he was determined to get through whatever was causing these problems, so he decided that when he finished work, he would see a doctor. He was totally mystified by these symptoms and rang the office, explaining his predicament and he asked if he could have a lift to work.

Debra kindly collected him but when she saw him she was horrified how frail and drawn he looked. She suggested that he should stay at home and get the doctor to visit but Stevens was determined to shake off the illness. However, after couple of hours he became so bad that Debra took him home and he went straight to bed, telling her that he would ring the doctor if he was no better the next morning. Stevens suffered all through the night and he knew something serious was developing and it frightened him.

On the Saturday morning, he literally struggled downstairs on his backside and with difficultly managed to get the milk from the porch and prepare his cereal with some tea. He didn't really want any, but he thought if he could eat something, it would help him recover.

His whole body was now in a cold sweat so he rang the doctor's surgery twice but couldn't get a reply. As he didn't seem any worse he decided to ring the doctor again on Monday.

On the Sunday, he was in pain but it was now worse. He did manage to get his milk and he had his usual cereal with tea and rested, however, later in the day his lower limbs became as cold as ice and now he simply couldn't understand what was happening, he was by now full of fear, the muscle spasms were more painful and frequent and his arms and legs seemed to be going rigid. He was now very frightened and realised he should have seen a doctor earlier.

As Stevens didn't come to the office on Monday morning, Debra rang him but there was no reply. She drove to the house and knocked on the door several times. She also shouted through the letter box and eventually it was opened by John but clearly with difficulty. She was shocked to see him bent almost double with excruciating pain. She got him into an armchair but he could hardly speak. He seemed to be in pain everywhere so she rang the doctor's surgery and was told that a doctor would come to the house immediately.

Whilst Debra sat with him waiting for the doctor, she was horrified how seriously ill John had become, even during the short time she had been there. Whilst she had been sitting with him his jaw seemed to have become locked, it seemed rigid and he couldn't speak. The only noises were forced groans and screams due to the excruciating pain. Suddenly he frightened her terribly when his eyes began to bulge as if they were coming out of their sockets and his face was slowly turning blue. She could see that he could hardly breathe and she was now petrified; she had never seen anything so horrific in her life. She prayed for the doctor's arrival.

Eventually the doctor arrived and as he entered the room, he was confronted with Stevens having the most violent convulsion, they had been happening every three or four minutes. He had no idea what was wrong with him but he took one look and rang the hospital immediately for an ambulance which came quickly. He was rushed to hospital and straight into intensive care but the muscles controlling his airways had become totally paralysed. Before he could be examined, Stevens suddenly had a most violent convulsion and gasped his last laboured breath. His body shook violently with dreadful groans coming from his mouth. Suddenly he became still and silent – he had suffered one of the most awful deaths imaginable.

It was what Henry was hoping for – payback time.

Sixteen

During the afternoon of Monday the 5th April, Henry had been patiently waiting for Jayne to arrive from the station. Mrs Moyle had supplied him with snacks and coffee and she had also prepared a nice meal for the two of them which only required to be heated up that evening. Henry had a nice surprise for Jayne as he had decided on a week's holiday in Marbella, and he was like an excited schoolboy, continually looking out of the window awaiting her return.

Eventually a taxi pulled into the drive and he was excited to see her getting out of the vehicle and the driver taking her luggage from the boot.

Jayne had removed the giveaway flight labels from her cases which would have revealed where she had been. Henry walked excitedly across as Jayne was hurriedly paying the driver. She was anxious for the taxi driver to go as she didn't want Henry to talk to him in case the origin of her taxi ride was mentioned.

To Henry, she looked stunning. She was tanned and wearing a smart bright blouse with white tight trousers and Henry thought she looked more like someone who had been on holiday rather than visiting a dying mother, nevertheless he was really pleased to have her to himself at last.

The taxi left and they embraced, with Henry attempting to kiss her lips but she simply pecked him on the cheek.

'How have you been, Henry?'

'Not too bad,' he said. 'I missed you a lot, how did it go with your mother?' he enquired, with genuine interest.

'She's bad and hasn't got long to live. I'm so glad I was able to see her one last time.'

Henry couldn't resist making an observation.

'You are really tanned and looking ever so well; you must have been in the sun an awful lot.'

Jayne explained as nonchalantly as she could. 'The weather in Australia is hot and sunny this time of the year; it's their summer and you can't really keep out of it all the time.'

Jayne wasn't really sure why she was lying anymore. She had made up her mind to tell him that she was leaving. However, she didn't feel like telling him as soon as she had arrived home and intended to deal with that awkward conversation later.

I'll do it tomorrow, she thought to herself.

Suddenly Mrs Moyle came out of the house with Candy who scampered across to Jayne. Excitedly Candy jumped up at Jayne and she picked her up and began talking to her in what Henry considered to be a silly voice, it amused him that she even asked the dog questions.

'Have you been a good little doggie then? Have you missed me?' As Jayne spoke, Candy aggressively licked her face.

When things settled down and when Mrs Moyle had gone home, Henry produced the meals that had been prepared and they sat down to eat and talk. He felt that Jayne was remote and agitated, as if she had something on her mind, and she seemed indifferent to him – he didn't like it. She ate some of the meal but was clearly feeling below par.

'Are you all right, darling?' he asked.

'Yes,' she replied rather coldly, 'just a bit tired. I think I'm going to have to go to bed early, do you mind?'

'No, dear, go when you like,' said Henry, sympathetically.

'I think the jet lag's got to me. I think I'll go up now. Let's talk tomorrow, OK?'

She left, giving Henry a peck on the cheek.

The following morning, Tuesday, they had breakfast together before Mrs Moyle arrived. Jayne was trying to pluck up the courage to drop the bombshell regarding a divorce. However, during breakfast, Henry kept asking her questions about Australia and he told her about some of the things he had been doing whilst she was away.

When they were both having a cup of tea after breakfast, Henry decided to spring his surprise in order to cheer her up. He began by mentioning the Marbella holiday.

'Jayne, there's something I want to tell you which you'll love–'

Jayne interrupted him sharply. 'I've a very important thing to tell you first.'

'No,' Henry said sternly but smiling, 'let me go first, please?'

'OK,' she reluctantly conceded.

Henry looked serious.

'You know I'm not going to work so hard now and I'm only going to take local cases, so we'll be able to spend much more time together. I've actually got some great days out arranged for this summer. In fact, I'm going to truly spoil you because I've also arranged for us to have a holiday in Spain.'

He began smiling broadly and continued. 'You'll enjoy that, won't you?'

Jayne looked totally astonished.

She was speechless for a few moments and thought to herself, *This is crazy. I've got to stop it now. This is the moment – do it!*

'Henry, it's finished!' She said it loudly, almost shouting.

Henry looked bemused and was clearly taken aback. 'What's finished? I don't understand.'

'Us, we're finished. Things were not right before I went away and I've had time to do a lot of thinking. Our relationship has all gone sour for me. It's no good, Henry, I just want us to finish.'

Henry sat totally astonished and bemused; he couldn't believe what he was hearing.

'Tell me this is a bit of fun, Jayne, a joke surely?'

Jayne looked at him with a serious look. 'No, Henry, it's no joke. I mean it.'

Henry felt the tears welling up in his eyes.

He looked at her and she could see he was pleading with her.

'Please don't do this to me, Jayne. I love you more than anything and I'd do anything for you. You must stay with me. You'll never find anyone who will look after you like I will. I'll never let you down. Please, please don't finish with me.'

Jayne truly felt sorry for him. Even she was surprised at how much he cared about her, but she knew she had to be strong to fulfil her dreams of being with Jonathan.

'No, Henry,' she said. 'It's over. I want a divorce.'

Henry was taken aback even more.

'A divorce, you must be joking, there's no way I'd ever agree to that. I love you too much.'

Jayne was getting excitable, she thought she had to tell him the truth.

'But that's what I want, I've met someone else.' Jayne was determined not to give in.

'Someone else? How long have you been seeing another man and who is he anyway?'

'It doesn't matter,' she replied. 'Think about what I've just said and we'll talk later. I am sorry, Henry, but that's how I feel and I want a divorce so that I can be with him. I'm going to take Candy for an early walk now – think about it.'

'I don't have to. I'll never divorce you!' he shouted after her.

Henry sat with tears in his eyes. His world was collapsing around him and he thought of the things he had done to keep the marriage together, the money he had lost, the risks he had taken.

'What a mess,' he whispered to himself through the tears.

To Henry, it was clear that the 'someone else' was John Stevens and as Jayne had been away, she wouldn't yet know he was in hospital and unlikely to recover in the near future. Stevens would be incapable of continuing their relationship, and when she discovered his plight, Henry was sure he could step in and win her back. She would find out soon enough, possibly even this morning, about Stevens's illness. There was certainly no question of Henry giving her a divorce despite her adultery, but the one thing he still couldn't comprehend was how she could bring herself to live with Stevens in his run-down semi-detached house.

Mrs Moyle came breezing in just before nine o'clock.

'Good morning, Elsie. Please sit down,' said Henry, sounding rather serious.

She sat down with a slightly worried look, and stared at him in anticipation.

'Elsie, I'm afraid things are not going very well with Jayne.' Henry had always confided in Elsie.

'Sorry to hear that. She's only just got back, hasn't she?' she replied, rather relieved it was nothing to do with her. 'Is there anything I can do?'

'No,' said Henry. 'I just wanted you to know why the atmosphere is a little frosty but just carry on as usual, please. I'll let you know how things develop. You might as well know that she's asking for a divorce but I'm not giving her one as I've done nothing wrong.'

Mrs Moyle had never liked Jayne so she was secretly delighted to hear this piece of news.

Henry felt tired and depressed. This was not how things were supposed to work out. However, he still hung onto his theory that when Jayne discovered that she wouldn't be able to live with Stevens, she would come running back to him. He went into the living room with a cup of tea and flopped in an armchair and soon dozed off.

Meanwhile, whilst Jayne was walking Candy, she stopped at the nearby call box and took the opportunity to telephone Jonathan.

'I've done it,' she exclaimed proudly. 'I've told him I want a divorce.'

'That's great.' Jon was clearly pleased. 'Well done. What was his reaction?'

Jayne was frustrated and annoyed.

'He said he wouldn't agree to a divorce, quite positive he was. I told him there was someone else but he still said no. It's crazy really because he now knows I'm screwing you yet he still wants me to stay.'

'You'll have to persevere and maybe he'll change his mind when he realises you're serious,' said Jonathan.

'Can I leave him now and come and live with you?'

'That's not a good idea at the moment, Jayne.' Jonathan spoke rather sternly.

'You need to work on him and make his life a bit of a misery. He'll soon change his mind then I'm sure.'

Jayne was disappointed with this response.

'But I want to be with you. That was the whole idea after such a wonderful two weeks together, wasn't it?' she said.

'Of course it was, but it's no good you living here now with me when you're still married to him – you need to be there badgering him, making it uncomfortable for him. I want you properly and completely so stay there and convince him. If you don't then nothing has changed so just get stuck into him – never be a loser.'

Jayne was disappointed and surprised. She was under the impression that Jonathan would invite her to live with him in his superb penthouse apartment and share her life with him immediately. However, she did understand his reasoning to some extent and so reluctantly agreed to stay at Tudor Manor and try to get Henry to change his mind about a divorce.

'OK, Jon, I'll do my best,' Jayne said sadly. 'I'm going to miss you a lot though because I won't be able to see you as much now he's not going to work away much in the future.'

'I get that but it helps to make his life a misery,' suggested Jonathan. 'We can meet up and just ignore him. He knows you are seeing someone so he'll just have to put up with it and that might help to make him change his mind about a divorce.'

'Yes, I see, that's a good thought.' Jayne felt a little happier. 'I thought the trip we had was absolutely wonderful. I can't stop thinking about it, can you?' Jayne added.

'Absolutely. I loved it. They'll be more trips to Las Vegas if you want to come with me because I have to go regularly due to my business out there.'

'Try to stop me.' She loved the sound of that.

Jonathan ended the conversation. 'We'll get there in the end, babe.'

'Speak to you soon when we can fix a meeting. Goodbye, honey.' Jayne hung up and walked back to Tudor Manor.

The next few days were very awkward all round for Henry and Jayne. She commenced her plan to make Henry's life miserable and as a result, he was more irritable and upset by her infidelity and her deliberately annoying attitude.

Also, whilst reading the local newspaper, he experienced a sudden panic attack when he caught sight of a small article.

Insurance representative dies.

The article reported the death of John Stevens. His death didn't worry Henry particularly as he considered the old saying "Dead men tell no tales" was true in this situation. He was totally convinced that he had taken every precaution to ensure that he would never be implicated. However, it brought home unpleasant memories of a situation he wanted to forget.

Reading the events of Stevens's death in print caused a churning feeling in Henry's stomach which was accompanied by a feeling of anxiety, the very feelings he was trying to eliminate. He was pleased to see that no mention was made of poisoning; it simply said that the cause of death was unknown.

Having read the article, he couldn't understand why Jayne was so unconcerned about her lover's death. He assumed she must know about it and yet she still talked about wanting a divorce to be with a deceased lover. This baffled Henry considerably.

Seventeen

Shortly after the death of John Stevens, the telephone rang on the desk of Detective Sergeant George Robinson at Henry's local police station. It was his Detective Inspector ringing from the Police Headquarters.

'George,' he said, 'I've got an unusual enquiry for you. I've just returned from a meeting with the Superintendent who told me that there has been a death at the local hospital. The post mortem revealed signs of poison in the body of the deceased but they weren't able to say how it got there.'

'Really?' George was curious. 'Was it murder, sir?'

'They couldn't say, apparently it could have been an accident, murder or suicide. The deceased is a young fellow named John Stevens who is mad on fitness training and weightlifting. He's got strychnine in his body but they can't tell how it got there.'

'Strychnine, that's serious stuff isn't it. How could it be an accident?' George queried.

'That's what I said, but they tell me that some fitness freaks use it sparingly to enhance their performance, never heard of that myself.'

'I see. I'm fairly clear at the moment, sir. Do you want me to have a look at it?' George liked the sound of this enquiry.

'Yes, George, I want someone like you who's switched on to establish what's happened here and to see if there's any skulduggery involved. I'll send someone over with the file we've started so that you can have a thorough read of the facts we have so far. He lived alone and he doesn't seem to have any family around.'

'Where did he die?'

'An ambulance was called to his house but he was so far gone he died almost as soon as he got to the hospital,' said the DI, 'obviously you'll have to search the premises, visit his place of work and check out any friends, contacts and neighbours, you know the drill.'

'Have we got the keys to his house?' asked George.

'The keys to his house will be with the file with the address. Take a detective constable with you and by the way, if you come up with anything suspicious come back to me and discuss it as we'll have to alter our approach and advise the boss.'

'OK, sir, I'll get straight onto it when I've got the file. Has anyone told the hospital to retain the clothing that the deceased was wearing?' George asked.

'Yes, it's been done and all of his clothing is in protective bags for the Scenes of Crime Officer.'

(A murder victim's clothing may carry evidence such as fibres, bodily fluids or possible other indicators as to who had been with him recently. However, DNA was not available to use in 1982.)

When the file arrived, George read it and familiarised himself with the situation. He decided to visit Lench Insurance Services first which was where Stevens worked. He spoke with Debra who was with Stevens during his last moments and also interviewed the other employees to establish their knowledge of the incident. He recorded a statement from Debra who was in the house and it was she who called the doctor.

His next move was to visit the address in Ely Street and he protected the house with no entry signs and barriers to preserve any evidence and spoke with the neighbours. He thoroughly searched the premises with Paul Davies, a young detective who was assigned to assist him. A scenes of crime specialist from SOCO was also in attendance. The search resulted in certain pertinent items being removed which were of interest, these were:

- Nine names and addresses written in an address book.
- A strychnine jar partly full, discovered in a shed. This was carefully removed for further examination for fingerprints and to identify its possible origin.

- An itemised telephone bill which covered the previous two month's calls made by Stevens. There were only 15 numbers but seventy one calls had been made spread amongst them.
- Two paid invoices for work done: one for a leaking tap and the other to repair a broken window.
- In addition the clothing worn by Stevens was now with SOCO.

No evidence of any foul play was identified at that stage so George collated the pieces of information and worked out an investigation plan. The plan would entail visiting all of the nine properties in the address book and interviewing all of the occupants of those properties regarding their relationship with the deceased.

The addresses relating to the 15 telephone numbers Stevens had called were obtained from the Post Office Communications. The two firms who carried out the repairs mentioned on the invoices would also have to be visited. Finally any findings arising from SOCO's examination of the strychnine jar found in the shed would need to be considered.

George decided that the first job was to interview those occupants in the 15 homes that Stevens had been ringing during the past two months. The breakdown of the calls to the 15 numbers revealed that the property that received the most calls was Stevens's workplace. The second was the property called Tudor Manor where Henry Walters was shown as the subscriber. As he was in the legal profession, his name was known by some police officers and George himself recognised it. He was intrigued to know why his home should have been telephoned so many times, but thought there would undoubtedly be a logical reason. However, he put this call on his own list to satisfy his curiosity. The voters' roll showed that there were a total of 34 people, including children, living in the 15 dwellings and all of them had to be seen.

George Robinson was a 41-year-old experienced DS who was an excellent interviewer. He was an overweight man with a large frame who smoked excessively. He liked a few beers nearly every day and didn't pull any punches. He was "old school" and he knew all the tricks to get to the truth. George believed that any person who had anything to do with the victim was initially a suspect, even the ones that had simply received a single telephone call. They would then be eliminated one by one when he was satisfied they were innocent. The remainder would be the subject of more attention and in police jargon would be "in the frame".

George was softly spoken for a big man with a style of questioning which made many interviewees feel uncomfortable – it was as if he knew what had occurred already so why was he asking these questions? In reality George often did know the answers to many of the questions he asked. The purpose of this tactic was to test the honesty of the interviewee, for if he or she gave the wrong answer, George knew the subject was lying and as a result, he or she would be placed in the group of serious suspects to be dealt with later. He was also always on the lookout for one of the most important elements of a murder enquiry – a motive. George rang the number on the telephone bill relating to Henry Walters. It was a few days after Jayne had returned.

'Good afternoon, sir. My name is Detective Sergeant Robinson from the local Criminal Investigation Department and I need to see you regarding an enquiry I am dealing with. I think you might be able to assist.'

Henry's throat started to go dry and his heartbeat quickened. He was overcome by a feeling of unease as he was not expecting this call. He told himself to stay calm and relaxed but he found it difficult.

'That's fine. I'll help you if I can. What's it about?'

Henry hoped it was something simple, nothing to do with Stevens.

'I can't tell you that over the phone, I'll explain when we meet.'

The detective's voice was calm with a slightly sinister tone to it.

'I'll come to your house if you wish, the sooner the better really.'

Henry's mind raced, he didn't want him at the house in case Jayne was around so he lied.

'I'm in town in the morning on business so would it be all right if I call at the station?'

'That would be helpful. I'm at the HQ station all morning so anytime would be fine.'

'Shall we make it 10.30?'

'That's OK with me, I'll see you then.' George rang off.

Henry did not like the sound of this at all as he felt sure it was to do with Stevens. He told himself again that there was no way he could be linked to his death. He tried to predict the questions that he might be asked, such as whether he knew Stevens, had he spoken with him or had he ever met him. He knew from his involvement with the police that they often ask questions when they already know the answers, so if these sorts of questions came up, he had to be ready with a logical reply. He spent some time doing just that but he was uncomfortable and worried.

The next morning, Henry arrived at the police station at 10.20 a.m. and asked for DS Robinson. He was shown into a bare room with a table and two chairs and the only other items in there were an ashtray and some notebooks and pens.

Within a few minutes, DS Robinson came in and apologised for keeping him waiting. He shook Henry's hand and asked if he wanted tea or coffee, Henry declined both.

'Thanks for coming in, sir. This shouldn't take long.'

Henry asked, 'What's it all about?'

'Well, I've got an enquiry going on and I just need to clear up a few points. I just need to ask you if you know a man named John Stevens, do you?'

Robinson gave no clue as to the answer he expected, but Henry's heart sank – it was what he dreaded. He tried desperately to act natural and prevent the sweat appearing on his brow.

'Why do you want to know?' said Henry, as calmly as he could.

'Does it matter, sir? It's a simple question.'

Henry did not want to raise Robinson's suspicions by making a fuss about his questions but knew his first response wasn't a good start. He had anticipated something like this and had decided that if he said he didn't know Stevens, Robinson might have somehow found out that he did and he would then know he was lying. To be safe he had to say he knew him.

'Yes, I do know the name but he's something to do with my wife, insurance I think.' This was his planned reasonable excuse.

'Insurance you say, what sort of insurance was it?'

Without appearing rude or intimidating, George seemed to be able to make Henry feel uncomfortable.

'She was organising a trip to Australia and needed travel insurance. He was the representative she dealt with as far as I can remember.' Henry explained.

He was really struggling to stay relaxed as Robinson seemed to have the ability to unnerve his witness. He was now just sitting pondering without saying anything and after a pause, he lit a cigarette and took a long draw.

'So you didn't get involved then?' he finally asked.

'No, I wasn't going; she was visiting her dying mother.'

Henry thought another try at opening Robinson up was worth it.

'Won't you tell me what this is all about – you're making me nervous.'

'No need to be nervous, sir. I'm sure in your profession you've been in more nervous situations than this.'

Robinson had a rather strange looking smile on his face as if he was teasing him.

'You know me then?' Henry asked.

'Oh yes, we sometimes follow barristers' cases for training; they are held in high esteem, including yourself. That's how we recognised your name,' he added.

Henry felt a little better on hearing that compliment.

'The thing is…' George started to speak as he took a deep draw on his cigarette. It was as if he deliberately wanted to leave Henry hanging, unnerve him whilst he was waiting for the next question, and it worked as he was now feeling very uncomfortable indeed.

George slowly continued. 'There were an awful lot of telephone calls made by this fellow to your house, did you ever speak with him?'

It dawned on Henry that the police had checked Stevens's telephone bill and he had no idea that Stevens had been ringing the house so many times, this was clearly their link to him and it could be a costly one. He was furious with himself for not picking up on it.

He knew he had to be very careful with this answer, so he thought quickly and decided to take a chance and say he had never spoken with Stevens, even though the DS might know otherwise. If he said yes, he would undoubtedly be asked some further awkward questions.

George noted the long pause. In his mind, that was a sign that the interviewee was struggling to find the most suitable answer – that caused George to be slightly suspicious as it was a simple question.

'No, I never spoke with him, it was all to do with my wife,' Henry said. 'There probably would have been quite a few calls as I know she was haggling about the price and other factors regarding the cover she needed.'

'When was this trip? It can't have been long ago considering the number of calls made recently.' George asked.

It wasn't meant to be like his. Henry had prepared a simple reasonable excuse for the calls but George seemed to be analysing everything to death and making things problematical for Henry.

'It wasn't a long time ago,' Henry said, 'she's only just returned. I think it was a Monday. Yes, she went on the 22nd for two weeks and returned home last Monday, the 5th April.'

George asked another awkward question. 'Did she take up the insurance with Stevens' firm?'

Henry kept things simple. 'I don't really know, I just left it all to her as I wasn't going.'

'OK, sir, that seems to be it.'

Robinson rose from his chair. 'I simply had to clear up why this chap Stevens rang your house so many times. Mind you, I still can't understand why there are so many calls. Anyway, job done I think as far as you're concerned.'

Henry felt relieved. *What a great result*, he thought to himself, but it was short lived.

'When can I see your wife?'

'Sorry.' Henry looked bemused. 'How do you mean?'

'Well, we have to speak with everyone who lives in the property to get their stories direct and as I said, there are a lot of calls so I need to speak with her as well. According to the voters' roll, there's only the two of you living at Tudor Manor I think. No one else. Is that correct?'

'Yes,' Henry confirmed.

'Well, as I think you realise, this is a serious investigation because this chap Stevens has died and we don't know the reason for his death,' explained George.

'Yes, I understand that,' said Henry, trying not to show panic, 'but I've told you what happened regarding the phone calls so it probably isn't necessary to trouble her, is it?'

'Sorry, sir, but it doesn't work like that. I have to obey the investigation rules and speak with everyone who may have picked up the phone. No problem seeing her, is there?'

Henry knew he couldn't give the impression he didn't want Jayne interviewed as it would look suspicious.

'No problem at all. She's in tomorrow afternoon. Is three o'clock OK?' Henry smiled as he spoke to give the impression he was pleased to assist.

'That's fine. See you then and thanks for coming in.' Robinson shook his hand, he seemed pleasant enough to Henry.

'Goodbye, officer,' said Henry. 'I'll ring if that time isn't convenient for her.'

He then drove to Tudor Manor worried to death.

Henry now had a serious dilemma so he started to think things through. He was sure that during George's interview with Jayne, her affair with Stevens would be uncovered because she wouldn't have an excuse ready about receiving all these calls. Anyway, she probably wouldn't give a damn whether George discovered her affair with Stevens or not as Henry knew she was seeing someone, and she wanted a divorce anyway – none of this was a secret anymore, it simply wouldn't matter to her. This was serious because if George discovered her affair with Stevens, George would have his motive so Henry realised that he must ask her to cover for him and use the travel insurance story as the reason for the calls – there was no other option.

That afternoon after Mrs Moyle had gone, Henry asked Jayne to sit down with him to talk. Jayne was intrigued and wondered if at last Henry was going to give her a divorce.

'Jayne, I've got a serious request to ask you.'

Jayne looked at him in anticipation. 'What is it?'

'Well, I've got a major problem. You've told me that you've been having an affair and I've discovered it was a man named John Stevens, who has recently died... I guess you know he's recently died?'

'Yes, I did hear something about him dying but I don't know why he died. It's of no concern of mine really; we finished our relationship a few weeks ago. How did you find out about him and me?'

'Never mind that... What do you mean you finished with him? You told me you wanted a divorce so you two could be together didn't you?'

Henry was totally shocked which showed in his face.

'I might as well come clean – it doesn't matter anymore; you know I want a divorce. The fact is that I did have an affair with John Stevens but it was more of a fling than anything. I've never wanted to live with him. I broke the relationship off a little while ago and I've been seeing someone else ever since.'

A terrible thought came over Henry. It began to dawn on him that he might have poisoned a totally innocent man. Henry couldn't speak anymore, he was dumbstruck and it took him a few moments before he could respond.

'I need time to take this in, Jayne. Let me think for ten minutes before we continue this conversation.'

'Whatever.' She shrugged with an air of indifference.

Henry was even more worried. He couldn't believe he had planned the destruction of an innocent man. Henry tried to work out how it could have happened but decided to think about that later. His priority was to get Jayne's interview with the police out of the way. He therefore reconvened the meeting with her.

'Jayne, the police are making enquiries about John Stevens's death and they saw me yesterday.'

'Really? Why would they see you?' Jayne asked looking very surprised. 'Surely you're not involved, are you?'

'Of course not,' lied Henry, 'but they have found a load of phone calls on his phone bill that he made to our house and they asked me why he made the calls. They want to see you tomorrow afternoon to ask you about the calls as well.'

'I'm not worried about that,' Jayne said nonchalantly. 'I'll just tell them I was having an affair with him and he rang me regularly when you were away, no problem.'

'No problem for you but it will cause a big problem for me,' Henry stammered, with a worried look.

'Why?' she said. 'You said you had nothing to do with it.'

'I didn't, but if they knew you were having an affair with him they may suspect that I had something to do with his death, plus the fact that my reputation goes down the pan. I'd rather you gave a false excuse, like saying you were asking him for help with your travel insurance for your trip to Australia. Would you do that for me?'

Jayne pondered for a moment and said, 'What's in it for me?'

'Does there have to be anything in it?'

'It's a big deal lying to the police. I think you owe me something if I do, don't you?'

'What have you got in mind?' Henry asked.

'I want a divorce, of course.'

Henry pondered for a few moments.

'Jayne, surely you will do this for me, won't you?'

'No, I'm sorry, I asked you for a divorce and you won't give it to me, why should I do something for you?'

'Let me think for a minute.' Henry simply had to get her to lie to George Robinson.

After a few minutes, he came to the conclusion that he had little choice. He had to give her a divorce as she was tacitly implying that she would tell the police about her affair with the deceased – he couldn't risk that. In addition, she was becoming extremely annoying and constantly unpleasant towards him. For the first time since they met he was beginning to think that he would be better off without her, particularly as he had other major problems to deal with.

'OK,' he said, sounding reluctant for effect.

'I'll give you a divorce but you must divorce me for unreasonable behaviour which I won't defend. That way your disgusting affairs won't come into it. If I agree to the divorce, will you tell the detective that you were simply discussing travel insurance with him?'

'Yes, I'm fine with all of that.'

Jayne hid her elation. In reality she could have jumped for joy.

She couldn't wait to tell Jonathan.

'What time is this detective coming did you say?' Jayne asked.

'Three o'clock tomorrow. He's a Detective Sergeant and I told him that you probably asked Stevens for quotes for travel insurance for your trip to Australia to see your mother. The reason there were so many calls was because you haggled about the price. I told the detective I never spoke to him, it was just you.'

Jayne wanted to confirm the agreement. 'So if I do this, you'll let me divorce you?'

'Yes, definitely,' confirmed Henry.

*

George had a meeting with his assistant DC Paul Davies after he had interviewed Henry. Paul had been busily interviewing the residents at some of the other addresses and he advised George that he had discovered nothing of importance. George wasn't too concerned about that because he was beginning to think he was onto something with Henry and Jayne.

'How did you get on with the barrister, Sarge? I'm glad you didn't give me that one.' Paul enquired.

'Not bad,' said George, 'but I can't help feeling there's something fishy about his story. He was a bit cagey at the start, and when I asked him why there were so many calls from the deceased, he claimed his wife was haggling with Stevens about the price of travel insurance.'

'What's fishy about that, Sarge?'

'Well, Stevens made these calls from his home telephone when they were work related, some were late in the evening. 'Why would he do that? He would probably have to pay for them. Also, Walters seemed concerned that I wanted to interview his wife. Maybe it's nothing. Anyway, I'm seeing her tomorrow afternoon so that should be interesting.'

George then rang Lench Insurance Services again and Debra answered.

'Hi, Debra, it's DS Robinson back again. I just need you to do something for me, please. Would you mind?'

'I'll help if I can. What is it?'

'Would John Stevens have normally kept the details of any prospective policies that he was working on, you know, like his notes in the form of a file or something like that, even if the quote wasn't taken up? I'm after details for a return flight to Australia on the 22nd March.'

'Like a file record or something of that nature, yes, there should be one?'

'Also, if you've got the latest itemised phone bill for the office I'd like to ask you a question about that as well if you can find it?'

'Sure, give me half an hour and ring me back, would you?'

George was pleased Debra was so helpful. 'Of course, thanks a lot,' he said.

George rang back after half an hour.

'Any luck?' he asked, hopefully.

'I can't find a thing about any Australian trip on the 22nd March.'

'That's strange,' said George. 'What about the itemised telephone bill?'

'Yes, I've got that. What do you want to know?'

Debra began to think there was something sinister about Stevens's death now that the police were getting more involved.

'If I give you a telephone number will you tell me how many times John Stevens used his office telephone to ring it over the period please?'

'Yes,' she said, 'that's fine.'

George gave her the number of Tudor Manor and he heard Debra counting.

'I've counted the calls up and he rang the number nine times from the office,' she said.

'Thanks,' said George, 'can I trouble you for something else?'

'Of course, what is it?'

'Well, suppose he rang a client from his home, would he get reimbursed for the call?'

'Certainly not, 'said Debra positively, 'there's no need for that as our business is done in working hours.'

'Debra,' George said, 'you've been really helpful, thank you.'

George was convinced there was something strange about Jayne's visit to Australia but he wasn't sure whether it was anything to do with the death of Stevens. Nevertheless, he intended to try to get to the bottom of the calls which did not seem to be work related.

The following afternoon, he arrived at Tudor Manor for his meeting with Jayne. Henry answered the door and welcomed him with a handshake.

'Good afternoon, Sergeant.'

'Good afternoon to you, sir. Everything all right?' said George.

'Fine,' Henry lied, he was not feeling good about this meeting at all.

'My wife Jayne is in the living room. Follow me.'

As they walked through the corridor, Henry put his head around the kitchen door where Mrs Moyle was cleaning the oven.

'Elsie, we're going into the living room. Please don't disturb us.'

'OK, sir,' she replied, wondering what was going on.

Jayne was sprawled out on the sofa reading with Candy lying across her legs. She put down her book, pushed Candy onto the floor, and started to stand up. As usual, she was looking radiant and Henry could see George was giving her the once-over with an admiring look on his face.

'No need to stand,' said George, holding his hand out which Jayne gently shook and sat back down.

'Pleased to meet you,' said Jayne in her usual sensuous voice. 'I understand you're a Sergeant, aren't you?'

Henry grimaced as her voice sounded so superior, almost as if she was talking down to him.

'Yes, I'm a Detective Sergeant investigating the death of a man called John Stevens whom I believe you have had conversations with. You are Mrs Jayne Walters, aren't you?'

'Yes, I am, please call me Jayne and have a seat. How can I assist you?'

Henry was amazed at Jayne's confidence when speaking with the detective. She waved him to sit in an armchair so George made himself comfortable. Henry then went to sit in another armchair, but as he did so George gave him a rather disapproving look.

'I'm sorry but I need to speak with your wife alone, sir, rules of investigation work I'm afraid.'

Henry was annoyed at not being involved in the interview but there was little he could do about it. He therefore slunk out of the room like a schoolboy who had been scolded and went into his office worried about what Jayne might say.

'Mrs Walters – sorry.' He corrected himself with a half smile. 'I mean Jayne.'

George couldn't help thinking to himself how attractive she was but Jayne was aware of that, she knew she had that effect on most men. George also had the feeling that this might be an awkward interview but he welcomed the challenge of the difficult ones.

'I think your husband has told you the reason for this meeting; it's about the considerable number of telephone calls you received from a man named John Stevens, who is now deceased. His death is the purpose of this investigation.'

George paused waiting for a reply but none came so he carried on.

'They're all shown on his itemised telephone bill, and I just need to clarify what they were about.'

'I thought my husband had explained the reason.' Jayne's expression hardened.

'Indeed,' George agreed, 'but your husband was speaking for you, the rules require me to ensure that what he said on your behalf was correct.'

Jayne sighed and rolled her eyes in frustration which George spotted. He felt she appeared to be disinterested.

'He was trying to fix my travel insurance for my trip to Australia, that's all. I thought Henry told you that, didn't he?'

'Yes, he did,' confirmed George.

Jayne followed up quickly showing impatience.

'Well, there you are then. What else do you want me to say?'

George leaned forward with a slightly menacing look – he was becoming irritated now and was not the sort of police officer to upset.

'I'll tell you what you can say. Listen carefully and start to take this seriously. I am investigating an unexplained death, and the person who has died has been ringing you from his home address, sometimes in the evening, using his home telephone which costs him money unnecessarily. OK so far?'

'Yes,' she seemed to be a little more attentive.

George continued.

'He rang 13 times from his home and 9 times from his office, and those calls are just the ones on the latest bill. Are you telling me that it needed 22 calls to arrange some travel insurance?'

Jayne frowned as she thought about her answer.

'I didn't realise there were so many calls, but if there were 22, there were 22.'

George openly looked in disbelief at her nonchalance and decided to turn up the pressure.

'I don't think these calls were anything to do with a trip to Australia. I believe there's something you're not telling me, isn't there?'

'No, I've told you all I know.' She was now biting her lip and starting to get flustered.

'I don't like being called a liar and I do believe you think I'm lying – is that so?' Jayne was getting annoyed.

'Of course it's so. I don't believe that you're telling the truth for one moment.' George kept up the pressure. 'Explain something to me, why is there no file about your quotation or anything else about your discussions in the insurance company's office?'

'I don't know,' was all she said.

'So did you accept the insurance quotation after all the haggling?'

Jayne looked confused, she wasn't sure what to say. 'What do you mean?' she said, playing for time to think.

'It's a pretty straightforward question. Did you accept John Stevens quote in the end?'

George was convinced she was struggling to keep up a lie. As he had told her that there was no paperwork relating to her trip in the office, she had to say she hadn't taken it up.

'No, I didn't take it up in the end.'

'So where did you get the insurance from then?'

'Does all this matter, I've told you what I know. In the end I didn't bother with any insurance.'

'I see,' said George with a smile showing disbelief. 'So you went to Australia with no travel insurance at all, is that right?'

'Yes, that's correct.'

Jayne was now flustered and she was losing her rather arrogant attitude.

George knew he was getting near to the truth.

'Where did you purchase your flight ticket?' George thought he would turn up the pressure with this question.

'Sergeant, I don't think I want to answer any more questions, if you don't mind.'

'Oh, but I do mind.'

George leaned forward again and looked deeply into her eyes.

'Listen, Jayne, let me tell you something,' George sounded threatening, 'I've been doing this job for many, many years and I've learnt a bit about people. I know that, due to the way you're dealing with this interview, you are in danger of digging yourself into a hole and that is highly dangerous because – listen carefully – you're in danger of being arrested.'

'Arrested?' Jayne looked bewildered. 'But I haven't done anything wrong.'

'That may be so but if I discover that you are impeding my enquiries by lying, I will arrest you here and now. You must bear in mind that this case involves a death, possibly murder and if you tell me untruths you will be in trouble.'

Jayne appeared to be paying more attention so George went on.

'If you tell me the truth now, we'll forget the rubbish you have just told me, but if you don't answer my questions truthfully then you will become a firm suspect regarding the death of John Stevens. Come on, tell me what the calls were really about.'

Jayne pondered openly and George knew this would be the breakthrough. She looked up at the ceiling in despair; she had given up.

'OK, you win.'

'Right, now tell me what's going on.'

Jayne knew she had little choice so she decided to come clean.

'I was having an affair with John Stevens but it was just a fling. He made these calls when we were seeing each other. I packed up with him recently because I'm in love with someone else.'

'Why didn't you tell me that in the first place?' asked George.

'It's embarrassing and it's not something I want people to know about. It's my private stuff.'

'You never discussed any travel insurance with him and you never went to Australia either, did you?' George was now smiling.

Jayne seemed to be showing him some respect at last.

'You don't miss much, do you? I went to the States with my new boyfriend, if you must know, but Henry doesn't know that.' Jayne was also smiling now.

'Please don't tell him,' she added.

'I won't tell him. Let me tell you something, Jayne,' said George in a reassuring voice, 'nothing you say to me will go any further unless it's to do with John Stevens's death.

'Thank goodness for that,' said Jayne feeling relieved.

'I guess your husband Henry must have been seriously upset when he found out about your affair though. Was he annoyed much?' George pursued the possible motive.

'I know what you're thinking,' Jayne responded, 'but he's not the type to do anything about my affair. He doesn't do violence, in fact he's only just found out about the affair. Between you and me we're now going to get a divorce.'

George rose from his seat. 'I'm not bothered in the slightest about your matrimonial issues. I'm just focussed on the reason for Stevens's death and whether anybody was involved.'

'Is that it then?' queried Jayne.

'Yes,' George smiled, 'if anything else comes up I'll be in touch. You've done the right thing telling me the truth.'

Jayne looked at him rather flirtatiously and smiled broadly. George looked at her with an amused look on his face and started laughing.

'Some interview that was, I quite enjoyed it really,' he said still chuckling, whereupon Jayne couldn't help bursting into laughter as well. Henry could hear the frivolity from his office and couldn't understand it.

George smiled and gave Jayne his card.

'I've really enjoyed meeting you, Jayne,' he said genuinely.

Jayne showed him to the door where Henry joined them.

'Thank you for your help, good afternoon to you both,' said George as he left.

Henry turned to Jayne, anxious to know how the interview went. 'How did it go?'

She gave Henry a dirty look. 'It was terrible at the start but OK in the end.'

'What was all that laughing about?' he asked.

'That detective was not a nice man to start with, he was very rude and he threatened me and all sorts of things. He got better as it went on but I'm afraid I had to tell him about my affair with John Stevens, I couldn't get out of it.'

Henry's jaw dropped.

'You did what? You told him, that means they'll think I had something to do with your boyfriend's death. Dear, oh dear, Jayne, I think you've really got me into trouble now, I'm most annoyed as that wasn't the deal.'

Jayne looked worried and she tried to explain.

'I had no choice, Henry. If you had been there you would have seen that. I hope this doesn't mean that you are changing your mind about the divorce? Let's be fair, I did tell the Sergeant that you didn't know about my affair with Stevens until after he was dead so he can't blame you for anything. Anyway, you said you didn't have anything to do with it, didn't you say that?'

'Of course I didn't have anything to do with it, it's just that they seem to think I did.'

'Anyway I really hope you're not changing your mind about the divorce.' Jayne looked concerned.

'No, I'm not. In fact I honestly thought I couldn't live without you but now I just want you out of my life completely.'

'That suits me,' said Jayne, although she was strangely sad that Henry felt that way.

Jayne was delighted she could get the divorce started and because she didn't care anymore, she blatantly rang Jonathan from the house telephone.

'Jon,' she said excitedly, 'something has happened which has made Henry change his mind; he's going to give me a divorce.'

'Fantastic news, Jayne. Can proceedings start immediately?'

'Yes, immediately.'

'In that case once they have started, you can move in with me at the Roman Rooms. How does that sound?'

'I can't wait,' she was so pleased.

Jonathan then spoiled her euphoria.

'Just one thing, Jayne, I can't cope with a dog in my club or apartment, I'm sorry.'

'Oh no,' Jayne was so disappointed, 'Candy is no trouble, I promise you, couldn't you just give it a try?'

'I'm sorry, Jayne. It's not that I don't like dogs, it's because I'm totally allergic to them. I know it won't work, I'd be ill all the time. I'm so sorry, babe, just try to find her a nice home to please me.'

Jayne was very disappointed but realised she had to find a home for Candy, as sad as that would be for her.

Eighteen

After George had interviewed Jayne, he returned to the police station and updated his progress report. He then went to his DCI's office to update him on the progress of the enquiry.

'The thing is, sir, I think Henry Walters, despite being a QC, must remain as a suspect. There's no real evidence to incriminate him, but I can't help feeling there's something going on. Until I get to the bottom of it, I can't rule him out.'

'Fair enough, George,' the DCI said. 'Keep at it, and good luck.'

'Here's my up to date report for you. I'm sure you'll need it for the superintendent.' George handed him the report and left.

DC Paul Davies was waiting for him in his office with some news.

'Sarge, we've got the result of the examination of the strychnine jar and there are no prints whatsoever on it. Forensic think it has been wiped clean by somebody as there would normally be some marks on a jar, but it's unnaturally squeaky clean.'

George pondered for a moment.

'The thing I can't get my head around is if Stevens was poisoned, how on earth did anybody get him to take the poison? I mean, from our enquiries, he just seems to eat on the hoof – you know, a sandwich at work, a steak he fries himself, no real friends or family and living alone, there's certainly no opportunity for someone to lace his food with strychnine on a daily basis. That's what makes me think it might have been an accident.'

Paul agreed. 'I get what you mean,' he said.

George had another thought. 'I wonder where these strychnine jars come from, you know, how are they controlled?'

'Do you want me to try to find out, Sarge?'

'Yes, Paul, see what you can do.'

The following morning whilst George was writing up his notes in his office, DS Robert Smart, one of his colleagues, came to see him, carrying a mug of tea.

'Got a minute, George?'

'Sure, sit down, Bob. What's up?'

Bob sat down and lit a cigarette.

'Well, it might be nothing but I'm dealing with a burglary where the householder was attacked and seriously injured, GBH it was. This attack took place early in the morning at number 22 Ely Street on a Saturday.'

George asked, 'Which Saturday?'

'The 27th March.'

George put his pen down and his face lit up in anticipation of some interesting news – he wouldn't be disappointed.

DS Smart went on.

'We're struggling with the investigation as the culprit ran from the scene, so we decided to do house-to-house calls in the street. I arranged for all of the occupants to be interviewed to establish if they happened to see anything suspicious at the time, bit of a long shot as it was around 6.30 a.m.'

'How do you think any of this helps me?' George asked.

'I don't know if it helps you but the thing is we couldn't get any response from number 14 and when I made enquiries as to why, I was told the occupant had died and you were looking into the circumstances.'

'Go on,' said George, becoming intrigued.

'Well, one occupant in number 12 said he couldn't sleep and went downstairs to make some tea. He saw a red Jaguar parked outside his house with a bloke sitting at the wheel and he said he was there for about 10 to 15 minutes but as daylight started to break, he drove off. The occupant of number 12 didn't know what the driver was doing there.'

'Any idea who it was?'

George eagerly awaited the answer as the DS took a gulp of tea.

'Yes, because we badly wanted to speak to the driver we contacted the DVLA and asked them to carry out an enquiry to establish how many red Jaguar owners there were on our patch. We only asked for our own patch initially and it turned out there were nine, I thought you might be interested.'

'Bloody right, I am.'

Bob continued.

'Well, as the car was near the deceased's house, I thought you might like to see the results. We've got a list of the nine owners of red Jags but we haven't spoken to any of them yet, I was waiting to see whether you might like to see it.'

'Where's the list?' asked George in an excitable voice.

Bob opened his file and pushed a sheet of paper across to him with nine names and addresses on it. George couldn't suppress his delight, there it was, the fifth one down was the address of Tudor Manor and the registered keeper of the vehicle was shown as Henry Montague Walters.

'Bingo,' said George.

'Sounds like it's a result for you, George. You owe me a pint, I think.'

'Bob, I owe you more than one I can tell you. I'm suspicious of this guy Walters and to a lesser degree his missus. She had been having an affair with the deceased but I can't really connect either of them to his death. This information is very interesting and I'm definitely going to have to have a more serious interview with him.'

'This bloke's a barrister, isn't he?' said Bob.

'Yes, but he was surprisingly nervous at the initial interview I had with him, that's what raised my suspicions. I'm even more suspicious now and I think the next interview will be under caution.'

Whatever Jayne had said to him, George knew Henry had a motive for harming Stevens and the fact that he had apparently been seen outside Stevens' address warranted a further interview.

George called Paul, his DC, to his office and told him about Henry's Jaguar being seen in Ely Street.

'Bloody hell, guv, that's a cracking bit of news. What's the next move?'

George had a determined look on his face.

'I'm going to interview him under caution at the police station, QC or not.'

Paul looked surprised.

'That's a big step, Sarge, particularly as he is a prominent barrister who is well versed in police tactics and the requirements of a cautionary interview.'

'I know that, Paul, and of course he'll know that by giving him the caution he will realise that I believe he may have committed an offence. Of course, he will also know that interviewees can remain silent and simply refuse to answer any questions at all.'

'Yes,' said Paul, 'but adopting that response would be dangerous for him because if the matter comes to trial, a jury may draw damaging conclusions. In other words, why wouldn't he answer the questions?'

'True. Well done, Paul. You're absolutely right. I'm going for it whatever.'

George rang Tudor Manor to arrange the interview and spoke with Henry.

'Good afternoon, sir, it's DS Robinson here again. Have you a moment please?'

Henry's jaw dropped, his heart started to thump and once again he had to compose himself. He was hoping it was nothing much, but he was wrong.

'How can I help you?'

'Well, something has come to light which needs clearing up. Would you be able to come into the station, please?'

'The station?' queried Henry, he didn't like the sound of that request. 'Is it necessary? What's it about?'

'I can't tell you over the telephone. I really need to see you, sir.' George sounded serious and Henry's mind was racing. He knew he had to comply as a refusal would raise suspicions.

'Very well,' he said, 'when should I come?'

'As soon as possible,' urged George.

'Is tomorrow morning any good? Say eleven o'clock?'

Henry was feeling uncomfortable about this meeting, he couldn't think of any reason for it.

'That would be fine, I'll see you then.' The call ended.

George spent a little time working out his questions to get the best results from them. He was looking forward to this interview but knew he must comply with all of the rules bearing in mind the legal knowledge that Henry possessed. Henry arrived at the station on time and was shown to DS Robinson's office.

'Hello again,' welcomed George. 'Thanks for coming. Shall we go into the interview room.'

Henry felt a little less concerned as the DS appeared to be very pleasant, however, Henry's worries soon returned when he heard George ask the receptionist to get DC Paul Davies to come to join them in the interview room. They sat down in the room and the DC came in with a third chair.

George introduced DC Davies to Henry.

'DC Davies will be taking notes which I'll get you to sign as a true record at the end of this interview. Would you like a tea or coffee, sir?'

'No thanks,' Henry replied. 'I don't suppose this will take long will it?'

Henry was hoping for confirmation to that question but there was no reply. He was feeling decidedly nervy as the interview was becoming extremely formal and although he was involved in law this was all unknown territory to Henry.

'OK,' George started, 'I have to tell you, sir, that certain information has come into our possession and this information, together with the fact that your wife was having an affair with the deceased, means that I am required to carry out this interview under caution. I'm sure that you know what that means?'

'Of course I know what it means but I haven't committed any offence so I don't understand why I'm being cautioned.'

'I think you will understand in a moment,' said George.

George became very serious as he looked Henry in the eyes as he cautioned him.

'You do not have to say anything but it may harm your defence if you do not mention when questioned something which you later rely on in court. Anything you do say may be given in evidence. Mr Walters, I have to ask you if you understand the caution and remind you that you are not under arrest or obliged to remain here. I also have to advise you that you may obtain legal advice and have a legal representative present if you wish.'

Henry was shocked as he had never experienced the other side of the law. He tried to be polite as he thought being cooperative might help him during the interview but deep down he was very annoyed and was unable to suppress his feelings.

'I've already told you I understand the caution,' Henry was almost snarling, 'and as for obtaining legal representation I wonder if you know who I am? I'll remind you that I'm one of the leading barristers in the area.'

George stayed calm. 'I know who you are and I respect that, however, under the law I have to advise you of these points.'

'Well you have advised me so let's get on with whatever it is you're going to ask me.'

Henry was furious and it showed in his face but he tried hard to calm himself down and concentrate on the questions.

'Now, sir, have you ever been to Ely Street, which is where the deceased lived. In fact have you ever parked in that street?'

Once again, Henry guessed that George probably knew he had been there so he had to tell the truth.

'Yes, I have a couple of times.'

'Have you ever been in John Stevens' house which is number 14?'

There was no way Henry could say yes to that. 'No, I haven't.'

He felt he had to chance that reply.

'But you have been in that street. Why was that?'

Henry now had to use his reasonable excuse which he had prepared.

'I take our dog out early in the mornings sometimes. I tend to go to different places for her walk and there is a park near Ely Street so sometimes I leave my car there and go in the park with her.'

George pondered for a moment. 'What sort of dog is it?'

'A poodle, you probably saw it when you came to my house the other day.'

Henry was managing to stay calm as he was now slightly relieved about the questions as he felt he had good excuses.

'On Saturday the 27th March you were parked in Ely Street just before daybreak for quite a while, can you remember?'

'Not really,' said Henry, trying to be casual. 'I just go to different places and I don't really take much notice of where I go or when.'

'You should remember that day as there were police cars in the street dealing with an attempted burglary and assault. You must have noticed.' George was about to turn the screw.

'Yes, I do remember that. There were two police cars.'

George's face hardened. 'You were parked there for nearly fifteen minutes, why was that?'

'I told you, I would have taken the dog for a walk.'

'But you didn't, did you? You didn't even get out of your car.'

Henry didn't like this line of questioning. 'I don't know, I was probably waiting for the commotion to settle down before I took her for a walk.'

'So you stayed in the car. Are you sure you weren't waiting for the police to go as you had something you wanted to do there?'

'I don't understand what you mean. I intended to take the dog for a walk, must have seen all the police activity and thought it might be better to go somewhere else with her – what's wrong with that? There's obviously something you are trying to get me to say and I object to the line of questioning.'

Henry was more annoyed than he appeared.

'When did you find out about your wife's affair with the deceased?' George was getting more suspicious of Henry due to his general demeanour.

'Only a few of days ago, my wife told me after he had died. If you're trying to suggest I had something to do with his death it's just not feasible because I only found out recently. Anyway, I heard he had been poisoned so I don't know how I could have been involved in that, I had no opportunity to poison him, and I've never even met the man.' Henry knew he had to lie regarding that issue.

George then challenged him.

'Why do you believe somebody poisoned him? There's no evidence regarding that. He may have committed suicide, accidentally poisoned himself or was poisoned by someone, we don't know. Our job is to get to the truth if possible.'

George wasn't happy, he was convinced Henry was hiding something. He decided to conclude the interview.

'That concludes the interview sir, DC Davies will write up the notes for you to check. If you agree with what was said perhaps you would sign them.'

'Where do we go with this now?' Henry enquired.

He had relaxed slightly now that the interview was over and he was pleased to hear the police confirm that they didn't know how Stevens was poisoned. He knew George suspected something but he was certain that there was no firm evidence.

He was surprised and relieved when George gave him a wonderful piece of news.

'Well, we don't really envisage seeing you again, sir. I'm sorry you've been inconvenienced. However, I'm sure you realise that as you appeared to have a motive, and you were seen at the Ely Street address, we had to see you formally.'

Henry was secretly elated by these comments.

'That's all right, Sergeant, you're only doing your job. I'm sorry I was so upset earlier.'

Henry wanted to apologise and be pleasant to George as he was delighted it was over. They shook hands and Henry left feeling very happy indeed.

George then sat with Paul Davies looking thoughtful.

'Get some tea, Paul, will you whilst I think about this.'

Paul left and came back with two mugs of tea.

George took his and looked at Paul quizzically.

'What do you think?'

Paul wasn't sure how to answer, he didn't really know what to make of it.

'I'm not sure really, Sarge, if I'm honest, you seem to have let him off the hook.'

'What do you mean?'

'Well,' said Paul in a disappointed voice, 'you told him you don't envisage seeing him again so I assume you consider that he is innocent.'

George lit a cigarette and took a swig of tea.

'Know what I think? I think he's telling a load of rubbish. I'm now more convinced than ever that he's involved in some way.'

'You just told him you don't think you'll need to see him again?' Paul looked confused.

'That was just small talk to make him relax and lower his guard. I'm going to get him somehow. By the way, what's happening regarding your enquiries about the strychnine?'

'It's going OK really, Sarge, you have to have a licence to get the stuff as it's strictly controlled. Farmers, racecourses and golf clubs all seem to use it but it's farmers who use it mostly. Not many have licences though, they use a professional and I'm waiting for the details of the main mole catcher for this area.'

'That's interesting, Paul. Chase them up will you; I'm anxious to get to the bottom of that strychnine jar. So there's a proper mole killer for this area then?'

'Yes, apparently he gets rid of the moles on about 25 farms in our county and I should have his details tomorrow. We can then interview him.'

'Good,' said George. 'If he doesn't come up trumps we'll have to see the others, can you get their details as well?'

'Yes,' said Paul, 'I'm on to it so if the main catcher's not involved, I intend to arrange for us to interview all the others to see if any of them have ever given strychnine to anyone who's not allowed to have it.'

'Is it definite that they mustn't give it to anyone else?' asked George.

'It's an offence if they do that, Sarge,' Paul confirmed.

George was pondering.

'Even so, the jar in the shed came from somewhere and if nobody can buy it he must have acquired it from someone with a licence surely?'

George was becoming obsessed with solving the mystery and it was keeping him awake at night. Even his wife was commenting on his sleepless nights.

*

After seeing DS Robinson, Henry returned to Tudor Manor where Jayne had been waiting to see him and she asked him to join her in the living room.

'Please sit down, Henry. I need to talk with you.'

Henry was feeling uncomfortable about this talk as Jayne appeared to be serious. He was concerned that another major problem was about to rear up.

'Henry,' she said, 'I've seen a solicitor and I'm now beginning divorce proceedings.'

'OK, that's what we agreed,' he said. He was pleased that it was nothing more serious.

'I'm just taking all of my clothes and stuff as nothing else belongs to me and I'm going to move it all in my car so I'll have to make several trips.'

'Whatever's best for you?' said Henry, nonchalantly.

'Can I keep my car?'

Henry thought for a moment.

'I suppose so,' he said, 'it's no good to me.'

'Now, Henry, I'm going to ask you a big favour. My boyfriend won't let me take Candy and I'm very upset about that. He's allergic to dogs.'

Henry gave a half smile. 'It's all one way, isn't it? I know what you're going to ask and the answer's no.'

'You're right, I was going to ask you to keep Candy. Are you sure you won't? Please, Henry, do that for me.'

Even now, despite what she had put him through, he still struggled to be unpleasant to her. He thought for a moment and reminded himself that things were different between him and Candy as she now responded to him. In fact, since she had been involved in his unlawful activity he quite liked her and thought perhaps she might provide a bit of company for him.

'All right, I'll keep her.'

'That's brilliant of you. Thank you so much, Henry.'

'When are you going?'

'I'm making a start tomorrow.'

Over the next couple of days, Jayne moved everything she owned over to Jonathan's apartment at The Roman Rooms. Jonathan got Ralph to help her but he himself kept away from Tudor Manor. Henry still didn't know who her boyfriend was and wasn't really that interested.

When she had moved the last car load, she was strangely a little sad as she had to say goodbye to Henry and Mrs Moyle. She found it awkward when leaving, she simply didn't know what to say so she made a quick departure.

'Goodbye, both,' was all she said and hastily drove off feeling uncomfortable. She couldn't face Candy at all and simply left without seeing her.

Elsie Moyle was a little confused and Henry took her into the living room and he told her briefly what was happening. Although she felt sad for Henry, she was secretly pleased that things were going to return to the days before Henry had met Jayne.

Jayne had been gone for over a week and Henry had become more relaxed. His worry about being connected with Stevens's death had receded since DS Robinson had told him that he was unlikely to be interviewed again. Tudor Manor was running much more efficiently now that Mrs Moyle did not have Jayne to worry about and Henry was beginning to enjoy life a little better. He attended a Masonic Lodge meeting, did some reading and walked the dog.

He had arranged some meetings with solicitors who had asked for his advice. However, his happiness was about to be destroyed.

He was relaxing and thinking in his favourite armchair when Elsie Moyle's voice suddenly jolted him from his thoughts.

'This envelope was pushed through the door, sir. There's nothing written on it except your name.'

Henry took the envelope and opened it.

'It's probably nothing,' he remarked casually. He would wish he had been correct.

As he pulled the piece of paper from the envelope, he saw a typed message on it which made his heartbeat quicken.

Payback time is coming – keep your wits about you as it won't be long. R.

Henry stared at the note trying to come to terms with what appeared to be a threat. There was only one person who could have been from – Rawlings. He read the note again – it gave him a dreadful sinking feeling.

Elsie Moyle noticed his sudden facial change.

'Is everything all right, sir?' she enquired.

'It's nothing,' he said, trying to appear casual whilst putting the note in his pocket.

He realised he now had this new worry to contend with. He had wrongly thought Rawlings would be no danger to him whilst in prison and he was shocked to receive this threat at a time when he was just getting over Stevens' death. He couldn't get the note out of his mind and he was so upset he decided to go to bed early in an effort to sleep and forget things. As he was preparing for bed, the telephone rang. It was about nine o'clock.

'Henry Walters speaking, can I help you?'

'Did you get the note?' a deep voice asked.

'Who is this?' Henry started to feel ill again.

'Never mind who it is, I'm asking you if you got the note?'

Henry wasn't sure how to handle the call.

'What is it you want?'

The man continued.

'I don't want anything except for you to suffer, so look out.' There was a click as he rang off.

Henry panicked; he was frightened and he wanted to speak with somebody so rang Bryan Mathews immediately.

'Bryan, it's Henry Walters. Sorry to ring so late but I've got a big problem. I've received a threatening note and a telephone call from Rawlings. I never expected this as he's in prison.'

'If you're sure it's him, you could go to the police, couldn't you?'

'The note's not specific enough, they wouldn't be interested,' Henry explained sadly.

Bryan made a suggestion. 'Let me make some enquiries in the morning as I have a contact at the prison that's holding Rawlings.'

'It's kind of you to do that? Thank you so much.'

'I'll ring you tomorrow,' said Bryan as he rang off.

Later the next day, Bryan rang a worried Henry.

'I've spoken to my contact at the prison and it seems they always have problems with Rawlings when he's inside. As you know, he's been in prison before and he has got several contacts on the outside who take orders from him when visiting, mainly in respect of his business activities.'

'That's terrible. Can't they stop it?' asked Henry.

'It's not easy. They don't seem to know anything about a vendetta against you but I'm afraid the people threatening you are likely to be his henchmen and they are not pleasant. Your best bet is to get away for a while and hope it blows over.'

'I don't know what to do, Bryan, but thanks for your help.'

The conversation ended with Henry wondering what to do about this latest worrying problem. There was little doubt that Rawlings was serious and the thought of being badly beaten up like Tomkins caused Henry's stress to return and he became very frightened. He remembered Bryan suggesting that he should get away for a while and Henry thought that was his best option. He decided to move to a hotel away from Nottingham but in the longer term, as Jayne had now gone, he decided to sell Tudor Manor and leave permanently for safety reasons.

Now that he intended to partially retire, he favoured making a new start in the south, perhaps Kent, so he quickly attended an appointment with his solicitors and changed his will. Henry was anxious to ensure Jayne inherited nothing once his divorce came through.

He then put Tudor Manor on the market and gave instructions to sell all of his investments and credit the money to his deposit account at his bank. He knew he must move fast as he had no idea when Rawlings' henchmen would carry out the threat.

Nineteen

When DS George Robinson's interview with Henry had concluded, he was more certain than ever that Henry had been involved in Stevens' death in some way. In an effort to cause Henry to relax, he had deliberately given him the impression that he was unlikely to be seen again. However, there was simply no proof other than circumstantial evidence and no obvious answer as to how poison could have been put into Stevens' food or drinks. However, he was about to be cheered up as his DC, Paul, knocked on his office door.

'Enter,' he said curtly, he was in a bad mood.

Paul came in smiling. 'I've got a bit of good news, Sarge.'

'I could do with some, shoot!' ordered George.

'Well, it's about this strychnine business. I've now confirmed that you just can't get the stuff anymore unless you have a licence and they are not easy to get but I've managed get the details of the man who kills the moles on most of our local farms; it's a fellow named Simon Bull and I've also got his address.'

'That's great,' said George, his mood improved immediately.

Paul went on. 'Although there are a few others with licences, they only help the odd farmers and golf courses. Bull, however, is the main man and he has nearly thirty farms in this area that use him when the need arises. His licence allows him access to all of the strychnine poison he needs for mole control.'

'You've told me all this before, Paul. The thing is have you got anything new?' George was getting frustrated again.

'Yes, I have,' said Paul rather excitedly. 'He's forbidden to give any to anyone, including farmers, as he must administer it himself but, get this, it has been known for special friends to get some from him for emergencies when he is on holiday or away for some reason.'

'Well done, Paul. This sounds promising. It seems to me that if we want to try to find out where Stevens got the stuff, we should start with this fellow Simon Bull. If we get no joy there, we could try the other smaller ones, do you agree?'

'Absolutely, that's exactly what I thought.'

'I like it.' George perked up. 'Well done, Paul. Let's do it.'

Paul's face lit up, he liked to please his boss.

Paul had the details of Simon Bull and George rang him. The call was answered by Simon Bull himself.

'Mr Bull, this is Detective Sergeant Robinson from the CID. We have an ongoing enquiry and wondered if it would be convenient to call on you as we think that you may be able to assist.'

'Sure,' he replied, 'when would you like to come? This week and next week are no good as I'm away working, but anytime after that is OK.'

'How about two weeks Monday in the morning?' George suggested.

'I'm here, is eleven o'clock, any good?'

'That's fine,' said George, 'shall we say eleven then?'

'OK, see you then.'

George was disappointed that he couldn't see Bull earlier but he put the appointment in his diary and worked out some questions for the interview. He looked forward to interviewing him as he had high hopes of a breakthrough.

Two weeks later, he drove to Simon Bulls' home accompanied by Paul as arranged. George had collected the strychnine jar from SOCO which was wrapped in see through foil for protection and he took the jar with him.

Bull's property consisted of a scruffy smallholding with some sheep, a few chickens and a couple of cows. There was a large vegetable allotment. The house looked more like a barn and they both dodged in and out of chickens to get to the door which was open.

George turned to Paul.

'Listen, no offence, but leave this to me. It's really important we get a result, just listen and learn.'

'OK, guv,' said Paul.

George shouted in the doorway. 'Anybody home?'

A middle-aged lady came to the door carrying a broom. 'What do you want?' she said, rather brusquely.

'We have a meeting arranged with Simon Bull, is he here?' George flashed his warrant card.

'Police is it? I'll get him, I'm his daughter and he's expecting you.'

The woman disappeared round the back of the house and returned with an untidy tall elderly man with a slight stoop.

'How can I help you?' he said.

George introduced them both.

'Thanks for seeing us. We are investigating an unexplained death which was caused by strychnine poisoning. We are hoping that you may be able to throw some light on how a jar of strychnine was found at the deceased's property.'

'I see.' Simon looked a little concerned. 'Am I in trouble for something?'

'No, we're just looking for your help. We understand that you are paid to kill moles and you have a number of farmers that are customers, is that correct?'

Simon invited them into the house and they sat down in a scruffy kitchen.

'Yes, I've got around thirty farms on my books and

when one of them has a lot of moles causing problems, I go and kill them with the poison. I am licensed to have it, you know.'

George reassured him.

'We know that, it isn't about you we just need your help. Do you ever give jars of poison to farmers if they want to kill the moles themselves, you know, like if you were away on holiday or something like that?'

'Good God, no,' he reacted sharply. 'More than my licence is worth that is.'

'Are you absolutely sure you've never ever done it?'

George was using his softly spoken scary voice whilst staring into Simon's eyes without blinking.

'Think carefully and be truthful.' He held the gaze.

Simon hesitated and George knew he was onto something; there was no need for him to hesitate if he hadn't given the jars to anyone.

'I can't remember doing that, I'm not allowed to.' Simon looked a little ruffled.

George kept the pressure on and Paul watched in admiration as George slowly began to get what he had come for. He leaned forward again and adopted a sort of threatening pose.

'Not remembering isn't really the answer, is it?' said George with a sinister tone to his voice.

'Either you have or you haven't, you must know. Let me make sure you understand what's going on here. This is a possible murder enquiry and strychnine's involved. If we later discover that this poison came from your stock you will be in trouble, impeding the police and possibly being an accomplice, very serious.'

'I don't want any trouble, I've done nothing wrong.' Bull looked frightened.

'We're not interested in giving you any trouble. If you cooperate and tell us if you have ever given any strychnine to anyone, then it won't matter at all, you'll be in no trouble. All we want is the truth, we're not interested in the rules you may have broken, just make sure you tell us the truth and you'll be OK. I'll ask you again, have you ever given any jars to any person?'

Simon paused again. 'I probably have on a couple of occasions but please let me keep my licence, it's my living.'

'Don't worry,' George reassured him again, 'if you cooperate we'll make sure your licence is safe.'

'OK, let me get my records.'

George winked at Paul.

Simon left the room and returned a couple of minutes later with a pile of untidy documents which he started shuffling through. He eventually pulled out a red ledger and opened it up.

'All of the stuff I do with strychnine is in here. If I've helped anyone out I like to record it but I'm the only one who knows what it means; it's in code as I'm not supposed to do it.'

He pulled out a sheet of paper.

'Right, here we are, I've had a few of my close friends ask me if they could have some as I was going away. They use the strychnine themselves because it's fairly easy to kill the moles with it. I've only allowed three close friends actually, what is it you need?'

'We need their details.'

Simon looked worried.

'This could be dodgy for me, couldn't it, because you're probably going to visit them, aren't you?'

'Yes, but it's only part of the enquiry, we won't tell anyone who matters so don't worry.'

'These are the three names and addresses of the farmers.'

George gave it to Paul. 'Write these down please,' he ordered.

George took from his bag the strychnine jar still wrapped in a see-through bag.

'Look at this, Simon.' He pushed it over the table to him. 'Does this look like one of your jars?'

'It's definitely the same as I use. Where did you get it?'

'From the deceased's home. Are they all the same as this?' asked George.

'Yes, they are, they are my old jars that I've already used. I mix the stuff up and put them in an old jar like this. I'm pretty certain this is one of mine.'

George took the list of three names. 'Can you remember how many jars you gave these three farmers?'

'It would have been a while ago,' he replied, 'but it would have only been one jar which had already been used, no more.'

'Did they all give you the jar back when they had got rid of the moles?' asked George.

'No, there wouldn't be much left so I told them to get rid of the jar safely; you know, bury it or something.'

'OK,' George said, 'we're done I think but Paul here will take a short statement. OK?'

'Sure.' Paul took the statement and Simon Bull signed it.

'Thanks, Simon. You've been really helpful,' said George. 'This is my card. If you think of anything else please ring me. In the meantime don't worry, we'll keep this discreet. Please don't tell anyone about our visit. Thank you very much again for your help.'

'Am I totally in the clear then?' Simon still looked concerned.

'Yes, totally, but we may have to use your statement later. The important thing is you must not tell anyone about this visit, OK?'

'I promise I won't,' Simon confirmed.

They drove back to the station and sat in the canteen with mugs of tea. Paul had clearly been impressed with the meeting.

'I learnt quite a bit today, Sarge, but where do we go from here?'

'Well, we need to interview these three farmers as soon as possible and find out if they used the jars. That was a great result today.'

Roger Spears was one of the three farmers.

*

As soon as the two officers had left, Simon Bull thought about the situation. He didn't believe that he had done anything seriously wrong concerning the poison. It all seemed trivial to him so he rang the three farmers on the list to warn them of a possible police visit. He also wanted to ask them if they had disposed of the empty jars safely.

Roger Spears was worried when he received his call from Simon.

'Roger, it's Simon Bull here. How are you?'

'I'm fine, Simon, nice to hear from you.'

'Listen, two police detectives came here this morning asking about the jar of strychnine that I gave you a while ago, have you used it?'

Roger was caught out. He needed time to think as he didn't want to tell Simon he had given it away. He paused thinking frantically.

'Are you there, Roger?' asked Simon.

'Sorry, I dropped the telephone. The strychnine jar you say, yes, I used it and disposed of the jar. I buried it for safety.'

'That's strange,' said Simon, 'because I only gave a jar to three friends and the other two still have theirs and you've buried yours.'

'Well that solves it then, doesn't it?' said Roger, somewhat relieved.

'Not really because the police have one of the jars, they showed it to me and asked awkward questions. I don't understand where it came from.'

Roger was beginning to feel a little uncomfortable. 'I don't get it either,' he said.

'Well, just to tip you off, the police will be coming to see you so for God's sake don't tell them I've rung you, OK? For some reason they seem to be making a big thing of it.'

'No, I won't mention this call. What are they after, do you know?'

'I haven't a clue,' said Simon. 'I'll let you know if there are any developments.'

Roger was concerned about the forthcoming police visit and he wanted to speak with Henry about the jar. He had been told not to speak to anyone but as he was a brother Freemason and a close friend, he considered it his duty to tell him what was going on. He rang him almost immediately.

'Henry, I don't know what's going on, but I've had a call from a fellow called Simon Bull. He is my mole controller, you know, the guy who poisons my moles.'

Henry felt his heart quicken, he could do without any more problems arising, especially as he was trying to escape from the threat that Rawlings was about to carry out.

'What's happened?' asked Henry sounding concerned.

'Well, Simon Bull tells me that two detectives arrived at his place today asking questions about a jar of strychnine poison. Apparently they asked him if he had given any of it to any of his farmers and he told them he'd given a jar to me.'

'What did he do that for?'

Henry was extremely annoyed as over the past few days the trouble-free lifestyle he was beginning to get used to seemed to be doomed as things were going decidedly wrong. He could feel his stress levels rising again.

'I don't know, he didn't tell me that much about it, I only spoke to him on the telephone.' Roger sounded irritated by Henry's response. 'Anyway, it doesn't matter that much does it?' he said. 'It's not really a serious crime to give someone a jar of it – after all, you only used it for the moles didn't you?'

'Of course,' Henry falsely assured him.

'You haven't done anything silly Henry, have you? I took a chance for you and helped you out – you did use it for the mole problem, didn't you?' Roger sounded worried.

'Of course I did,' Henry stressed, untruthfully. 'I told you that.'

Henry felt guilty and upset to have let down a member of his Masonic Lodge and a true friend but he couldn't help that now.

Roger was clearly agitated. 'It just seems over the top to me for detectives to be making enquiries about a jar of mole poison, that's all. I'm just warning you that you will get a call from the police later on because they are clearly coming to interview me.'

'Does that mean you're going to tell them that you gave the jar to me?' Henry asked, with desperation in his voice.

Roger's reply was rather curt. 'Of course I will, why not? What else can I do?' Roger was secretly annoyed that somehow or other Henry had let him down and he wasn't up to trying to protect him.

'OK, thanks for the tip off,' said Henry, realising Roger was annoyed.

'Listen, Henry, you mustn't tell anyone about this call, get it?'

'I won't,' he said.

Henry now had to consider what options he had to escape detection. He was worried because he knew that after the police had seen Roger Spears they would be convinced Henry was involved in Stevens' death. It was a certainty that he would face awkward questions about the strychnine jar found in the shed. He realised that he had to act quickly as they would be after him immediately they had the damaging information from Spears.

As if that weren't enough, he had continuing worries about the threat of being seriously beaten up by Rawlings' henchmen. He made an instant decision, he would move to Spain permanently instead of simply moving out of Nottinghamshire and he would try to organise it immediately. The idea of just getting away and leaving it all behind appealed to him greatly but he had to move very quickly.

Henry decided to try to use his connections in Marbella, Spain. His close Spanish friend, Diego Garcia, lived there and Henry and Jayne had spent some wonderful times with him when they enjoyed holidays in Spain years earlier. Diego had always mentioned to Henry the benefits of retiring to Spain. He constantly told him that he would enjoy a more healthy and enjoyable retirement in the sun. Diego was a wealthy man who owed his freedom to Henry and he was sure he would help him to find a suitable home so he rang him to see if he would assist him and made the call through the International Operator.

'Diego Garcia.'

Henry recognised the voice.

'Diego, how are you, this is a voice from the past, it's Henry Walters.'

'Henry, how are you, amigo? Fantastic to hear your voice. Are you coming down?'

Diego was genuinely pleased to hear from him, he had always liked Henry. They used to spend hours together talking when Henry visited him in Spain and Diego liked that as it helped to improve his English which became very good indeed.

'I'm going one better than that; I'm coming to live in Spain permanently. I've been thinking about the advice you gave me years ago and now I'm retiring, I've decided to emigrate.'

'Wonderful news. I hope you come to live in Marbella. When are you coming?'

'Well,' said Henry choosing his words carefully, 'I'm selling my home here in England and I want to stay in a hotel in Marbella temporarily until I find the right property. I have to move quickly as I've sold Tudor Manor quicker than I thought and the buyers want possession.'

He was not prepared to tell anyone the real reason for his haste.

'Stay in hotel? You joke, you must live in my, how you say, annexe? Live in it until you find place to buy. What does Jayne think of this move, she pleased?'

'We've split up, she's not with me anymore, that's another reason why I'm leaving and another story.'

'Sorry to hear that Henry, that sad, tell me about it when you come. When are you leaving?'

'I've been planning for a while and I meant to ring you earlier. Anyway, I've got a few loose ends to tie up and then I'm driving down and I should be with you within a week.'

'Good God! You not hang about, do you? Make sure you come straight to my place, I have annexe ready for you. How long the journey?'

Henry had had a sneaky feeling Diego would offer him his annexe so he was delighted when he did as he would have a place to stay in Spain on arrival which was a bonus.

'It's quite a long journey, Diego, I've got to drive to Dover and go on the cross channel ferry to Calais. From there I will drive through France and then on down through Spain to Marbella so it will probably take me at least three or four days.'

'You alone, Henry, no girlfriend?' Diego chuckled as he spoke.

'Yes, there's nobody going to be with me. I've not met anyone since Jayne left. I'll be fine on my own. I'll stop a couple of nights on the way.'

'Look forward to seeing you, Henry.'

'Brilliant, Diego. I'm so grateful. See you soon.'

'Adios, amigo, drive carefully.' Diego hung up.

His main priority was to get across the Channel before Roger's disclosure was revealed to George, plus he needed to escape from Rawlings's henchmen quickly.

He had to move fast so he rang his bank straight away and arranged an appointment with his friend Graham, the manager. He arrived and was escorted through to his office.

'Lovely to see you, Henry, come in and have some coffee.'

'Thank you, Graham.'

Henry made himself comfortable and made small talk until the coffee and biscuits arrived.

'Graham,' he said, 'there's no easy way to tell you this, I'm going to emigrate to Spain and I need your help.'

'Really? That's a shock, Henry. We'll be upset to lose your friendship and, of course, your account.' He smiled as he added that last remark. 'Why are you leaving us, I thought you were just moving down south?'

'It's just that having split up from Jayne I'm trying to start a new life. As you know, I'm quite wealthy so I'm going to retire and enjoy some nice weather and enjoy a relaxing life.'

Henry had decided to keep the real reasons to himself, he decided not to share them with anyone for safety.

'You're quite young to retire, aren't you?'

'I'm 51 but so what? I have the money so why work anymore?'

'Fair enough,' Graham acknowledged. 'How can I help?'

'Well, although credits are being made to my account from the sale of shares, there will be substantial sums arriving soon from more sales and from the sale of my property.'

'You're selling Tudor Manor, are you? You'll get a tidy sum for that for sure.'

'I think I will,' Henry confirmed, 'so I will have plenty of money as I'll only need a small place down in Spain.'

'We'd be pleased to handle it all for you,' said Graham.

'Thanks for that but I do want to open an account in Spain and have money transferred into it from here, is that possible?'

'Of course, if you give us the bank and the account details you can simply ring and make a transfer. We'll just set up a password to use when you ring.'

'That's fantastic, thanks.' Henry was pleased.

Graham smiled. 'So you're not closing your account for a while, I'm pleased with that, it's a big one for me to lose.'

'No, I'll not be closing it for a while. Is it possible for you to arrange for me to collect £20,000 in cash tomorrow please?' Henry asked, hopefully.

'That is a tidy sum, Henry. If you're taking it with you could be in trouble,' warned the manager.

'I'm going to open an account with some of it in Marbella and I need some cash to buy what I need. Once the account is open, I can transfer more when I next need money.'

'I assume you're driving down, you could be stopped by customs and questioned about the large sum of cash.'

Henry agreed. 'I know, but I'm going to chance it.'

Graham looked serious for a moment. 'I can't sanction that idea so I know nothing about your plan, OK?'

'I understand,' said Henry. 'Thanks for your help.' He then left.

Twenty

Whilst Henry was furiously making arrangements to drive to Spain, George was equally anxious to see the three recipients of the jars of poison. Together with his DC, Paul, he began to interview the three farmers and the first two were able to explain that they had successfully killed most of the moles on their land using the strychnine. Moreover, both of them still had the partly full jars, which George confiscated and carefully put them in protective bags. George told them that they were now eliminated from their enquiries.

When they visited the third farmer, Roger Spears, he appeared nervous. George introduced himself and showed him his warrant card and they were both invited into his scruffy kitchen where they sat at the table. George detected the apprehension before he had hardly said anything so he therefore decided to use a different approach. He immediately produced the strychnine jar which was still in the see-through wrapper and put it on the table in front of him.

Roger was clearly shocked by the sudden appearance of the strychnine jar and the rather aggressive manner of George, who came straight to the point.

'We are investigating a serious incident and this jar forms part of the enquiry. Have you ever seen it before?'

Roger stared at it with a look of surprise, and hesitated for a few moments before answering. He looked terrified.

'Well, yes, I've seen one like it.'

'What does that mean?' George asked.

'I had a jar like that for killing my moles.'

'What do you mean, you *had* a jar like this, where is it now?' demanded George.

Roger was all over the place and was clearly nervous.

'I don't really know what to say. I haven't got it anymore. Is that what you want to hear?'

George did his leaning forward routine and it was as if his eyes were boring into him. Paul looked on almost like a student and said nothing.

'Now listen,' George said quietly, 'I'm sure you don't want any trouble so just cooperate with us and you'll be OK. Don't go trying to protect people. This is a serious enquiry so just tell us where your jar went – you got it from Simon Bull, didn't you?'

'Yes, he gave me a jar some time ago and I used some of it.'

'Where is it now?' asked George looking threatening.

Roger paused, it seemed that he was trying to think of the best way of responding.

George stared penetratingly into his eyes.

'Think very carefully, Roger, because this is a serious enquiry,' said George slowly. 'You don't want to get drawn into anything nasty, do you? Make sure you tell the truth.'

'Well,' said Roger, 'a friend of mine wanted to kill the moles in his garden and as there was still some poison in this bottle, I let him have it. I didn't think it was that serious.'

'It isn't,' George agreed, 'but what was this person going to do with it, that's what you didn't know, isn't it?'

Roger went quiet; he didn't really know how to respond to that remark.

'You say you gave him this bottle,' said George, 'that suggests that this is the bottle you gave to a man named Henry Walters?'

'How did you know who I gave it to?'

'We know more than you think so just tell us what you know. Is this the jar you gave him?'

'I think so, it looks exactly the same as the one I gave him and I've never had it back. Simon Bull makes his own liquid strychnine which he mixes and puts in his own bottles – I'd say this is the jar I gave Henry.'

Roger was cooperating and George certainly liked this piece of information.

'So let's get this straight – you were asked by Henry Walters to give him some strychnine to kill his moles and you gave him a part-full jar which you are sure is this one. Is that correct?'

'Yes,' said Roger. 'What's Henry done and what's going to happen to me?'

'Nothing's going to happen to you, we all know what you did was wrong but we're not reporting that, all we're interested in is what Henry Walters did with the jar, nothing for you to concern yourself about.'

Roger felt relieved.

'We need a statement to that effect.' George turned to Paul. 'Will you take his statement now, Paul?'

The statement was written by Paul and Roger signed. They thanked him for his help and stressed that he shouldn't talk to anyone else about the case. They then went back to the station.

*

Whilst George had been successfully moving his enquiry along, Henry had collected the £20,000 from the bank as arranged, and concealed it in his car hoping to avoid being questioned about the large amount at customs. He wanted the sum to use in Spain until his estate was liquidated after which he could then transfer further funds as and when required. He also had attended an appointment with his solicitor, instructing him to complete the sale of Tudor Manor with the help of Mrs Moyle. In case he needed to speak with him, Henry gave him Diego's telephone number in Spain on the strict understanding that he would never passed it on to anybody.

The only other job he had to do was to explain to Mrs Moyle that he was emigrating and ask for her help. He saw her the next day.

'Elsie, there's no easy way to say this, as Jayne has left me I want a fresh start and I'm going to live in Spain.'

She was visibly shocked. 'Spain?' she gasped. 'I thought you were going down south?'

'I'd like to retire completely now and start a new life where I can enjoy some nice weather. I'm sorry to spring this on you.'

'When will you go?'

'Tomorrow evening,' Henry replied casually.

'Tomorrow! So soon. Why is that?' Elsie looked surprised.

'I was persuaded by my Spanish friend who is helping me. He has an annexe free and if I go quickly I can use it.'

Henry lied blatantly as he still wasn't prepared to share any of his problems.

'Would you kindly do me a favour, Elsie? Would you stay in touch with my solicitor regarding the sale of Tudor Manor?'

'Of course I will.'

'Also, here is my telephone number in Spain. It's Diego's villa and you can ring me there if there are any problems. Please keep the number totally to yourself, it's important.'

'I won't give it to anyone, I promise.'

'Elsie,' he said rather sadly, 'you've been marvellous to me over the years and I do thank you very much indeed. Everything must come to an end and now I'm retiring, I just feel I want somewhere nice to relax and forget Jayne and the problems I've had.'

'I don't blame you at all,' said Elsie tearfully. 'I can only wish you well for the future. I'm so sorry to see you go, we go back such a long time. I'm 67 myself now so I think I'll join my husband and also retire.'

Henry handed her an envelope with £1,000 in it. 'I want you to accept this to help with your retirement.'

Elsie Moyle was touched, tears welled in her eyes. She had never had so much money.

'Sir, this is so generous. I can't thank you enough.'

She then did something for the first time in all of the years she had worked for him; she threw her arms around him and kissed his cheek. She was gently weeping, and Henry was so touched he responded by putting his arms around her, and the two of them embraced for several seconds.

'Thank you again,' Henry said.

'Don't worry about the house or the sale, I'll come in every day as usual until things are finalised and I'll ring you if there are any problems.' Elsie pulled herself together and said, 'I'll put your dinner on before I go home.'

'Elsie,' Henry said with a pleading sort of look, 'I've another difficult problem and that's Candy. When the house has been sold and you have gone is there any chance you could find her a home?'

'I would be thrilled to have her myself. She's a lovely dog and I'd be delighted to take her home.'

'Wonderful, thank you so much,' he said gratefully.

Henry felt more comfortable now, but he couldn't relax totally until he was on the ferry. He knew that either Rawlings or George Robinson could strike at any time.

The following morning Henry packed and successfully collected the cash from the bank. He left as planned that evening and drove to Dover where he stayed in a hotel near the port but remained nervous as he wasn't yet on the ferry.

*

As Henry was speaking with Elsie, George Robinson had just returned from the interview with Roger Spears and was attempting to fix a meeting with his DCI as soon as possible. He was anxious to advise him of the breakthrough but was told that the DCI was on a course for two days. He therefore made an appointment to meet with him at 9 a.m. as soon as he was back in the office. As Henry was a prominent barrister who might have to be arrested, George wanted to be sure his superiors agreed with his intended action. He therefore put copies of the statements taken, including that of Roger Spears's, onto the DCI's desk so that he could read them before they met.

Paul, his DC, was uncomfortable about the delay.

'Sarge, it's probably not for me to say but don't you think we should see Henry Walters immediately. He could be tipped off and scarper?'

George looked at him somewhat annoyed.

'You're right; it's not for you to say. I know you mean well but I told Spears to say nothing and as we have an appointment with the boss early the day after tomorrow it'll be OK, trust me.'

'Shouldn't we just take his passport or something now?' Paul pleaded.

'I've told you, no, it'll be all right, trust me.' George was getting irritated.

Two days later, the DCI saw George and Paul first thing in the morning having read the statements.

'Well, I've read these statements and I must say you have done a brilliant job, very impressive. I believe we have enough to question him with a view to a charge and possible arrest.'

'Thank you very much, sir,' said George smiling.

'That's the good news, George. Here's the bad news. I cannot for the life of me understand why you didn't go straight to Walters' house and question him, or at least get his passport. You've had this info for a couple of days now and you had enough to detain him immediately. I'm truly worried that he's disappeared if either of these two witnesses have tipped him off.'

Paul looked at George with an "I told you so" look but he avoided his gaze.

'I'm sorry, sir, but I stressed to both of them that they mustn't speak to him and as it's only been a couple of days, I'm sure it will be OK – in fact I still do. I just wanted to be sure you agreed with possibly charging him, after all, he is a QC. That's the reason I waited.'

The DCI looked at George grimly.

'I hope you're right, George, because I've got a feeling that the superintendent will take a dim view of this delay if we fail to clear this death up as a result.'

George looked despondent and said nothing. He had never been criticised in his whole career and he found it hard to take. He was desperately hoping he could repair the damage.

'Listen,' said the DCI, 'go to his house right now and bring him in. There can be no more delays. Go now.'

They both left the meeting and hurried to Tudor Manor where Elsie Moyle answered the door.

'Good morning, madam. Is Mr Walters at home? We need to see him urgently.' George showed Mrs Moyle his warrant card.

'Police, good God, what's happened?' she was shocked.

'Never mind what's happened, where is he?' Paul detected desperation in George's voice.

'He's not here, I'm afraid. He's emigrated; he's gone to live in Spain permanently.'

George's heart sank and he was truly annoyed with himself. He now realised that he shouldn't have waited for his DCI to return from his course – he should have interviewed Henry immediately the interview with Roger Spears was finished.

'When did he go?'

'Yesterday afternoon, can I help?'

Mrs Moyle was intrigued to know the reason for the police visit.

'What's it about?'

'Nothing to concern yourself with, madam, we just think he may be able to help us with something.'

Elsie felt better after that explanation.

'Do you know how he was travelling to Spain?'

'Yes,' she replied, 'he's driving. He drove to Dover and stayed there last night, intending to catch this morning's ferry to Calais.'

'Do you know where he's going to in Spain and if he's returning to clear up any affairs?' George asked hopefully.

'I don't know exactly where he is in Spain but I know he's not coming back as he's asked me to deal with the sale of this house.'

George was looking desperate. 'If you are assisting him with the sale of this property surely you know where he is going, I mean, you must have to talk to him?'

'I've got a contact telephone number, that's all I've got. He's not coming back though, he put his affairs in order before he left and I helped him. I'll give you the telephone number if you like.'

Although Henry had told her not to give the number to anyone, she didn't feel she could obstruct the police.

George gladly took the phone number. 'So you don't have an address in Spain for him?'

'No, I've only got this telephone number.'

'OK, thanks for your help,' said George. 'We'll be in touch if there's anything else.'

As they drove back to the station George was gloomy.

'I've really slipped up here, Paul, and in fairness, you were right. I wanted to discuss things with the DCI after the Spears interview but I wrongly chose to wait for the DCI's return to the office. It's all buggered up now as he's scarpered to Spain as you warned, Spears or someone must have tipped him off.'

'I don't know what to say, Sarge. I'm sorry for you.'

Paul was secretly pleased to have received the compliment but it was the first time he had ever known his DS to make the wrong judgement.

George was clearly very upset.

'Unless he comes back I'm right in the shit and I could get a bollocking, I can't believe I've slipped up like this.'

'I don't know what to say, Sarge. I'm sorry for you. Can't we get him back from Spain?' asked Paul.

'No chance, there's not enough evidence to extradite him. Anyway, we haven't got a treaty with Spain anymore. We had a one-hundred-year treaty but it ended in 1978 and nothing has ever been renewed. I bet he's in the Costa del Sol, somewhere like Marbella.'

Paul looked bemused. 'Why should he be there?'

'There are all sorts of bloody criminals taking advantage of the lack of an extradition treaty and that's where they nearly all are. They don't call it the Costa del Sol now, they call it the Costa del Crime so we've got no chance with Walters.'

Paul didn't know what to say, he felt sorry for his boss.

'Right, let's be positive,' said George sounding serious, 'we have his car number so get onto the ferry terminal at Dover and try to get him stopped. We're probably too late but it's worth a try.'

'I'll get onto it straight away, Sarge.'

George pondered for a moment.

'I think I'll leave him time to get to Spain and then I'll ring him on the number that woman gave us. Mind you, I don't think I'll get much joy because he'll be well up on the law being a barrister, I'll give it a go anyway.'

George and Paul then encountered two more disappointments as Paul's telephone enquiries at the ferry port revealed that Henry and his car had passed through that very morning. George had a last forlorn hope as he frantically tried to contact the police in Calais, but what with the language difficulties and the time constraints, there was little to convince them to get involved.

Later, George was called before the Superintendent regarding his misjudgement concerning the delay in acting on Roger Spears' important tip-off. It was a formal disciplinary meeting, and he received his first reprimand. George was now totally depressed and annoyed with himself. It was the worst experience in his career.

Meanwhile, that very morning, Henry had driven his Jaguar onto the ferry and was delighted when he looked back to see the white cliffs of Dover fading into the distance as the ferry made its way across the English Channel. Henry was of little interest to the customs in Calais and he passed through without incident.

As he began his long drive to Marbella, he felt totally different within himself, he was deliriously happy and was looking forward to a new life without worry.

*

Henry arrived in Marbella in his beloved red Jaguar which did not look out of place in the growing smart and fashionable Mediterranean resort. He had driven off the Dover to Calais ferry without a hitch, with the £20,000 cash being undetected in the boot. As he left Calais, he smiled to himself and heaved a sigh of relief.

"George Robinson will struggle to get to me now," Henry quietly said to himself.

Since leaving Dover, he had taken two overnight stops to complete the leisurely journey, staying in modest bed and breakfast lodgings. On the second night, he stayed in Alicante and after an early breakfast he telephoned Diego to tell him that he would be arriving around lunchtime.

Henry left Alicante early that morning to face the five-hour drive and arrived in Marbella early in the afternoon.

As he drove through the town of Marbella to Diego's beautiful villa, Henry felt a tremendous feeling of elation, the escape from all the worries at home made him feel so much better. He was impressed by the wonderful weather greeting him, the expensive-looking homes and the way the people were dressed – casual but tasteful. He liked the upmarket feel of it all and he somehow knew he was going to really enjoy his new life here. He hadn't been to Diego's villa for years but he remembered its location just outside of the town by the sea, with stunning views and a delightful beach at the rear of the property.

Diego had named the villa *Paraiso Enconrado* meaning *Paradise Found* and an elaborate sign to that effect was at the entrance. Henry always thought the name was a little cheesy but he kept that to himself. In his view, giving it a name like that was typical of Diego. The villa was as beautiful as he remembered. It was a ground floor property standing in nearly two acres of well-maintained gardens kept in pristine condition by a gardening firm Diego used.

There were four en suite bedrooms, an expensively furnished lounge with a baby grand, a twelve-seated dining room, large conservatory, gymnasium, sauna, steam room and modern kitchen. The whole property was air conditioned throughout and it had a very nice self-contained annexe which Diego had offered to Henry. Beautifully furnished terraces surrounded the property, and there were outside dining areas and barbecue facilities together with a 10 x 5 metre swimming pool.

Before entering the drive, Henry stopped momentarily to admire the impressive home.

Henry had known Diego ever since he had successfully defended him from imprisonment years earlier when he was tried for fraud in London. He secretly suspected that Diego's fortune came from the proceeds of that fraud and that was the reason for his many shows of appreciation towards Henry. The fact that he was found "not guilty" might have been the wrong verdict, but Henry was just doing what he was paid for. At the time of the trial, Diego was married to a Spanish lady called Mariana, but when she found him in bed with her best friend, she divorced him, fair enough Henry thought.

Diego had always been a handsome womaniser and with plenty of money. He was tall, slim and despite being 48 years of age still had his own shining black hair. Henry was never sure whether he dyed it or not. Diego had a typical continental look and spoke near perfect English with a sexy accent. After his divorce he had countless affairs and one night stands. He had no trouble attracting women and younger girls despite the dreadful way he treated them but he never seemed to have any desire to remarry. Despite that, Henry liked him a lot but could never understand why women fawned over him. Diego's theory was that many women like to be treated rough. 'Try it sometime with Jayne,' he used to say to Henry, 'you'll be surprised.'

Henry drove along the drive through the beautiful gardens and parked outside the villa. Diego heard the car and came bounding out with his usual free-and-easy style, smiling broadly, he was clearly delighted to see his old friend.

'Henry, it is so good to see you again, amigo.' Diego gave Henry a strong embrace and kissed him affectionately on the cheek.

Secretly Henry was not a fan of this continental style of greeting.

'I am so pleased to see you, Diego, and thank you so much for helping me.'

'Do not mention it. Let us have a drink. Un momento, you wait here.'

He went inside and returned with two chilled bottles of San Miguel which they enjoyed on the sunny terrace whilst catching up on each other's activities since their last meeting. Diego then took Henry into the annexe.

'You remember this, Henry? I had it built when I was married. I built it for Mariana's old mother and when she died, we finished our marriage and, how you say, got divorced? So I don't bother with it anymore.'

'I remember,' said Henry.

'You can stay in here as long as you want. I will enjoy your company,' he proclaimed. 'Put your car in the other garage.'

'That is very generous of you, Diego.' Henry was delighted to have a readymade self-contained home as soon as he had arrived.

'Get sorted out and we can take some sun and talk by the pool. Later we go to dinner at a nice restaurant. You

324

must be tired so no need to dress up. We can just have a nice meal and a chat, you can then sleep when you like. Tomorrow night there is a party at a club with food and I would like you to come with me, OK?'

Henry was a little surprised at the precise pre-arranged agenda but as a grateful guest, he felt he had to conform to Diego's wishes.

'It all sounds very nice to me,' Henry replied, with uncertainty.

'The only thing is, Diego, I must go to the bank tomorrow with my passport and open an account to deposit some money that I've got with me. I can then draw pesetas as and when I need them.'

'That OK,' said Diego, 'you can put the money you have in my safe for tonight, get unpacked and I'll see you on the terrace for another beer.'

Henry unpacked and had a shower. He was delighted with the annexe as it had everything he needed and he soon joined Diego who was lying on a sunbed. Henry sat under a parasol in the shade.

'Henry, why you don't take off your shirt and get some colour, much better for getting the ladies, you will find?' Diego had a cheeky grin on his face.

Henry was a little uncomfortable as taking his shirt off wasn't something he did. Neither was 'getting the ladies', as Diego put it. Henry therefore hesitated.

'Come on,' insisted Diego, 'get your shirt off, you are in Spain now. You must not be, how you say, stuffy?'

That comment reminded him of Jayne, she was always trying to get him to 'loosen up' as she put it. Henry reluctantly took off his shirt and lay on a sunbed in his trousers. The sun was warm and he found it surprisingly pleasant with his beer on a table next to him.

'Have you got swimming trunks?' asked Diego.

'I never thought about it,' said Henry. 'I don't really go in the sun.'

'You need to get some colour, Henry, and some swimming, it will do you good. We'll get some trunks tomorrow.'

Henry was beginning to feel slightly controlled and out of his comfort zone and found this slightly disturbing as he had only just arrived.

That evening, Diego drove them to a very nice restaurant facing the sea where he seemed to be well known not only by the management, but even by some of the customers. Diego and Henry were shown to a nicely decorated table on an outside terrace which was festooned with lovely assorted flowers. It had a lovely view of the yacht harbour.

Henry loved al fresco dining and particularly so when the restaurant seemed to cater for well-dressed high-class diners, it was just what he loved.

A smart waiter came over carrying menus and a wine list and as they were perusing them the manager appeared.

'Buenas tardes, Diego,' he said, broadly smiling.

Diego responded. 'Buenas tardes, Matias.' He turned to Henry. 'This is a very good friend of mine from England who is staying with me.'

Matias shook Henry's hand. 'Welcome to El Gastronomo, senor.'

Henry turned to Diego. 'What does that mean in English?'

'The Gourmet – that is restaurant's name in English,' Diego explained.

Henry turned to Matias. 'This is a beautiful restaurant in a lovely setting. I'm very impressed.'

'Thank you, sir. I hope you enjoy our food. Call me when you are ready to order. Can I get you some drinks whilst you are choosing?'

They ordered gin and tonics, chose their food, and requested a fine bottle of red Rioja wine.

'Diego,' said Henry, 'I'm very impressed with what I've seen in the short time I've been here. To be able to enjoy such lovely surroundings in a restaurant of this quality makes me very excited about living here.'

Henry was genuinely pleased.

'You have seen nothing yet, there are many restaurants like this in Marbella. It grows all the time. You will love it here and I know the people that matter.'

Diego came across as being really proud of his status in Marbella.

Over dinner, they discussed a number of topics and during the conversation, Diego suddenly surprised Henry.

'Why bother buying property here, you can rent the annexe from me if you want, it is hardly ever used these days. You can have your own key, your own telephone, and it is OK by me to invite any lady friends overnight, if you want to.'

Diego broke into his cheeky looking grin as he said it.

Henry wasn't really used to talking about things like that.

'I think I'm too old for that sort of thing, Diego. In any case, I can't speak the language.'

'Nonsense.' Diego kept smiling. 'Have some fun, Henry, while you can. You do not worry about speaking Spanish, a lot of British live here and many others come on holiday. Nearly all who come to Marbella are... how you say, classy? Many local people speak English as well. This is the growing resort on the Mediterranean, there are many things to do and lots of single ladies.'

Henry looked embarrassed.

'Diego, you keep talking about ladies but as I've told you, I'm too old for that sort of thing.'

'Rubbish, you'll be OK with the ladies, and you'll love the place. It has fantastic restaurants, clubs and hotels like the Marbella Club which is superb. I will take you there sometime. Lots of well-known people have been there like Cary Grant, Audrey Hepburn, Teddy Kennedy, the Duke and Duchess of Windsor, as well as Sean Connery. Now the current famous people come as well.'

Henry found it sounded exciting but a little overwhelming.

'It is impressive I must say – I think your offer of the annexe is very generous, Diego, and I'm looking forward immensely to being with you – it's an adventure for me.'

'Good,' said Diego. 'That's settled then. I don't want much rent, I'm glad of the company, you make yourself at home.'

Henry was getting tired and suggested turning in for the night so Diego insisted on paying the bill. Henry objected but Diego just brushed him aside.

'Get it next time,' he said nonchalantly. Henry noticed the handsome tip he slipped to Matias.

Diego and Henry drove back to the villa where Henry slept like a log in the comfortable annexe.

Twenty One

Back in the UK, Detective Sergeant George Robinson couldn't wait to ring the Spanish number given to him by Mrs Moyle. He was still smarting from his ticking off and the fact that he had let Henry escape. The first time he rang, he spoke to Diego who told him Henry would be back later.

It disturbed Diego slightly that the police had rung but he thought it was probably concerning a trial that he had handled.

Henry had been busy opening a bank account and depositing his money and when he returned, Diego looked serious.

'Henry,' Diego said, 'the English police have just telephoned asking for you.'

Henry appeared to be unperturbed, he wasn't unduly worried as he was now safely in Spain.

'I wonder what they want,' he said, calmly.

'There's nothing dodgy going on, Henry, is there?' Diego sounded concerned. 'Only the police seemed anxious to speak with you, they're ringing back.'

'It's probably nothing, it will be a query about a court case I have been handling I expect, no problem.'

Henry was aware that he had no problem lying these days.

Diego looked relieved. 'Oh good, I just get worried about the police, bearing in mind my past involvement with them.'

A short while later, the phone rang again and Diego answered.

'Just a minute, he's here.' He passed the phone over to Henry who put his hand over the mouthpiece and looked at Diego whilst hesitating to speak. As a result, Diego guessed that he wanted some privacy so he left the room.

Henry's heartbeat quickened as he recognised the voice.

'Mr Walters, I'm sure you remember me, Detective Sergeant Robinson.

'Yes,' was all Henry said, he remembered him all right.

'Well, we need to talk to you concerning a further important piece of evidence that has come to light concerning the death of John Stevens. When will you be in England next so we can have a chat, sir?'

Henry guessed what the further piece of evidence was and he wanted absolutely nothing to do with it. He knew he was safe as long as he was in Spain and so he decided to take no nonsense from George whatsoever.

'I'm afraid I've retired and I've emigrated to Spain. I'll be living here permanently now so I don't intend to return to England.'

Henry was calm and positive. He didn't feel nervous anymore as he knew George couldn't do anything meaningful.

'Not even for a holiday?' George enquired.

'Why would I go on holiday in the UK? The weather is lovely here, I have no family, my wife has left me, and I'll have to put up with you tormenting me over a death which I had nothing to do with. Why should I want to come back?'

'That's disappointing, sir, because what we have discovered is very important indeed so what we could do is come and see you in Spain. At least we could then clear this up.'

George suggested this with tongue in cheek, he knew he was struggling to get anywhere with the former barrister.

'There's no point. I don't want anything more to do with the incident so I will be declining an interview if you come. I have no further comments to make and that will be my response to any questions you may ask.'

George decided to have one more try. He knew he had messed up and was desperate to retrieve his credibility.

'This evidence we have seriously implicates you in this matter. It's in your interest to clear it up and if you refuse we may have to think about trying to bring you back to England.'

Henry blatantly chuckled down the telephone, he was quite enjoying tormenting George now he was safe; he felt the shoe was on the other foot.

'Are you serious? Aren't you forgetting who I am? You haven't got a cat in hell's chance of bringing me home and you know it. I know the extradition laws better than you so let me remind you that the one hundred-year treaty between our country and Spain ended in 1978 and has never been renewed.'

George knew he was totally correct and before he could answer Henry brought the conversation to a close.

'In fact, you probably know that there are scores of British criminals living down here and you can't touch any of them. Some of them have been charged and others ran away from court. I haven't even been arrested.'

'Yes, but–'

Henry interrupted him immediately. 'I'm saying nothing more on this matter whatsoever, good day to you.'

He then hung up.

George was embarrassed and accepted the situation. He did however discuss the circumstances with the Crown Prosecution Service but they confirmed that any further action would simply be a waste of time and money. Unless Henry returned to the UK, there was nothing that could be done. They recommended that he revisited the case periodically to see if there was any sign that Henry might come home for some reason in which case action could be considered. George was bitterly upset and annoyed with himself especially when he was advised by his DCI that the police would not be looking for anyone else with regard to Stevens' death.

*

The next morning after a good night's sleep, Henry took his passport and drove to a bank Diego had recommended where Henry opened an account using Diego's address. Henry deposited the £20,000 and drew out some pesetas.

When he returned to the villa, he rang his UK bank, giving them the details of his new Spanish account, his address in Spain and his telephone number.

In the evening, Diego was ready to go to the party at the club. He was anxious to leave and called Henry through the annexe door.

'How's it going, Henry? Are you ready?'

'Just coming,' said Henry, as he walked out of his bedroom.

Diego looked Henry up and down with a shocked look on his face.

'You are not going to the club like that, are you?'

Diego was grinning broadly. He was referring to Henry's choice of dress as he was dressed for the trendy club wearing a Harris Tweed jacket, a formal-looking shirt, a pair of brown brogues, and a tie.

'What's wrong?' asked Henry.

'What's wrong, you say. Look at me.'

Diego stood with his arms open inviting him to check his dress. He had a short sleeve yellow shirt, thin white trousers, soft slip on shoes and a smart belt. He also sported a gold necklace.

'What do you think?'

Henry looked him up and down.

'I guess it is more comfortable but I couldn't dress like that. I'm 51, I'd feel silly.'

'You can't go out like that in this temperature, besides, you'll be a laughing stock. I don't know why you keep on about your age so much; you're only three years older than me.'

'I know, but I haven't got anything else to wear.'

Henry was thankful as he didn't really want to dress like Diego.

'OK, let's go,' Diego said, disappointedly.

Diego had two cars and he drove his open top yellow sports car which Henry thought was a trifle flashy.

'There's a lot of yellow in your life, Diego. Is there any reason?' Henry queried.

'I love yellow. I'm known as the yellow man because I love the colour,' Diego was laughing again. 'Come on, jump in, and let us go to the party!'

They arrived at a very high-class looking nightclub which was exclusive to members and as they entered two well-dressed but burly doormen shook Diego's hand and opened the doors for them.

Inside, Henry could see that the revellers were a mixture of ages and he felt a little more relaxed as he thought they would all be youngsters. The music was not ear shattering or unpleasant either, in fact *Imagine* by John Lennon, one of his favourites, was softly playing. He had expected rock and roll music blasting out, making conversation impossible.

The rather lavish and impressive bar area was separate from the dance floor and played soft music, it also had plenty of comfortable armchairs and sofas. Henry had never been anywhere like this in his life and although he would be reluctant to admit it, he quite liked it.

Everyone seemed to know Diego and as he and Henry pushed their way through the crowd, several lovely looking women of differing ages spoke with him, pecked him on the cheek or kissed him. Lots of men seemed to know Diego too – Henry was amazed how popular he was. Diego introduced Henry to some of them explaining that he was a friend staying with him.

One girl thought he had been in a show as it was clear that his formal looking attire caused some curiosity. This made him feel embarrassed. Another lady in her late thirties actually asked Henry to dance with her but he blushed and quickly declined. He felt really out of place, especially when he heard someone else say to Diego, 'Who's your square friend?'

Diego was clearly well respected in the club, so much so that he and Henry were taken to a private VIP area where they sat in plush armchairs and ordered gin and tonics from one of the attractive waitresses. Diego lit a cigarette and turned to Henry with a smile.

'What do you think of it so far?' he asked.

As he spoke, the waitress poured the drinks. Diego pulled a wedge of money from his pocket and paid her with what appeared to be a generous tip.

'Well, you were right about my style of dress, that's for sure,' observed Henry.

'I think you would be more comfortable if you dressed down a bit,' said Diego, 'don't you think?'

Henry thought for a moment.

'Yes, you're probably right.'

'I want to know something important as you are going to stay in Marbella – would you come here again?'

'Well, I have to say that this club surprises me because I expected a lot of scruffy youngsters leaping about, loud rock music and a general uncomfortable experience but this is quite classy with smart clientele – it's good.'

Diego went on to explain. 'Nearly all of the clubs and restaurants are upmarket here. It's not Benidorm or Magaluf because it's more expensive and so the people expect quality. Come on, Henry, let's go to the dance area.'

They made their way through some double doors and once inside, the music was louder but not unpleasant and neither was it too crowded but Henry still wasn't comfortable, especially when a smart-looking lady in her thirties grabbed his arm somewhat aggressively.

'Come on, Dad, get your jacket off and let's have a dance,' she said, rather playfully.

It was difficult for Henry to get out of it so he reluctantly shuffled around on the dance floor, copying others as best he could for a few moments, but he was totally out of his comfort zone. He was also becoming extremely hot so he apologised to the lady and told Diego that he wanted to get a taxi back to the villa.

Diego was disappointed but he took the annexe key from his key ring.

'Here you are, Henry, take this key and keep it for the future. I'll be home late so I'll see you tomorrow.'

Henry left the club and hailed a taxi.

When he was back at the annexe, he had a coffee and went to bed.

The next morning, he made himself some breakfast of cereal and toast but there was no sign of Diego.

About 9.30 a.m. he came in just as jauntily as the night before; Henry wondered how he could stay so bright and cheerful all the time.

'Sorry, Henry,' Diego said, with a cheeky smile. 'I met a lovely looking girl last night and she looked after me all night, very nice too.'

Henry said nothing, he simply smiled, rather embarrassed.

'You didn't get on with last night's action, did you?' Diego sounded disappointed.

'I felt out of place. I know you don't agree, but I still think I'm too old for clubs like that.'

Diego looked somewhat irritated. 'Listen, Henry, can I make a suggestion, you won't like it but I'd really like you to consider it?'

'OK, go ahead.' Henry was curious.

'Look, you have to get yourself a life here and I think if you change your rather old fashioned approach you'll enjoy Spain much better – no offence meant.'

'I've never been any different, it's difficult for me.'

Diego looked at him intently.

'The thing is, Henry, you're not a barrister anymore, you're retired, but you're lucky because you've retired very early leaving yourself plenty of time to enjoy yourself. I think you should change your approach to life, you should try to be different.'

Henry looked at him quizzically.

'I don't understand what you mean.'

'Well, there are all sorts of exciting things you can do here: learn golf, swim, take walks, read, plus two or three nights a week you could enjoy the classy clubs here with me. You can do a bit of dancing too. What's wrong with that? You thought the club was OK, didn't you?'

'Yes, I was pleasantly surprised but I seemed out of it.'

Diego pushed on with his plan. 'Yes, but the reason you felt out of it is due to your old fashioned attitude, what you need to do is take a few years off yourself – I could make you look forty one not fifty one.'

'Nonsense,' said Henry, 'I can't believe that.'

'It's true.' Diego was adamant.

'This is what I want you to do. The first thing is for us to go into town and buy you some new clothes and shoes. Secondly I want you to come to my hairdressers and he will sort out your hair. You have got plenty of hair but it's just lank and it needs conditioning and styling.'

Henry was intrigued and was listening intently.

'I also want you to go to the local opticians and get some contact lenses and get rid of the spectacles.'

'Really?' Henry was having mixed feelings about these ideas.

Diego went on quite excitedly. 'I have a gym in the villa, go in there and work out on the equipment. If you do that your fat belly and flabby chin will be gone in two or three weeks. Then you should round the exercises off with a good swim in the pool.'

'How often should I use the gym?'

'Every day without fail, be committed. The other thing you must do is get some colour, don't overdo it, just sunbath for fifteen minutes at a time most days, you'll be amazed how different you will look and how confident you will become.'

'It's a big thing for me to do, Diego, a massive change.'

'Yes, I know, but your life is going through a massive change and you must adapt, will you do it for me? If it doesn't work you can go back to your old ways.'

Henry thought for a moment. 'All right, I'll give it a try,' he said with some apprehension.

'One more thing: I want you to call yourself Harry, Henry is too, how you say, posh.'

Henry looked bewildered.

'Why would I want to change my name?'

'You're not changing your name really, Harry is the other name for Henry. You'll be in good company if you use Harry because most of your English Kings and Princes never used Henry as their name, they were often called Harry.'

'I don't know about all this, I really don't.' Henry was still sceptical.

'Trust me, Harry, just give it a try, and do it for me, please.'

'Very well, but does this mean you're going to call me Harry from now on?'

'I'm afraid so,' said Diego with a grin.

'Just one more thing.' Diego looked serious. 'Try to change your speech, you know, speak a bit more down to earth, not so toffee nosed, is that the correct term? Do you know what I mean?'

Henry didn't take offence, he knew what Diego meant.

'OK, I will try. In other words, I'll give it my best shot.' They both laughed at Henry's attempt.

'That's it.' Diego looked pleased. 'That's the sort of talk we want more of.'

Later that day, they visited several men's outfitters where Henry purchased shoes, shirts, trousers, swimming trunks, and other bits and pieces under Diego's guidance. He also bought belts, a new watch and an unpretentious men's necklace. He also had his hair styled by Diego's barber who washed and conditioned it. Henry thought he would be there forever but he did see a distinct improvement when it was finished.

The next day, he visited the opticians and purchased contact lenses which would be ready in three days. In addition, he commenced his sunbathing and workouts in Diego's gymnasium.

A few days later, after Henry had collected his contact lenses, Diego invited him for dinner followed by a visit to a different nightclub called Pablo's. Diego considered this club to be the best and he expected Henry to begin his transformation. He got him to put on a nice silk lemon short sleeved shirt, black slacks, white belt and soft white shoes. His shirt was open neck revealing his necklace with an 'H' on it and he also wore a classy looking new watch. Although he felt a little peculiar, he was more comfortable. He went to the full-length mirror and couldn't help feeling pleased with the transformation, particularly as he was now sporting the start of a nice tan. He was apprehensive but determined to give his new look a try.

'Harry,' said Diego, 'I want you to come to another nice restaurant tonight which I have booked. I had to do that as it's Friday and it gets busy. You OK with that?'

'Absolutely.'

When they arrived, Harry noticed that once again he seemed to know the manager well as he came to greet him as they entered.

'Diego, buenas tardes,' he said, shaking his hand with a beaming smile.

'Pedro, it is nice to see you. Let me introduce you to my very good friend from England, Harry.'

Henry shook his hand. 'Good evening,' he said.

'Are you staying in Marbella for long?' Pedro asked.

'I'm actually living here now permanently.' Henry was delighted to be able to say that, it made him feel good.

'Bueno,' said Pedro. 'Let me find you a nice table.'

They were given a table outside on a terrace where they had a sumptuous meal accompanied by a bottle of red Rioja. Once again they talked incessantly about the past and they rounded the meal off with a couple of large brandies with cigars. Henry insisted on paying the bill on this occasion and he followed Diego's practice of giving the waiter a decent tip.

Diego and Henry then went on to Pablo's club which was clearly very popular as there were many people in a queue waiting to pay at the door. The doormen recognised Diego as they approached the club and waved for them to come to the front where they were both shown straight into the bar area. As usual, everyone seemed to know Diego. Henry was impressed with this club as it seemed very sophisticated and catered for a slightly older clientele, he guessed some of the ladies were in their thirties with a few possibly in their forties.

There was a group of three nicely dressed girls at the bar who seemed to know Diego and he introduced Henry to them.

'Girls, this is my good friend Harry who's staying with me.'

He turned to Henry and pointed to each one.

'This is Gina, Sophia, and Barbara, am I right?'

'Very impressive, Diego,' said Gina with a lovely smile. 'What a memory.'

She turned to Henry.

'Hi, Harry. How long are you staying in Marbella?' Henry was oblivious to her remark.

'Harry!' she said, more determined. Diego nudged him and Henry suddenly remembered the change of name.

'I'm sorry,' Henry was annoyed that he had forgotten. 'I'm staying here for good. I'm retired now and I'm making my home here. Diego is helping me.'

'Retired?' she exclaimed sounding disbelieving, 'Christ, you must be loaded if you can afford to retire at your age.'

Henry felt really good having heard Gina's response. Perhaps Diego was right about the changes he had made. He liked her.

'Are you on holiday, Gina?' Henry was gaining confidence and a few drinks had helped.

'No, I work here for a British travel firm, I am the representative who looks after their customers during their holidays.'

'That's interesting. Do you stay here just for the summer?' asked Henry.

'Yes, just the summer.' Gina pointed to an empty sofa. 'Let's get some drinks and sit over there, Harry.'

Diego interrupted. 'Harry, I've already ordered large whiskies, I'll bring them over.'

He was so delighted to see Henry getting on so well he wanted to help.

Henry sat with Gina on the sofa in a quiet corner of the club and Diego brought their drinks over. Gina told him she was 38 years of age and Henry thought she was totally charming.

A few minutes later, she looked into Henry's eyes.

'Do you fancy a dance, Harry?'

Her voice was sensuous and she reminded him of Jayne, especially with her blonde hair tumbling over her shoulders. She was a beautiful young lady, slim and shapely.

'Why not?' he said, trying to appear laid back.

As they moved onto the dance floor, the music changed to a slow ballad and Henry found himself enjoying a slow romantic dance, something he hadn't enjoyed for years. He seemed to have more confidence, no doubt assisted by the large brandies he had enjoyed at the restaurant. They were more or less embracing on the dance floor now, her head resting on his shoulder and Henry thought the aroma from her blonde hair was divine. Their hips were swaying from side to side, moving to the soft music which was deep and strong – Henry had never felt so relaxed for years and he loved the experience.

Diego happened to glance over and was surprised but delighted to see Gina literally wrapped around Henry, they seemed to be in their own world; oblivious to the other dancers around them on the romantically lit dance floor. Diego turned to Gina's friend Barbara with a chuckle.

'Your friend Gina looks like she's in love the way she's dancing with Harry.'

Barbara smiled and said, 'She's always been into slightly more mature guys, Diego. Harry seems really nice.'

The music stopped and they sat back down. Gina then surprised Henry.

'Can I see you again?'

Henry couldn't believe she was asking him.

'If you want to, I'd love to see you,' he stuttered.

She opened her handbag and took out a card. 'This is my business card, give me a ring and we'll fix up something.'

Diego came over and whispered in Henry's ear.

'I've struck gold with this Barbara and I'd like to go off with her, do you mind?'

'Fine,' said Henry, 'don't worry about me, I'll get a taxi.'

Henry spent the rest of the evening with Gina and took her home in a taxi. When they arrived at her rented apartment, he asked the taxi driver to wait a moment whilst he walked her to the door.

'Don't forget to ring me,' she said. It sounded like an honest request.

'I won't.' As Henry spoke, she moved forward and kissed him passionately on his lips and he responded immediately.

'I can't ask you in, Harry; it's a shared lodging.'

'Don't worry, I'll give you a ring and arrange something.'

'Thanks, Harry, I'll look forward to that.'

Henry got in the taxi and returned to the villa.

When he got back to the annexe, there was no sign of Diego so Henry made himself some coffee and sat down to deliberate on the evening. He couldn't believe what was happening to him and he couldn't help thinking about Jayne. She had always wanted him to be like this but he could never understand what she meant. Now he had enjoyed such a wonderful evening following the changes he had made, he was beginning to think that Jayne and Diego were right, he did need to permanently change –

and change he would. He now vowed to totally accept his name change and decided to drop the name Henry for good. He was now Harry and life was looking up.

At 8 a.m. on Saturday, the following morning, Harry woke up to another beautifully sunny day. He dressed in his sporting attire and spent his usual thirty minutes in the gymnasium, intending to have his daily swim after breakfast. As he walked into the kitchen, he was startled to see Barbara from the previous night sitting casually at the breakfast table eating cereal and wearing a pair of Diego's pyjamas.

She looked up at him looking completely unperturbed.

'Hello, Harry, how's it going?'

He quickly composed himself. 'I'm OK,' he said, wondering what was going on.

Diego came through the kitchen door wearing only his shorts. 'How's it going, my amigos, OK?'

'I had a great night, Diego,' said Barbara. She then turned to Harry and said, 'How did it go for you last night, Harry? What happened with Gina?'

She gave him a saucy smile as she said it.

This way of living was alien to Harry as he had never experienced the informal and casual way Diego lived his life but had to admit that he was beginning to enjoy himself in this new world. Harry tried to respond to Barbara more casually, using a more down-to-earth tone as suggested by Diego, so he paused slightly to think of suitable wording.

'Gina was great, we had a ball and she gave me her card so I'm going to give her a bell later to try to fix something up.'

'That's brilliant,' said Barbara. 'She likes you, she told me that.'

'I'm really pleased to hear it,' said Harry, casually but inside he was secretly overjoyed at that piece of news.

Diego was listening and was delighted to see Harry getting into his newly formed character, he was hoping that he would continue to develop the change and relish the new fun life he had found. As it was Saturday, Diego had arranged to spend the day with Barbara and he made a suggestion.

'Gina gave you her number, did she, Harry? Why don't you ring her and see if she can join us today? It's Saturday so she won't be working.'

This caught Harry off balance; his life up to now had always been planned.

'I can't do that, can I? It's too late.'

'Of course it isn't,' said Diego. 'She's on day off. I think she would love to be with us.'

Harry paused for a moment, 'What would we do?'

'Well,' said Diego, 'I'm taking Barbara on a boat trip along the coast and stopping for lunch at a restaurant in a lovely, what do you call it, a cove? We're swimming a little and coming back this evening. It will be a nice day.'

Harry liked the sound of that. 'Shall I ring her then? Are you sure we won't be in the way?'

Diego handed him the telephone. 'Go ahead, it will be great to have you with us.'

Harry rang the number on Gina's card and she answered in a sleepy voice. 'Hello.'

'Gina, it's Harry here from last night.'

'Blimey, Harry, you didn't take long to ring. Is everything all right?'

'Absolutely. Listen, Diego and Barbara are going on a boat trip up the coast for lunch, I wondered if you fancied joining me and we'll go with them?'

Gina was excited to get the call; she'd had a boring day ahead.

'Count me in, Harry. I'd love to come.'

Harry turned to Diego. 'What time must she get here?'

Diego took the telephone from him.

'Gina, we need to leave by eleven o'clock so if you can drive here quickly, you can leave your car at my place. By the way, bring something to swim in.'

'Where does the boat trip go from?' Harry asked.

'It's not a boat trip like that, Harry. It's my own Sunseeker yacht which is moored in Puerto Banus down the road a bit. I own it. We just drive down there and I'll sail it to wherever we want to go.'

Barbara added, 'It's a lovely yacht, Harry. It's even got a bedroom in it,' she said, smiling cheekily. 'We know about that, Diego, don't we?'

An hour later, Gina pulled up in her sports car. She was wearing shorts and a tight pink blouse which showed off her ample breasts and Harry thought she looked truly appealing. To his delight, she walked straight up to him and kissed him firmly on the lips, and he responded. The kiss lingered for several seconds. He found her charming and she reminded him of Jayne in the early days when she was nicer towards him.

'Right,' said Diego laughing, 'let's go unless you two want to go to the bedroom first!'

Harry felt embarrassed.

They all got into Diego's larger car and within ten minutes they arrived in Puerto Banus, a small port a couple of miles from Marbella. Harry could see it was different to the ports he had seen previously as it was more up market. Beautiful yachts and boats were moored in a busy harbour lined with quality restaurants and clubs and there were many expensive designer shops catering for expensively dressed and trendy people of differing ages.

Diego parked and took them to his yacht which was impressive as it was motorised and relatively new. Harry could see that it must have been expensive, and this added to his belief that he had successfully defended a guilty man, saving him from a certain prison sentence so avoiding the confiscation of the stolen money. However, once again he told himself that he had only done his job – after all, Diego always claimed he was innocent to him and that was all that was required for him to be able to accept the defence case.

They boarded the yacht which had a dining area on the deck, sunbeds, a living room inside, one bedroom and a shower room with a toilet.

Diego steered them past various resorts and Harry could feel the wind through his hair and the sun on his face as they sailed through the azure blue waters of the Mediterranean. They were drinking champagne which Diego had chilled in his on-board refrigerator and as they sailed close to the shore the views from the yacht were stupendous.

Harry had never felt so happy and relaxed in his life. The worries of arrest by DS Robinson, a probable beating from Rawlings and the constant stress of pleasing Jayne had all vanished and it was a wonderful feeling to be free of them. He was now determined to totally embrace this new world and his new identity.

They sailed into a pretty little cove which had a stylish al fresco restaurant facing the sea. Diego anchored the yacht and treated them to a delicious lunch of paella with chilled white wine. Gina was very affectionate to Harry, holding his hand and giving him the occasional kiss, and he loved the attention so much that he began to respond to her romantic gestures. He liked her a lot and wanted to see her again.

After swimming off the yacht and sunbathing, they returned to Puerto Banus later that afternoon where they enjoyed dinner at the well-known Silks Restaurant. The meal was accompanied by Harry's favourite red wine and he was pleased to pay for everything. They then returned to Diego's villa where they enjoyed coffee with fine Cognac during the evening. It was one of the best days he had ever experienced.

Diego faked a yawn. 'I don't know about anyone else but my bed is calling. Are you going to stay here with me tonight, Barbara?'

'If that's OK, I'd love to,' she replied with a mischievous look.

'Let's go then,' said Diego, rising and taking her hand. They walked hand in hand down the hall and into his bedroom.

Harry felt slightly awkward but Gina took over.

'Can I stay tonight as well, Harry? It's Sunday tomorrow so I've no work in the morning.'

Despite still feeling awkward, he really wanted her to stay.

'Of course,' he said. 'You know I live in the annexe and there's only one bedroom though, don't you.'

He wasn't sure how to handle things but he needn't have worried.

'We only want one bedroom, don't we?' She smiled as if she knew he was out of practice so she rose from her armchair, took his hand, and gently took him towards the front door.

'Let's make love,' she said brazenly as they made their way to his bedroom in the annexe.

Harry found making love after so long required some concentration as he had never been with anyone else since Jayne and he found it a little difficult. However, Gina was sexually active and pretty adventurous in bed, and Harry soon began to enjoy the steamy night with her.

In the morning they all had breakfast together and Gina and Barbara got ready to leave about 10 a.m.

'Will I see you again, Harry?' Gina looked at him with anticipation.

'Absolutely, I'll ring you soon,' Harry said genuinely.

Gina smiled. 'Make sure you do, I've had a wonderful time.'

'Adios,' said Harry, trying to maintain his new style of informal speech. They kissed as she left the villa.

Diego was delighted that he had been right in transposing Henry to the life of Harry.

'I'm proud of you, you'll have a great life here and I guarantee you won't want to return to England,' he said.

Harry thought he was a little emotional as he said it but he was completely correct and he continued to enjoy his new lifestyle. There were other women, but it was Gina who he saw more than anyone. His paunch and double chin had both gone and he looked slim. Also he had a nice tan and his hair had become slightly bleached by the sun. He still went to Diego's hairdresser to ensure it always looked healthy. He looked good and had become known around Marbella with affection. He was 'playing the field', as they say, something he would never have thought would happen in a million years.

An incident in a bar greatly pleased Diego. Harry was talking to a young lady when Diego heard the lady ask him a question.

'What's your name?' she enquired.

He paused for a moment before replying.

'Harry,' he said.

Diego whispered to himself, 'Yes, he's got it.'

Things were going well as the sale of Tudor Manor had now been completed and the substantial sale proceeds had been transferred to Henry's new Spanish account. He also had the funds from the sale of his stocks and shares so he was a very wealthy man indeed.

However, things were about to become very difficult indeed.

Twenty Two

In Nottingham, Jayne was enjoying a wonderful lifestyle too, a lifestyle that she had always wanted. She had managed to get the wealthy man she had always been looking for and, unlike Henry, he had the good looks as well. He was prepared to give her anything she desired and she firmly believed that she had finally achieved what she had always wanted – Henry was now just a distant memory.

One evening, shortly after she had moved into Jonathan's lavish Roman Room's apartment they had dinner in the club restaurant with some nice wine, followed by coffee and brandy. Jonathan lit a cigar and said he wanted a serious talk with her.

'Jayne, now that we are properly living together I've got a few personal wishes which I'm hoping you will respect.'

'Of course I will, darling,' she replied. She was somewhat intrigued.

'Babe, I have to go to America periodically as I have a lot of stuff going on over there. When I'm away I would suggest that you dine in the club and have what you like. Alternatively you can go to a restaurant if you prefer but when you eat in the club, you can just sign the bill and there's no charge, OK?'

'That's fabulous, thank you very much, Jon.'

'Of course, when I'm here we can eat where we like or have my cook rustle us something up in our apartment.'

'You won't be away that much though, will you? What are we talking about time wise?'

'Don't worry, I'll only be away occasionally,' he was smiling. 'I couldn't bear to be away from you for long so if it's more than a couple of days you can always come with me if you like.'

'I'd much prefer that, darling. Is that it?"

'No,' Jonathan handed her a bulky envelope.

'I've ordered you a nice new silver Mercedes – I know you prefer that colour and I hope you like it. In this envelope is £14,000 so go to the garage and buy it for yourself.'

Jayne was shocked and delighted. 'That's fantastic Jon, how generous of you. Is there a reason that I should pay in cash?'

'No, not really, but I prefer to do all my business using cash, it's just a habit of mine.'

'I'm so pleased Jon, I can't get over it.'

'Well, there's something else as well. In addition, I'm going to arrange for a monthly payment to go into your bank account. We have no real overheads as all of our own food shopping is just linked into the restaurant deliveries.'

Jayne was overwhelmed. *A new Mercedes*, she thought, *things were getting better all the time*.

'That's really nice of you, thank you so much, darling,' she was truly appreciative.

'I can tell you that your monthly payment is only pocket money, but it will be generous. Incidentally, the club's cleaner does our apartment so there's nothing to do there, she even makes the beds.'

Jayne was beginning to think that she had gone to heaven, she couldn't believe how marvellous her life was going to be, and she felt this was the closest she could ever get to living like royalty. She also noticed that he said "our apartment" which pleased her greatly.

'Another point,' Jonathan went on, 'your divorce will come through soon so we can plan our wedding, and I intend to pay for a really luxurious event. You can shortly start looking at venues and all the other usual stuff. I'll leave it all to you, if you're OK with that.'

What woman wouldn't be OK with that, Jayne thought to herself.

'I really can't wait for our wedding day, Jon,' she sounded excited and added 'I think I'll get rid of Jayne Walters and go back to my maiden name which is Grant.'

Jon looked at her with uncertainty.

'It'll be a nuisance doing that because you'll have to change everything like passports and then you'll have to do it all again when we marry when you will become Mrs Bond.'

'You're right, I'll leave it for now but I can't wait to be Mrs Bond.'

Jonathan suddenly sounded serious.

'Now, I've just got a couple of requests. You can go into the club whenever you like and I've told Keith that you can have food, drinks and enjoy yourself. However, I must ask you not to interfere with any management decisions or the general running of the place when I'm not around, just tell me about any possible problems you have spotted when I'm back.'

'I get it, it's not my business,' she sounded understanding.

They finished their brandy and Jonathan had a mischievous look and Jayne knew what he was thinking.

'I know what you want,' she said playfully, 'let's go.'

They went up to the apartment using the inside lift in the club and straight to the bedroom. They both knew that mad passionate lovemaking was on the agenda and Jayne loved every minute of it.

Most of the time, Jonathan was at home and they enjoyed some wonderful times together. They visited race meetings, went to shows, had the odd night away at the coast, visited some of Jonathan's many high profile friends and sometimes just stayed at the Roman Rooms enjoying the superb apartment with its nice pool. As it was early summer, sometimes Jonathan would occasionally put on a sumptuous barbecue around the pool terraces with all types of lovely food was on offer with a variety of drinks and cocktails including champagne.

The barbecues went on into the night and sometimes there were thirty to forty invited guests. Jayne noticed that people were honoured to be invited to one of these events, and Jayne milked her position as the host's future wife. To her delight, she was able to invite her own friends and Moira and others sometimes attended. Jayne loved the chance to show off her newfound wealthy life but when Jonathan had to go to Chicago for ten days in May, Jayne was upset.

'Don't be upset, babe,' he said. 'I have to go as my work maintains our lifestyle. You don't want to jeopardise that, do you?'

'Of course not,' she said trying to sound understanding, 'it's just that I'll miss you. You said I could come if it was a long trip.'

'I'm sorry, I'd take you with me if I could but I have loads of meetings and a couple of business dinners so you would be left on your own a lot.'

Jonathan was being apologetic but it was clear that he would be going alone.

'What sort of business meetings are they?' Jayne asked a little tentatively.

Jonathan gave her a disapproving look. It was the first time she had seen him looking slightly annoyed.

'Please don't ask about my business in America, Jayne.' It was a curt reply and Jayne dropped the subject.

'Tell you what, babe,' Jonathan was now smiling broadly, 'why don't you treat Moira to a few days abroad, go to Sorrento or somewhere. That would be nice, wouldn't it? I'll pay for you both.'

Jayne was always up for a holiday and as Moira's husband worked a five-day week, he might let her go for a few weekdays.

'Are you serious, Jon? That's a great offer.'

'Yes, I'll give you the dates that I'm away and you can go and book something.'

Moira was delighted and her husband said it would do her good so she took up Jonathan's offer and they went to Sorrento for a full week. They had a wonderful time and for Jayne things just got better and better.

When Jonathan was away, she ate in the club restaurant, and during the days, if the weather was good, she would read by the pool, swim or have a friend or two around for drinks.

Two weeks after Jayne returned from Sorrento, Jonathan had a proposal to make.

'Listen, babe, Antonio Rossi has got VIP tickets for the Heavyweight Boxing Championship of the World for his wife Martina and two other guests. The fight takes place on the 11th June in Caesars Palace, Las Vegas – that's where we stayed in March. Do you fancy going?'

'Do I fancy going?' Jayne looked totally exhilarated and excited. 'Just try to stop me.'

'Great,' said Jon, 'Larry Holmes is defending his title against a boxer called Gerry Cooney, and if we go we can make it a two-week holiday, is that OK?'

Jayne had no idea whatsoever who these boxers were but she didn't care, she could go back to Las Vegas and that was all that mattered.

'That is absolutely fantastic.'

On the 8th June, they flew first class, and Antonio and Martina met them at Las Vegas airport. Once again, they booked into a luxury suite at the lovely Caesars Palace hotel. They enjoyed swimming and sunbathing with fine food in the evenings and they went a top show one night with the best seats. Jayne loved the razzmatazz of Vegas and the weather in June provided hours of sunshine every day.

On the evening of the World Championship boxing, Jonathan suggested that Jayne should dress up smartly.

'Dress up smartly, it's only a boxing match, Jon.'

'Listen, babe, we're going to a formal reception before the fight with drinks and nibbles. There will be celebrities there and it's all black tie, you can't dress down for something like this, it's the world championship. Anyway, I thought you liked dressy functions?'

Jayne looked pleasantly astonished.

'I do, I do!' she exclaimed, 'I just didn't realise it was like that, I just thought it was a boxing match and nothing more.'

This threw a different light on things for Jayne, black tie reception, celebrities attending, she realised she had underestimated the importance of the event and immediately started sorting out some of her more stylish clothes.

When she was ready, she poured herself a whiskey from the mini bar and sat on the balcony. Jonathan soon appeared looking splendidly smart in his elegant dinner suit and a fashionable bow tie.

'You look lovely. Are you ready?' he enquired.

'You're looking good, Mr Bond. I feel like someone should be playing your theme song.' She was laughing as she said it and looking at him admiringly.

'You don't look so bad either. Let's go.'

They took the lift to one of the downstairs bars where they had arranged to meet Antonio and Martina and they had another drink before making their way to the reception which was exciting for Jayne as it was only for VIPs. These included several celebrities and as usual, Jayne made an effort to speak with some of them. Eventually they were taken to the fight venue and she was surprised to be led to an outside arena. However, it was a warm and pleasant evening and they had the best front row seats.

The crowd was massive, nearly 30,000 people, the highest number ever to attend a prize fight in Las Vegas, and Jayne found the whole experience really exciting.

During the fight, she sometimes got carried away, shouting and urging the fighters on, totally out of character.

In round thirteen Larry Holmes stopped Cooney and the fight was over. They made their way back to the hotel, had a nightcap and turned in. Once again, an experience that Jayne didn't think she would like, turned out to be fantastic.

The following day, they were sunbathing by the pool when a waiter came across to Jonathan advising him that Keith, his manager, had rung from England asking him to call him urgently. Jonathan went to the reception and returned to the pool after he had made the call.

'Bad news, I'm afraid.' Jonathan looked depressed.

'What is the matter?' asked Antonio. Jayne looked on anxiously.

'I'm afraid I have to get a flight back straight away; there's a big problem at my club.'

Jayne was worried. 'What sort of problem?'

'I don't know many details but it seems to be something to do with the books. The authorities are at the premises this morning. I'll see if I can get a flight.'

'What about me?' Jayne asked, looking a little uncomfortable.

'I think you should stay and finish your holiday. There's nothing that you can do if you come back early.'

'I'll have to get a taxi to St. Pancras and get the train home, won't I?' Jayne queried.

'Yes, that's no problem though, is it?'

'Not at all. If you're sure, Jon, I'll stay.'

That's what she wanted, having a week in Las Vegas doing what she liked appealed to her.

Jonathan gave her a wad of notes.

'Use this for your spending money, I'll pay the hotel bill now.'

He managed to fix a flight for the next morning and they said their goodbyes at the hotel. Antonio drove him to the airport and Jayne sprawled out on a sun bed by the pool thinking about what she would do during the week. Antonio and Martina were never going to stay longer than the first week as they had family commitments to attend to, so Jayne said her goodbyes to them as well. Martina was worried about Jayne being alone but she assured her she would be fine, after all, Jon's minders were still hovering around. Secretly she was pleased that Antonio and Martina were leaving.

Jayne spent the first few days simply reading and sunbathing around the pool as she loved the sun and was by now showing off a lovely tan. She could never stop posing and flirting which inevitably attracted male attention but despite the young attractive looking men who propositioned her, she resisted any advances as there was no way she wanted to upset the wonderful life Jonathan gave her. Knowing the wide range of contacts he had, plus the minders she now knew were about, she was sure he would know if she strayed and that would cost her dearly. She remembered what happened the last time she was there.

She tried to ring Jonathan after a few days and was upset to receive no answer on the Roman Room's number. Later that day, she tried three more times, but still nobody picked up the phone. Jayne couldn't relax properly until she had spoken with Jonathan to make sure he had got home OK and that the problem with the books was resolved. She had paid a deposit on a couple of trips, one of which was for a day in San Diego, which included a visit to the famous zoo. San Diego was about an hour flight from Las Vegas but the lack of contact with Jonathan bothered her immensely.

She couldn't stop thinking about him and so she had one more attempt before she was due to join the group going to the airport for the San Diego flight. This call caused her intense concern because the Roman Room's telephone was dead. She rang several times and then asked the international operator to check the line. The operator shocked her by advising her that the line had been closed down. This worrying discovery caused her to cancel both trips as she knew she would never be able to enjoy them in the circumstances. Her flight home was now three days away and she spent them lying on a sun bed worrying terribly about Jonathan. She kept telling herself she was probably concerned about nothing, but she wasn't convinced.

Jayne just wanted to get home and she couldn't wait to board the aircraft. She had a seat in first class and Jonathan's seat next to her was empty. She advised the airline staff at the check-in that he would not be travelling. She realised the he couldn't have been bothered about it at all as he hadn't given her his ticket or cancelled. She had a comfortable flight with plenty of space as a result, but her mind was in turmoil and her stomach was churning. She had persuaded herself that something terrible had happened.

On arrival at Heathrow, she took a taxi to St. Pancras and then a train to Nottingham.

She got in a taxi at Nottingham Station and the driver knew the Roman Rooms.

As they drove off, her heart jumped when the driver suddenly spoke to her.

'There's something going on at the club, isn't there?'

'Like what?' said Jayne feeling extremely agitated.

'I don't really know, but it's closed at the moment because I took a customer there last night and we couldn't go in.'

'Really?' said Jayne casually but inside she was panicking. She sat quietly in the back of the taxi for the remainder of the journey worried to death as to what she would confront.

Her worst fears were confirmed as they approached the elaborate gates as they were shut with police barriers across the entrance to the property. The barrier across the entrance had a sinister sign on it.

POLICE LINE – DO NOT CROSS

There was a police car parked outside the gates and two officers were protecting the entrance. She stared at the scene feeling sick to the stomach with jumbled thoughts flashing through her mind.

'That'll be two pounds, please.'

The taxi driver's voice jolted her from her thoughts and she hurriedly paid him whilst he took her two suitcases from the boot. The terrible situation she found herself in was just dawning on her. As she stared at the club car parking area, she could see various boxes being loaded into white vans. Jayne looked on in disbelief at what was happening and approached one of the police officers.

'What's going on, officer? Could you tell me, please?'

Her voice was filled with apprehension as to what the answer would be which caused the officer to think that she was connected to the property.

'Who are you, madam?'

'I live here,' Jayne replied.

'I didn't ask you that, madam. Who are you?' he repeated the question.

'My name is Jayne Walters and I live at this property. Won't you tell me what's going on?' She looked positively stressed.

'What is your relationship to the resident of this property?' the officer asked.

Jayne hesitated for a moment and realised that she had no official connection whatsoever. 'I live here, I know the owner.'

'You're a lodger then, are you? Do you rent a room here or something like that?' The officer was getting irritated.

'No, I'm getting married to the owner.'

'You're his girlfriend then, is that it?'

'I suppose it is, but we are arranging to get married and I have been living here for sometime. Won't you please tell me what's happening?'

She was getting more stressed by the minute.

'I can't tell you much as it's a crime scene and nobody is allowed in, I'm afraid.'

The officer seemed unsympathetic.

'But this is my home, my belongings are in there, and that's my silver Mercedes by the garages.'

Jayne was pointing to her car whilst begging him to let her in.

'I assume your boyfriend is Mr Jonathan Bond who is the only person shown on the voters' roll. However, it is actually owned by his bank and in view of the circumstances they will undoubtedly be repossessing the property when we have finished our investigation.'

Jayne had no idea that the bank owned the property.

'Where is Jonathan then? I need to see him.'

'I'm sorry to tell you that he's been detained.' The police officer seemed more compassionate. 'I'm afraid you won't be able to see him at this time.'

'Detained, my God, what for?' she was bewildered and unable to think clearly.

'I'm not permitted to give you any facts at this time I'm afraid, madam.'

Jayne couldn't control herself any longer; she broke down with tears streaming down her cheeks in front of the police officer. She dropped to her knees with her hands over her face, sobbing uncontrollably. She tried to speak but the words were indecipherable. This display was totally out of character as Jayne had always been a strong woman.

The officer looked shocked and his officious attitude turned to one of sympathy. Kneeling down, he put his arm around her shoulders trying to console her and managed to walk her to his vehicle where he sat her in the front passenger seat and he got into the driver's seat.

Jayne sat sobbing and trying to take in what was happening.

'What property do you have at the premises?' the officer seemed to be more understanding.

Jayne composed herself. 'My car, my clothes, and a few personal items, that's all.'

'I may be able to arrange for you to take them all if you can prove the car is yours, you can then put your belongings in it and leave.'

Jayne took her keys from her handbag and shook them at him.

'The key to my Mercedes is on this ring, is that enough proof? I also have the log book in the property.'

'That should be OK. I'll just go and check with my boss.'

Jayne sounded desperate and she gave a pleading look.

'Before you go, will I be able to sleep here tonight? I've just come straight from the airport having flown in from America. I can't believe this is happening to me.'

'You won't be able to sleep here; this property is sealed off.'

He now seemed to feel sorry for her.

Jayne looked horrified and started crying again.

'Where am I supposed to go? This is my only home and I have no family.'

'Haven't you got a friend that you could stay with?' the officer suggested.

'Not really, I don't know what to do.'

'Let me see if we can get your possessions out – wait here.'

The officer went into the property and Jayne sat in his car trying to come to terms with the terrible dilemma she faced. Her mind was racing and it didn't take her long to realise that for the second time, her perfect world was collapsing around her.

The officer returned with a man in civilian clothes.

'This is DC Baxter, CID. Follow him and he'll help you collect your things.'

The detective kindly helped Jayne with her two cases and they both went through the gates with them.

'Thank you for your help,' she said as she followed the CID officer.

When they reached her car, he asked her to verify that the car was hers by unlocking it. He then put the cases in the boot for her.

'I understand you've just returned from America so you must have your passport. Can I see it please?'

She took it from her handbag and he examined it.

'OK, let's go in.'

The CID officer led her into the club and she noticed some men in white coats carrying out some sort of examination. When they got to Jonathan's apartment there were more searches going on in the rooms of his penthouse.

Jayne was still struggling to come to terms with the life-changing scenario that was being played out before her. Momentarily, she felt she was having a dreadful dream but unfortunately she knew it was all real. It took her quite a while to sort out all of her clothes and personal items and having done so it was clear that they wouldn't all fit in the car.

'Where are you going?' said the officer.

'I haven't a clue. I'll try a couple of friends to see if I can stay with them tonight whilst I sort myself out. This has come as a terrible shock to me. Can I leave the rest of my stuff and pick it up later?'

'I don't see why not, but you mustn't leave it too long.'

'OK,' said Jayne. 'I'll come back when I've decided what to do.'

The CID detective showed pity on Jayne.

'Stay a moment to collect your thoughts before driving.'

He then led her to a seat in the club.

'I'll get you some tea.'

Jayne went to the ladies' room in the club before sitting down with a cup of tea. Whilst in there, she caught sight of herself in the mirror.

'My God, what's happened to me?' she whispered.

She looked worn out and thought that she had aged ten years.

When she had sat for a while, she composed herself and decided to try to accept her fate – what's done is done. She must think positively. Her best bet for help was definitely Moira and although she didn't get on with Moira's husband very well, she had recently enjoyed a free holiday in Sorrento with Jayne and they had been friends for many years. Jayne would have to swallow her pride as for years she had boasted about the life she enjoyed; the fantastic holidays and her wonderful homes with swimming pools. Now she had nothing, what a climb down. She realised that some people might be pleased about her downfall but she would have to rise above that.

Whilst she sat there, she was surprised to see Jonathan's employee Ralph walk in with a suitcase.

'Ralph!' she exclaimed.

He stopped and walked over. He didn't seem surprised to see her.

'Isn't it terrible,' he said in a low voice. 'I can't get over what's happened.'

He was staring at her, shocked by her appearance.

'What's happened to you? You look awful.'

'Thanks for that, Ralph. I landed today after a long flight from the States and I've walked straight into this mess – I guess I'm entitled to look awful.'

'Sorry, I wasn't thinking. I've just come in to collect some stuff I had kept here, where are you going to stay? This place is finished for us.'

'I'm just trying to fix something up with a friend.'

'You could stay at my flat, if you like. I'll have to sleep on the couch though. You could then have my bed for a few days until you get sorted out. It's not much but beggars can't be choosers.'

Jayne didn't fancy that. 'Can I come back to you on that, Ralph. It's really kind of you?' she said, trying to protect her options.

'Do you know what's happened, Ralph?' she said hopefully.

'I think so. I had a conversation with Mr Bond's manager Keith who has been questioned a lot by the police. It seems that this has been generated by the FBI in the States who have suspected for years that Mr Bond and some associates have been involved in organised crime here and in the America.'

Jayne was shocked. 'What sort of crime?'

'Drug trafficking, extortion, money laundering, prostitution and, dare I say it, violence. I even heard murder mentioned. They are talking about extraditing Mr Bond to the States and a possible 20 years' minimum term in prison.'

'Christ, Ralph, that's serious. He's kind of tricked us, don't you think?'

'I'm pissed off as I've got no job now.'

Jayne said, 'What about me? I've lost my home, we were getting married – bloody hell, what a mess.'

Jayne was in danger of breaking down again but pulled herself together.

When she was ready to leave, the police allowed her to make a telephone call so she took the opportunity to ring Moira, praying she was at home. Jayne was in luck so she told her briefly what had happened and although Moira was shocked, she seemed sympathetic about her plight.

'I'm so sorry, Jayne. This is terrible. What can I do to help?'

'Well, I really don't know what to do, I've nowhere to stay, have you any ideas?'

Jayne had her fingers crossed, hoping Moira would help.

'You can stay at my place tonight, no problem, but rather than discuss it over the telephone, shall I drive straight over and help you with your stuff. Is your car there?'

'Yes, so I can stay with you tonight, that's so kind but what about your husband?'

'Oh sod him, he'll do as I say, don't worry. I'm on my way.'

Twenty minutes later, Moira arrived and the police allowed them to load both cars whereupon they drove in tandem to Moira's house. Her husband was still at work. Moira poured two large whiskies.

'Take this,' she said to Jayne, handing her one, 'you need it.'

Jayne leaned back in the armchair and told her the whole story.

'Good God, what a mess.' Jayne couldn't help constantly saying it.

Moira appeared to be totally dumbfounded. 'What a shit.' She was truly disgusted.

'What are you going to do long term, any idea?' asked Moira.

Jayne hesitated. 'I simply don't know. I've got some money in my bank account but not a lot. One thing's for sure, I won't get any monthly money now from Jon as they're sure to freeze his accounts. Apparently a money laundering investigation is going on.'

'Do you want to stay here longer? You can stay until you've sorted yourself out if you like?'

'Really, could I?'

Jayne had been hoping and praying she would offer.

'Of course, you can have the spare room for a bit, that's the least I can do.'

'Thank you so much, Moira, you're a true friend. Are you sure about your hubby, will he be OK?' Jayne was apprehensive about him.

'Don't worry about him' said Moira confidently 'I told you, he'll do what he's told.'

Jayne stayed with Moira overnight and the following day she contacted the police asking whether it would be possible to see Jonathan. The officer she spoke to took the details and said he would call back.

Later that day the police rang and Moira handed Jayne the phone.

'Miss Walters?'

'Yes, speaking.'

'Regarding your request to visit Jonathan Bond, I'm afraid he has declined to see you.'

Jayne found it hard to believe.

'Are you sure, we were to be married shortly?'

'I'm sorry, madam, but if a prisoner declines to see a visitor there's nothing we can do about it.'

The man was quite positive and blunt.

'So what can I do?'

'Nothing,' he said, 'you can try again in a few weeks if he's still here, but at the moment you have no chance. Anything else I can help you with?'

'No,' Jayne sounded disappointed and hung up. She began to think that she would never see Jonathan again.

'How could he do this to me, Moira?'

She was livid and stomping around the living room. Moira had never seen her so upset, she was clearly bewildered by what was happening.

'He won't even see me,' she snarled.

'Forget the bastard,' said Moira. 'You're going to have to move on.'

Jayne composed herself and decided to sit down and discuss things again with Moira.

'Moira,' she said, 'I'd welcome your honest perspective on my position.'

She sounded as if she truly valued Moira's opinion.

'Can we talk please?'

'Of course. Let me make some tea and then you can fire away.'

Moira returned from the kitchen with two teas and a plate of biscuits.

Jayne sounded very serious. 'The first thing is I can't stay here for long, I know that.'

She looked at Moira for a response. Jayne was fishing to see how long she had before she had to find somewhere.

Moira nodded. 'You're right, because we sometimes need our spare room and so my husband will soon start moaning. I reckon you've only got about two to three weeks.'

Moira sounded a little apologetic and guilty.

'The thing is, Moira, I realise I've messed up big time.' Jayne was demoralised.

'I wanted to have the good life, get a rich man who could give me a life living like royalty. I vowed I would never work, I just wanted to get myself a life of leisure, totally selfish I am but the thing is I got that life, I had everything I wanted with Henry except the enjoyment of sex.'

Jayne was rambling but despite feeling sorry for her, Moira was finding these personal disclosures very interesting indeed.

'Really,' she said, 'there was no sex then?'

'Nothing to speak of, in fact I honestly think that Henry would have closed his eyes if I'd have had the odd bit of rumpy pumpy elsewhere if I'd wanted it. In fact, he more or less said that to me once.'

'Really,' said Moira, 'go on.' She was full of curiosity and was astonished by Jayne's openness – she wanted to hear more.

'Well, I had plenty of money, a swimming pool, gym, beautiful home and a nice new car and Henry paid for it all. I now feel that I threw it all away, thinking I could get something even better and I thought that I had when I met Jon, but now that's gone wrong as well and I've finished up with bugger all. Deep down I did think there was something dodgy about him; a couple of things happened that worried me a bit but I dismissed my fears and just enjoyed myself.'

Moira noticed Jayne had a tear trickling down her face and she couldn't help feeling sorry for her.

Jayne carried on.

'I've been a fool, I had it all but I'll be thirty shortly and I doubt if I'll ever have the opportunity again. What the hell can I do?'

Moira held her hand.

'Listen, let me ask you something. If you could turn the clock back would you have stayed with Henry?'

Jayne sobbed a little and nodded.

'He wasn't a bad man, nobody could ever love me like

he did. He would have given me anything; he was totally obsessed with me.'

She was becoming very nostalgic.

'Well, my advice is – go and try to get him back.' Moira spoke in an authoritative voice, it was like a command.

Jayne managed a limp smile, suggesting that she thought the remark was nonsensical.

'I mean it,' said Moira positively 'I'm not joking.'

Jayne looked at her as if she was mad.

'There's no chance of that happening, apart from anything else, he may well have been arrested by now.'

Moira looked at her in amazement.

'Arrested, whatever for?' Moira nearly came out of her seat.

'Well, between you and me, the last time I talked to Henry he was getting pressure from the police about the death of a boyfriend of mine who died under suspicious circumstances. They thought Henry may have had something to do with his death, in fact he was interviewed under caution the last I heard. Once I'd left him I don't know what happened.'

'So you had a boyfriend?' Moira had a look of astonishment. 'I didn't know that. Were you having it off with him while you were married to Henry?'

'Yes. I kept it quiet. I didn't even tell you but you nearly caught me out when you came round that evening with my wedding anniversary present, do you remember?'

Moira thought for a moment.

'Yes, I do remember, you told me you were in the middle of having a bath I think.'

'Yes, well he was upstairs in my bedroom when that happened and now he's dead and I think they suspected Henry.'

'Bloody hell, Jayne, you are a cunning little devil, aren't you? Moira looked astounded.

'You could have told me you know, you obviously didn't trust me but I really wouldn't have said anything.' She looked hurt and annoyed.

Jayne was concerned she had upset her and couldn't risk that at this delicate time.

'Of course I trusted you, Moira, you're my best friend, you must believe that. I didn't tell you because I didn't want you dragged into the sorry mess – it wouldn't have been fair.'

'Oh, I see,' Moira looked satisfied with that explanation, 'I understand.'

Jayne looked depressed again. 'He's dead now anyway, poisoned, and I think they suspected Henry but I'm sure he didn't do it.'

Moira had a sarcastic look. 'No, he hasn't got it in him to bump someone off,' she said scornfully. 'Why don't you just go round to Tudor Manor and throw yourself at his feet, tell him you made a mistake, tell him you can't stop thinking about him and tell him you've left Jonathan.'

'But I didn't.'

'He won't know that will he? I mean, even if he's heard of Jonathan's arrest you could say you'd decided to leave him before he was arrested. Does he know anything about Jonathan?'

'No, I don't think he even knows who I left him for.' As she spoke, Jayne started to think that perhaps Moira had a point – what had she got to lose?

Moira was persistent. 'Listen, he's loaded and you've lost everything, why don't you give it a try?'

Moira was not giving up.

'Think of it Jayne, if you pull it off at least you would get back to the luxury living you enjoy. I know it won't be with Jon but it looks like that's just as well.'

'I can see your point.' Jayne was warming to the idea. 'Let me sleep on it.'

The next day, Jayne told Moira at breakfast that she was going to Tudor Manor to plead with Henry as she had suggested. She left fairly early as she thought she might have more chance of catching him in as he had probably retired. Driving into the Tudor Manor property seemed strange as the memories came flashing back, and she felt a little tearful looking at the beautiful property and the lovely gardens. She couldn't help being annoyed at what she had lost.

She was disappointed that Henry's Jaguar was not on the drive and neither could she see it in the open garage.

She rang the doorbell and after a few seconds, an elderly man opened it – things didn't look promising.

'I'm looking for Henry Walters. Does he still live here?'

The man looked her up and down in a suspicious way.

'No, we bought this house from him a while ago. I've no idea where he's gone.'

Jayne was very disappointed. 'So you can't help me at all as to where he is living?'

'No, I'm afraid not.'

He then simply closed the door with no further comment.

'Rude sod,' Jayne said to herself.

Jayne sat in her car thinking about what to do and soon realised that the most likely person to know of Henry's whereabouts was Elsie Moyle. Jayne knew where she lived and so she drove straight to her modest semi detached property a few miles away. She was sceptical about the welcome she would receive as she and Mrs Moyle had never got on very well but she had to try.

She arrived at the house and knocked on the door which was opened by Mrs Moyle's husband.

Jayne was determined to be positive despite any ill feelings.

'Is your wife in?'

The man shouted back into the house. 'Elsie!'

It was strange to see her old adversary once again as Mrs Moyle strode purposefully towards the door.

'Oh, it's you. What on earth do you want?'

She sounded irritated and Jayne was not hopeful for any help.

'I'm trying to locate Henry, and I wondered if you could help me?' Jayne was secretly praying she would be able to assist.

'Henry has gone and you won't find him. What's it about anyway?'

Jayne had been prepared for that question. 'It's in his interests to see me; I've got to pass him some important information I have.'

Mrs Moyle looked at her suspiciously.

'I can't tell you where he is but I do have a telephone number of a friend of his who takes his messages. If you give me the information I'll pass it on to him.'

'I can't do that; it's personal,' said Jayne.

'Please yourself. I'm not giving you the number,' she replied curtly.

'So you do know where he is then?' Jayne hoped for something positive from her reply.

'Yes, I know he's in Spain but I don't know where. I just ring him now and again on the number as I've been helping him sell Tudor Manor and stuff. I don't know where he is in Spain so I couldn't help you if I wanted to. Sorry.'

'So you won't give me the number?'

'Definitely not; he told me not to give it to anyone. Are we done?'

Mrs Moyle started to shut the door.

Jayne was disappointed. 'Yes, we're done.'

She went to her car and sat for a while thinking things through. If he's in Spain, Jayne was sure she could guess where he had gone.

She returned to Moira's house and told her what she had discovered.

'So he's definitely in Spain.' Moira pondered for a moment. 'That means he won't know anything about Jonathan's arrest and he won't be troubled by the police anymore.'

'Why ever not?' asked Jayne curiously.

'Because all the criminals are heading over there as the extradition arrangements have all gone wrong. Pity you don't know where he is in Spain because you might be able to pull this plan off if you could find him.'

'I'm pretty sure I could find him in Spain.' Jayne looked pleased. 'I think he'll be in the Marbella area.'

'What makes you say that?'

'He's got a close friend there and we've been several times to his place. He's called Diego. In fact we even had our honeymoon there. He helped this Spaniard to get off of a big fraud in the UK so he owes Henry big time. I'd be amazed if he didn't know where he was, in fact he's probably helping Henry down there.'

Jayne sounded excited. 'Old Moyle wouldn't know all this, she thinks I wouldn't have a clue but she's wrong, Diego will know where he is for sure, trouble is how do I get in touch with him, she won't give me his number?'

'What about the International Operator searching if you know his address,' suggested Moira.

'I don't know the address other than the name of the villa so I don't think that will work. In any case talking on the telephone won't be enough to get back with him. It's a bloody nuisance he chose to live abroad.'

'I guess you're right.'

They both sat for a moment looking thoughtful and Moira suddenly made a suggestion.

'I'll tell you what you could do,' Moira looked apologetic for suggesting something so silly. 'You might think this is mad but why don't you just drive down there and turn up at Diego's place? He'll tell you where he is, won't he? He obviously still lives around there because that's got to be the number Moyle's got and if she rings it Henry's got to be somewhere nearby.'

'Oh come on, Moira, help me out here. I'm trying to be serious. It's no joke,' said Jayne, smiling.

'I'm not joking, I'm serious. Just drive down there.' Moira looked positive. 'You've got nothing to lose and nowhere to live so what does it matter? It'll only cost you some petrol and a few nights in a cheap B and B.'

Jayne started to think about the idea more seriously.

'Bloody hell, Moira, you could be right. You've been a great help to me, I don't think I'd have thought about these options without you. Mind you, I haven't got a lot of money, but I could afford the ferry, petrol and a couple of nights in a cheap hotel. You think it could be worth it, do you?'

'Of course it would. You may get him back.' Moira looked at her with a serious look. 'Listen, if you could find him, you could stress that you left Jon, give Henry all the stuff about how he's always been the love of your life, you made a mistake, you didn't realise how much you loved him, and all that blarney.'

Jayne was listening intently, she was beginning to think this might work.

Moira went on. 'You might get your life back and it would be in the sunshine, imagine that. You know he must be loaded because he must have got a fortune for Tudor Manor. He won't know that you're in the shit because of Jon's arrest; Henry's been in Spain so he won't know anything about it. Why don't you go for it?'

The more Jayne heard, the more she knew she should do it. Her mind was made up; she was going to Marbella immediately.

'Moira, I'll go. You've been really helpful.'

The next morning, Jayne filled the petrol tank of her car and went to the bank early, drawing out some French francs and Spanish pesetas. She then returned to Moira's house where she took as many belongings as she could get in the car, including her passport. She thanked Moira for her assistance and said she would ring her from Spain.

As she left, they had a lingering embrace and tears trickled down Jayne's cheeks, Moira was also emotional.

'I truly hope you get a result, Jayne, but you really have nothing to lose anyway other than a few quid.'

'Thanks for everything, my dear friend.'

Jayne drove off that morning waving from the open car window. She felt slightly sad to leave her friend so promptly but she wanted to get to the ferry at Dover that afternoon. She put her foot down and as she drove, she began to feel a little better now that she was doing something positive.

She had a successful ferry crossing and was able to drive to a village just north of Paris, arriving in the evening where she stayed in a cheap boarding house.

The next morning, she left early and reached Barcelona that evening where she stayed in a hostel overnight. The following day, she left early again and it took her all day to drive down to a village about an hour north of Marbella, arriving that evening. She had no intention of going straight to Diego's home looking tired and dishevelled so she found another cheap hotel for the night.

When she awoke she spent some time sprucing herself up. She had a shower, washed her hair, put on makeup and selected some nice summer clothes to wear. She just had a feeling that if she was really lucky she might find Henry that very day and if so she wanted to make the best impression possible and look as stunning as she could.

She booked out of the hotel and drove to Marbella where she started the search for Diego's villa. Her heart was beating a little faster than usual but that was mainly due to the excitement and anticipation as she knew her future was in the balance.

Twenty Three

Jayne remembered that Diego's villa was called *Paraiso Enconrado* because when she first went there with Henry, they were amused by the rather cheesy name. She also remembered that the villa was near the well known and exclusive Marbella Club Hotel so she made her way to that area. She had written the name of the villa in Spanish on a piece of paper, and she stopped the car and began showing it to anybody who looked like a resident. Eventually she found a man who knew Diego's property and he drew a simple map for her as he didn't speak English.

Twenty minutes later she was parked outside *Paraiso Enconrado*.

Jayne sat staring at the villa from the road. She had always thought it was a beautiful property and it seemed even more gorgeous than she remembered. What she was about to do filled her with apprehension and nervousness. Nevertheless, she was determined to go through with it – she had no choice having travelled this far. If Diego could tell her where Henry was living it would be a fantastic result.

She looked in the car mirror and made some unnecessary adjustments to her hair and makeup. She thought she looked good in her brightly coloured silk top, nice white slacks with high-heeled shoes. She had conditioned her hair in the hotel and as her sunroof was open, she was pleased to see a lovely shine on her hair. She was ready to go but decided against appearing presumptuous by driving up the drive, so she left her car by the quiet roadside. She took a deep breath and started to walk confidently along the drive towards the villa.

Diego's decorative paving slabs enhanced the drive which had borders either side filled with lovely flowers. The drive meandered up past the swimming pool and through two flower gardens to the main elaborate wooden double doors of the villa. Nobody seemed to be around except a man lying on a sunbed by the pool, but she noted that it wasn't Diego. She reached the door which had a nice brass Gothic style hanging bell with a rope pull and she pulled the rope and the bell rang. The heavy doors were opened and there, standing in his swimming trunks, was Diego. Jayne recognised him immediately. He stared at Jayne as if he had seen a ghost.

'My God, I don't believe it. What are you doing here? It is you, Jayne, isn't it?' Diego had a look of total astonishment.

Jayne smiled and tried to stay calm.

'Sorry about the shock, Diego, but yes, it's me.' She smiled broadly and tried to stay as relaxed as she could.

'You look fantastic. What are you doing here?' Diego leaned forward and kissed her on both cheeks still looking shocked.

'Well, it's a long story but I'm hoping you can help me. Henry has come down here to Spain as we've had some problems and I wondered whether he had been in touch with you.'

She secretly gritted her teeth and crossed a couple of fingers behind her back whilst she waited with baited breath for his reply.

'Didn't you see him? He's by the pool – you must have passed him?'

'Really, I saw a man by the pool but it wasn't Henry.'

Jayne was over the moon to hear Henry was actually here.

'No it wasn't Henry,' said Diego laughing, 'it was Harry.'

'Sorry,' Jayne looked quizzical, 'who is Harry?'

'I'm afraid it's your former husband; he's changed his name like the royal Henrys did.'

'I don't get it, the guy by the pool doesn't look anything like Henry.'

Diego pointed towards the pool.

'Go and see him then. I remember you saying you wanted him to shake off his old-fashioned ways, well I've done it for you but it's too late now because I understand you've, how you say, dumped him?'

Jayne felt embarrassed but she wanted Diego to know the situation.

'I've dumped the "someone else" now as well now so I've buggered things up if you want the truth.'

'He has told me you are divorced, does that mean you're going to try to get him back? Is that what this visit's all about?'

Jayne couldn't help smiling. 'Harry, his new name, it's hilarious but I love it. Yes, I'm going to have a go at getting him back – does that bother you?'

'Not at all,' said Diego. 'I liked you as a couple so try to do it. Mind you, he will take some persuading as he's having a great time here playing the field.'

'Really? Do you mean he's had other women?'

Diego smiled. 'I'm not getting into that but I have taught him a few of the good things in life.'

Jayne looked astonished. 'I don't believe that, Diego, no way.'

'Whether you believe me or not doesn't matter. Go and see for yourself.'

'I can't believe he's changed that much, I know him too well. He's always listened to me and I have a way of getting him to give me what I'm after.' Jayne sounded rather proud of her hold over him.

'Anyway, whatever, I'm going to try to get him back.'

'Best of luck with that. I don't think it will be as easy as you think.' Diego said it like a challenge.

'We'll see, wish me luck,' Jayne said, smiling.

Diego grinned. 'I just did. I'll keep out of your way.'

Jayne looked in the hall mirror, tidied herself up again and made her way to the pool.

The sun was shining the man was lying flat out sunbathing on a bed with his eyes closed. She couldn't believe it was Henry so she looked around the pool for someone else, but there was nobody, it had to be him.

She noticed his hair had been groomed and treated with gentle enhanced colouring and the bags under his eyes were gone. He wasn't wearing spectacles anymore and there was no double chin or paunch, in fact he looked muscular and fit. The patchy body hair she hated had all been waxed off and his body was toned and tanned. He was wearing a gold pendant displaying the letter 'H' on it and he was sporting a pair of stylish yellow swimming trunks. Jayne stared down at him in disbelief, she thought he looked in his early forties, the transformation was truly amazing to her and she was struggling to take it all in.

Why couldn't he have done this for me when we were married, she thought to herself. She took a deep breath.

'Henry,' she said quite loudly.

It startled him and he opened his eyes and looked at Jayne in total bewilderment. He was speechless.

'It's me, Henry, or should I say Harry.' She smiled mischievously as she used his new name.

'What the bloody hell's going on? I'm dreaming am I?'

He had a look of total astonishment on his face and he ignored her weak joke. He sat up abruptly and stared at her with a furious look on his face.

Jayne was taken aback by his response – he would never have acted like that to her when she was with him.

'I've come to see you.'

She spoke in a mild and tender manner as she was frightened of upsetting him but she could now see Diego was right; he was different.

'I don't get it. What are you doing here?' He seemed to be almost snarling at her.

'Aren't you pleased to see me?' Jayne was struggling to deal with the conversation.

'Why should I be?' He seemed annoyed. 'You left me for someone else, is he with you, are you trying to wind me up, is that it?'

'No, I'm on my own; I've left him, left him for good.'

Henry looked confused but said nothing for a moment before replying.

'So you found me here and thought you could just come down and pick up where we left off, is that it?'

'No, that's not how it is at all.'

Diego was hiding behind the door of the swimming pool changing room fascinated by the situation that was unfolding, he loved it. He was within earshot and wanted to know how this battle was going to end.

Jayne wasn't happy with the way things were going, and her mind went back to Moira who had advised her to throw herself at Henry and make an impassioned and emotional effort. She took a deep breath and put on her puppy-dog face by tilting her head down with her eyes looking up as if she were about to cry. It gave her a look of innocence and it was a ploy she had used many times, particularly with him when she wanted something. She then launched into her pre-planned explanation.

'My darling, I've done it all wrong. I didn't realise how much I loved you until I'd left you. You're the only man for me, I know that now, I really do. I just can't understand why I was stupid enough to be persuaded to leave you. He just kept on and on to me about leaving you and in the end I stupidly gave in.'

She kept going and poured it on.

Listening from his hiding place, Diego was impressed; he thought she was giving a superb performance.

'I love you and I always have. I can't stop thinking about you and I don't want anyone else ever. I've wanted to walk out on him for a while. Please take me back. I've learnt my lesson. Won't you take me back, please, please?'

Whilst Harry was listening to her emotional and rather sad outburst, he was also taking in her wonderful looks which had never faded. To him, she had always been outstandingly beautiful. She was the most gorgeous woman he had ever seen and as she declared her undying love for him, he couldn't help slightly warming to her pleas. He had never really fallen out of love with her, he had always been totally obsessed with her and she had simply abused his weaknesses and had taken advantage of his generosity.

When she had finished pleading she sunk slowly to her knees on the grass and took hold of his hands. She looked into his eyes with tiny teardrops trickling down her cheeks, her face looked sad and full of innocence and regret.

'Won't you please take me back, darling?'

She knew he was weakening so she kept going.

Diego peered around the wall in admiration of the dramatic way she was handling her appeal.

'I'm so sorry for what I've done, I don't want to be with him anymore – I only want you.'

Harry broke off the conversation.

'Listen, Jayne, I understand what you're saying but I need time to think. It's taken me a while, but I've finally got over you and just when I have, you turn up like this. I'm living in the annexe here now so I'm going to my room to think. Please ask Diego for a drink and sit out here for a while. I'll be back in half an hour or so.'

Jayne went to say something but Harry cut her short.

'No, say no more, let me think, I'm totally shocked.'

As he walked away, Jayne shouted after him and he stopped.

'I have to say that I can't believe how you look. I would never have recognised you as you look absolutely fantastic.'

Harry ignored the comment and walked into the annexe closing the door behind him but secretly he loved the compliment Jayne had given him.

Diego appeared from the changing room and called to Jayne, 'Would you like a drink?'

Jayne shouted, 'Have you got a San Miguel, please?'

'Sure, I'm surprised you didn't ask for something stronger after that performance.' Diego was grinning broadly.

He went inside and returned to the sunbeds with two chilled bottles of San Miguel.

'I think you may have done it, you were terrific.'

'Do you think so?'

Jayne was encouraged by the compliment. 'I really hope so because I shouldn't have left him. I made a mistake and I have been waiting for the right moment to tell my boyfriend that I was leaving him. I genuinely think it would work with Henry, or rather Harry, especially now you've changed him.'

'What do you think of the changes?' Diego was proud of what he had achieved.

'Absolutely amazing. I find it hard to believe, the only thing is though he's not such a pushover now, he seems a much stronger character. Also, I notice that he doesn't talk so posh, is that down to you as well?'

'I'm afraid so,' said Diego proudly.

Harry appeared about twenty minutes later and he seemed to have cooled down a little.

'I've done some thinking and firstly, Jayne, let me ask Diego if it's all right for you to stay here tonight.'

Diego just shrugged. 'Of course, I've got several bedrooms, that's no problem.'

'The thing is I want you to accept that I'm now called Harry – the name Henry is dead and is not to be used anymore.'

'Fair enough, if that's what you want,' said Jayne.

'Great.' Harry looked serious, 'Jayne, what I'd like is to take you out to dinner tonight and discuss things a little more, are you OK with that?

'I'd love it, but can I get a bit of shut eye this afternoon as I've done a lot of driving.'

Jayne wanted to be wide awake if her future was being discussed.

'Of course, that's no problem. Is that your nice looking Mercedes down on the road?' asked Diego.

'Yes, can I bring it up here? My stuff's in it.'

'Drive it up and then come with me, I'll show you to a bedroom you can use to shower and put your stuff in.

I'll make you a sandwich if you would like one and you can have a sleep, OK?'

'Brilliant.'

She was delighted to be able to stay and was pleased with the way things were going. She knew now that Moira had been right and was glad she had listened to her as she would never have thought of coming to Spain.

'Are you coming with us tonight, Diego?'

Jayne felt she should ask him but hoped he would decline.

'No,' Diego said, 'you've got stuff to discuss privately. Anyway I've got a date.'

Jayne drove the car up and Diego showed her to a nice bedroom.

Harry said he was going to have a swim, and it was agreed that Jayne and Harry would leave for dinner about 7.30 p.m. after she had slept for a while.

*

When Jayne woke up she spent some time getting ready and she made a special effort with her hair and makeup. She deliberately dressed sensually wearing a low cut dress with the expensive necklace that he had bought her for their wedding anniversary.

When she was ready she checked herself over in front of a full-length mirror and was confident that she looked appealing, that was her main aim.

She had arranged to meet Henry by the pool and when she arrived he was already there having a beer with Diego. He looked really dapper in white trousers, black open neck shirt wearing stylish sunglasses. Diego handed Jayne a beer and they sat making small talk until they left for the restaurant.

Harry thought Jayne looked absolutely radiant in her outfit and even though he was uncertain about taking her back, he was looking forward to showing her off at his local haunts. He walked her to Diego's large garage and as the automatic door was rising, Jayne giggled as his trusty red Jaguar came into view.

'Harry…' she hesitated and smiled, 'I can't get used to calling you that name?'

'Harry is best now,' he said. 'That's what they all call me these days.'

'Well, Harry, I was just thinking of the memories that this car brings back.'

'I couldn't part with it; it's a great car,' he said. 'Come on, get in and let's go.'

He drove straight to the seafront promenade and parked near The Gourmet restaurant and as they entered Matias, the manager, spotted Harry and came straight over to greet them.

'Harry,' he exclaimed, eyeing up Jayne whilst smiling broadly, 'how are you and who is this ravishing beauty?'

Jayne took an instant liking to the manager as he had a sexy Spanish accent and of course, anyone flattering Jayne was an instant hit with her.

'I'm fine. Let me introduce Jayne.'

Harry introduced her with a hand gesture and Matias leaned forward and lightly kissed her on each cheek.

'Welcome to our gourmet restaurant and may I say that you look absolutely divine?' he was smiling almost lecherously.

'Well, thank you, kind sir,' Jayne purred in her usual sensual voice.

Harry had seen it all before.

'Let me show you to a nice table on the terrace,' he said.

They followed him to one of the al fresco tables which Harry was fond of as it overlooked the harbour.

Jayne was impressed by the lovely restaurant with its crisp tablecloths, napkins, crystal glasses and carver chairs. She noticed that the staff seemed to respect Harry, he seemed so much more in command, it reminded her of Jonathan and she couldn't get over the change in Henry.

They had large gin and tonics and chose their meals. Whilst they were waiting they both relaxed with cigarettes and Jayne couldn't wait to go back to the aim of her visit, to persuade him to take her back.

'Have you thought any more about us getting back together, Harry?' she asked, tentatively.

'I'm still working on it. The thing is, Jayne, if you were to stay, it would be forever. I can't go back to the UK and I think you know why.'

'What happened with the police eventually?'

He chose his words carefully. 'Well, they tried to pin the death of your boyfriend on me but I got fed up with the hounding so I cleared off down here, they can't really get to me in Spain so as long as I don't go back to England, they can't touch me.'

'Did you do it, you know, get rid of John?' she asked cheekily.

'Absolutely not, and I'm surprised you would even think that. It's really upsetting to hear you say that.' He looked annoyed but he would never tell anybody the truth, not even Jayne.

Jayne realised she had said the wrong thing and tried to recover.

'Sorry, Harry, it was just a joke.'

'The trouble is they wouldn't believe me so they kept trying to find something to be able to charge me with.' He looked frustrated. 'I couldn't stand it anymore.'

'I never thought you'd done it, Harry, I really didn't,' but she didn't really know either way.

They finished the excellent meal, which was followed by coffee and Spanish brandies. Jayne lit a cigarette and Harry joined her by choosing a fine cigar.

Jayne looked at him with her usual sultry gaze, she was trying to get him back to the annexe.

'Perhaps we could go back to the villa, Harry, you know, have a drink in privacy. You never know what may happen.'

She spoke in a sensual voice trying to tempt him, hoping he would get the message. She was intending to try to seduce him at the villa as she thought this might get her the result she was after, but Harry wasn't ready for bed yet, he'd got used to a different lifestyle.

'It's been a lovely evening. Do you fancy finishing it off by going to a club for a nightcap?' he suggested.

'You, a nightclub? It's unheard of?'

'Listen, Jayne, you must know I've changed. Being retired and living here several months with Diego has opened my eyes to a new world, one I enjoy. If you don't fancy a club, I'll drop you off at Diego's and go on my own.'

Jayne was taken aback as she wasn't used to him speaking to her in such a forceful way. 'I never said that, no way. I'm coming with you. It's just that you would never go to a nightclub when we were married.'

'Well, I do now,' said Harry sharply.

Jayne hadn't finished her quest, she still didn't know if Harry would invite her to stay with him in Spain for good so she had no intention of leaving him that night if she could help it.

'Just before we go,' said Jayne, 'let me say, Harry, that the changes in your personality really suit you. You look ten years younger and it's something I was trying to get you to do for ages – it suits you a lot and I love it.'

'Well, thanks, Jayne. That means a lot to me but there was no way I could have changed like this working in the law courts. The other thing is the culture is so much different down here and that's why I'm not leaving. In fact I'm thinking of buying my own villa down here soon.'

Jayne's ears pricked up.

'Really, we could have a wonderful time living here together, don't you think?'

Harry wasn't giving anything away.

'Yes, I think we could but there's a lot of temptation for people to stray around Marbella and that would worry me for a start.'

'I would never cheat on you again, Harry. I promise you that. So do you think you'll let me stay?'

'We'll see,' he said. He still sounded undecided but Jayne thought his response was promising.

'Right,' he said, 'let's go.'

He drove to Pablo's club and Jayne noticed the size of the queue at the door.

'We'll never get in here, is there anywhere else?'

Harry parked the car. 'Come with me, and don't worry, it's no problem getting in.'

As they approached the club, the doorman saw Harry and waved them to the front of the queue where he shook his hand like a long-lost friend.

'Nice to see you, Harry. How's it going?'

'I'm fine,' he replied.

Jayne noticed that Harry secretly slipped the doorman a peseta note of some sort as they shook hands.

Jayne was surprised and impressed because they simply walked straight past the cash desk without paying.

Harry simply nodded to the girl behind the counter and she gave him a respectful smile.

'Hi, Harry,' she said.

'How come you don't pay to come in, Henry?' Jayne queried.

'I'm a member and I spend a lot of money here. By the way, stop calling me Henry. I'm getting fed up with it now.'

Jayne thought that was the first time in all their years together that he had scolded her. 'I'm sorry. I'm struggling to get used to it, it won't happen again.'

As she followed him through the club, she couldn't help being impressed by the elegant surroundings and the trendy stylish clientele. Jayne got some admiring glances herself from many of the men they passed and as usual, she loved that but she also couldn't help noticing the amount of people who seemed to know Harry.

'Hi, Harry' and 'How's it going, Harry?' was what she heard several times and it reminded her of going to places with Jonathan. He too was known and respected and it was as if Harry was turning into him. She knew that it was down to one thing really, money. Jayne knew that he must be extremely wealthy now that he had sold Tudor Manor.

In the bar area, Jayne thought all of the waitresses must have been handpicked for their looks as they were all young, attractive and smartly dressed. A lovely blonde approached them.

'Good evening, Harry. Would you like an alcove table?' she asked giving him a rather sultry smile.

'Thanks, Maria. That would be nice,' he said.

They were shown to the VIP area with armchairs and sofas tucked in a recess away from the hub of the action.

'We can talk privately in here,' said Harry. 'Shall we have a bottle of champagne?'

'Thank you. I'd love that.'

'I'll bring you a bottle of your usual Moet, Harry.'

'How come so many people seem to speak English around here?' asked Jayne.

'You have to speak English in all the upmarket places here. Very few people don't speak it.'

Harry became slightly uncomfortable when he saw Gina with two of her friends being shown to a table nearby. Just as they were sitting down, Gina spotted him and sidled over.

'This is cosy, Harry,' she said with a playful look.

Harry looked embarrassed.

'Hi, Gina. This is Jayne, we go back ages.'

Jayne thought to herself, *Bloody right we do. What an understatement.*

Gina looked Jayne up and down. 'Nice to meet you, Jayne. How long are you staying?'

Jayne hesitated. 'I'm not really sure.'

She glanced at Harry, hoping he would give her a clue but she was disappointed that he said nothing.

'Well, have a nice evening. I'll no doubt see you sometime, Harry – be good and don't leave it too long.'

As she said it, she looked into Harry's eyes knowingly, which Jayne spotted.

Gina went back to her friends.

'Who's she, Harry? Is she your girlfriend or something?' Jayne was curious.

'I have been out with her a few times.'

'Really,' said Jayne in a disbelieving voice.

'Don't seem so surprised. I do have a life down here, you know.' Harry sounded annoyed.

'Sorry, I didn't mean to sound rude but it's just that you're so different. I can't get my head around the way you've changed. You'll be telling me next that you've been bonking her.'

Harry looked slightly irritated and responded totally out of character.

'If you must know, I've bonked her several times, as you so nicely put it.'

Jayne went quiet and she seemed to become a little sullen.

'Don't tell me that you're jealous,' said Harry with a laugh. 'I don't believe it.'

'I just didn't expect it, that's all. I suppose I'm surprised at what you get up to here.'

Harry looked stern and hurt. 'You've got a bloody cheek, bearing in mind what you got up to when we were married. I'm enjoying my life down here and what I do is up to me.'

Jayne panicked inside. She knew she was handling things very badly. She had never known him to talk to her like this, she used to be able to twist him round her little finger but not anymore it seemed. If she didn't approach this in a more understanding manner she guessed she would blow her chances of getting back with him.

'I'm sorry, Harry. I'm being silly. Of course you must enjoy your new life.' She was trying to pull things around.

'OK, Jayne. There's nothing serious going on with Gina. She's just someone I see now and again, that's all. Come on, let's finish this Moet and go back to the villa. Is that OK with you?'

'Absolutely.'

Jayne couldn't help wondering whether anything would happen between them when they got back and she desperately hoped so.

After the champagne was finished, they went back to the villa and as they approached the door, Harry stopped.

'I'm staying in the annexe. Would you like to come in for a nightcap before you go to your room?'

Jayne said to herself under her breath, 'Yes!' She was elated as this was her chance to persuade him.

'That would be nice, Harry.' She tried to sound casual.

They went into Harry's living room in the annexe which was nicely furnished and comfortable.

'What would you like to drink?' he asked.

'Have you some Scotch with ice?'

'Yes, we'll both have one.'

He poured two generous portions and dropped a couple of ice cubes in each from the fridge.

They both sat on the sofa.

'This is a lovely annexe, Harry. Will you stay here for long?'

He thought that she was fishing for information.

'I'm not really sure what I'm doing as I haven't made my mind up yet.'

'I've had a wonderful evening and it's been so great to see you.'

She moved slightly nearer to him and rested her hand on his knee. 'I do think a lot of you, I never realised how much until I'd left you. Do you think anything about me?'

Harry responded to her obvious advances. 'Yes, of course, sometimes.'

Jayne moved her face nearer to his and stared provocatively into his eyes. It was clear that sexual tension was rising and suddenly, without a word being spoken, they were embracing and kissing passionately. Jayne clumsily pulled off his shirt and was kissing his body somewhat frantically – he suddenly broke it off.

'Let's go to the bedroom.' Harry sounded excited.

He took her hand and led her in, they both eagerly stripped off their clothes completely and fell on the bed ravishing each other and constantly kissing.

They passionately made love in a way Jayne had never experienced before with Harry. She knew he had gained some experience from somewhere and she loved it.

It was nearly an hour when they both reached an orgasm, unheard of when they were married, and they fell back on the bed exhausted.

'Wow!' Jayne exclaimed, 'that was really something.'

Harry smiled. 'Yes, it was fantastic.'

Jayne realised that it wasn't just his looks that had changed; it was his whole attitude to life, the way he spoke and now the way he made love. She desperately wanted to stay with him in Spain as she had nothing to her name if she went home. She turned to him to discuss their future but he was fast asleep so she went into the living room and finished the whiskey whilst thinking for a while about the important conversation she would be having with him the next day.

Afterwards she returned to the bedroom and slept.

In the morning, before they went to the villa to make some breakfast, Jayne woke up Harry with some coffee which she had made and brought it back to the bedroom.

'Good morning, Harry. Are you all right?'

'I'm great, what a super night that was.'

Jayne was pleased to hear that. 'I thought so too and that's how it would be if we were living here together, don't you think.'

Harry had made his decision. 'Listen, Jayne, I've made my mind up about the future.'

Jayne looked at him with nervousness and hope. 'Are we back together, darling?'

The unexpected bombshell shocked her to the core.

'No, we're not, I can't do it.'

Jayne stared at him truly believing it was a joke. 'What? Are you serious? Surely not.'

'I'm serious I'm afraid, I just don't want to do it, it's as simple as that.'

'What about last night?' she queried, 'what was that all about, one for the road?'

'No it wasn't, you wanted it as well as me,' said Harry.

Jayne started the waterworks, tears started rolling down her cheeks.

'Please, I've nowhere to go and I've got no home, please take me back, please, please.'

She had a look of desperation but Harry was adamant.

'Sorry, Jayne, if you've got nowhere to go you must go back to your boyfriend and sort something out.'

Without thinking, she said, 'I can't.' She stopped herself from saying anything else.

'Why can't you?' he asked.

'I just can't.'

Harry looked at her suspiciously. 'Why can't you go back, you told me you had left him?'

'I have, but I don't want to be with him anymore, I want you.'

'Well, you should have thought of that when you cheated and left me.'

Jayne started crying but Harry was unmoved.

'I'm sorry, Jayne, but that's my decision. If it had been several months ago it might have been different, but I've changed and I'm really enjoying my new life. I don't want to be tied down now because I'm having such a great time. I'm sorry but that's my decision – end of story. I never asked you to come down here.'

He then left the annexe and went into the main villa where he sat with Diego explaining what had happened.

After a while, Jayne came in. 'I suppose he's told you, Diego. What do you think?'

Diego looked uninterested. 'Nothing to do with me, love. You're both adults.'

Deep down, Diego was pleased, he had been enjoying having his buddy around for company.

'What happens now?' Jayne asked the question rather sheepishly.

Her eyes were still wet but Harry was unmoved.

'I'm going to help you financially, Jayne. I'll give you two grand in sterling which will help you until you find a job. I expect you to drive back to England tomorrow or I can get you a flight if you don't want to drive. In that case I'll buy your car and sell it down here. It's up to you which way you get back to the UK.'

'Please reconsider.' She was pleading again but Harry was having none of it.

'Listen, I'm not doing it and that's that. Be careful, Jayne, I don't have to help you in this generous way. I'll remind you again, I didn't ask you to come here; you're the one who decided to come.'

Jayne realised it was over. 'When do you want me to go?' she asked tearfully.

'Tomorrow, I'll get you the money this morning. How will you get back?'

'I'll drive,' she said in a miserable voice.

'I'll get the money and you can leave tomorrow. There's nothing more to be said.'

Jayne accepted the situation and kept quiet in case he changed his mind regarding the money.

The following morning, Harry went to the bank and took our two thousand pounds and a few pesetas which he gave to Jayne. Diego told him he was a soft touch.

'Don't give her anything,' he said, 'you didn't ask her to come. It all sounds a bit fishy to me, but I didn't like to say anything as it's nothing to do with me.'

Jayne was tearful and miserable as she packed her car but she didn't make too much fuss as she wanted to keep the money Harry had given her.

As she drove out of the villa's driveway, Harry and Diego both waved her off but this gesture was hollow, it just seemed the right thing to do.

When she was out of sight, Diego showed Harry how to do a high five and they both smiled – they were pleased to be on their own again.

Jayne would never see Harry again.

Harry had been obsessed with Jayne ever since he met her but he truly didn't want to give up his new life. He turned to Diego grinning broadly.

'Where are we going tonight, amigo?'

Diego smiled. 'You were never going to take her back, were you?'

'No, I wasn't,' he confirmed. 'For one thing I'm not

really convinced about the story. It's more likely that she's been kicked out rather than she left him. I suppose I'll never know and I don't really care.'

'Still,' Diego said cheekily, 'at least you got, you know, your leg over, isn't that what you say?

'That's not very nice is it?'

Harry was laughing too – what a change in his mannerisms.

'I think we deserve a night out together, don't you?'

'Absolutely,' Diego totally agreed, he was delighted with the outcome.

That evening they went to dinner and then on to a club where they danced with girls, had plenty of drinks and simply enjoyed the evening. Now that Harry had found this new life he wanted to keep it. As far as he was concerned, Jayne had caused her own downfall and he now had no sympathy.

Jayne drove home the same way stopping twice overnight. She was devastated by his decision and realised that her hold over him had gone. She had nowhere to live but she went back to Moira's who kindly put her up until she found a flat a few days later. Deep down, Jayne was grateful for the two thousand pounds but she would never get over the mistake she had made.

Conclusion

Most of the people involved in this story were either unlucky or met a tragic ending.

The first was *John Stevens*, an innocent man who met a horrific death in excruciating pain.

The second was *Jayne* herself, who was eventually reduced to taking a job as a waitress in a café, but she was asked to leave due to her rude manner with customers. She then worked behind the bar in a public house but that didn't end well either. She struggled along but her options grew less as she became older. Despite trying, she was unable to find a third wealthy man and she never achieved her goal of living like royalty – that dream had been thrown away twice. She was reduced to simply getting through life the best she could living mainly in rented flats.

Mrs Moyle was simply unlucky. Two years after she retired, she fell ill and died aged 69. Harry only found out as his solicitor rang him with the news and suggested that he should change his will. He dare not return to England for the funeral as he was worried that George Robinson might reappear.

Detective Sergeant George Robinson resigned from the police and took an early pension. He never got over his reprimand or the mistake he made in allowing Henry to leave for Spain. George was quite rightly convinced that Henry had poisoned John Stevens, and George blamed himself for letting him get away with it. It was something he never forgot and it haunted him until his dying day.

Jonathan Bond sat in his cell in the Southern Nevada Correctional Center which was located 30 miles south of Las Vegas. In his cell were a bunk bed, sink and toilet with a small window. He had been extradited to America and tried for crimes connected with drug trafficking, grievous bodily harm, fraud and income tax evasion. He declined to see Jayne before he left as he simply couldn't face the embarrassment. Sometimes he sat for hours on his bed staring into space wondering what went wrong. He was shocked at his arrest as he was convinced that as he only made occasional visits to America, he was safe from arrest as he lived most of the time in England.

At his trial, he was facing 20 years imprisonment without remission but as he was involved with organised crime syndicates, the police offered him a deal. The prison term would be reduced to ten years if he would "Turn State Evidence" meaning he would be required to assist in the prosecution of his accomplices, this would include Rossi.

As Jonathan felt safe in prison, he took the deal. One day, whilst in the exercise yard, a prisoner contrived a reason to talk to him. Whilst in conversation with him he felt a sharp piercing pain in his back as a crude homemade five-inch blade sank in. The attacker withdrew the blade and both he, and the person speaking to him, quickly melted into a crowd of prisoners. Jonathan slowly slid to the ground in terrible pain; he bled to death within 30 seconds.

Henry, or Harry, was initially facing disaster in his life but he now found himself transformed into this new identity, one who was enjoying life to the full. He was correct in thinking the police could not touch him but in July 1985 a new extradition treaty was signed by the UK with Spain, and this generated the arrest of many British criminals on the "Costa del Crime" as it was comically called. However, unbeknown to Harry there was no interest in him as DS Robinson was the only officer who tried to pursue him and when he retired, all police interest petered out. After all, Henry had never been charged with anything. The police at that time had far bigger problems than Harry to worry about such as the Brinks Matt robbers who stole millions of pounds plus many other serious criminals who had escaped to Spain.

He was now having a wonderful new life enjoying good health and plenty of money. He and Diego got on extremely well so Harry abandoned his plan to purchase a property and he made the annex his own. He insisted on paying Diego the going rate for his rent. The two were inseparable, so much so that some people suspected that they were gay. However, the majority of people knew the number of women they both bedded and laughed off the idea.

Life was one big party with holidays in Mexico, Thailand and many other exotic places and they only stayed in the best hotels. At home their parties at the villa became renowned, and people felt privileged to be invited. They were lavish affairs with a mixture of chosen females and males of all ages. Superb buffets and copious amounts of drink were freely available, and there was loud music and skinny-dipping in the pool. Harry and Diego had some wonderful times on his Sunseeker which remained moored at Puerto Banus and their world opened up even further as sometimes they sailed way up the Spanish coast, stopping at various ports and they often slept on the boat in its small but adequate bedroom.

This lifestyle confirmed to Harry that he had made the right decision regarding Jayne. Ironically he believed that it was his obsession with Jayne that had led him to this wonderful new life which he now enjoyed so much. His obsession with her was what caused him to punish Stevens. Had he not done so, he would still be sitting in Tudor Manor living life in his boring old fashioned way.

Jonathan Bond had frequently used the saying "never be a loser" but that saying would now probably be more appropriate for Harry to use, as he was the only winner in the end.